He must have sensed her approach for he suddenly turned.

When their gazes connected, his eyes lit, then turned dark and smoldering. The small thrill became a rushing river of awareness. All at once, Adele knew why Ty had called her to meet him and what he wanted. She didn't hesitate going to him.

Dropping the reins, he came forward. Luckily, Hamm was placid by nature outside the arena because another horse might have spooked when Adele flung herself into Ty's open arms.

"I've been waiting a week for this," he said as his mouth came down on hers.

Only a week? It felt to Adele as if she'd been waiting forever. For this kiss. This moment. This man.

WYOMING

COUNTRY LEGACY

A COWBOY'S REDEMPTION

New York Times Bestselling Author

Cathy McDavid

Rebecca Winters

Previously published as *The Comeback Cowboy* and *The Wyoming Cowboy*

HARLEQUIN

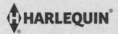

ISBN-13: 978-1-335-46774-4

Recycling programs
for this product may
not exist in your area.

Wyoming Country Legacy:
A Cowboy's Redemption
Copyright © 2020 by Harlequin Books S.A.

The Comeback Cowboy
First published in 2011. This edition published in 2020.
Copyright © 2011 by Cathy McDavid

The Wyoming Cowboy
First published in 2013. This edition published in 2020.
Copyright © 2013 by Rebecca Winters

This edition published by arrangement with Harlequin Books S.A.

For questions and comments about the quality of this book, please contact us at CustomerService@Harlequin.com.

Harlequin Enterprises ULC
22 Adelaide St. West, 40th Floor
Toronto, Ontario M5H 4E3, Canada
www.Harlequin.com

Printed in U.S.A.

CONTENTS

The Comeback Cowboy   7
by Cathy McDavid

The Wyoming Cowboy   243
by Rebecca Winters

Since 2006, *New York Times* bestselling author **Cathy McDavid** has been happily penning contemporary Westerns for Harlequin. Every day, she gets to write about handsome cowboys riding the range or busting a bronc. It's a tough job, but she's willing to make the sacrifice. Cathy shares her Arizona home with her own real-life sweetheart and a trio of odd pets. Her grown twins have left to embark on lives of their own, and she couldn't be prouder of their accomplishments.

Books by Cathy McDavid

Harlequin Western Romance

Mustang Valley

Cowboy for Keeps
Her Holiday Rancher
Come Home, Cowboy
Having the Rancher's Baby
Rescuing the Cowboy
A Baby for the Deputy
The Cowboy's Twin Surprise
The Bull Rider's Valentine

Harlequin Heartwarming

The Sweetheart Ranch

A Cowboy's Christmas Proposal
The Cowboy's Perfect Match
The Cowboy's Christmas Baby

Visit the Author Profile page at Harlequin.com for more titles.

THE COMEBACK COWBOY

Cathy McDavid

To Libby and Connie.
I always knew you would make great critique partners. What I didn't know was how much your friendship would enrich my life.
Thank you for making the last ten years not just a journey but an adventure.
I love you both.

Chapter 1

Welcome to Seven Cedars Ranch, Home of Cowboy College.

He sat immobile, staring at the large sign with its horse-head logo, his jaw tightly clenched.

Up until the moment he drove through the main gate, he'd been able to deny how really low he'd sunk in the last six months and how really far he'd have to climb to get back on top.

No more. The time to man up had officially arrived.

He reached for the door handle on his pickup—only to have it abruptly wrenched open. Startled, he turned to look into the face of a kid no older than eighteen or nineteen.

"Welcome, Mr. Boudeau. We've been expecting you." The kid waited, a gosh-I-can't-believe-it's-you grin plastered across his freckled face.

"The name's Ty." He removed the keys from the ignition and climbed out.

"A real pleasure to meet you, Ty." They shook hands. "Folks 'round here call me Stick." The kid stepped back, and Ty could immediately see how he'd earned the nickname. Stick could get lost standing behind a flagpole. "Right this way. Adele's waiting for you."

Ty hesitated, the doubts he'd successfully kept at bay during the four-hour drive across Wyoming gaining ground. He needed help, that was a fact. But from a woman? One who made a living instructing amateurs at a glorified dude ranch. For a professional tie-down and team roper like himself, the idea was ludicrous. Certainly not "genius," as his younger sister had professed.

And yet he'd come.

"Okay to leave the truck parked here?" His Ford F350 dually and horse trailer blocked all six of the available spaces in front of the rustic two-story lodge.

"No problem."

Being a minor celebrity, even an undeserving one, had its privileges, he supposed.

Grabbing his wallet, Ty followed Stick up a stone-lined walkway, across a sprawling porch and through the front entrance of the lodge. With each thunk of his boots on the hardwood floor, his gut clenched tighter. This place was his last-ditch effort. If it, and Adele Donnelly, couldn't figure out what he was doing wrong, then he might as well kiss his roping career goodbye.

"Here's the main lobby and that way is the business center," Stick informed him as they crossed the spacious room with its vaulted ceilings and pine beams. Ten-foot-high windows looked out onto rolling green grounds dotted with thick stands of trees. "The front desk is where you check in and out, get the weekly schedules, sign up for classes." He shot Ty a guilty look over his shoulder. "Not that you need any."

"You never know." He definitely needed something.

"There's a lounge with a TV over there for guests." Stick pointed. "It's got satellite."

"Oh, good. Can't miss my daily dose of CNN."

His attempt at sarcasm went right over Stick's head, who didn't stop talking long enough to take a breath.

"The dining hall's that way. Breakfast is served from five-thirty to seven, lunch from eleven-thirty to one and dinner from six to seven-thirty. Social hour starts at five. 'Course, if you're hungry, Cook's always got a pot of stew or chili on the stove."

"I'll remember that."

Ty didn't anticipate doing much socializing during his four-week stay. He was here to rope. Though competent in other rodeo events, steer wrestling and team roping mostly, tie-down roping was what he excelled at.

Make that *had* excelled at. Everything had changed last December.

Stick escorted him to a long counter resembling a hotel registration desk, only on a much simpler scale. "You in there, Adele?" he called.

Ty caught a glimpse of a desk with a phone and computer through the open door behind the counter.

When no one answered, Stick tapped the bell on the counter. It promptly dinged. "Huh." He pushed his cowboy hat back, revealing a shock of red hair, and scratched his forehead. "Guess she's not here."

"We can come back," Ty offered, in no hurry to meet the owner and manager of Cowboy College.

In the next instant, he mentally kicked himself. He hadn't come all this way to chicken out at the last minute.

"But we have to get the key to your guest cabin. How else you gonna unpack your stuff?"

"It'll wait," Ty assured him. The poor kid was trying so hard and deserved a break. "How 'bout we head to the barn and unload my horse. Maybe Adele will show up by the time we're done."

Stick immediately brightened. "Sure thing," he said, only it sounded more like "shore" thing.

Back outside, they hopped in Ty's truck, and Stick directed him down the dirt road to a row of three barns. Across the open area in front of them was a large arena complete with holding pens, boxes, chutes, bleachers and an announcer's stand. A handful of riders were honing their roping skills with the help of some wranglers. Situated behind the barns were two smaller arenas, a pair of round pens, and endless acres of fenced pastures in which dozens of horses grazed on fresh spring grass. About a half mile beyond that, at the base of a valley, afternoon sunlight glinted off a large pond.

"How's the fishing?" Ty asked.

"Plenty of bass and bluegills. But if you're hankering for some serious fly-fishing, Little Twister Creek's the place to go. It's not far, about a mile or two from here. My cousin and I go every chance we get."

"You up for some company sometime?"

Stick's face exploded into a huge grin. "Just name

the day." As they approached the row of barns, he indicated the largest one. "Here we are."

Ty pulled up in front of an old-fashioned hitching post and parked. His horse, Hamm, greeted him with a shrill whinny and a bang on the trailer sidewall when he went around the back and unlatched the gate. Eager to be free after the long drive, the large gelding piled out of the trailer. Once on solid ground, he raised his head high, took in his new surroundings and whinnied again. Mares with young foals in the far pasture ran to the fence for a closer look at the newcomer.

"He's a beaut!" Stick gazed at Hamm admiringly.

"That he is." Holding on to the lead rope with one hand, Ty patted the horse's neck. Plain old sorrel didn't begin to describe Hamm. With four perfectly matched white stockings and a three-inch-wide blaze running down the entire length of his face, he was striking.

"Bet he can chase calves down like lightning streakin' across a meadow."

"He's fast all right." Ty didn't elaborate. His problem, the reason he'd come to Cowboy College, had nothing to do with Hamm and everything to do with him.

"This way." Stick started toward the barn opening. After several steps, he turned, gave Ty's horse another adoring once-over and whistled low. "That big boy can sure walk out."

The barn housed at least forty horses. Every one of them charged to the door of their stall and hung their head out to observe the visitors. A few of the braver ones stretched their neck out to either sniff Hamm or give his rump a quick nip. Ty assumed some of the horses belonged to Cowboy College and the rest to guests like himself.

Midway down the aisle, Stick stopped and opened the door of an empty stall. "Here you go."

Being accustomed to traveling, Hamm entered his new quarters without balking. He quickly inspected the stall's perimeter, then buried his head in the feed trough. It was empty, and a second later his head shot up in obvious displeasure.

Given it was late afternoon, Ty supposed the stable hands would be feeding soon. Still, he asked, "You got a little grain or pellets we can give him until I go over his diet with the barn manager?" Hamm liked to eat, and a snack would help him adjust to his new surroundings.

"Be right back." Stick took off and promptly returned with a small bucket of oats.

Fifteen minutes later Ty and Stick were parking his trailer behind the barn. When they were done, Ty pulled his truck around front.

Stick sat forward in the passenger seat. "There's Adele." He hitched his chin toward the arena. "Come on, you can meet her."

Horses and their riders had gathered at the south end of the arena. Ty picked out a trim young woman astride a stout paint mare, a blond braid snaking down her back from beneath her battered cowboy hat. Despite the distance, he recognized her immediately. No surprise; he'd been staring at pictures of her on Cowboy College's website for weeks while deciding to come or not.

"She looks busy."

"Naw." Stick dismissed his concern with a wave. "She won't mind."

They selected a spot along the fence and settled in to watch, their forearms resting on the top rail.

"Hey, folks."

Stick's friendly greeting was returned by all except Adele. She was preoccupied with lining her horse up in the box. The mare, obviously new at tie-down roping, didn't like being enclosed in such a cramped space. She danced nervously, snorting and pulling on the bit. With firm hands and a honeyed voice, Adele brought the animal under control.

"Good girl." She placed the pigging string in her mouth, checked her rope and shifted in the saddle. Ty knew she would cue the wrangler manning the chute only when she and the horse were completely ready. That moment came a second later.

"Go!"

The wrangler slid open the gate, and the calf bolted for freedom, running in a straight line away from the chute. Adele's horse might not have much experience, but its instincts were right on the money. The mare exploded from the box at a full gallop, following the calf with the persistence of a heat-seeking missile. Adele's arm came up. In the next instant, she threw her rope. The noose landed right where it should, squarely on the calf's horns, and she leaped from the saddle even before the mare had come to a complete stop.

Ty watched, completely captivated as she raced to the calf and dropped it effortlessly to the ground, securing its legs with the pigging string. She worked efficiently, not a single motion wasted. And yet there was a natural, fluid gracefulness about her.

It was then Ty noticed the mare. Rather than backing up and stretching the rope taut, as was her job, she moved aimlessly, allowing the rope to hang loosely. The lack of assistance, however, didn't appear to hamper Adele's performance. She threw her hands in the air, signaling she was done—in less than eight seconds, according to Ty's internal stopwatch. The students watching at the end of the arena broke into applause. He and Stick joined them.

Stick beamed. "Isn't she something?"

"Pretty good." Ty rocked back on his heels, absorbing what he'd just seen and thinking how much he hated admitting his sister might be right about Cowboy College.

Adele stood, exhibiting that same dancer's grace from earlier. The calf, now free, trotted off, only to be rounded up by one of the wranglers. Suddenly, Adele turned and glanced in Ty's direction. Their gazes connected, and the same recognition he'd experienced when he first saw her was reflected in her dark green eyes.

"Glad to see you made it, Mr. Boudeau. I'm Adele Donnelly."

"Glad to be here."

"Did you get your horse situated?"

"Stick's taken fine care of us."

At the compliment, Stick puffed up his skinny excuse for a chest. "Ty still needs to get checked in."

"I'll be up to the main lodge in a bit."

She walked over to her horse, calmly collecting her rope and winding it into a coil. With the ease and confidence of a practiced athlete, she swung up into the saddle and rode out of the arena.

Ty stared after her. Despite hearing of her skill, he'd

half expected—make that half hoped—the stories about her to be hype.

They weren't.

Adele Donnelly could not only show him a thing or two about a sport in which he'd been a top World contender mere months ago, she could quite possibly beat the pants off him.

"Hey, Dellie." Adele's grandfather joined her behind the registration counter. "What are you doing?"

"Hi, Pop." She straightened from her hunched position and rolled her cramped shoulders. "I'm just going over these schedules."

"I heard Tyler Boudeau arrived."

"About an hour ago."

"You meet him yet?"

"Briefly, at the arena."

"Which cabin did you assign him?"

"Number twenty-two."

Pop grunted. "The honeymoon cabin is bigger."

"It's booked. Number twenty-two is our next largest cabin, and the view from the back balcony's the best on the ranch."

"It's kind of far from the barn."

She studied him curiously, wondering what was up.

He rarely concerned himself with a guest's accommodations, preferring to leave the administrative functions of the ranch and roping school to Adele. On most days, when his acute arthritis didn't confine him to bed or the couch, he could be found at the barns and arena, teaching classes, overseeing the livestock and supervising the ranch hands. He still put in a full day's work when he could, but the last few years he'd come to depend more and more on their barn manager to pick up the slack.

"So, what do you think of him?"

Adele paused before answering the question, unsure of her response. Having a professional roper stay at the ranch, particularly one of Ty Boudeau's caliber, was certainly a boon for business. But the explanation he'd given for his month-long stay, that of training his new horse, hadn't rung true.

"We exchanged only a few words, and those were pleasant enough."

"Humph." Pop seemed disappointed.

"He should be here any minute."

His eyebrows shot up, momentarily erasing the deep wrinkles creasing his brow. "You don't say?"

Adele almost laughed, with surprise, not humor. Her grandfather was starstruck and couldn't wait to meet their semifamous guest.

"In that case, guess I'll get me a cup of coffee in the kitchen and wait for him."

"Decaffeinated," Adele called after his retreating back, and resisted adding, "You know what your doctor said."

A few minutes later, she looked up from her work to see Ty stride through the lobby door. She had to admit he wasn't hard to look at. And taller than she'd expected. Picking up the house phone, she paged the kitchen and said, "Tell Pop he's here," when Cook answered.

Reaching the counter, Ty removed his cowboy hat, and an unruly lock of sandy-blond hair promptly fell across his tanned forehead. His attempts to push it off his face were wasted…and also charming.

"Welcome again, Mr. Boudeau." She gave him her best professional yet friendly smile.

"Please, call me Ty."

"And I'm Adele."

The registration process didn't take long. When she finished, she put together a stack of papers, including a brochure, maps of the ranch and the nearby town of Markton, the current week's schedule of classes and events and a list of rules and regulations.

"Please read through this the first chance you have." She pointed to the papers stapled together on top. "You can't begin using the facilities until we have a signed copy on file."

"Tell me, am I signing away all my rights?"

Adele thought she detected a twinkle of amusement in his dark brown eyes. Perhaps he wasn't all-business, as she'd first suspected.

"No. You're just agreeing to abide by the rules and regulations. Very standard stuff. We already have the liability waiver and insurance certificate you faxed last week."

Ty signed the form without reading it and slid the papers across the counter.

"Let me make you a copy." She went into the office, where she kept a desktop copier, and returned shortly. "Here you go."

"Thanks." Ty folded the sheets in thirds and slipped them in his shirt pocket, again without reading them.

Oh, well, she'd done all she could.

Her grandfather appeared from the entryway leading to the kitchen, his chronic limp barely noticeable for once.

"Hey there, young fellow." He extended his right hand. "I'm mighty glad to make your acquaintance."

"Mr. Donnelly." Ty's glance fell for the briefest of seconds on Pop's hand before clasping it in a firm shake. "It's a real honor to meet you, sir."

Adele liked that Ty didn't appear put off by her grandfather's missing right thumb, a casualty of a roping accident that had happened long before she was born.

"The honor's mine," Pop said. "I've been watching your career since you were competing in junior rodeo."

"And I've studied yours."

"You have to go back a lot of years for that." Pop laughed, but it was filled with warmth.

"I'm counting on you teaching me a thing or two while I'm here. It's one of the reasons I came."

Pop stood a little taller. Most of their guests were recreationists and wannabe cowboys. Some were high-school students hoping to eventually compete on the professional rodeo circuit. Almost none of them knew about her grandfather's once impressive and long-ago rodeo career. Not until they got here and saw the photos and framed buckles on the lobby wall.

"I doubt there's anything I can teach you." Pop chortled. "Now Adele here, she's likely to have a trick or two up her sleeve you can use."

"I saw her earlier at the arena," Ty said. "She's good."

"She's the best in the state, man or woman." Pop's voice rang with pride.

Adele loved her grandfather, but at the moment she

wanted to cringe. "Mr. Boudeau is one of the best in the world, Pop."

"Doesn't mean he can't learn a thing or two from you."

"I agree," Ty answered good-naturedly. "Getting help, from both of you, is the reason I'm here."

Adele wondered if he'd added the "from both of you" for her grandfather's sake, considering how hesitantly the words had rolled off his tongue.

"Pop, why don't you show Mr. Boudeau to his cabin? You two can swap stories on the ride."

"Nothing I'd like better. Except I'm due to meet the boys in thirty minutes."

His regular Thursday-night poker game. She'd forgotten about that. "I'll call Stick."

"Adele, maybe you can take me?" One corner of Ty's mouth lifted in a grin. A very potent grin. "I'd be much obliged."

"Certainly."

"Good," Pop said, with more satisfaction than the situation called for. "That's settled, then."

As Adele left the lodge with Ty, she couldn't shake the feeling that her grandfather had set her up. She should be mad at him, but when she hopped onto the truck seat next to Ty, being mad was the furthest thing from her mind.

Ty slanted a glance at Adele, wondering what she was thinking. They'd both been relatively quiet during the five-minute drive through the main part of the ranch, except for the occasional item of interest she pointed out.

"Is this my home away from home?" he asked when she directed him to an attractive cabin atop a rise.

"Yes." She removed an old-fashioned hotel key from her pocket. No key cards for Cowboy College. "You'll love the view from the back patio."

They climbed out of the truck, and Adele led him along a split-fence-lined walkway to the front porch. Unlocking the cabin door, she swung it wide, and went ahead only when he indicated for her to precede him inside.

Ty took in the cabin's spacious and charmingly appointed interior, which appeared to have every amenity he could possibly want. "Very nice."

"If you aren't happy here, we can always move you to a different cabin."

"Are you kidding? This is great."

"It's a little far from the barn and arena." Adele walked over to the drapes on the other side of the living room and opened them, revealing a sliding glass door that looked out onto a calendar-perfect view of the nearby pond and distant mountains.

He joined her at the door and scanned the horizon. A glorious red sun was starting to dip behind one of the mountain peaks.

"It's worth the extra distance just for this."

Adele eased away from him, piquing his interest. Women generally acted the opposite, hanging all over him if possible. It was either a hazard or a perk of his profession, depending on a guy's perspective. Ty mostly found it wearisome. Except in Adele's case. Sharing the same air space with her had definitely been enjoyable.

Apparently not so much for her.

"There are two bedrooms," she said, walking past the fully equipped kitchenette. "The master and a small guest room. The couch also folds out into a bed. Your rental agreement allows for overnight guests up to three consecutive nights, but you have to report them."

"Dana will be glad to hear that." Was it his imagination or did a glint of curiosity flash in Adele's eyes? "My little sister's been bugging me to come here and take lessons from you."

"Oh, really? We'd love to have her," Adele said, so smoothly that Ty figured he'd been mistaken.

Perhaps because she was so different from the women he usually met, or that she was a roper like himself, he found himself trusting her. Enough to reveal the real reason he'd come to Cowboy College.

He hadn't expected he would, the idea of enrolling in a roping school for amateurs being hard to swallow. Taking instructions from a woman made it worse. But she'd impressed him in the arena, demonstrating a core of steel.

Like the one he had lost.

"It's not just my horse," he said abruptly. "It's me."

"What?" She turned to face him, her expression puzzled.

He cleared his throat, freeing the words stuck in it. "The horse I'd been riding the past four years suffered a fractured metacarpal last December in a fall. Right before the National Finals Rodeo. I was ranked second at the time."

"I know, I read about it in *Roper Sports News*."

"I lost more than a gold buckle and a title that day.

Iron Grip Ropes had signed me for a sponsorship deal. A very lucrative sponsorship deal."

"Which was contingent on you winning," she correctly guessed.

"I competed on a friend's horse, but lost the championship by one-point-eight seconds." Ty swallowed. Six months later, the bitter defeat still stung. "I bought Hamm in February after an extensive search. He's an incredible horse. Big, athletic, strong, fast and smart as a whip. Everything I could want." Ty paused.

"What's wrong, then?"

"That one-point-eight seconds. No matter what I do, no matter how hard I train, whatever trick I try, I can't seem to perform any better on Hamm than I did on my friend's horse. And I don't know why."

"Sometimes the partnership between a rider and horse is off."

"I'm hoping that's all it is. Because the alternative, that I've somehow lost my competitive edge…well, let's just say it's not acceptable."

He went to Adele and took her hand in his. The calluses on her palm from years of roping were in stark contrast to the silky smooth skin on the back of her hand. *Like her*, he thought—tough on one side, soft on the other.

"This isn't easy for me to ask, Adele. But I need your help."

She gazed at their joined hands for several seconds, then lifted her eyes to his. "I'll do my best."

"Good. Because the Buffalo Bill Cody Stampede Rodeo is less than four weeks away, and I *have* to win."

Chapter 2

Adele stood with Pop on the fence beside the chute and watched Ty position his horse in the roping box. People who weren't involved in rodeoing had no idea how many hours were spent training for the sport by studying others from the sidelines.

"What do you think?" Pop asked.

"Good-looking horse."

"Real nice looking."

So was the rider, but Adele kept that opinion to herself. Ty sat tall in the saddle, his Stetson angled low over his eyes, his Western cut shirt stretched taut across his broad shoulders. She wondered if he'd object to having his picture taken for their next website updates.

Almost immediately, she changed her mind. Ty had come to Cowboy College because of a problem, one he hoped to correct. It would be thoughtless and insensitive of her to take advantage of his misfortune in order to advance the ranch.

Ready at last, Ty signaled the wrangler, who pulled back the gate on the chute and released the calf. Ty's run, over in the span of a few heartbeats, was a good one. Not, however, spectacular. And spectacular runs were needed to win World championships.

"What do you think his problem is?" Adele asked her grandfather as Ty exited the arena.

"Not saying yet." Pop waved to Ty and pointed at the box, indicating for him to take another run.

Ty's admiration of her grandfather yesterday afternoon wasn't unfounded. Pop had been National tie-down roping champion for three years straight in the late 1950s, and again in 1963, before permanently retiring. Granted, things were done a little differently in those days, but the basic sport had remained the same.

One aspect not the same was the popularity of tie-down roping. That had grown tremendously in recent years, especially among amateurs. Not only did horse people with an interest in roping participate, so did thrill-seekers looking to try something new, urbanites wanting to experience the cowboy life, and even companies offering team-building retreats for their employees.

The increase in popularity was what had given Adele the idea to start Cowboy College. Her business savvy combined with her grandfather's experience made a winning combination. Together they'd turned a run-down ranch into a thriving enterprise.

Seven Cedars hadn't always been in trouble. For three decades after her grandparents bought the place, they'd run a modestly successful cattle business. Then, during Adele's junior year at university, her grandmother had died unexpectedly from an aneurysm. Pop sank into grief, letting the ranch go. Adele's father wasn't able to leave his job and move his second family from Texas to tend the ranch. Until Adele arrived after graduation, no one realized how bad the situation at Seven Cedars, and Pop's depression, had gotten.

Cowboy College not only breathed new life into the ranch, it gave her grandfather a purpose again. Within a year, they'd opened their doors, and had grown steadily in the six years since. Guests came from all over the country now, spending anywhere from a long weekend to weeks on end.

Ty Boudeau, however, was their first ever professional roper.

His horse, Hamm, lined up in the box with only the smallest amount of urging. "Go!" he shouted. As on the first run, the wrangler released the calf and Ty successfully roped it in a respectable time.

"He could do this all day and it wouldn't be any different," Adele commented.

"I'm afraid you're right." Pop rolled the toothpick stuck in his mouth from one side to the other. He was rarely without one since giving up chewing tobacco years earlier. Another of his doctor's mandates.

"The horse isn't taking one wrong step," Adele commented, "and Ty's doing exactly what he should be doing."

"But the magic just isn't happening."

"Could his problem be lack of confidence?"

Pop shrugged. "Possibly. Losing a world championship when you're as close as he was could set anyone back."

"Except Ty doesn't strike me as lacking confidence."
In or out of the arena, thought Adele.

But then, he'd lost much more than the championship. Sponsorship deals, good ones, didn't grow on trees, and had launched more than one athlete on a successful post-competing career.

"You never know," Pop mused out loud. "He could be putting on a good front. My guess is it's the horse."

Adele shot her grandfather a sideways look. "You just agreed Hamm's a nice horse."

"But he isn't Ty's other horse. Don't get me wrong. The boy was always a good roper, one to watch since he began competing in junior rodeo. He didn't come on strong until four years ago, when he got that horse. It was a perfect partnership. Now he's lost that partner."

"I think Hamm has the potential to be every bit as good as Ty's other horse."

"Maybe even better."

Adele nodded in agreement. "He just has to realize that."

"I'm thinking he already does." Pop's expression became pensive. "Recovering from a loss isn't easy, be it someone you've loved or a dream you've held. Something inside dies. There's no miracle cure and no set timetable for recovery. Ty will come back when he's ready." Pop turned a fond smile on Adele. "Or when someone shows him the way."

She patted his hand in return, recalling their early days of Cowboy College. "You could be right."

Stepping off the fence, she pushed a damp strand of hair off her face. The temperature might be only in the low seventies, but the bright morning sun beat down on them, warming her through and through. "If he were anyone else but Ty Boudeau, I'd recommend the beginners' class. The best way to get to know your horse is by starting with the basics."

Pop also stepped off the fence. "Why not Ty?"

"He's…one of the best ropers out there. He doesn't need a beginners' class."

"Are you sure? Could be just the ticket."

"He'll laugh in our faces, then pack his bags."

"He won't laugh if he's committed." Pop moved the toothpick to the other side of his mouth. "And Ty strikes me as a man with a mission."

"Excuse me for disagreeing."

"Relax, Dellie. You know it's a good idea. Ty Boudeau has everything it takes to be the next World Champion. And when he is, he's gonna be thanking you and me."

"Okay," she grumbled. "But I'm not going to be the one to tell him he has to take the beginners' class. *You* are."

"Isn't this place great? My husband and I arrived just a few days ago. We've never been here before. Have you?"

The woman astride the horse standing beside Ty had been rambling nonstop for five minutes solid, not caring if he answered her question or not before going on to the next one.

It was different being around people who didn't recognize him. Different and unsettling. When had he become so accustomed to the attention?

"How'd you get into roping? My husband rodeoed some when he was growing up. We saw a show on cable TV about couples roping, and decided to give it a try. And now we're hooked. Me, not so much."

The woman paused to take a breath. Ty used the lull to observe Adele.

She stood on the ground giving instructions to the group, which was comprised of about a dozen beginner ropers. Ty only half listened. He was quite familiar with the training technique she described—a fake calf head attached to a bale of hay and pulled by a wrangler driving an ATV. The group had assembled in one of the smaller arenas beside the barn, away from the ropers practicing in the main arena, in case the ATV spooked their horses.

"I can't believe I'm actually taking a roping class." The woman untangled her reins for the third time.

"Me, either."

When Pop had proposed the idea that Ty participate in the afternoon beginners' class, he'd balked. Then he learned Adele would be teaching it. That, and the arguments Pop had presented about getting back to basics, convinced Ty to give one—and *only* one—class a try. He told himself it wasn't because he found Adele attractive. Rather, he wanted to see if she could teach as well as she roped. His decision to remain at Cowboy College depended on the outcome.

She continued explaining how the wrangler would take off on the ATV, and that the riders should allow their horses to follow the calf head and bale of hay, rather than attempt to direct them.

Yeah, yeah. Ty suppressed a yawn.

His cell phone rang a minute later, coming just when he thought he'd reached his boredom threshold. Unclipping the phone from his belt, he checked the screen. A photo of his younger sister appeared with her name above it.

"Sorry, I need to take this call," he told the students nearest him, and nudged Hamm into a fast walk away from the group. Stopping about twenty feet away, he answered the call. "Hey, Dana."

From his chosen spot, he could see Adele frowning at him. Too late, Ty realized there was probably something in the rules and regulations he hadn't yet read about no cell-phone calls during class. Oh, well, he'd already screwed up.

"How's it going, bro?"

"Not so great."

"Why?"

"Because I'm sitting here in a beginners' class."

"Really! Doing what? Showing the students how it's done?"

"No, attending. Actually, attending as little as possible."

"I guess a refresher course never hurts."

He should have figured Dana would agree with Pop's suggestion, being it was her idea to come to Cowboy College.

"Right. I could be doing this in my sleep."

"So prove it."

"You're not serious." He laughed.

"I am, Ty. You need to figure out what's not working, and fix it. Taking a beginner class might seem ridiculous, but you need a new perspective, and I'm all for trying anything. You should be, too, if you want to win that championship."

Ty tamped down his rising annoyance. It had been a long time since anyone had lectured him. A long time since he'd felt he deserved a lecture.

A quick glance at Adele confirmed yet another talking-to might be in store for him. She looked about as happy with him as his sister sounded.

"This isn't easy for me, Dana." The admission came with an uncomfortable tightening in his gut.

"I know, honey. But I'm one of the people who has your back, remember?"

"And I appreciate it."

"You couldn't have two better experts there."

"I agree with you about Pop Donnelly. And I wouldn't mind half so much if he was teaching the class."

"What's wrong with Adele Donnelly?"

There was nothing wrong with her that Ty could see. It was his ego having the problem. Granted, he'd asked for her help yesterday, but that was in a weak moment. This morning, when he'd faced himself in the bathroom mirror, he wished he'd asked Pop for help instead.

It wasn't too late. He'd get through this one class and seek out the older man. Maybe then he wouldn't feel like so much of a loser. Or have an entire group of people witnessing his shame.

"You practice with a woman roper," Dana prompted.

"It's different with you."

"Because I'm not competing against you in the same sport?"

"Yikes." Ty grimaced. "That smarts."

"Give Adele a chance before you hightail it out of there."

How did his sister know he'd been contemplating leaving? "Fine. I promise to stay another couple days."

"You said a month." Her tone dared him to defy her.

"Okay, okay. You win."

"Call me if you need anything."

"I will." They disconnected after saying goodbye.

Ty silenced his cell phone and walked Hamm over to the group, smiling apologetically to his classmates and Adele, who blatantly ignored him. All right, he deserved that. Leaning forward and propping a forearm on the saddle horn, he made an effort to really listen to her. After several minutes passed, he had to agree she knew her stuff. She certainly had the attention of all the students.

"Are we ready to try? Who wants to go first?"

Hands shot into the air, none of them Ty's.

"All right, how about you, Mike?" She picked the husband of the woman Ty'd been talking to earlier.

He sat quietly on Hamm, watching Mike and the others take their turns one by one. He easily and quickly spotted the errors with each student. Adele did, too, and patiently explained it to them in laymen's terms the students could comprehend. When everyone had done it, Adele's gaze landed on him.

"You're up next, Ty."

He moved into position behind the bale of hay. Hamm pawed the ground, far more eager to get started than his owner.

"Wait. We're going to do this a little differently with you. Put up your rope."

"My rope?"

"Then drop your reins and kick your feet out of the stirrups."

"You're kidding."

"No hands, no legs."

"Why?" he asked.

"You don't think you can stay seated?" Her green eyes flashed up at him.

He attached his lasso to his saddle with the rope strap. "Ma'am, I can break a green horse riding bareback and with one hand tied behind my back."

"Then this should be a cakewalk for you." She stepped away from him.

With a shrug of his shoulders, his hands resting on his thighs and his legs dangling, he waited for the wrangler to take off on the ATV.

"One more thing," Adele said, the lowered brim of her cowboy hat partially hiding her face. "You have to do it with your eyes closed."

"Excuse me?"

"Eyes closed, Mr. Boudeau."

Was she smiling?

Ty decided to go along with her rather than put up a fight. He'd promised Dana, and besides, the students might learn something from watching him.

"Go!" he told the wrangler.

Hamm took off after the bale of hay as if it were the real thing. Because the wrangler didn't drive the ATV very fast, Hamm's gait was an easy lope rather than a full-out gallop, as it would be in the arena.

Ty set down deep in the saddle, adjusting himself to the horse's rhythm. Trying to, he amended. It wasn't as easy as he might have guessed. Not with his eyes closed and his legs dangling. As the driver zigzagged, mimicking the course a calf might take, Ty felt—*really* felt— the nuances of Hamm's muscles bunching and releasing when he changed directions. Ty shifted accordingly, to compensate for the horse's movements, thinking about it rather than doing it instinctively as he should.

After thirty feet, the wrangler slowed to a stop.

Hamm also slowed. Opening his eyes, Ty used the pressure of his legs to guide his horse in a circle and back toward the group. Once there, he stopped and rubbed his neck, contemplating what had just happened.

"You look perplexed," Adele said, studying him.

"Not that so much," he answered.

She'd put him through a very basic exercise, one, he realized in hindsight, he should have tried himself. Perhaps if he had, the results wouldn't be quite so startling.

Ty trusted himself as a rider. What he'd learned today was that he didn't trust Hamm. Not entirely and not enough. His other horse's accident had robbed Ty of that vital component to a successful rider-horse partnership, and the tiny fear that it would happen again was causing him to hold back.

"Ty?" Adele asked.

He grinned suddenly and waved to the wrangler to come back around.

"I want to go again."

"Hey, Adele, hold on a minute."

Hearing her name, she stopped and turned to see Ty hurrying after her.

Uh-oh. He was probably annoyed at her for what she'd pulled on him during class earlier. Squaring her shoulders, she waited for him to catch up, committed to defending her actions.

"Can I help you with something?" She smiled, pretending she didn't notice the Ben Affleck–like perfection of Ty's strong, dimpled chin or the fluttering in her middle that ogling his chin caused. "Perhaps a copy of the rules and regulations you obviously lost."

"I guess I deserve that." He returned her smile with a healthy dose of chagrin. "No more phone calls. You have my word."

She was glad to see he didn't take offense at her more-serious-than-humorous jest. Rules were rules, in place for a reason, and Ty Boudeau didn't get to break them just because he was a professional roper.

"You're allowed one mistake before we start giving demerits. Ten demerits, however, and you're kicked off the ranch."

His startled expression was so comical, she almost laughed. "I'm joking."

The hint of a twinkle lit his eyes. "You're good, you know."

"I've had a lot of practice keeping unruly students in line."

"No denying I'm one of those unruly students in need of lining out, but that's not what I meant."

"Oh?"

"You're good at spotting what a person's doing wrong. Me included."

She knitted her brows in confusion. "I didn't notice you doing anything wrong."

"Maybe not exactly. But the exercise helped me understand some things about myself. Things that need fixing."

"Not many competitors at your level would admit to that. I'm impressed."

"Don't be. I'm usually thickheaded. A good suggestion could be driving a Mack truck straight at me, and I'd ignore it."

"I'll remember that next time."

He moved closer. "I just wanted to thank you for the help."

"You're welcome." She worried that he was going to take her hand again. Relief flooded her when he didn't. One intimate encounter was more than she could handle. "Have a productive remainder of your day, Mr. Boudeau."

"If you don't mind, I'd like to pick your brain sometime when you have a minute."

She debated refusing his request. In the end, she decided to grant it. He was a paying guest, after all, and part of the fees they charged entitled students to "pick her brain," as he said.

"I'm heading over to check on one of our expectant mares. You can come with me if you like."

His dark eyes, arresting to begin with, lit up. "I would."

"I'm not keeping you from anything important, am I?"

He fell step in beside her. "Only the horde of adoring female fans waiting for me in the lobby."

She momentarily faltered. "If you have to go…"

"I'm kidding." He flashed her his heart-stopping grin.

It appeared she was just as gullible as him.

He surprised her during their walk with the questions he asked, which were detailed and thought provoking. Did tie-down straps really help horses stop faster, or hinder them? How did she feel about the new Professional Cowboy Association regulations, and did they affect her teaching methods? What kind of personal fitness regime, if any, did she recommend for her students?

More than once, Adele found herself examining the

techniques of roping from a different and enlightening perspective.

"Here's where Pop and I keep our private stock," she told Ty when they entered the smallest of the ranch's three barns. At the end of the aisle, they came to a double-wide stall separated from the other horses by twenty feet and a six-foot wall.

"And this is Crackers," Adele said by way of introduction.

Upon seeing her, the heavily pregnant mare nickered softly and lumbered over from the corner where she'd been standing, to hang her shaggy head over the stall door.

Adele stroked the animal's neck. "She was my first barrel-racing horse. Gosh, was that really fourteen years ago?"

"Did you compete professionally?" Ty asked. He stood beside her, his elbow propped on the stall door.

"A little in college."

"Any good?"

"All right."

"Why'd you quit?"

She absently combed her fingers through Crackers's mane. "I came here after graduation to help Pop with the ranch. He'd turned seventy, and his arthritis was getting bad. He needed help, and I needed a job." She didn't mention her grandmother's death. "I've always loved Seven Cedars, and spent a lot of time here when I was growing up."

"Did your parents rodeo?"

"My dad. Though he never did all that well, and moved to Texas years ago. My mom traveled the rodeo circuit considerably longer than Dad, but not to compete."

Adele didn't elaborate. Despite Ty's friendliness, she wasn't ready to confess that her mother had taken up with whatever cowboy would have her, dropping Adele off with her grandparents if her father wouldn't have her. As her mother aged and her looks faded, those cowboys went from being competitors to bullfighters to stock handlers. In between men, she'd find a small place to rent for herself and Adele, but only until another man came along. For a young girl feeling unloved and unwanted, Seven Cedars became a haven in an otherwise turbulent childhood.

"So, Pop taught you to rope."

"He was a man ahead of his time. In those days, women didn't rope. Period." She opened the stall door and went in to give Crackers a closer inspection.

"She looks close," Ty observed.

"Soon." The foal had dropped considerably in the last week, but otherwise, Crackers showed no signs of delivering. "She's due this week."

"Her first?"

"Second. Up until a few years ago, we used her steadily for beginner students. When her stamina began to fade, we decided to breed her." Adele patted Crackers's rump, then left the stall and shut the door behind her. "She's got good lines, and she's a good mama."

"And she's your first horse."

"Pop bought her for me when I was a freshman in high school. There were always plenty of horses to ride wherever I lived, but she was the first one that was truly mine." Latching the stall door, she met Ty's gaze. "Cook will be serving dinner soon, and I need to get back to my office first."

"Will I see you in the dining hall?"

"Absolutely."

Adele made a point of sharing dinner each evening with the students, often moving from one table to another. That way, she got to know them on a more personal level. Breakfast and lunch, however, were hit-or-miss and often consumed on the run.

At the entrance to the barn, she and Ty separated, each heading to their own vehicle. Hers was parked closer, and she hesitated before climbing in, stilled by the sight of Ty striding to his truck.

It had been a very long time since Adele had met a man who gave her that uncomfortable yet deliciously thrilling feeling every time she got within ten feet of him.

She silently warned herself to proceed with caution. Ty Boudeau had all the makings of a heartbreaker, and as much as she might want to get to know him on a more "personal level," she was far better off keeping her distance.

Men who spent inordinate amounts of time on the road didn't make good husbands. It was one of the many lessons her parents' failed marriage and her mother's endless stream of lovers had taught Adele.

Chapter 3

Ty drove through the small town of Markton, the closest community to Cowboy College. It could hardly be described as a metropolis, but he liked its grassroots country charm, its one stoplight at the intersection of Main Street and Brown, and the way everybody waved at everybody else.

Markton was a far cry from Santa Fe, where he'd grown up. He couldn't say *lived* because once he'd left home to rodeo full-time, he traveled six to nine months a year. When he needed to crash for a while, he stayed at his older sister's place. His fifth-wheel trailer parked behind the barn was, sad to say, the closest thing he had to a permanent residence.

He drove along Main Street at the posted speed of thirty-five, enjoying his free afternoon and taking in the various sights. The Spotted Horse Saloon. The feed store. Bush's General Store. The elementary school. The barbershop and its counterpart, Goldie's Locks and Nail Salon.

He'd often thought he might like to settle down in a town like Markton, and as he drove through it—end to end in less than five minutes—he contemplated where to stop first.

The feed store, an always familiar stomping ground, looked to have possibilities. Ty pulled into an empty space across from a sign advertising a popular brand of dog food. Inside the store, he was greeted by the middle-aged man behind the counter, whose double take was almost comical.

"Ty Boudeau?" he asked with raised brows.

"On a good day," Ty joked.

"We heard you were in town." The man came around from behind the counter carrying a pen and piece of paper. "Name's Henry Parkman."

"Pleased to meet you."

"If it's not too much trouble, the wife would sure love to have your autograph."

"No trouble."

It felt good being asked. The requests for autographs had tapered off since he'd lost at Nationals. Ty preferred to think it was because he hadn't been competing of late, not that he'd fallen from grace.

As he scribbled his name on the notepad, Henry Parkman produced his cell phone, held it at arm's reach, leaned in close and snapped a picture of him and Ty.

"For the wife." He grinned sheepishly. "Anything special I can help you with today?"

"Just browsing."

"Holler if you need me," he said to Ty, returning to his place behind the cash register.

Ty gravitated to the back of the store where the saddles and a rather impressive assortment of lariats hung on the wall. Though he wasn't in the market for another one, he removed several from the wall display and tested them for weight and flexibility.

For reasons he chose not to address, he avoided the Iron Grip Ropes—though it probably had something to do with the face smiling at him from the rope's cardboard wrapper. Garth Maitland. The man who'd beat out Ty for the championship last December.

"Mr. Boudeau?" The cracking voice belonged to a teenager who bore a striking resemblance to Stick.

"Hi."

"Hate to bother you, sir," he said, his exceptionally large Adam's apple bobbing as he talked, "but could I trouble you for an autograph?"

"Are you by chance related to Stick over at Cowboy College?" Ty asked as he signed the kid's ball cap with a black marker.

The teen's eyes went wide. "He's my cousin."

"Well, he's a pretty good worker. But don't tell him I said so."

"I—I won't," the kid stammered, and made a beeline for the door.

Ty wasn't in the market for a new pair of boots, either, but he checked out the selection just for something to do. The front-door buzzer went off every few minutes as customers came and left. Deciding he could possibly use a new leather belt, he picked one out and headed to the counter.

While he completed his purchase, the door buzzer went off again. Bidding the store owner goodbye, he turned…and came face-to-face with Adele.

"Oh!" She drew back. "Hello. I didn't know you were here."

"Just seeing what the town has to offer." He glanced at the attractive young woman beside Adele, whose stylish clothes and painful looking four-inch heels were more suited to a stroll down Hollywood Boulevard than Main Street in Markton. "I'm Ty Boudeau."

"This is my friend Reese Carter. She's engaged t-to…" Adele stammered, then recovered. "She lives on the ranch next door."

Ty's chest suddenly constricted, and he cautioned himself not to jump to conclusions. Markton boasted more than one rodeo family; Seven Cedars had more than one neighbor.

"Nice to meet you," he said, and shook the hand Reese offered. "Are you ladies in the market for horse pellets?"

"We were just killing a little time before going for lunch at the Spotted Horse."

"They serve food?"

"Surprisingly good food." Reese smiled brightly.

She sure didn't look as if she'd grown up on a ranch, not with her high heels and the designer sunglasses propped on her head.

"Well, it was nice running into you." Adele looked ready to bolt, and clamped on to her friend's arm. "See you later at the ranch."

"Would you like to join us for lunch?" Reese asked.

"I'm sure he's busy," Adele cut in before Ty could answer.

Because she seemed in such an all-fired hurry to get away from him, he answered, "I'd like that very much. Appreciate the invitation."

Adele's mouth, usually lush and pretty, tightened.

Finding her discomfort amusing, Ty followed the ladies to the door and held it open for them. They crossed the street at the corner and went up half a block to the saloon entrance.

Inside, Reese informed the hostess her fiancé would be joining them.

"I'll show him to your table."

"That won't be necessary." Reese peered past the hostess, her face alight. "Here he comes now."

Everyone looked over to see a handsome cowboy making his way toward them, his swagger confident.

The same anxiety that had gripped Ty that first day at Cowboy College, the one he thought he'd successfully conquered, returned with a vengeance. Too late, he realized his mistake—he'd misread Adele completely. At the least, he should have asked Reese her fiancé's name before barging in on her and Adele's lunch date.

Then he wouldn't be stuck sitting across the table from the man who had beat him in team and tie-down roping last December, stealing the title of World Champion and the Iron Grip sponsorship deal from him.

Each bite of Ty's Swiss-cheese-and-mushroom burger tasted like paste and sat in his stomach like a lead ball. He couldn't fault Garth Maitland for his unappetizing meal. The guy had been nothing but decent all during lunch. He always was, even when Ty lost to him at Nationals.

Until then, Ty and Garth had been friendly rivals, getting along well, real well even, when they weren't competing. Not the same could be said when they were in the arena. Both of them were out to win, and a mutual liking and respect of each other's abilities went only so far. After losing the title, Ty had kept his distance from Garth. Not because he resented the man; Garth had won fair and square. The problem was Ty's, who felt he was staring his personal failings square in the face each time he looked at Garth.

The lunch conversation, stilted at first, soon settled into a congenial rhythm, carried mostly by his companions. Ty injected a comment every now and then just to keep anyone from noticing his discomfort.

Except one person did.

"I'm sorry," Adele whispered under her breath, when Garth and Reese were busy speaking to each other and momentarily ignoring them. "I tried to—"

"Not your fault," Ty whispered back. They were seated together in the booth, the only positive thing about lunch as far as he was concerned. "It's okay."

"Really?" She appeared genuinely distraught.

He flashed his best interview smile, hoping to reassure her. "Really."

She'd tried to avoid this disaster earlier at the feed store. He had no one to blame but himself.

"What brings you to Cowboy College, Ty?" Reese asked, her demeanor curious but friendly.

Instantly, silence descended on the table. Adele

gnawed her lower lip. Garth's eyebrows raised in curiosity.

Ty got annoyed—with himself and the situation. Okay, he'd lost the world championship title and a profitable sponsorship deal. To the man with whom he'd just eaten lunch. No reason for everyone to act as if he had an incurable disease.

"I apologize if I said something wrong." Reese looked contrite.

"You didn't." Ty gave her credit for not ignoring the sudden tension. "I came to Cowboy College for Adele's help with my new horse." The glossed-over explanation sounded better than the truth.

"It was a shame about your other horse," Garth said sympathetically. "And bad timing."

"It was. But these things happen."

"They do. My old partner fell and busted his kneecap last September. He won't be competing again until this fall, and even that's iffy."

"Here's to this season." Ty lifted his mug of beer in a toast.

"To this season," Garth repeated, and lifted his own, a glint in his eyes. He was obviously looking forward to the next time they went up against each other.

Determination surged inside Ty. Residing next door to his rival might have some advantages. At the very least, the constant reminder would help motivate him and keep him focused on his goal.

Reese's glance traveled from one man to the other. "Is something going on here I don't get?"

Garth chuckled.

Ty wanted to but wasn't able to let his guard down enough to explain.

The remainder of their meal went well, until it came time to pay the server.

"I've got it." Ty reached for the bill.

"No problem." Garth beat him to the punch by a scant second. "I already told the waitress lunch was on me." He signed the slip with a flourish.

"All right. I'll buy next time."

"Deal." Garth grinned, and for a moment they were friends again.

Outside the saloon, they made plans to go their separate ways.

"You need to head back to the ranch right away?" Reese asked Adele.

"If you don't mind. I've got a bunch of work at the office stacked up."

"It's Sunday. Don't you ever take any time off?"

"I just did."

"You work way too hard," Reese scolded, and slung an arm around Adele's shoulders. "Come on, we'll drive you home."

"She can ride with me," Ty offered. He'd assumed Adele had driven herself, or he would have offered earlier.

"You don't have to," she answered a little too quickly.

"No problem. I'm going that way."

"I hate cutting your trip to town short."

"You're not. I was just thinking of heading back to the ranch." In truth, he'd been planning on driving down the road to Little Twister Creek and the fishing spot Stick had mentioned earlier. Noting Adele's hesitancy,

Ty couldn't help himself and pressed the point, if only to see if she'd rather inconvenience her friends than ride with him.

"Why don't you come by one day for a visit?" Garth suggested. "Have a look around."

Ty had seen pictures of Garth's place in various rodeo publications. It was a roper's dream. Part of him wanted to go, just to check out the setup and salivate. The other part of him resisted. He would, after all, be walking into the enemy's camp.

"Thanks. I may take you up on that one day."

"Bring your horse. When you and Adele have worked out the kinks," he added.

Ty bristled. With competitiveness, not anger. He recognized a challenge when it was issued, and would like nothing better than to take Hamm over to Garth's and show him what he could expect to see on the circuit next month.

"I'll do that. Soon."

"I'm looking forward to it."

"I don't know about you," Reese said to Adele with exaggerated weariness, "but I've had just about as much testosterone as I can handle in one day." She looped her arm through Garth's. "It was really nice meeting you, Ty. And I do hope you'll come for a visit. With or without your horse. Bye, sweetie." She blew Adele a kiss. "Call me tomorrow."

"You okay?" Ty asked Adele as they were heading to his truck. "You've been awfully quiet."

"A little tired. I ate too much at lunch."

"We can walk a bit if you want."

"I really should get back to work."

He was pretty certain there was more to her subdued mood, but didn't ask, opening the passenger side door instead.

"Sorry about me and Garth back there," he said as he drove. The ranch was only about a fifteen-minute ride from town. Ty didn't intend to spend it all in silence. "We probably got a little carried away."

"It's understandable. All things considered, I think you two behaved quite well."

"Meaning he could have rubbed his championship belt buckle in my face?"

"That, and you could have retaliated with something equally petty. It had to be hard for you, sitting there, pretending you weren't bothered."

"Not as hard as watching him win last December. You have no idea how much I wanted his rope to land short that day."

"I do," she said absently, staring out the window. "I've watched men compete in roping for years, and known that no matter how good I was, no matter how hard I trained, I'd never be allowed to compete against them."

"Do you want to?"

"I do and have. In local jackpots where women are allowed to enter. But it's not the same as a professional rodeo."

"You're the exception. Not many women can go head-to-head with a man in this sport."

"Not yet."

Ty had to smile. He had no doubt if a member of the fairer sex could break into professional tie-down roping and pave the path for others, it would be Adele Donnelly.

Which was why he should probably give her every opportunity to help him with his problem.

"Selfishly," he admitted, "I'm glad you're not competing professionally."

"Why's that?"

"Because after the last few days, I'm thinking you're the only person who can help me." Her expression softened. So did a place in Ty's heart. "Unless you think it's a conflict of interest. Garth's your neighbor and friend."

"No conflict. He understands business is business."

"Just out of curiosity, have you ever beaten him in a one-on-one match?"

Her green eyes sparkled. "Frequently."

Ty burst into the first true belly laugh he'd had in months.

Moments later, they pulled up in front of the main lodge. He put the truck in Park but left the motor running.

"Thanks for the ride." Adele had her hand on the door handle but made no move to open it.

Was she also reluctant for their afternoon encounter to end?

"Thanks for letting me tag along during your lunch," Ty said.

"Are you serious? It couldn't have been that much fun for you."

"There were a few high spots." Like the seating arrangement.

"Next time I try to warn you—" she gave him a stern look "—pay attention."

"How 'bout next time we go to lunch just the two of us?"

The pause that followed lasted a little too long.

"I...uh..." She inhaled slowly and squared her shoulders. "Thank you for asking, but I don't date guests."

He hid his disappointment with a joke. "Is that one of those rules on the list I haven't read yet?"

"No, a personal one. Less messy that way when the guest leaves." Without another word, she pushed open the passenger door and hopped out, giving him the briefest of waves as she climbed the steps to the lodge entrance.

Her abrupt departure had Ty wondering if she'd been there and done that, and been left behind with a wounded heart.

And since he was leaving after the Buffalo Bill Cody Stampede, he certainly couldn't argue the logic behind her rule.

"What's wrong?"

"Nothing, Pop." Adele had practically steamrolled her grandfather in her haste to get inside.

"You sure?" He studied her with concern.

She suspected he'd been watching her and Ty from the lobby window. "Absolutely. Why would you think there was?" She made her way around the registration counter and into the sanctuary of her small office.

Pop followed her, shutting the door behind them except for a narrow crack—just in case someone rang the bell.

"You're upset, and Ty looked none too happy, either."

She was never any good at hiding her feelings.

"Reese and I ran into him at the feed store. He wound up joining us for lunch. Garth was there, too."

Pop harrumphed. "Guess I can't blame the boy for being a touch prickly after that."

"Actually, he handled it pretty well." She gave her grandfather a brief account of the lunch.

"Then why are you acting like you two tangled? Is he mad about taking the beginner class?"

"Not at all."

Pop lowered himself carefully into the office's single visitor chair, wincing slightly. When he was settled, he let out a long groan. "Damn hip's giving me fits today. Must be the rain."

It hadn't rained in over two weeks and didn't remotely look like it was going to anytime soon. "You taking the new medicine your doctor prescribed?"

"Yes, and quit nagging me." They both knew he should have hip-replacement surgery, but Pop insisted he wasn't going under the knife unless it was a matter of life and death.

Adele thought his refusal had more to do with her than any fear of hospitals. He worried about leaving the entire responsibility of the ranch and Cowboy College to her.

"And quit changing the subject," he scolded.

"What?"

"From you and Ty." His wizened features softened. "You like him."

Hoping to distract her grandfather, she shook her mouse and roused her computer from its hibernation. "He's just another guest."

"You don't date enough. You need to get out and have a little fun now and then."

"I went to lunch today."

"With friends. That's not the same."

No? It had felt a little like a date. Part of the time, anyway.

"You've haven't gone out with anyone since that Joe kid from Phoenix."

"Yes, I have."

"When? Who?"

Adele searched her brain and came up blank. "I'm sure I have."

Pop just grunted. His way of saying he was right.

She skimmed the contents of her email in-box, hating to agree with her grandfather. Joe had been her last relationship, and it could hardly be called serious. In fact, none of her relationships since she'd graduated high school had been serious.

"Ty's a good man," Pop continued, oblivious to her diversion tactics. "And he's taken a shine to you. I can tell by how he looks at you."

"I'm not interested in him except as a guest of this ranch and a student in my class."

Pop chuckled. "I guess that's why you were walking away from him earlier like a bee flew up the back of your shirt."

"I was not!" Adele's heated denial was met with another grunt. She clicked on the unopened emails in earnest, ignoring her grandfather.

He abruptly sobered. "Is it because he's a professional roper?"

She didn't respond.

"They're not all bad," his said, his gravelly voice dropping in pitch.

"I know." She turned and gave him a soft smile. "But men like you are the exception, not the rule."

"It's been a lot of years, Dellie. Time you moved on. Put your parents and what they did behind you."

"I don't want to talk about them. Not now."

"Just because your mom and dad were lousy parents is no reason to shut yourself off from love. I won't be around forever."

"Don't say that!"

"You need someone besides an old coot like me to dote on. A husband. Children."

"You're more than enough."

"Get to know Ty. Don't let him being a professional roper put you off."

Her grandfather had hit the nail on the head, and they both knew it. Work was simply an excuse. The main reason Adele didn't date much was because the vast majority of single men she met were unsuitable. Markton was a small town and the pickings slim to begin with. Making it worse, she didn't date employees or, as she'd told Ty, guests. Most others close to her age were either rodeo men or wannabe rodeo men.

After watching her parents destroy each other's lives *and* hers, she'd vowed not to become involved with anyone remotely connected with "the business."

"He's leaving in a few weeks, Pop. Even if I wanted to give him a shot, I wouldn't."

Before her grandfather could comment, the bell on the reception counter rang. Adele sprang to her feet and called, "Be right there."

As there were no new guests scheduled to arrive today, she fully expected to see one of their current students standing at the counter, waiting to inform her of a need. At the sight of the lone, middle-aged woman wheeling one small suitcase, Adele came to a sudden stop, every thought flying instantly out of her head.

"Who is it?" Pop asked, hobbling out the office door. He, too, drew up short. But unlike Adele, he wasn't at a loss for words. "What the hell are you doing here?"

Adele wanted to know the same thing.

"Oh, Pop," Lani Donnelly chirped. "Is that anything to say to your daughter-in-law?" She turned to Adele, a too-sunny-to-be-real smile on her face. "Don't just stand there, baby girl, come give your mom a hug."

Chapter 4

Adele didn't move right away. She couldn't. Waves of hurt, anger and resentment hit her all at once and kept her rooted in place. She was vaguely aware of a guest coming out of the business center and leaving through the lobby entrance. She was *acutely* aware of her grandfather standing beside her. For a man with debilitating arthritis, his spine had snapped as straight and rigid as an iron bar.

"Please, baby girl." The pleading in her mother's voice penetrated the haze surrounding Adele.

She shored up her defenses, only to discover they weren't as impenetrable as she'd hoped. The sad and neglected little girl inside her still longed for the comfort of her mother's arms and the reassurance that she was loved.

"You okay, Dellie?"

At Pop's question, Adele glanced down, to see that her hands were shaking.

"I'm fine." And she was fine. Pulling herself together, she wrung the tremors from her fingers and raised her chin. No matter what, her mother wasn't going to hurt her again. Not after Adele had worked so hard to create a good life for herself.

"Hello, Mom."

They each took a step, then two, and met in the middle. The hug Adele offered was reserved. Not so for her mother, who clung to her, then burst into great racking sobs.

Adele wanted to remained unaffected, but couldn't. Years of mistrust and disappointment, however, enabled her to extract herself from her mom's desperate grasp.

"What's wrong?" she asked.

"Nothing." Lani dabbed at her eyes. "I'm just so happy to see you. It's been months."

Almost two years, but Adele didn't bother correcting her.

They were about the same height and had once possessed similar figures. A weight loss during the last two years had left Lani painfully thin. Combined with her rough-around-the-edges appearance, she looked years older than her actual age. Her green eyes, highlighted with too much makeup, darted around the lobby with the desperation of a starving animal seeking its next meal.

"You should have called to let us know you were coming." Adele struggled to keep bitterness from creeping into her voice. Her mother may have hit rock bottom—the only reason Adele could think of to explain the unexpected visit—but that didn't erase all the bad memories.

"The battery died on my cell phone, and I haven't had a chance to replace it."

She was lying. Adele could feel it in her gut. Her mother had probably been unable to pay her bill without the help of a man.

Was else was she covering up?

"You look good, Pop." Lani smiled at Adele's grandfather, though her eyes were still filled with tears.

"You don't." Leave it to Pop to cut to the chase.

"This last year's been pretty hard on me." She swallowed.

He hobbled closer. "Is that why you just showed up out of the blue?"

"I, ah…"

One of the housekeeping staff entered the lobby pushing a cart laden with cleaning supplies, fresh linens and a vacuum. After a hesitant glance at them, she changed direction and went into the TV lounge to begin her work.

Lani rolled her suitcase from one side to the other. Uncertainty clouded her features, and she blurted, "I need a place to stay for a few days. Maybe a few weeks. I know it's a lot to ask, and Lord knows you have every reason turn me away, but I've got nowhere else to go. I'm willing to work off my room and board."

Adele took a step back, stunned by her mother's request. She didn't know what shocked her more—that her mother had the gall to show up unexpectedly and ask for a favor, a big one, or that she was actually willing to work. Lani hadn't voluntarily sought employment that Adele could recall.

"I don't know, Mom," she hedged. "We're kind of full right now."

"I can always sleep on your couch." The offhand remark came across as desperate. "You'll hardly know I'm there. I swear."

Adele almost choked. Her mother sleeping on her couch? Not in this lifetime. "Mom—"

"She can stay in room nine." Pop stepped around Adele.

She started to protest, not wanting her mother anywhere near Seven Cedars, only to shut her mouth when Pop took hold of her mother's suitcase.

"Come on, we'll take you there now. Dellie, grab the key and bring the golf cart around."

Though they ran the ranch together, it technically belonged to Pop. Adele might disagree with his decision, and would tell him later when they were in private, but the choice to let Lani stay was his to make.

She promptly spun on her heels and fled to her office without glancing back.

In addition to eighteen fully equipped cabins, they had a building with nine hotel-like rooms behind the main lodge. Number nine was on the end, the smallest of the rooms, and contained only a twin bed. For that reason, it was usually vacant. The room had been reserved for the upcoming weekend, but the guest had canceled.

It looked to Adele as if they wouldn't be renting number nine out even if they did get a last-minute request.

Removing the room and golf cart keys from a cabinet

in her office, she exited the lodge through the kitchen's back door. The cart was parked under the large cedar tree where she'd last left it. She preferred driving ATVs, and used the golf cart mostly to transport guests and their luggage.

Not once had she imagined that her mother would ever be a guest.

The reason Lani had given for her unannounced visit didn't ring true. Though it was obvious she was in dire straits, Adele couldn't shake the sensation there was more going on than a run of bad luck. The question was what?

"Here we are," she announced when they pulled in front of room nine.

The three of them climbed out of the golf cart's one bench seat with noticeable relief. Pop insisted on removing Lani's bag from the back and wheeling it inside.

Adele opened the door to the room and handed the key to her mother with some reluctance.

"Thank you." Lani's voice cracked and her eyes welled with fresh tears. "Both of you."

"Come on, Dellie." Pop patted Adele's shoulder. "Let's give your mother a chance to get settled. Dinner starts at six," he told Lani. "If you want, after you eat, you can go to the kitchen and help the staff clean up. They're always shorthanded. Cook will tell you what to do."

Lani simply nodded and quickly shut the door behind them.

Her mother's hurry to be alone might be because she was going to start crying again, Adele thought, and her determination to remain unaffected battled with concern. Not caring was easier when Lani lived hundreds of miles away.

"She's in sorry shape," Pop said once they'd gotten back in the golf cart and were putt-putting down the road to the lodge.

"Is that why you agreed to let her stay on?"

"Partly."

"You're not usually such a softy. Especially where Mom's concerned."

In fact, the last time Lani had dropped Adele off at Seven Cedars, Pop had told Lani that Adele was staying with him for good and for her not to set foot on the place again. Adele had been fourteen at the time, but she remembered their huge fight as if it had been last week.

Lani had respected Pop's demand and never come back. Until today. Adele had finished out high school in Markton and then left for the University of Wyoming, seeing her mother only on occasion. When she'd returned to Seven Cedars after graduation, it had been like coming home.

"Maybe it's time to let bygones be bygones."

Adele wasn't so sure about that. There were too many bygones to let go of easily.

They reached the lodge, and she parked the golf cart under the same tree. Pop started to get out, but she stopped him with a hand on his arm.

"Considering the way Mom's always treated you, you have no reason to show her the tiniest kindness, much less forgiveness."

Pop sighed, removed an unused toothpick from his front shirt pocket and stuck it in his mouth. "Your mom's made a lot of mistakes in her life, but she did one thing right. For which I'm very grateful."

"What's that?"

"She gave me and your grandmother legal guardianship of you back when you were fifteen. She didn't have to do that."

"She gave you guardianship?" Adele's jaw went slack.

"Your dad signed off, too."

"Why didn't you tell me?"

"Lani didn't want you to think your parents had abandoned you."

"But they did," Adele insisted. A year after that dreadful day and terrible fight.

"Depends, I guess, on how you look at it. They weren't such bad parents that they didn't realize you needed a real home and someone to take care of you."

With that, her grandfather left Adele sitting alone in the golf cart, reeling from her second shock that day.

All this time, she'd believed her grandparents had wanted her. Had fought to have her.

Instead, her mother and father had simply handed her over, like an old set of golf clubs or a broken TV.

Worse, none of them, not even Pop, had had the decency to tell her.

A wall of chilly air greeted Ty the moment he stepped outside his cabin. For a moment he considered driving to the barn, then decided a brisk walk would jump-start his sluggish system.

Normally an early riser, he was up and at it even earlier than usual thanks to a restless night. The reason for his tossing and turning was the same as his trip to the barn at half past the crack of dawn. Hamm hadn't been himself yesterday and appeared to be favoring his right front leg. After having his other horse suffer a debilitating injury, Ty was cautious when it came to Hamm. Some might say overly cautious.

In his mind, he had good reason. He couldn't afford another setback. Not this far into the rodeo season.

He briefly considered stopping at the dining hall and grabbing a cup of coffee. They weren't scheduled to start serving for another twenty minutes, but as Stick had promised on Ty's first day, Cook was very accommodating to the guests. Ty's concern for Hamm took precedence, however, and he made straight for the main barn.

The ranch hands had just begun feeding when he got there. While Hamm was happy to see him, he was more interested in breakfast. The big horse paced back and forth in anticipation as the feed wagon moved slowly down the aisle. Ty used the opportunity to observe the worrisome front leg.

Hamm grabbed a bite of hay even before the thick flake was dropped into his feed trough. He then ignored the hay in favor of the grain that followed, snorting lustily.

Now that he was standing still, Ty entered the stall and ran his hand over Hamm's front leg, paying particular attention to the knee area. It looked normal. No swelling or bruising. Next, he hefted Hamm's foot and, using a penknife, checked under the shoe. Hamm didn't so much as blink during the entire examination. Could be because he was fine. Could be because he was too busy eating to care about a little tenderness.

After another minute and a pat to Hamm's rump, Ty decided to get that cup of coffee in the dining hall and come back when the horse had finished eating. Then he'd take him to the round pen, work him a few minutes and get a better look at the leg, just to be one hundred percent sure.

Maybe he'd ask Adele to join him and give an opinion. She had a good eye when it came to both riders and their horses. It also gave him an excuse to see her. She'd missed dinner the previous evening. He assumed whatever work she'd mentioned at lunch with Garth and Reese must have kept her busy.

In the dining hall, the aroma of breakfast proved too tempting to resist. When one of the waitstaff brought out a tray of freshly baked cinnamon rolls, two somehow made it onto Ty's plate before he realized it. He no sooner sat down to eat then he noticed Adele cutting across the large and noisy room toward the kitchen.

Her gaze didn't waver from the floor in front of her, which was certainly strange. She was often in a hurry, especially in the mornings. But she always had a wave or smile for the guests. Ty's curiosity lasted only until she disappeared behind the kitchen's double doors and he took his first bite of the warm and gooey cinnamon roll.

Thirty minutes and one full stomach later, Ty was back in the barn. Haltering Hamm, he led the horse to the round pen. There, he put him through his paces, mostly satisfied that whatever had been bothering him yesterday, if anything, was no longer an issue. Nonetheless, he'd watch Hamm closely during morning class.

After walking him several times around all three barns to cool him down, Ty returned the horse to his stall. Class didn't start until nine, leaving a good hour to kill. Not really enough time to go back to his cabin. Ty supposed he could grab another cup of coffee in the dining hall.

It was then he saw Adele heading into the small barn where she and Pop kept their private stock. Even at a distance, she still appeared distracted. Then it hit Ty. Her mare—Crackers?—was due to deliver any day. That could explain Adele's unusual behavior, especially if there was a problem with the birth.

On impulse, Ty followed her into the barn and, as he'd guessed, found her at Crackers's stall. She had her arms resting on the door and was staring, unseeing, at the mare and newborn foal standing by her side.

"She had the baby," Ty said, approaching quietly.

Adele started at the sight of him but recovered quickly. "Sometime last night. A filly."

The foal, initially wary, relaxed enough around her human visitors to begin nursing. Ty noticed she stood straight and that her weight was good. A blanket of white spots covered her hind end. "She looks healthy."

"Seems to be. The vet is coming out later this morning to check on her."

"Nice markings, too. Going to be an Appaloosa like the mare."

For the first time that morning Adele looked Ty fully in the face. He was momentarily taken aback by the dark smudges beneath her eyes. She hadn't slept well, either.

"Are you okay?" The question slipped out automatically.

"I'm fine." She tried to smile, but it was lopsided. Then it wobbled.

"Adele."

All at once, she let out a sob. Her attempts to swallow a second one failed.

Ty responded without thinking. Reaching for her, he pulled her into his arms.

Her immediate response was to stiffen and draw back, as if she suddenly realized what she'd done.

"It's okay," he murmured, and she relented, burying her face in his shirt.

"I'm sorry."

"Don't be." He patted her back.

Normally, Ty avoided crying women, or at least kept his distance. Like a lot of his male brethren, he supposed, he didn't know what to say or how to act. His confusion was ten times worse if he was the cause of the woman's distress.

For some reason, it felt different with Adele. And not just because he was relatively certain someone else was responsible for her being upset.

He guessed she didn't often let down her guard. That she did so in front of him, allowed him to offer her comfort, showed just how much she trusted him and—was it possible?—liked him.

Tilting her head back, she looked up at him, blinking back the last of her tears. "I can't imagine what you think of me." Her damp lashes had formed tiny spikes that surrounded her liquid green eyes.

Ty was captivated. Driven by a force he couldn't resist, he lowered his head and pressed his mouth to hers.

Just one taste. One tiny sip of her petal-soft lips. He wanted more. Any man in his right mind would. But even this infinitesimal piece of heaven was more than he was entitled to. Whatever upset Adele had left her vulnerable, and he wasn't one to take advantage of that.

With a last featherlight brush of his lips against hers, he drew back—only to have Adele stop him with a tug on his jacket. Clutching the thick fabric in her hands, she drew him closer.

Clearly, her emotions had gotten the better of her, and she wasn't thinking straight. If Ty were a gentleman, he'd tactfully disengage himself from her embrace. At the first touch of her tongue to his, however, *his* emotions got the better of *him*. When he heard Adele's soft moan and felt her arms circle his neck, he was a lost man.

The longer their kiss lasted, the more difficult it became for him to restrain himself. She felt exquisite, a maddening combination of taut muscles and soft curves. She tasted even better, like biting into another one of those freshly baked cinnamon rolls.

Just when the last of his restraint threatened to snap, she broke off their kiss, stepped back and placed her palms on his chest. Both of them were breathing hard. Her tears, he noted, had dried.

"Adele."

She shook her head and shushed him with a finger to her lips.

He hoped she wasn't planning on apologizing, because he sure wasn't sorry about what had happened. No way.

"If you're—"

She silenced him with another head shake, and cut her eyes to a place just over his shoulder.

All at once the hairs on Ty's neck rose, and he sensed they weren't alone.

"Shoot," he muttered.

"Yeah," Adele agreed.

A moment later Ty heard a loud voice say, "What in tarnation is going on here?"

He turned, expecting to see Pop.

What he didn't expect was the woman accompanying him, her face an older, harsher version of Adele's.

Grinning saucily, she gave Ty a thorough once-over. "Well, ain't you something."

Behind him, Adele softly swore.

"Is she your mother?"

"Yes."

"You look kind of alike."

Adele grumbled to herself. If Ty had so easily spotted the resemblance, so would everyone at the ranch.

"She here for a visit?"

"Sort of." After only two meals, dinner last night and breakfast this morning, Lani was fast becoming useful in the kitchen—a surprising turn of events that didn't make Adele one bit happy.

"How long is she staying?"

"Not long." *Better not be.*

"I'm sorry about putting you in a, ah, compromising situation back there," he said.

They were walking toward the main arena, though walking was a loose term. Adele was practically running, and Ty, even with his six-foot-plus height, was forced to take long strides in order to keep up with her. She didn't want him accompanying her, but after getting caught kissing him, by her grandfather and mother, it didn't seem fair or right telling him to beat it.

"You weren't the only one participating in...what happened."

He chuckled. "For which I'm damn glad."

"I shouldn't have—" She swallowed to clear the lump in her throat. Allowing her emotions to run amok was what had landed her in this jam in the first place. Why had her mother chosen now to show up? Why had she shown up at all? And why did Ty have to be such a good kisser? "I shouldn't have allowed things to go as far as they did."

"What now?" There was a hint of amusement in his voice. "Are we going to pretend we didn't kiss?"

Adele would like nothing better. However, she was relatively certain she'd remember kissing Ty for the rest of her life. In vivid detail.

"I think we should try."

He laughed out loud.

She frowned and trudged ahead.

They reached the main arena and went in through the gate. Beginner class was scheduled to start soon. Some of the students were already warming up their horses in the adjoining, smaller arena.

Ty followed Adele to the holding pen that housed the

calves, and busied himself checking on the gate while she reviewed a list of instructions with the wrangler. When they were done, she made an effort to shake Ty by suggesting, "Go ahead and saddle up if you want. Class starts soon."

"What about your horse?"

"Stick's supposed to be taking care of that for me." Fingers crossed, the kid was doing his job. Adele dreaded going into the barn, just in case Pop and her mother were still there.

And speaking of Pop and her mother, just what the heck were they doing together? In her embarrassment and haste to get away, Adele had forgotten to ask. Anybody else and she'd have believed they were wanting a peek at the new filly. But Pop and Lani didn't take strolls around the ranch together.

As soon as class was over, she intended to find her grandfather and pester him until she got an answer.

But before then, she was going to have to relieve herself of Ty's company. Covering the last item on her list with the wrangler, she left him to join Ty at the gate. Subtleties hadn't worked, so she tried being direct.

"You need to leave now," she told him. "To get ready."

"I will leave." He flashed her that killer sexy grin again. "As soon as you agree to meet me after class. We need to talk."

She cast a furtive glance at the wrangler, who appeared to be occupied with his task of separating the calves, but was probably hanging on their every word. "I thought we agreed to pretend that didn't happen," she hissed.

"I meant about your mother."

She drew back, completely caught off guard. "Hell no."

His grin widened. "You owe me that much. For allowing things to go as far as they did," he said, quoting her.

"You started it."

"I admit, I'm a man and a pushover when it comes to a crying woman."

She glanced over her shoulder at the wrangler and grimaced. How long until this piece of juicy gossip made the rounds of the ranch?

She conceded to Ty's request only to get rid of him. "I'll meet you in the barn office at eleven-thirty."

"I have a better idea."

She didn't like the glint in his eyes.

"Take me on a tour of the ranch."

"A tour?"

"Our horses will already be saddled. And I've been wanting to see the place since I arrived."

"Fine," Adele reluctantly agreed.

She just wished part of her wasn't thrilled and eagerly anticipating a ride with him.

Chapter 5

Ty collected Hamm from where he'd left him tethered in the barn. Tired of standing, the horse practically knocked Ty over in his haste to get outside. Ty didn't mind. He admired the horse's natural athleticism and endless energy. If they could just get in sync like him and his last horse, they'd be unbeatable.

A quick stop at the water trough proved to be a waste of time. Hamm wasn't interested in drinking. He did no more than splash water with his snout, reminding Ty of that old saying about leading a horse to water.

Adele hadn't specified a meeting place, so Ty led Hamm toward the open area in front of the barns, figuring he'd see her eventually. He ran into two of his classmates near the smaller practice arena—Mike and his wife, the woman who talked a lot during class. Thankfully, her name came to Ty a split second before she hailed him.

"Hey there, Ty."

"How you doing, Sandy? Mike? Getting some extra practice in?"

The couple was taking turns tossing ropes at a stationary practice dummy.

"Yeah." Mike grinned sheepishly. "I can't quite figure out what Adele was trying to show us this morning." He wound his rope into a loose coil.

Sandy laughed. "I can't figure *any* of it. But it's still a hoot." Of the two of them, she was the less serious and the less coordinated. That didn't stop her from enjoying herself, a trait Ty admired.

He wondered what it would be like to have the kind of affectionate and supportive relationship Mike and Sandy did. He met a lot of women on the rodeo circuit, but most were either competitors focused on their own careers or buckle bunnies with a personal agenda that didn't appeal to Ty.

Like Adele's mother.

He hadn't said anything to Adele, but he'd recognized Lani the moment he saw her. No surprise, really. Rodeo folk might be spread from one corner of the globe to the other, but they were also a small community unto themselves. Everybody knew everybody, or at least had heard of them. Lani had been a member of the rodeo world far too long for Ty not to have run into her now and again through the years.

He was no authority on reading people, but he'd wager Adele wasn't close to her, judging from the look she'd given Lani earlier.

"You think you could watch me throw a few and see what I'm doing wrong?" Mike asked.

"If you don't mind," Sandy hurriedly added. "We don't want to keep you."

"Sure. Why not?" Ty was early and Adele was nowhere in sight. "I can spare a few minutes."

"Taking a ride?" The woman's attention strayed to Hamm, who was pawing the ground impatiently.

"Thinking about it."

They didn't need to know he was touring the ranch with Adele. And if she failed to show up as promised… well, he could always ride around the ranch by himself.

Tethering Hamm to a nearby post, he perused the open area one last time. No Adele.

"Go ahead." Ty turned his attention to Mike. "Show me what you've got."

The man raised his arm over his head and swung his rope in a circle before tossing it at the fake cow head. The lasso just missed.

"Dang." Mike shook his head in disgust. "I think I might need glasses."

"Do it again." Ty studied him closely while he repeated the exercise, and came to the same conclusion he had the first time. "This time, try shifting your weight just slightly to your left foot."

Mike did and his next toss landed where it should, if a little lopsided.

"All right!" He beamed.

"One more time."

Mike threw the rope again with the same results.

"Good job." Sandy clapped.

"Can you feel the difference?" Ty asked.

"Yeah." Mike rolled his right shoulder as if testing it.

"Your center of gravity was off."

He laughed and shook his head. "Sounds too simple."

Ty didn't comment. He was too busy replaying his statement to Mike over and over in his head.

Center of gravity. He should have picked up on that in the beginners' class, when Adele had had him riding with his eyes closed. He'd repeated the exercise several times since, until he felt he knew which way Hamm would turn even before the horse did. But Ty hadn't paid attention to his center of gravity while throwing the rope.

Another point-two second gain in his time was staring him smack in the face.

What was wrong with him that he hadn't seen these mistakes before? He was hardly a novice. Blaming four years of competing exclusively on one horse was beginning to sound like a lame excuse. In reality, Ty's inflated ego and overabundance of confidence had gotten in the way, convincing him he needed to retrain Hamm rather than retrain himself.

While Ty was absorbed with this latest revelation, two things happened. Mike continued to throw more successful tosses and Adele emerged from the barn astride the paint mare she'd usually rode.

"Hey, I've got to go," he told Mike and Sandy.

"See you at dinner?" Hope shone in Sandy's eyes.

"You bet."

"Thanks for your help." Mike extended his hand, and Ty shook it.

"My pleasure."

And it was. Ty had enjoyed giving Mike pointers. On top of that, he'd learned something valuable about himself.

From the corner of his eye he spotted Adele riding in

his direction. Memories of their kiss returned, and he forgot all about Mike and Sandy and roping and pretty much everything else except her.

Riding to meet her halfway, he ignored the stares of nearby wranglers. He couldn't be the first guest Adele had taken on a tour.

"Where would you like to start?" she asked, as Hamm tried to make friends with the mare by stretching his head out and sniffing her. The mare responded by pinning her ears back and playing hard to get.

"How far is Little Twister Creek?" Other than that one afternoon in Markton, and walking to and from his cabin, Ty had seen almost nothing of the countryside.

"A few miles. More than we can fit in this afternoon."

"Then how 'bout just around the ranch?"

She took him through three gates. At each one, she opened the latch and swung the gate wide without dismounting. When they were both through, she pushed it shut and relatched it, also without dismounting.

"You've been working with her," Ty said as they rode across the big pasture.

"Bella can be a bit flighty, but she's learning." Adele nudged the mare into a slow trot, but not before he glimpsed her eyes warming with pleasure at his compliment.

"How long have you had her?"

"A month or so. I'm training her for a client."

"You do that often?"

"Sometimes. Depends on the horse and the client."

With Adele riding in front, they picked their way along a winding trail toward a manmade stock pond.

"Did your grandfather raise cattle long?"

"A lot of years. He bought Seven Cedars back in the

sixties after he retired from rodeoing. The ranch isn't as large as some of the other ones in the area, but he did pretty well until about eight years ago."

"What happened? The economy?"

Adele hesitated briefly before answering. "My grandmother died."

"I'm sorry."

"It was hard on Pop."

It had been hard on Adele, too. Ty could tell. "When did he lose his thumb?"

"Oh, gosh, over forty years ago. That was the reason he quit rodeoing."

"A roping accident?"

"Yeah. His thumb got twisted in the rope. The horse went one way and the calf another."

"Some guys still compete without a thumb." The loss of a digit wasn't entirely uncommon with ropers.

"Pop says he was ready to retire, anyway."

"Well, this is a nice place to retire to."

Winged insects, buzzing in the warm midday sun, flitted over the pond's glassy surface, dipping occasionally to take a sip of moisture. Suddenly, there was a small splash in the center of the pond. Ty had the urge to bring his rod and reel another day and go after one of those bass making a meal of the flying insects.

"So, when did you come here to live?"

"I visited Pop off and on ever since I was a kid. We didn't start Cowboy College until after I earned my business degree." More hesitancy before answering. Whatever else there was to the story, she wasn't saying.

They'd passed the pond and were now on a slightly wider trail that allowed Ty and Adele to ride side by side. The arrangement also pleased Hamm, who continued trying to win Bella over with little love nips. Unfortunately for him, she remained indifferent.

"I like what I do." Adele gave Ty a shy smile. Her eyes, however, were lit up, their brilliance captivating him. "Technically, it's work, but most days it feels a whole lot more like playing."

"Can't blame you. This is a great place to work. Wish I'd thought of opening a roping school."

"We're a little remote for some people."

"That's what makes it so nice. I could see myself living here." His gaze traveled to the distant mountains, their tops peeking through a blanket of wispy white clouds.

"Not some big fancy ranch?"

"If you're referring to your neighbors, no." He gave her a wry smile. "Though I admit I wouldn't mind heading over to Garth's place one day just to check it out." His grin widened. "Maybe you can take me."

"We'll see." Her expression instantly closed.

Had he pushed her too far, reminding her of their kiss earlier? He wanted to talk about it, but gut instinct told him she wasn't ready.

After several minutes of riding in silence, Ty asked, "Do you have any other family in the area?"

"You mean besides my mother?"

He didn't react to the bitterness in Adele's voice. "Here or anywhere."

"My dad's in Lubbock, Texas. He moved there about fifteen years ago after marrying my stepmom."

"Did your dad rodeo, too?"

"For a while. He quit when I was young."

The careful answers Adele delivered told Ty more about her and her childhood than the sparse and rehearsed information she provided.

"Do you see much of them?"

"No," she answered, with a finality that implied the subject was closed.

He took the hint and gave her some space.

"I read somewhere you're from Santa Fe," she said after a few minutes. "Is your family still there?"

"Most of them. A few years ago my folks sold their place and bought a smaller one closer to town."

"Were they rodeo people, too?"

"No. Dad's a mortgage broker and Mom's a real estate agent. They've always ridden, so we had horses growing up."

"How did you start rodeoing?"

"Friends. I got serious in high school. About that and football. I had trouble deciding between the two after graduation."

"What made you pick rodeoing?"

"I won All Around Cowboy at the National High School Finals Rodeo my senior year. I was hooked after that. Luckily, my family's supported me or I wouldn't have made it. Financially or emotionally."

Rodeoing wasn't cheap, and until he'd started winning, Ty, like a lot of competitors, had depended on his family to supplement his income.

"Losing the Iron Grip Ropes sponsorship cost me more than a career opportunity," he continued. "I was counting on the money that came with it to pay back my parents."

"Does your younger sister rodeo?" Adele asked. "You said she wanted to learn to rope."

"She tried barrel racing for a while, but didn't stick with it. My older sister's a single mom with two little girls."

"That must be rough."

"She's doing okay. She has her real estate license and works with our mom. I keep a fifth-wheel trailer at her place and stay there when I'm not traveling. The rent helps. She and my mom have been struggling these last couple years, what with the real estate market being so up and down. Mom's worried about keeping the business afloat. And Dad's job is just crazy. Changing every day."

"I bet."

Ty pushed down on his right stirrup, adjusted his saddle, which had shifted slightly, and said determinedly, "Another reason I don't intend to lose the championship a second time."

"Is your little sister coming out?" Adele asked.

"She'd like to, but probably not. Right now, she's doing an internship with a large animal surgery center."

"She's a vet?"

"Officially, not until next month, when she graduates school." A wave of nostalgia struck Ty, and he made a mental note to call his family tonight.

"Hey, check that out." Adele reined in her mare and pointed to a cluster of trees. Behind the grove, the land sloped down into a small draw. "Is that what I think it is?"

Ty stopped beside her and peered into the trees. He immediately spotted the small face staring at them from between low hanging branches. "One of yours?"

"Has to be. Two head went missing a couple weeks ago, when they got through a hole in the fence during the night. I figured they'd gotten lost or…" She grimaced.

"At least one of them has escaped being a meal."

"You game?" Challenge glinted in her green eyes.

"Are you kidding? I'm always game."

They both untied their lassos from their saddles. The calf, about forty yards away, observed them warily.

All at once Adele shouted, "Go," and the chase was on.

Adele pressed her legs into Bella's flanks. The mare immediately went from a standstill to a full gallop. With Ty right beside her, they bore down on the lone calf. Because Bella was smaller and quicker than Hamm, Adele took the header position. Ty remained a length behind, in the heeler position. Team roping wasn't her specialty, but she'd done enough of it through the years to hold her own, even with someone of Ty's caliber.

Considering they were unaccustomed to roping as a team, they worked well together, automatically anticipating and compensating for each other's moves. The calf, spooked into action, had spun sideways and was hightailing it through the trees as fast as his stubby legs could carry him. He headed toward the narrow draw, bawling loudly, then dropped out of sight beneath the rim. Adele and Ty bent low on their horses' necks and flew down the side of the draw.

An exuberant "Yee-haw" erupted from her throat before she even realized it, then "Come on, Bella," when the calf unexpectedly cut to the right.

Her mare's front hooves hit the ground at the base of the draw like a ton of bricks. Adele hung on, the resulting jar to her system acting like a shot of adrenaline. A quick glance over her shoulder assured her Ty was having no trouble keeping up. Pure unabashed joy lit his face. Her own jaw hurt from smiling so hard.

Chunks of dirt exploded from beneath their horses' hooves as they gained ground on the tiring calf. In the next few seconds, they closed the distance to mere feet. Sensing the moment was right, they reached for their lassos. Adele threw hers at the calf's head a heartbeat ahead of Ty. He aimed his for the animal's rear feet. Her lasso landed where it should, around the horns. Ty's didn't, falling instead to the ground.

The calf jumped and twisted, shaking his head and fighting to break free. Adele reined Bella to a stop and backed her up to bring the line taut. Ty collected his rope and wound it into a coil, a sour expression on his face. He obviously didn't like missing his throws.

Giving their heavily breathing horses a rest, they dismounted. By then, the calf stood quietly, nostrils flaring and flanks heaving, resigned to the fact that his wandering days were at an end.

"Don't look so miserable, buddy." Adele removed her rope, wrapped it around the calf's neck and tied a knot, one designed for safely leading him back home. "We just saved your life. With all the wolves, bears and mountain lions in this area, I can't believe you've survived this long."

Feeling Ty's gaze on her, she looked up, momentarily stuck by what she was doing here with him. She didn't act spontaneously. She certainly didn't tear across the countryside chasing down calves with men she hardly knew. On a bet, for crying out loud.

She didn't normally kiss them, either, but she'd done all those things with Ty, in the same day, no less.

When he didn't say anything, she asked, "What?"

"You look happy."

"That was fun." Okay, she'd confessed, and the ground hadn't opened up to swallow her whole.

"You should do it more often."

"Catch stray calves?" She laughed.

"Have fun. And laugh." His brown eyes bored into hers, studying but not judging. "I'm thinking you don't do either enough."

According to her grandfather, she also didn't date enough. Had she really become that much of a stick-in-the-mud? And when had it happened? Adele didn't like the momentary glimpse of herself through another's eyes.

"Sorry about missing earlier," he said with what might have been embarrassment.

"I doubt that happens much with you."

"No. And I'm not sure why it happened now."

"Mind if I make an observation?"

"That's why I came here."

"Hamm takes aim with his right eye."

"He does?" Ty pushed back his cowboy hat, scratched his head. "I must have watched a half-dozen films of myself on Hamm, and I never noticed."

"You might not if you weren't looking."

He closed his eyes, his brow furrowed in concentration. Adele imagined he was mentally replaying his run, feeling the barely noticeable tug on the reins as Hamm turned his head to the left in order to see better. Realizing he should be loosening the reins and shifting his weight.

"You're right." He opened his eyes and grinned. "You can spot me any day."

Pleasure coursed through her. Satisfaction at helping a student improve—that was her job, after all. But something else. Something having to do entirely with Ty.

"We'd better get this little fellow back home," she said, to cover her sudden rush of emotions. Leading the calf behind her, she mounted Bella and dallied the rope around her saddle horn, glad to be returning home. Ty had an infuriating way of unsettling her.

He also mounted. "Maybe we can finish our tour of the ranch tomorrow."

Of course he would remember.

"We'll see."

Adele clucked to Bella, who obediently began walking out. Ty fell in step beside her, and the calf brought up the rear, not liking the rope, but having no choice in the matter. Soon enough, he settled down.

Their slow climb up and out of the draw wasn't nearly as thrilling as galloping down into it had been.

At the top, Adele pointed to a trail. "This one circles back around to the east pasture."

They slowed their pace to accommodate the calf's exhausted state and recalcitrant nature.

"What made your grandfather pick this place?" As they meandered along, he took in the rolling green landscape and startling blue skies.

"Pop was friends with Garth's grandfather. He told Pop about the vacant land bordering his ranch being for sale. Pop and my grandmother had visited a few times and liked the area. They wound up buying the land sight unseen."

"My mother would never recommend that to a client, but in your grandfather's case, he made a wise decision."

"He and my grandmother lived in a camper for six months while the original ranch house was being constructed. The crew barely finished before the first snow hit. Lucky for Pop, because Grandma might have left him otherwise."

"Can't say I'd have blamed her. It must get pretty cold here in winter."

"Twenty degrees on a warm day. But it's really pretty in a primitive way."

"I'd like to see that."

"There's some good skiing up north."

"I was thinking more along the lines of sitting in front of a roaring fire." Ty's eyes locked with hers. "Snuggled under a blanket."

"Oh." Adele required several seconds and a fair amount of throat clearing to recover. "Pop, um, built the stock barn and the main arena the following spring."

Ty didn't resist her efforts to return the conversation to their earlier topic. Thank goodness.

"When did you start Cowboy College?"

"About seven years ago. We began with the main lodge and the inn building. The cabins came later, a few each year as we grew."

"That was quite a risk you took."

"Pop's the one who took the risk. He invested his life's savings in Cowboy College. And it's paid off."

"You've worked hard." Ty sent her an admiring glance.

Adele waited for the wariness that usually overcame her when a man showed signs of interest. Only it didn't happen, and she couldn't help wondering why. Ty was a poor choice for any romantic entanglements, short-term or long. She should be doubly cautious.

Then it occurred to her that maybe his leaving soon was the reason she felt less on guard. No way would she be stupid enough to let herself fall for him, only to be hurt later. She was too smart for that. Too careful. Knowing she'd keep her heart under lock and key allowed her to let loose a little. Laugh. Chase calves.

Because he was...safe.

She relaxed, her newfound discovery giving her confidence—until he looked at her with a much too endearing expression on his handsome face.

"Do you like to fish?"

"I used to. Pop would take me sometimes when I was young."

"You want to go one day? I hear the fly-fishing's pretty good at Little Twister Creek."

"I, ah..." Feeling safe with Ty—make that *semi*safe—didn't mean she was ready for a date. "We're so busy right now, I really can't afford the time off."

"Well, if you wind up with a free morning or afternoon, let me know. The invitation's always open."

For just a moment, she indulged her imagination and pictured the two of them whiling away a lazy afternoon on the banks of Little Twister Creek. It could be—here was that word again—*fun*.

The discussion changed to roping and the upcoming Buffalo Bill Cody Stampede Rodeo. Ty gave his opinion on who he considered his toughest competition, which included her neighbor, Garth Maitland.

"Will you come watch?" he asked.

"I wouldn't miss it. We usually take a group of students along, too."

They reached the first gate, and once again, Adele opened it without dismounting. When she went to close it, Ty stopped her.

"Can I try?"

"Sure." She backed Bella up to give him and Hamm room. When he succeeded in closing the gate with no problem, Adele tipped her head appreciatively. "Nicely done."

"We're learning to work together, too."

The calf abruptly let out a noisy bawl.

"Guess he's glad to be home." She started forward. This time the animal followed willingly, in a hurry to be reunited with his pals crowding together at the fence in order to get a look at him.

"He's not the only eager one." Ty had to hold Hamm back from running a race to the barn.

They rode first to the calf pen and dropped off their charge in the care of the assistant stock manager, then walked their horses to the barns. When they reached the place where they would separate—he was going to the main barn, she to the smaller one—they stopped as if on cue.

"Thanks for the tour," he said, with that sexy half smile she'd seen countless times in magazines, on cable television and the big screen at rodeos. Only this time, the smile was directed at her. "I know I kind of tricked you into it."

"Kind of?"

"But if we hadn't gone, we wouldn't have found the calf, and you wouldn't have shown me how Hamm takes aim."

Or had such a good time team roping, she thought.

"I might have shown you. Eventually," she said with a grin, and quickly escaped to the quiet seclusion of the barn, where she could give her wildly beating heart a chance to slow.

Who was she fooling, thinking Ty Boudeau was safe? He was as dangerous as they came, especially to someone like her, a country girl with little experience around men like him.

Just as Adele was latching the door to Bella's stall, a woman's voice sounded from behind her.

"That's one fine looking cowboy."

Her mother, of course, would notice, having made fine looking cowboys the focus of her entire adult life. Still, Adele couldn't disagree.

"I suppose."

"He likes you." Lani accompanied Adele to the tack room in the center of the barn, where she hung the mare's bridle on a peg. "You like him, too."

"He's a student, Mom." Adele bristled, the remark hitting too close to home. "And a guest of the ranch. That's all."

She walked away, well aware that her reaction was over the top. But hell would freeze over before she'd discuss Ty with her mother.

"Wait," Lani called after her, struggling a little to catch up, her breathing shallow and raspy.

Smoking and hard living did that to a person.

Only now that Adele thought about it, she hadn't seen her mother with a cigarette or a drink since she'd arrived. Knowing her, she'd probably gotten better at hiding her vices.

"You have every right to be mad at me," Lani said.

The admission was the last thing Adele had expected to issue from her mother's lips. Ever. It brought her to a standstill.

"I have to get to the office," she said, fighting an unwelcome rush of emotion. "Some new guests are arriving this afternoon."

"I'd really like to talk to you."

Adele inched away. "Not now."

"You can't keep avoiding me."

"Why not, Mom?" She spun around. "You avoided me for years."

"I guess I deserve that."

Whatever else Lani intended to say was cut short by Stick barreling down the barn aisle toward them, his shirttail flying and his freckled face flushed beet-red from exertion.

"Adele, Adele! Come quick."

"What's wrong?" she asked, alarmed by the sight of him.

"It's Pop," he said, holding his sides. "He fell. And he's hurt bad."

Chapter 6

Adele reached her grandfather first, ahead of Stick and her mother. He lay flat on his back on the muddy ground near the water trough. Ty, of all people, was kneeling beside him. Where had he come from and how did he get there ahead of her?

"Pop, are you okay?" Breathless from running, Adele bent at the waist and braced her hands on her thighs.

"I'll live," he muttered, his chest rising and falling.

"You're lucky you didn't crack your head open on the trough."

Pop groaned when Ty lifted him to a sitting position.

"Careful," she warned. "He may have broken something." She thought of Pop's hip, the one that was always giving him trouble.

"Quit being such a mother hen."

She ignored her grandfather's comment and came

closer, intent on verifying for herself his claim of being uninjured. "What happened?"

"That damn spigot's been leaking for days. Figured I'd fix it." His face twisted into a painful grimace when Ty stood and hauled him to his feet. Putting out a hand in protest, Pop said, "Give me a minute, would you?" in a strained voice.

"Sorry." Ty relaxed his grip but didn't let go.

Good thing, because Pop swayed unsteadily.

"Maybe we shouldn't have moved him just yet." Adele hovered, the mud her grandfather had slipped in pulling at her boots and sucking her in. It also covered her grandfather from head to toe, probably soaking through his clothes.

Several more guests and the assistant barn manager had come over to investigate, crowding around them. Their anxious chatter and proximity grated on Adele's already frayed nerves.

"Can everyone step back, please. He needs room."

"Don't mind her," Pop told Ty. "The least little thing sets her in a tizzy."

"This is hardly the least little thing," she retorted hotly. "You're hurt."

"I'm fine."

"Can you walk?"

"I'm getting to it."

Distressed by the sight of her grandfather's ashen complexion and his attempts to dismiss what could be a serious injury, she confronted Stick. "Why didn't you help him when he fell?"

"Ty got there first. Pop didn't want to tell you, but Ty—"

"You weren't going to tell me?" Adele demanded of her grandfather.

He shot her an isn't-it-obvious-why look. "Don't know what all the fuss is about. I just had the wind knocked out of me."

"And now you can hardly stand, much less walk."

"The hell I can't walk." He shook off Ty's hold.

Adele watched, biting her lower lip. To her relief, Pop didn't topple, but neither did he attempt to take a step. She sent Ty a worried glance behind her grandfather's back.

He nodded reassuringly, letting her know he wasn't moving from Pop's side.

The seconds dragged by. Finally, Pop attempted a step—and his knees went right out from under him. Ty easily caught him when he pitched forward. Thank goodness.

Adele panicked at the sight of her grandfather's pale face. "I think we should call 911."

"You'll do no such thing."

"You need to see a doctor. You could have broken a rib or sprained an ankle."

He made a sound of disgust.

"She has a point," Ty said.

"That's enough out of the both of you."

"I have an idea." Adele turned to Stick. "Find Mike Scolari and bring him here. His cabin number is fourteen. If he's not there, go to the office and have Gayle pull up his reservation record. His cell phone will be listed under guest information."

"Mike? The husband of Sandy, who talks nonstop?" Ty asked.

"Yes." Adele nodded, her attention remaining on her grandfather.

"What can he do?"

"Mike's a doctor."

"You're kidding!"

"I don't need a doctor," Pop groused.

"Yes, you do," Adele insisted. To Stick, she said, "Hurry."

"Take one step and you're fired."

Stick's gaze traveled between Adele and her grandfather. "Sorry, Pop," he said, and dashed off to do her bidding.

Smart kid.

"What's the matter with you?" she asked Ty, who continued to gape at her.

"I just can't believe Mike's a doctor."

"Because his wife talks a lot?"

"Because roping is a dangerous sport. I can't believe he'd risk injuring his hands."

"Mike's a pediatrician."

Wrong thing to say.

Pop exploded. "I ain't letting no kiddie doctor examine me."

"Then I'm taking you to the emergency room."

"The hell you are."

"Pop, please." She couldn't help the sob that infected her voice.

To her amazement, he conceded. "All right, all right."

"Mom." Adele reached into her jeans pocket and fished out her keys. "Can you pull my truck around?"

"Of course, sweetie." Lani hurried off. A few minutes later, she returned in the truck.

After arranging a horse blanket on the front seat to protect it from all the mud, Ty helped Pop climb in. It was a struggle for both of them.

"Thank you, Ty," Adele said softly when they were done.

"I'll ride with you, just in case he needs help getting out."

She didn't want him along, but knowing her grandfather, he'd be more cooperative with Ty than her. "Okay."

He opened the rear passenger door and climbed in.

"I'll come, too," Lani said, and before Adele could stop her, she'd hopped in the rear driver's-side seat.

"Great." Adele's next thought vanished with the ringing of her cell phone. She recognized the number and quickly flipped the phone open. "Stick, did you find Mike?"

"Sure did."

"Meet us at Pop's house." She slid in behind the steering wheel and reached for her seat belt. "We're on our way."

Pop's house bore little resemblance to the modest structure he'd built over forty-five years earlier. Along with a room added on the back for Adele when she was eight, he'd constructed a new master bedroom suite and completely remodeled the downstairs, including the kitchen. Soon after his wife's death, however, he'd moved back into their old bedroom, and as far as Adele knew, no one had slept in the master bedroom since.

"Down the hall," she instructed Ty as soon as they entered the house. "Second door on the right."

"The family-room couch will do just fine," Pop grumbled.

"You need to lie down."

"What I need is a less bossy granddaughter."

Ty, his strong arm supporting Pop, changed direction, away from the hall and toward the family room.

"Hey!" Adele chased after them. "Ty," she pleaded when neither of them listened.

"It's his house," he said gently. "He has a right to go where he wants."

"I knew there was something I liked about you." Pop grunted as Ty lowered him onto the leather couch. "You ain't afraid of her."

"Are you kidding?" Ty bent close to Pop's ear and whispered loudly, "I'm counting on you to protect me."

Pop laughed, and Adele breathed a sigh of relief. Maybe he wasn't badly hurt, after all.

Stick showed up with Mike Scolari. Adele wanted to stay with Pop during the examination, but he'd have none of it.

"Can't you give an old man some privacy?" he complained.

She and Ty joined her mother and Stick in the kitchen.

"A glass of water, anyone?" Lani asked.

She flitted around Pop's kitchen, making herself comfortable—which rankled Adele.

"No, thanks," she mumbled.

"I'll take one, if you don't mind." Stick accepted the tall glass Lani prepared for him, and guzzled it down.

"Your grandfather will be fine." Ty joined Adele at the table. The same table she had sat at whenever her mother dropped her off at Seven Cedars to stay. She'd been four the first time, and her feet hadn't touched the floor.

Seeing Lani standing by the sink unleashed an onslaught of memories Adele had been all too happy to shove to the back of her mind. For a moment, she became that little girl again, crying her heart out as she watched Lani's beat-up Mercury pull away from Pop's house and drive away.

Her mother had returned weeks—or was it months?—later. But she'd left Adele with her grandparents again the next year. Then again six months later. The pattern had been repeated with increasing frequency until Adele was fourteen. That summer, Lani and Pop got into a huge fight like never before, and Lani hadn't come back. From then on, the only time Adele saw her mother was during the holidays, when she flew out to wherever Lani was currently living, and only because her grandparents had insisted. Those visits stopped when Adele turned eighteen. After that, Adele saw Lani only when their paths happened to cross at some rodeo.

Looking back, she realized she hadn't visited her father any more than she had her mom. Her trips to Texas, at least, weren't strained, and peppered with petty outbursts. Her father had tried to include Adele in his life, which was more than she could say about Lani.

Mike entered the room, disrupting her thoughts. "You can see your grandfather now."

She stood, vaguely aware that Ty did, too. "How is he?"

"Tough as nails."

"Will he be all right?"

"I'm sure he's strained his back, though he won't admit it hurts."

Adele sighed.

"I gave him ibuprofen, triple the regular dose, told him to soak in a hot bath for an hour and to take it easy over the next couple of days."

She wondered how in the world she would manage that.

"I doubt anything's broken," Mike continued, "but I'd advise a trip to his regular doctor."

"Yeah." Yet another challenge to test her.

"I also offered him a lollipop, like I do my regular patients. He refused that, too."

"Are you making a joke?"

Mike chuckled and put a hand on Adele's shoulder. "He'll recover. Falls aren't uncommon with the elderly. Luckily, the ground was soft, and he didn't hit the water trough on his way down."

Elderly? Pop had always seemed ageless.

"If he has a bad night or appears worse in the morning, don't hesitate to call me."

Adele nodded. "Stick, take Dr. Scolari, Mr. Boudeau and my mother back to their cabins, please."

"How 'bout I stay?" Ty offered in a soft voice. "Pop may need some help."

He might, even if it was just to undress for bed or get that hot soak in the tub. God knew Pop wouldn't accept Adele's assistance with those things.

"Okay."

"I want to stay, too, baby."

Her mother's show of concern was about two decades too late. "Don't you have to be at work?" Adele asked.

Lani's mouth compressed into a tight line, the reminder of her place at the ranch clearly stinging.

Adele didn't care. Pop was her top priority at the moment, and her mother wasn't anyone he wanted around.

More than that, *she* didn't want her mother around.

"Come on." Ty took Lani's elbow and gave her his most disarming smile. "I'll walk you to the truck."

She relented. Lani was always a sucker when it came to good-looking men.

Stick and Mike said their goodbyes, then followed Ty and Lani out the door. Adele didn't wait. She crossed the threshold into the family room before the kitchen door was closed.

Pop sat propped in a corner of the leather couch, his head tilted back, his eyes closed. She approached quietly, not wanting to disturb his sleep.

Only he wasn't sleeping, just resting, and he opened his eyes the instant she neared.

"I feel like a fool."

"You?" she chided, and perched gingerly on the opposite end of the couch to avoid causing his back discomfort. "A fool?"

"I suppose you think it was stupid of me to try and fix the spigot with all that mud."

"To be honest, I wouldn't have given it a second thought."

"I lost my balance, is all."

"Could've happened to anyone." She reached across the couch.

For several seconds he stared at her outstretched

hand, then clasped it in his. Adele felt the world lift from her shoulders.

"Pop, can I ask you a question?"

"Sure."

"Why'd you agree to let Mom stay? And to give her a job?"

He raised his bushy silver eyebrows. "I told you, I think she's ready to make amends."

"I know. But when she left that summer I was fourteen, you told her to never come back."

"That's not entirely right."

His statement shocked Adele. "I was there. I heard the two of you fighting."

"You didn't hear everything." He expelled a long breath, readjusted his position and winced.

From pain or regret?

"What did I miss?"

His gaze turned inward. When he spoke, it was as if he was talking to Lani on that long-ago day. "I said 'if you ever come back, it had better be because you're ready to be a real mother to your daughter.'"

Adele remained quiet, not trusting her voice.

"The way I figure it," Pop continued, "if she finally got the nerve to face me, maybe she's finally ready to be that real mother to you."

If only Adele agreed with him.

Ty opened Pop's back door and stepped out onto the porch. In the distance, the sun was making another spectacular exit, sinking behind the mountains in a blaze of vivid reds and golds. What would it look like in winter, with snow covering those mountains and blanketing the land? Adele's earlier description tempted him to find out.

He wasn't usually one to notice nature's bounties, being too busy most of the time. It was different here at Seven Cedars. His frantic pace slowed enough for him to appreciate sunsets, and the smell of damp earth after a sudden shower, and the taste of freshly ground coffee enjoyed over a leisurely breakfast.

"How's he doing?" Adele rose from the rocker she'd been occupying.

He hadn't seen her sitting there, and tried to hide his delight. "Complaining up a storm."

"Complaining's good. It's when he doesn't that I really worry."

Ty held out the bottle of beer he'd carried with him. "Want a sip? Pop said to help myself."

"I don't usually drink beer." She took the bottle anyway and returned to her rocker.

Pulling up one of the empty stools, he sat beside her, the aged rattan seat creaking beneath his weight.

"Is he in bed?" Adele took a long swallow of Ty's beer.

He studied her every move. "Watching TV. Said no one had helped him take a bath since he was three, and he'd be damned before someone else does again."

"I'm sorry he was so uncooperative." She returned Ty's beer to him.

"No problem." He paused, studying the bottle in his hand, intensely aware of where her lips had been seconds before. Savoring the sense of anticipation for a tiny while longer, he finally put the bottle to his mouth and drained a third of its contents. "You really should call his doctor tomorrow."

Adele stopped rocking. "Is something wrong?"

"This isn't the first time he's fallen. He accidentally mentioned it during one of his grumblings. I thought you should know."

Frowning, she rubbed her forehead.

"Someone with his severe arthritis is bound to fall now and then," Ty said.

"I know. I just wish he wasn't so stubborn about getting hip replacement surgery."

"He wants to see you taken care of first."

Adele shot Ty a sideways look. "Did he tell you that?"

"He didn't have to. I can see it plain as day."

"This is ridiculous." Her voice cracked when she spoke. "I'm worried about him, he's worried about me. What a pair we are."

"You okay?" Ty touched the back of her hand. Just a quick, gentle brush of his fingertips

Laying her head back, she stared at the sky. "I know it has nothing to do with you, but ever since you arrived, my life's been turned upside down."

He didn't ask about Lani and how much she'd contributed to Adele's topsy-turvy state. "I understand. It was like that for me last December when my horse was injured. I felt like I'd lost control of my life, and nothing I did seemed to help."

"What happened to your old horse?"

"I gave him to a buddy of mine for his teenage girls."

"So, he's not permanently crippled?"

"No. But he can't be used for anything except easy riding, which makes him a perfect family horse."

Ty held out his beer, offering her another sip. She declined with a shake of her head.

Too bad.

"What made you decide to turn Seven Cedars into a guest ranch?" he asked.

She relaxed, maybe for the first time that day. "I became serious about roping in college. Entering local jackpots was a way for me to make extra money, especially during the summers."

"You won a lot?"

"Yeah, I did." The hint of a smile touched her lips. "I would talk to the other competitors about where they were getting their training. A lot of them wished they had access to a more intensive program, one with equipment like professional ropers."

"And Cowboy College was born."

"Pop came up with the name." Her expression softened. "I was so nervous when I suggested the idea to him. I'd spent two months putting a business plan together, with the help of one of my instructors. But Pop, he was behind me one hundred percent from the beginning."

"Sounds like he's always been there for you."

"Always." She stood. "I think I'll go check on him. If he'll let me."

"I should get going." Ty also stood. "I've got an early class, and my teacher is a stickler for starting on time."

Her eyes warmed. "I really appreciate all you did for Pop."

"If you need anything, just call. I don't mind coming back."

"Thanks."

"Let me give you my cell number."

"I already have it."

He extended his hand. "Let me plug it into your phone. Save you a trip to the main lodge to look it up."

"I have it," she repeated in a quiet voice.

Pleasure shot through Ty as the implications of her statement sunk in.

"I'll be right back." She cut past him and went inside, but not before he caught sight of her pink-tinged cheeks.

He waited for her in the kitchen. She returned shortly, brandishing a key ring.

"I'll drive you back to your cabin."

They took Pop's old pickup. Ty wished the ride would last longer than it did. Too soon, their evening together ended.

"I hope I'm not one of those things that has turned your life upside down," he said, referring to her earlier remark.

Their gazes held.

"You are," she murmured.

He was surprised she admitted even that much. "I'm sorry. That wasn't my intention."

"Don't be." She shifted the truck from Neutral to Reverse. "I'm not entirely sure I didn't need a good shaking up."

He considered her remark long after she'd left, hoping it meant what he thought it did.

Chapter 7

Ty watched as a truck and horse trailer bearing the Maitland Ranch logo rolled past the open area in front of the barns. Maintaining a steady speed of five miles an hour, it continued to the pasture designated for visitor parking. The distance was too great for Ty to identify the driver of the truck, but his gut told him it was Garth Maitland, and that the two of them were in for a rematch today.

Friendship aside, this time Ty intended to win. Garth also wouldn't have it any other way.

On the second Saturday of every month, Cowboy College hosted a roping jackpot competition. Unlike professional rodeos, jackpots were open to anyone, regardless of gender. Participants paid an entry fee and competed against other individuals ranked the same as them. At the end of the competition, the pot was divided among the top three competitors in each group. The more participants, the bigger the pot—and the tougher the competition.

Ty couldn't wait to put into practice everything he'd learned since coming to Wyoming, and have his best time ever on Hamm.

"What are you standing there for?" Pop hobbled toward Ty. "That horse of yours won't saddle himself."

"You're right." Ty started off toward the barn, then slowed when he realized Pop was tagging along. "How you feeling?"

"The next person to ask me that is going to feel the sole of my boot in their arse when I kick them off this place."

"Better, then?"

"I slipped in the dang mud. Not like I fell off the roof."

The fall might have been minor, but not the aftereffects. Pop's arthritis had flared, confining him to the couch for several days. He'd finally gotten up and around yesterday, refusing to miss the monthly jackpot.

"Looks like we got a decent turnout," Ty commented.

"Right decent."

They entered the barn, the shade offering immediate relief from the midafternoon sun beating down. The spectators filling the bleachers were already cooling themselves with whatever they could convert into a makeshift fan, and guzzling cold drinks from the snack bar, run by the local Boy Scout troop.

"Garth Maitland's here," Pop said.

"I saw."

"He'll be riding his new horse. One he's never roped on before."

Ty opened Hamm's stall door. The big sorrel was raring to go and pawed the ground relentlessly while Ty snapped on the halter. "Garth's horse any good?"

"So I'm told."

Adrenaline built in Ty while he saddled Hamm. He ignored it, focusing all his mental energies on the upcoming jackpot. He'd learned long ago that the way to win was to treat every competition, big or small, local or National, like a World Championship.

"You're busy." Pop clapped Ty on the back. "How 'bout I catch up with you later."

Ty had momentarily forgotten he wasn't alone. "Any good advice before you go?" he asked, mounting Hamm.

Pop rolled the toothpick he was always chewing on from one side of his mouth to the other. "Forget about Garth. The only person you need to be concentrating on is yourself."

Ty nodded. He was right.

"You can beat him."

"Thanks for the vote of confidence."

Pop chuckled. "Well, a piece of humble pie wouldn't hurt Garth Maitland none."

Ty couldn't agree more.

At a slight pressure of his legs, Hamm trotted briskly from the barn. "See you at the winner's table," Ty called over his shoulder.

Outside, he made straight for the warm-up arena. From the nearby bleachers, the crowd cheered as the first group finished. Participants in the second group were lining up behind the boxes, while wranglers readied the calves.

Hamm, picking up on Ty's mood, shook his head and snorted, his front feet dancing.

"He's ready to go."

Ty looked up and smiled. He hadn't seen much of Adele since the night at Pop's house. "We both are." He pulled on the reins, slowing down so she could fall in step beside him.

"Where's Bella?" he asked, indicating the unfamiliar bay gelding she was riding.

"With her owner. He's giving her a go today."

"I'd like to see that."

"You will," she answered smoothly. "He's competing against you."

Realization dawned on Ty, and he smiled at his own gullibility. "You've been training her for Garth."

"Worried?"

"Not at all."

"You sound pretty sure of yourself."

Did he? The truth was his ego hadn't fully recovered from his loss to Garth last December. If he lost again today, he didn't want Adele knowing he'd failed despite having a newly acquired weapon in his arsenal.

"Care to make a wager?" he asked.

"Shouldn't you be talking to Garth?"

"I'm not interested in having dinner with him."

"Dinner!"

The idea had been a spontaneous one, but the more Ty thought about it, the more he liked it. "If I win, you take me to dinner."

"And if you lose?"

"I take you to dinner."

She pondered the wager. "That sounds more like a win-win situation for you."

It could be for both of them. "You want to raise the stakes?"

"Change them."

And here he thought she was going to turn him down. "To what?"

"You win, I go to dinner with you."

"Take me," he corrected.

"Okay, take you."

"And if I lose to Garth?"

Her eyes glinted with michief. "You teach the beginners' class for one week."

Ty's hand must have jerked on the reins, for Hamm suddenly slowed and bobbed his head. He didn't like being restrained.

"You kidding?"

"Not in the least." She smirked, obviously having fun with this.

"Why? Are you taking a vacation?"

"No. I just think the students would benefit, learning from a professional."

"The bet seems a little lopsided."

"Only if you're afraid of losing."

That got him, which was probably what she'd intended. "You're on. Make sure you have plenty available on your credit-card limit, because I have expensive tastes," he said, and broke into a slow trot.

Her laughter followed him as he circled the arena.

At the gate, Ty came face-to-face with Garth Maitland riding the paint mare. Both men nodded. Garth wore a wide, confident grin. Ty didn't let it faze him.

"Good luck, pal."

"Same to you."

This, Ty thought as he continued on, was going to be an interesting jackpot...for many reasons. And he had never been more ready.

Adele didn't stand on the fence railing behind the box with the other ropers. She'd be welcome; that wasn't the reason. Mostly, she didn't want Ty to see how nervous she was, waiting for him and Garth to finish their runs. To avoid any potential embarrassment to herself, she waited—make that hid—in the announcer's booth. While old Larry Fisher provided color commentary, his wife, along with the help of their oldest granddaughter, monitored the electronic timekeepers and kept the scores. If they were curious about Adele's presence in the booth, they didn't say.

Each contestant was allowed three turns. Their scores were then added together and averaged. The person with the highest average was the winner. After two rounds, Garth led, with Ty coming in a close second. Chase, a newcomer, wasn't far behind in third place. It remained anybody's game.

She still wasn't sure she wanted Ty to win or lose. Beating Garth would do Ty good and restore some of his lost confidence. On the other hand, Adele had worked hard training Bella, and the horse was performing well. A win for Garth could potentially bring her new clients.

There was also the matter of her bet with Ty. Having dinner with him would be a mistake. Mind-boggling kissing and long, lingering glances aside, he was leaving soon. Regardless of how attracted she was to him, and she was seriously attracted, she wasn't about to engage in a temporary fling. Her mother had done enough of that for both of them.

Try as she might, however, Adele couldn't put the idea of dinner with Ty from her mind. Joe from Phoenix, as Pop had pointed out recently, was Adele's last serious romance. Sadly, it hadn't ended well. For either of them. Mainly because she wouldn't leave Seven Cedars.

Nothing had changed since then. She was as rooted at the ranch as always.

Anticipation at the final outcome of the jackpot had her standing on her toes to see better. Garth rode into the box and positioned Bella. Chase had taken his run moments before, and currently held the first place position. Dismounting, he hopped onto the arena fence alongside his buddies to wait out the rest of the competition.

Down in the arena, the gate to the chute flew open, releasing the calf. Garth followed in hot pursuit. Bella performed flawlessly. Even so, Adele tensed. Seconds later, it was all over. Prompted by his wife, Larry called out Garth's time, which was quickly added to his other two times to determine his final standing.

"That run, ladies and gentlemen," Larry said, his voice blaring from the speaker, "will put this here young man in first place."

Adele hadn't doubted the outcome. The question was, could Garth maintain it?

"Our last contestant for the day is Ty Boudeau." The crowd applauded. "Come on, folks," Larry coaxed, "don't be stingy. This cowboy needs more encouragement than that if he's going to take home the prize money." The audience broke into cheers.

Adele chewed on her bottom lip, studying Ty's every move as he lined up his horse in the box.

Why had she agreed to such a stupid bet?

Larry's wife swiveled around in her chair. "You doing okay, honey?" she asked Adele.

"Yeah, fine."

"You sure? 'Cause you've been fidgeting something awful."

Had she? Adele willed herself to relax.

Her efforts were wasted. A moment later, the calf sprang from the chute. Hamm went from zero to sixty in one second flat. Ty raised his arm high and threw his rope. It sailed through the air like an arrow, straight and true.

Her hands balled into tight fists, Adele watched Ty jump from Hamm's back and hit the ground at a dead run. In the next instant, he'd roped the calf and was throwing his arms up in the air even as he climbed to his feet.

She knew without looking that his time was a good one. Better than his first two runs. A glance at the digital display confirmed it, as did Larry's announcement.

"Ladies and gentlemen, weren't that a pretty run? Give it up for Mr. Ty Boudeau. Your winner today."

Happiness for Ty swelled inside Adele. This competition might be nothing more than a two-bit local jackpot, but he'd needed the win. To prove he still had what it took. To prove he'd picked the right horse when he bought Hamm. To prove coming to Cowboy College was the right decision.

Larry turned away from the microphone. "Adele, tell Pop when he's got a second—"

"I'll get him for you."

She used the excuse to flee the announcer's booth.

Only it wasn't Pop she went looking for when she reached the bottom of the stairs.

Ty wasn't hard to locate. A group of people, mostly fellow students and wranglers he'd come to be friends with, surrounded him and Hamm, offering their congratulations, shaking his hand and giving him hugs. Adele held back, a sudden and acute bout of shyness cementing her feet to the ground.

Slowly, the group thinned. Before the last person had departed, a lone cowboy approached. Garth Maitland. Adele was relieved to see he was wearing his usual grin.

"Good run, Boudeau." Garth extended his hand.

Ty shook it. "You, too."

"It'll be better at the Buffalo Bill Rodeo."

"I'm counting on it."

"Why don't you come by my place this week? Check out the facilities."

"I'd like that."

"Bring Adele with you."

Ty glanced over, caught her gaze and winked, giving her reason to think he'd known all along she was standing there. "I will."

Humph! What made him so convinced she'd go?

Because she wanted to, and he'd probably seen as much in her eyes.

"Give me a call," Garth told Ty, then turned in Adele's direction. Touching his fingers to his hat, he said, "See you later, Dellie."

Great. He'd known she was there all along, too.

Eventually, the last of Ty's fans left. The bleachers had emptied out and the Boy Scouts were packing up the snack bar. Only Ty and Adele remained. She stood there, still unsure what to do or say. He didn't seem to share her problem. Tugging on Hamm's reins, he closed the distance separating them, a happy smile stretching across his face.

"I'll start tomorrow, if you want."

"Start what?" she asked.

"Teaching the beginners' class."

"Why? You won."

"Yeah, but I'd like to, anyway. I've been working with Mike, giving him some pointers, and enjoying it."

"Really?"

"Took me by surprise, too."

"Seriously, Ty. You're not under any obligation. And you're here to work on your own skills."

He wasn't taking her to dinner. The stab of disappointment cutting through her was far stronger than she would have liked it to be.

"I owe you that much."

"For what?"

"Figuring out that Hamm takes aim with his right eye." Ty scratched behind his ear, the boyish gesture charming Adele. "The thing is, I was scared. Thinking somehow I'd lost it. Roping came so easy for me on my other horse. I took that for granted. The harder I tried with Hamm, the more I screwed up. Overcompensating, I suppose. Whatever was going wrong, I kept getting more and more tangled up in it. Coming here, focusing on the fundamentals, well, it's cleared my head and put me back on track."

Adele could see the admission hadn't come easy for Ty, and she valued it that much more.

"I'm glad." She returned his smile with a tentative one of her own.

In every direction, wranglers were hard at it, moving the calves to their regular pens, feeding the stock and cleaning up the arena. On the other side of the bleachers, Pop and Larry conversed. Too late, Adele remembered she hadn't informed her grandfather that the announcer wanted to speak to him.

"So, how's seven-thirty?" Ty asked, distracting her. "Does that give you enough time to change and get ready?"

"For what?"

"Dinner tonight."

"But I thought...you said you'd teach the beginners' class."

"That's a favor." He eased closer. And though he didn't touch her, Adele swore the bare skin on her forearms tingled as if stroked. "I still won."

Yes, he had.

"I intend to collect my dinner date," he added.

She could decline. Ty had coerced her into the bet, and she doubted he'd insist on holding her to it if she flatly refused.

"Seven-thirty will be fine," she answered in a low voice. "I'll meet you in front of the main lodge."

Ty shook his head, his eyes glinting. "Nothing doing. This is a date. I'll pick you up at your place."

"All...right." She swallowed. "See you then."

"I'm looking forward to it."

So, Adele realized, was she. More than she should.

Chapter 8

Flowers.

Adele accepted the bouquet—fresh picked and tied with a ribbon—from Ty's outstretched hand, her movements tentative.

"Thank you."

As she cradled them to her chest, she tried to recall when a man had last given her flowers. The only incident to come to mind was a pink carnation corsage at her senior prom.

That long ago?

"Come in," she said, and stepped back to admit him, hoping he didn't notice the tiny catch in her voice.

He glanced around her smallish but, she liked to think, comfy living room. "Nice."

"Let me put these in water." The excuse was a good one and got her the minute she needed to compose herself.

Why didn't men give her flowers? Was it their un-romantic nature? Her hesitancy to commit to a serious relationship? Maybe she was too much of a tomboy, and men assumed she didn't like flowers.

Except for Ty.

Her heart melted a little as she pulled a glass jar from the kitchen cupboard, filled it with water and arranged the flowers. Smiling to herself, she set them in the center of the table, then moved them to the breakfast bar, where she could see them first thing in the morning when she stumbled in from the bedroom.

"I'd have brought you roses, but there's no florist in Markton."

At the sound of Ty's voice behind her, she momentarily froze. "These are lovely," she said, covering her reaction.

The flowers were perfect, in fact.

Repositioning a daisy that wasn't out of place to begin with, she swallowed and turned to face him.

He looked good, doing justice to his jeans and Western dress shirt, which hugged his broad shoulders. The only place to eat a sit-down dinner in Markton was the Spotted Horse Saloon, and cowboy wear was practically required to get in the door. She'd picked her newest pair of jeans, her most flattering shirt, and left her usually bound hair loose to frame her face. Ty seemed to appreciate her changed appearance, given he'd yet to take his eyes off her.

"You ready?" She hesitated, feeling on unfamiliar territory. Entertaining men in her small apartment behind the main lodge wasn't something she did. "Or would you like a cold drink first?"

Cold drink! She mentally kicked herself for sounding like a waitress.

"We should probably get a move on." Ty flashed her a disarming smile. "We've got eight-o'clock reservations."

"Reservations?"

"It's Saturday night. I figured the place would be packed after the jackpot, and I wanted to make sure we got a table."

Ty was going out of his way to make their date special.

And it *was* a date, despite starting out as a bet. Her tingling insides confirmed it.

"Let me grab my purse."

Outside, Ty opened the passenger door of his truck for her and supported her elbow as she climbed in. Adele was about to protest that she climbed in and out of trucks all day long and didn't need help. At the last second, she shut her mouth and just enjoyed his chivalrous treatment.

Fifteen minutes later, they reached the Spotted Horse Saloon. Adele expected the place to be crowded, and she wasn't disappointed. It took them as long to find a parking spot and walk to the front entrance as to drive there.

"We have a reservation," Ty told the young hostess. "For Boudeau."

"Right this way, please."

Piped in country and western music accompanied them to a dark booth tucked in the corner. The band was scheduled to take the stage soon, and by nine o'clock the place would be hopping.

Ty stood and waited while Adele slid into the booth.

He sat beside her—close—and the hostess passed them menus.

"Enjoy your meal."

Ty squinted at the menu, not easy to read in the dim light. "Are the specials any good?"

"Actually, most everything is." The cowboy-type fare at the Spotted Horse was simple but tasty. "I like the grilled chicken, and the fish and chips aren't bad."

Their dinner progressed comfortably, and the mood, much to Adele's relief, was definitely casual, with conversation centering mostly on Cowboy College and the students.

"We'll be taking a group of whoever wants to go to the Buffalo Bill Stampede Rodeo," she mentioned, while buttering a roll. "Pop, of course, wouldn't miss it."

"I'm already entered. Tie-down roping and team roping."

"Who's your partner for team roping?"

"A buddy of mine. Louis Garcia."

"I've heard of him. He's good."

She thought she might have detected a bit of tension in the lines around Ty's mouth. Was he nervous about competing? It was hard to tell over the mounting noise, a combination of the lively crowd and the band warming up on the stage. Adele recognized several ranch guests among the saloon patrons, as well as locals and out-of-town jackpot contestants. From where they sat, she could see almost as many people packed into the bar area.

"I don't think you ever told me what you do when you're not rodeoing." She fully expected him to answer horse trainer or wrangler or stock breeder. Those professions went hand in hand with rodeoing. She didn't see him following in his parents' footsteps by going into real estate.

"I apprentice at a saddle shop."

"Seriously?" She imagined a small, independently owned shop like the ones she'd visited before. "I don't remember ever reading that about you."

"You've read up on me?" A twinkle lit his eyes.

"I subscribe to horse and rodeo magazines. You're in them." She didn't mention the online searches she'd conducted before he'd arrived in Markton, afraid—make that *convinced*—it would go to his head.

"You're in them, too."

She felt his gaze on her and cleared her throat. "So, you build saddles?" she asked, as casually as if asking if he built bookcases in his spare time.

"A few. Mine, for one. Pop has a couple of old Charlie's."

"He does?" She stopped chewing. Pop owned a lot of custom-built saddles. But Ty had used only one, and she'd recognized the maker immediately. Could it be? "What's the name of the shop?"

"Kingston Saddlery."

"As in Charles Kingston?" She almost choked on her chicken. "You're kidding!"

Ty broke into an amused grin. "Not at all."

There wasn't a serious horse enthusiast alive who hadn't heard of Kingston Saddlery, and many wanted to own what was considered to be one of the finest custom built saddles available.

"That's where you work?"

"Yep. When I'm not rodeoing."

"And you make saddles. Actually *make* them?"

He laughed. "I actually make them. Though I'm still considered an apprentice. If you ask old Charlie, he's not sure I'll ever amount to anything else."

"How come you never said anything?"

"It's not a secret. Just something I don't publicize. Old Charlie's shop is one of the few places I can go and just be myself." His voice dropped. "So's Seven Cedars."

"Wow." Adele shook her head dumbly, still absorbing Ty's remarkable news.

"Is it so hard to believe I'm learning a trade?" He turned his head and eyed her with a mixture of humor and curiosity.

"Well, saddle construction does take a lot of…" She scrunched her mouth to one side.

"Skill? Craftsmanship? Ingenuity?"

"I was going to say patience."

That earned her another laugh.

"And meticulous attention to detail. I suppose you also have to be good with your hands."

"You have no idea."

Too late, she realized her mistake. He immediately sobered, and the comfortable mood that had prevailed up till now vanished.

Oh, brother. She'd stepped right into that.

"Much as I like rodeoing, chances are I won't be doing it forever," Ty said philosophically around a bite of fish. "I may need a backup career."

Adele breathed easier at the change of subject.

"Besides, I'd like to be on road less, some day. Put down roots. Get married and have a couple of kids."

So much for breathing easier.

"I know a lot of guys—and women, too—who leave their families for months at a time, but I couldn't do it. Raising kids is hard enough for two people. It's got to be darn near impossible for one." He paused, suddenly catching himself. "I'm sorry, I wasn't criticizing. Your dad and mom—"

"It's okay. I agree with you." Adele tried to maintain a light tone. "I wouldn't want to be married to someone who was on the road for months at a time, either." And she wouldn't, not after seeing what that lifestyle had done to her parents' marriage. To her.

"When I do finally have kids," Ty continued, his gaze meeting hers, "I want to be there every moment. From the first visit to the baby doctor to the day they graduate and leave home."

Adele couldn't look away if she tried.

Fortunately, the band chose that moment to begin the first set. Despite being good, the music was loud, and limited conversation. Ty made up for it by sending her smoldering glances between bites. Adele polished off the last of her meal in a rush. This thing happening between them, whatever it was, couldn't go anywhere, and she needed to put a halt to it once and for all.

She was just setting her fork down and hoping they'd be leaving soon when the band launched into a slow number, one of George Strait's more popular hits.

"Let's dance," Ty abruptly said.

"I…ah…"

Her senior prom was the last time a man had given her flowers. It was also the last time she'd danced to such a slow song.

He stood and tilted his head toward the band. "Come on. I won't bite. Not on a first date, anyway."

Was he joking?

Walking ahead of him, Adele tried to convince herself she wasn't making a huge mistake. Just look what had happened the last time Ty had held her in his arms.

"Relax," he said into her ear, and pressed his palm against the center of her back.

She tried. It wasn't easy. The man smelled too darn sexy for his own good.

"Afraid I'm a little more comfortable on a horse than the dance floor," she confessed.

"It's not all that different than riding. You just have to find the rhythm and settle in."

He couldn't be more wrong. Dancing was entirely different than riding.

On horseback, she was in complete control. Wrapped in Ty's arms, she was a stick being carried along by a rushing, storm-swollen river.

But after an awkward minute, she did indeed find the rhythm, and stopped inhaling sharply every time their bodies gently collided, either from a misstep on her part or another couple bumping into them. No sooner did the tension start to ebb than the song ended.

"Wait," Ty told her when she began to pull away.

"The song's over," she murmured. The realization that she rather enjoyed staying right where she was made her nervous all over again.

"They'll play another one."

And the band did, this one also slow. Had Ty known?

Without any prompting on his part, she slipped back into his embrace, her earlier suspicions that they were headed for trouble solidifying into absolute certainty. He felt good. Strong and sure of himself. And those hands he'd bragged about were holding her as if he had no intention of ever letting her go.

As the song played on, she discovered that following his steps wasn't all that hard. When he lowered his head to brush his temple against hers, she didn't retreat or tell him to stop. Stranger still, when his hand moved from the center to the small of her back, she turned her head and rested her cheek on his chest as if she'd done it a thousand times before.

Maybe her lack of finesse on the dance floor had less to do with talent and more to do with not having the right partner.

As they moved to the seductive beat, Ty's heart rate slowly increased. She could sense the pounding more than she could hear it over the loud music. When her fingers walked gingerly from his shoulder to the back of his neck, his heart rate accelerated even more.

People were looking at them, Adele noticed through slitted eyes and a dreamy haze that had begun to surround her. Not that she could blame them. As Pop had pointed out recently, she hardly dated, much less glided across a crowded dance floor in the arms of an incredibly attractive rodeo star. One who also worked for the best custom saddle and leather shop in the Southwest.

She was still trying to wrap her brain around that piece of news when Ty suddenly swung her in a half circle in order to avoid colliding with Mike and Sandy.

"Whew!" It took Adele a moment to regain her balance.

"Sorry," Mike called over the music before he and his wife were swallowed by the other dancers.

"You okay?" Ty asked.

Adele looked up at him, and her own heart began racing. At close range and in the dim light of the honkytonk, his brown eyes were dark as ebony. They studied her with the intensity of a man with an agenda. An agenda that involved the two of them alone in a secluded place, those talented hands of his discovering the curve of her hips and the texture of her skin.

Adele averted her gaze. She had little experience with the kind of supercharged sexual currents running between her and Ty.

He let go of her hand and, tucking a finger beneath her chin, lifted her face to his. Dancing became impossible, so they stopped, staring into each other's eyes right there in the middle of the dance floor. The people moving beside them were just blurs to Adele, who only had eyes for Ty.

Leaning down until their foreheads touched, he said, "I want to take you home. Right now."

She withdrew slightly, his remark swiftly bringing her back to her senses.

"I—I don't… I can't…"

He wanted her. And she returned the feelings. But she wasn't ready for *that*. Not yet.

He looked stricken. "I wouldn't take advantage of you, Adele." He blew out a breath and, giving her a gentle tug, pulled her back into his arms. "God, I screwed that up." They started dancing again. "I want to kiss you." He caught her gaze once more. "You can't imagine how much." His mouth curved up in an apologetic smile. "I just didn't want to do it here, and figured if I took you home, I'd have my chance."

"I see," she muttered softly.

"This keeps getting worse and worse. I should just shut up."

"No. It's all right." Adele gathered her courage and made a leap she never had before with a man. "Because I want you to kiss me."

"You do?" Ty's grin widened.

She nodded, and said, "Let's get out of here," just as the music stopped.

Unfortunately, several people were close enough to hear her. Including Mike and Sandy, who both smiled knowingly.

"Good idea." Mike waggled his eyebrows and flashed Sandy a look that left no question as to his own intentions.

Adele groaned inwardly. She rigorously strived to keep her private life just that. Tonight, however, she'd broken that rule.

"You've got an early morning tomorrow," Ty said loudly enough for everyone to hear. "And Pop's waiting for you." With a gentlemanly touch to her back, he guided her off the dance floor.

"Thank you," she said, when they reached their booth. Ty had done his best to make it clear he and Adele weren't spending the night together. She liked him for that. More than liked him.

"I'd say I was sorry, except I'm not going to get in the habit of apologizing, or thinking I should apologize, every time I kiss you."

Something about his tone caused a tingle to skip lightly up her spine. Almost like the gliding of fingertips. *His* fingertips.

"You say that as if we're going to kiss a lot."

"A man can hope."

The dinner tab had been placed on their table while they were dancing. Adele reached for it, but Ty beat her to the punch.

"Hey, I'm supposed to pay."

"I'll get it."

"We had a bet."

"You can pay next time."

"Who says there's going to be a next time?"

"There is if you owe me dinner."

"You're impossible!"

Ty removed his wallet and place several bills inside the folder containing the dinner tab. His gaze held hers as he replaced it on the table. "Don't think this gets you out of kissing me tonight."

"It never crossed my mind," she said softly, reeling from more of those sexual currents.

Despite her earlier vow to keep her personal life private, she didn't object when Ty clasped her hand in his. Together, they wove through the throng of boisterous patrons.

With each step, she tried convincing herself not to get involved with Ty. His return to the rodeo circuit loomed ahead. Unless she could be satisfied with seeing him a few days here and a few days there, engaging in a romantic relationship could only end with her being hurt.

No amount of warning, however, lessened the anticipation building inside her at the prospect of their next kiss. How could she refuse him? Especially when she might not have another chance?

To reach the front entrance, they had to pass the bar area. Typical for a Saturday night, people stood two and three deep. If a big burly man hadn't chosen that exact moment to back away from the bar, Adele might have left without ever having spotted her mother parked on a stool near the end.

The sight of Lani hefting a beer wasn't enough to stop Adele in her tracks. She'd seen her mother in bars before. It was the man she sat next to, with her head bent close to his in what was clearly an intimate conversation, that left Adele chilled.

Henry Parkman, owner of the feed store.

Married Henry Parkman. And until this moment, Adele had thought him happily married.

His wedded state, however, didn't seem to make a difference to Lani. She flashed her white teeth at him before tipping her head back and laughing uproariously.

Adele's mother had always gone after men; that was nothing new. Somewhere along the line she'd apparently moved to married men. Adele felt sick to her stomach.

Every thought fled her head save one: getting the hell out of the Spotted Horse. Legs shaking, she sidestepped Ty and brushed past another couple in her haste to reach the entrance, her escape fueled by an incessant roaring in her ears.

"You don't have to get out," Adele said when Ty opened his truck door and pocketed his keys.

"I'd like to walk you to your door, if you don't mind."

He assumed the good-night kiss they'd teased about at the Spotted Horse—the one that had sent his pulse skyrocketing—wouldn't materialize. That didn't stop him from wanting to see her safely inside.

Adele's mood had plummeted the moment she saw her mother with Henry Parkman, the owner of the feed store. And understandably so. Ty had remained silent on the subject during the short ride home, commenting on the weather and upcoming rodeo, and not pressuring her when she didn't respond. It had been obvious from the day he first saw Lani in the barn with Pop that any discussion of Adele's mother was off-limits.

From somewhere nearby, one of the ranch's many dogs barked. Ty sat behind the steering wheel, absently tapping a foot.

When Adele didn't immediately exit the truck, he waited another moment, then shut his door. She continued sitting in the passenger seat, staring into the darkness at a row of sprawling cottonwood trees, standing like a black wall against a silver sky.

Strange behavior for someone who'd been in an all-fired hurry to get home not twenty minutes earlier.

Okay, maybe she did want to talk. Or not be alone. When she still didn't move or speak, he hunkered down in his seat, pushed back his cowboy hat and scratched his forehead. The intricate workings of a woman's mind had often eluded Ty, and he'd long ago developed a system to use in situations like this one. When in doubt, wait and say nothing.

"I'm sorry," Adele finally muttered.

"For what?"

"I know this isn't how you expected the evening to end."

"Don't sweat it."

"From the day my mom arrived, I've been trying to figure out why she showed up. I should have guessed it was to find a new man. She doesn't go long without one. I just hadn't realized she'd lowered her already low standards and was including married men in her pickings." Hurt and disappointment roughened Adele's voice.

Ty decided to go out on a limb. "Don't take this wrong, but are you sure your mother was going after Henry Parkman?"

Adele turned her head to gawk at Ty with disbelief. "You saw the two of them at the bar."

"I did." He scratched his forehead again. "Can't say there was much going on between them other than talking and laughing."

"If she'd been sitting any closer to him, she'd have been in his lap."

"The place was pretty crowded. Hard not to sit close to someone with people crammed in all around you."

"Why are you defending her?"

"I'm not defending her. Only saying I didn't see anything more than two people having a friendly conversation."

"Yeah. *Real* friendly. That's how it always starts with her."

Ty let the remark pass, returning to his original plan to say nothing. Women were talkers, he reminded himself, and men were fixers. She probably didn't want his advice, just a sounding board on which to vent her frustrations. At least, that was what his sisters used to tell him when he opened his mouth once too often with unsolicited advice.

Several more moments passed with Adele sitting silently. Ty leaned back, content to be patient, and determined to be what she needed, even if he couldn't figure out exactly what that was.

"You have a perfect family," she murmured, staring out the window again.

"I wouldn't call them perfect."

"Your mom and dad are still married after, what, thirty years?"

"Something like that."

"They not only raised three kids, they both have successful careers. I'd call that pretty perfect."

"They've had their share of rough patches." Some of them a direct result of Ty and a few rather rebellious teen years.

"My parents divorced when I was three." She heaved a sigh. "I don't really know why. My dad refused to talk about it, and the reasons my mom gave always sounded a bit…manufactured." Adele turned toward Ty. "Do people really grow apart?" Without waiting for him to answer, she resumed gazing out the window. "I think she just got tired of him." Adele's voice hitched. "Like she got tired of me."

"That's not true."

"How would you know?"

"All right, I don't." That's what he got for trying to say the right thing. Back to plan one: be quiet and listen.

"She left me here every chance she got. Every time she found a new man to latch on to. What kind of mom does that to her own kid?"

"Maybe she was trying to protect you."

"From what?" Adele asked, her expression incredulous.

Ty ground his teeth, cursing his inability to shut up.

"From *what?*" she repeated when he didn't respond.

He was probably going to regret it later, but answered her anyway. "From the lifestyle she was living. From the men she was with. From the constant liquor and partying and living on the road in a motor home or in a hotel room. I can't imagine any mother wanting to expose her child to that."

"Then why didn't she just stay home and get a regular job? Why did she dump me off at my father's or grandparents' every chance she got?"

"You should be asking your mother these questions."

Clearly, he'd blundered, for Adele sprang into action, wrenching open her door and jumping out.

Ty went after her, but she'd gotten a solid head start on him. He caught a break when she fumbled with her keys at the front door.

"Adele, I'm sorry." He came up beside her. "I shouldn't have said that." Dang it all, she was crying. "Oh, sweetheart." He placed a comforting hand on her shoulder.

She went into his arms so fast he momentarily lost his footing.

"I hate being one of those pathetic people with mommy issues," she said, her face buried in the front of his shirt.

"There's a reason Lani came here." Ty put an arm securely around Adele. When she didn't retreat, he tugged her closer.

"That's what Pop says, too," she muttered. "He thinks I should give her a chance to explain."

"Your grandfather's a smart man."

"Not about everything. He overdoes it and falls."

"Well, that's true."

Ty forced himself to concentrate. It was hard holding Adele—feeling her body fitted snugly against his—and not responding. He ached to taste her lips, glide his palms along her supple curves. When his hand inadvertently slipped off her shoulder and down her back, he quickly pulled it away.

"You're right about me talking to my mom," Adele said, her head nestled in the crook of Ty's neck as if it belonged there. "It's just that we've never been close, and talking about anything serious..." She gave a small laugh. "We don't."

"When's the last time you tried?"

"I don't even remember. How sad is that?"

She sounded so forlorn, he couldn't resist, and placed a tender kiss on the top of her head.

Big mistake.

"Ty." She immediately pushed away from him.

"My fault, I got carried away."

"It's not that. I do...want to kiss you again." She settled her palms on his chest. "Just not when I'm all weak and weepy and an emotional mess. Been there, done that, and once was enough."

He brushed aside a stray lock of her hair. "I'm willing to wait."

Using the key still clutched in her hand, she opened her front door. "Thanks for dinner. I really did have a nice time."

"Nice enough to do it again?"

"You're leaving soon."

"Which doesn't give us time to waste."

In response, she stood on tiptoe and kissed his cheek. He expected her to immediately retreat, but again she lingered, her lips soft on his skin. If she'd wanted to torture him, she couldn't have devised a more effective method.

"Good night, Ty," she whispered.

Unable to control himself, he dipped his head and inhaled the incredible scent of her. Sweet and flowery, like peach blossoms.

"Good night, Adele."

Difficult as it was, he stepped back. Giving her one last look, he touched his fingers to the brim of his hat and returned to his truck.

On the drive to his cabin, he remembered she hadn't given him an answer about going on another date. He wasn't worried. She'd mentioned wanting to kiss him again.

And Ty had every intention of taking her at her word.

Chapter 9

Adele sat at the folding picnic table outside the camper she and Pop were sharing during their long weekend at the Buffalo Bill Cody Rodeo. Cheers from the crowd carried across the parking lot to the open field where they and a hundred or so other people had constructed a makeshift RV park. Though it was normally reserved for contestants, Pop and Adele stayed there because of his long-standing involvement in rodeos and his previous championships.

Once a member of the rodeo community, always a member.

Pop opened the door of the camper and climbed down the steps. While Adele had been woolgathering and listening to the distant cheers, he'd been inside taking a short, midafternoon nap.

"Aren't you going to mosey over and watch Ty compete?"

"I will soon." She knew from the schedule on the table that Ty's event wasn't starting for another twenty-five minutes.

"Have you seen him today?"

"Earlier. After the team roping."

As Pop sat down across from her, the lightweight picnic table seesawed, ceasing to move only when he did. "I bet he's mad at himself. A new partner and a new horse are a difficult combination."

Ty had partnered with an old friend for the event. They'd done passably well on Saturday, but bombed the final round today, making several avoidable mistakes.

"Don't tell that to Ty."

Pop chuckled. "I bet he's a nervous wreck about now."

"And doing a poor job of hiding it, from what Mike and Sandy tell me." Some of the students attending the rodeo had reported back to her, too.

"He'd better get ahold of himself if he wants to do well in tie-down roping."

"He will. He's a pro, and committed."

"I figured you'd be down there offering him moral support."

Adele ignored her grandfather's penetrating gaze. This was hardly the first hint he'd dropped that she and Ty had a romantic thing going.

They didn't. In fact, they'd spoken only in passing the last two weeks. He'd been busy teaching the beginners' class, practicing for the rodeo at every opportunity, and fussing over Hamm as if the horse were a newborn baby. She'd given Ty his space so as not to distract him.

Or so she told herself.

In truth, he'd asked some hard questions the night of their date—she'd stopped thinking of it as anything else—and seeing him only reminded her that she had no answers for the questions, and probably never would. Not without talking to her mother, as Ty and Pop had both suggested.

Except Adele could hardly bring herself to say hi to her mom, not after seeing her with Henry Parkman, and avoided her at all costs.

"Pop, why did my parents get divorced?"

His brows shot up. "Where in blue blazes did that come from?"

"I've been wondering about it ever since Mom showed up."

Lani hadn't accompanied the small group of students to the rodeo. Initially, Adele had been relieved; her mother wouldn't be attempting to attach herself to a new man. Then Adele panicked. What if Lani was staying home in order to be with Henry Parkman?

Adele rubbed her eyes and sighed. Ty was wrong. That conversation in the bar hadn't been casual. Adele had seen her mother in action too often not to know when she had her game on.

"What did your folks tell you?" Pop asked.

"Dad never talked about it."

"That doesn't surprise me. Warren was always one to keep his hurt to himself."

"Why did Mom leave him? Was he such a bad husband?" Adele had always suspected it was the other way around—that her mother was a bad wife.

"She did move out, but you couldn't fault her. Not

really." Pop massaged the knuckles of one hand, then the other, a sign his arthritis was acting up. "They were young when they got married. And Warren was on the road a lot. I don't think rodeo life is good for a marriage."

Adele couldn't agree more. It was yet another strike against Ty, despite her attraction to him.

"Add a baby, plus a drinking problem on top of that, and it's a lot for two inexperienced kids to handle."

Adele frowned. "Mom's always liked to party, I know, but I don't remember her drinking *that* much. Not while I was around."

"She didn't. Warren's the one with the drinking problem."

"What?" Adele almost slipped from her seat. "Dad doesn't drink. Not a drop."

"He used to. Like a fish. That's what put an end to his rodeo career. One too many drinks, way too many losses. A shame, too, because he had real talent."

"I… I can't believe it."

Sorrow shone in Pop's eyes. "Warren went on a binge to beat all binges about a year after he and your mom separated. Crashed his truck into a billboard pillar and damn near killed himself."

"Where?"

"On the highway twenty miles outside of Markton."

"I don't remember any accident."

"Your mom took you to Cheyenne, where she had some friends. After the accident, she brought you to the ranch, but didn't tell you about your dad being all banged up. You were just a tyke, and she thought seeing your father in such bad shape would give you nightmares. He recovered and has been on the straight and narrow ever since."

Adele sat back, her head swimming. All these years, she'd assumed her father left Wyoming and ran off to Texas to escape her mother. Or, as a small part of her heart had feared, because he hadn't wanted her. In reality, he'd done so in order to turn his life around.

"Why didn't he tell me?"

"It's hard for some folks to admit their mistakes. Especially to their kids. It's one of the reasons he didn't fight your mother for joint custody of you, much as I wanted him to. He found a good woman who keeps him in line. Reminders of his past, well, they seem to tempt him too much. He falls into old habits."

"I'm not a child anymore," Adele said with a trace of bitterness. "Yet he still refuses to include me in his life."

"That goes both ways."

Pierced by guilt, she averted her glance.

"Someone's got to take the first step," Pop urged.

Hadn't Ty said almost the same thing about her mother?

Adele rubbed her temples, which were throbbing now from her taking in so much at once. Had she been wrong all these years about *both* her parents? The possibility sobered her.

"None of us likes the idea of being a disappointment to our children." Pop's expression softened. "Take it from me."

"You've never disappointed Dad. Or me."

"I did. When I let the ranch practically go to ruin after your grandmother passed."

"That was understandable."

"So is what happened to your parents."

Adele said nothing.

"Could be why your mother came back. Hoping to set things right with you."

She stared at the rodeo grounds across the parking lot. People and vehicles poured in and out, as they had all weekend long. Even at a distance, the tourists were easy to spot, with their shorts, T-shirts, sneakers and souvenirs. Children walked beside their parents, balloons bobbing at the end of strings.

"It took a lot of courage for Lani to show up," Pop said gently. "She had to know you'd still be mad at her."

"I thought you didn't like my mother."

"That's not true. I despised what she did to you, carting you off to some new place on a whim, leaving you on your father's doorstep or mine whenever the mood struck. But then, I knew she was unhappy and that Warren had caused a lot of it. I also remember her the way she was when your dad and she first met. Your mother was the prettiest, sweetest little gal."

No one, as far as Adele knew, had ever described her mother as pretty or sweet. She must have been, however. Pop didn't usually hand out compliments where Lani was concerned.

"Why are you telling me all this now? Why not before?"

"I wasn't altogether sure you'd listen."

Adele *was* listening. Understanding, however, was a different matter. "We're a miserable lot, when you think about it."

"Doesn't have to be that way. Which is why I let Lani stay." Pop reached across the table and patted Adele's hand. "It's not too late for you and your mother to mend some of those bridges."

"I don't know," Adele said wistfully. "I don't think I can, not while she's up to her old tricks."

"What tricks?"

"I saw her at the Spotted Horse last week with Henry Parkman."

The toothpick Pop had been rolling from side to side in his mouth stilled. "Are you sure?"

"Of course I'm sure."

"They were together?"

"Sitting at the bar, big as life."

"I can't believe that. Henry and Carmella have been together over twenty years."

"I know."

"He's devoted to her."

"When Mom goes after a man, she's hard to resist." Adele could still see Lani smiling up into Henry's face, hear her boisterous laughter. "I'm worried that's why she didn't come to the rodeo, so she could be with Henry without the rest of us around."

"Except he's here."

"He is?" Adele's eyes went wide.

"Him and Carmella both. The feed store's one of the sponsors."

"I haven't seen them all weekend." Though she had noticed the store's colorful banner hanging in the main arena.

"Well, they're here. You've probably been too busy with the students and Ty."

Adele wanted to object. She'd been so certain her mother had returned to her old ways.

"What did you see Henry and Lani doing at the Spotted Horse?" Pop asked.

"Sitting close. Talking. Laughing and smiling at each other."

"That all?"

"Don't say it like it's nothing." Adele scowled. "Mom was flirting with him, and he didn't seem to mind."

"Flirting is a far cry from having an affair."

"It's still wrong."

"Are you sure it wasn't the other way around? Henry could've been flirting with your mother."

Adele started to answer, then clamped her mouth shut.

Two people had now told her she may have been jumping to a wrong conclusion. As much as she hated to admit it, the possibility was looking more and more likely. Were her feelings for Lani so negative and slanted that she was quick to assume the worst?

Doubts came rushing in. Adele had been comfortable for years living with her anger at both her parents. Just because the time for change might be at hand didn't mean she was eager to embrace it.

A cheer went up in the stands. It was followed by the announcer's voice, telling the audience to stay seated for the final round of tie-down roping, due to start after a ten-minute break.

"We'd better get a move on." Pop rose from his seat, causing the small picnic table to seesaw again.

Adele also stood. Her grandfather could move only so fast, and they had a fair distance to cover—which gave her plenty of opportunity to think…and reconsider.

* * *

During the walk to the main arena, Adele pulled herself together, only half listening to Pop's chatter and half noticing the endless stream of people, participants and horses. Tantalizing aromas from the concession stands and brightly painted signs atop vendor booths vied for their attention. She practiced smiling, wanting to present a relaxed demeanor to the students sitting in the section of bleacher seats they'd reserved. Pop would head on down to the chutes and boxes to watch the tie-down roping and give last-minute advice to the participants he'd mentored through the years.

The first competitor had just finished his run by the time Adele climbed the bleacher stairs, saying hi to the students and hoping they didn't notice her distracted state. Luckily, their gazes were centered elsewhere.

She sat in the only available seat, which happened to be next to Mike and Sandy. They were leaving Cowboy College the next day, and Adele would be sad to see them go. They'd been two of the ranch's more enjoyable and memorable guests.

"I was pleased to hear about Pop," Mike said, leaning forward to converse with Adele around his wife.

"What about him?" She automatically searched for Ty, finally spotting him behind the chutes and boxes. He sat astride Hamm, waiting his turn and watching the competition from that vantage point.

"The report from his orthopedic surgeon."

Adele squinted curiously at Mike. "What report?"

"When he saw his doctor last week." Understanding and then embarrassment flashed across his face. "You don't know."

"What did the doctor say?"

Mike shook his head. "I'm sorry. I can't tell you."

"But he's not your patient."

"Even so." He looked miserable because of his blunder. "I thought Pop had discussed the report with you."

"Well, he didn't." At the moment, she wasn't sure who to be more agitated with, Pop or Mike.

"Ask him," Mike urged.

"Tell me this much. Do I have anything to be worried about?" Anything *more*. Between Ty's event and the revelations about her parents, she'd reached her stress limit for the day.

Mike broke into a grin, and repeated, "Ask him. But in the meantime, feel free to sleep easy tonight."

That much was a relief.

"Next up," the announcer called, his voice blaring from the speakers, "is a young man all the way from Missouri."

Young was right. He didn't look any older than nineteen. At twenty-seven, Ty was one of the older competitors. He was also one of the more experienced, and that counted in his favor.

When Adele glanced back over at the box, she noticed he was gone. She didn't think much about it, assuming he was warming up Hamm. But when Ty didn't reappear a few minutes later, she started to worry. His turn was fast approaching.

Great, yet another thing to weigh on her mind. She'd be glad when this weekend was over and she could go home, retreat to a quiet place and think things through. Maybe talk to her mother.

Maybe.

The sudden ringing of her cell phone took her by surprise. She tried but couldn't read the display in the bright sunlight. Giving up, she answered the call.

"Hello."

"Come meet me by the stock pens."

She recognized Ty's voice immediately, and a jolt shot through her. "What's wrong?"

"Just come. I need a favor." He sounded anxious.

Various scenarios played in her head. A problem with Hamm or an equipment malfunction. A last minute strategy powwow. Something significant, or else why would Ty call her so close to his run?

"Be right there," she told him, already on her feet and squeezing past people on her way to the aisle.

Ty stood exactly where he said he'd be waiting, holding Hamm's reins. From a distance, everything looked fine. His equipment was intact, the horse appeared calm and uninjured, and Ty's features were composed, reflecting determination and—this was a good sign—confidence.

Adele wove in and out of the throng of people, hurrying to get to him as fast as she could. She didn't question her sense of urgency or why her heart was suddenly turning somersaults. The last forty-five minutes had delivered one emotional bombshell after another. The entire week, really. No wonder her nerves were a tangled mess and her anxiety level through the roof.

Anxiety? Or excitement?

No denying it. The small thrill winding through her as she drew close to Ty had more to do with attraction than trepidation. Much more.

At last she broke free from the crowd. Feeling like a fish escaping through a hole in a fisherman's net, she slowed down, covering the remaining thirty feet separating her and Ty at a walk. Until that moment, he'd been staring at the arena, his head cocked slightly to one side as he listened to the announcer's evaluation of the last contestant's run—a good one, according to the score. Ty would have to give everything he had and then some if he intended to win.

He must have sensed her approach, for he suddenly turned. When their gazes connected, his eyes lit up, then turned dark and smoldering. The small thrill became a rushing river of awareness. All at once, Adele knew why Ty had called her to meet him, and what he wanted. She didn't hesitate going to him.

Dropping the reins, he came forward. Luckily, Hamm was placid by nature outside the arena, because another horse might have spooked when Adele flung herself into Ty's open arms.

"I've been waiting two weeks for this," he said as his mouth came down on hers.

Only two weeks? It felt to Adele as if she'd been waiting forever. For this kiss. This moment. This man.

Forgetting all the obstacles facing them and the fact that he was leaving soon, *very* soon, forgetting the crowd, which had dissolved into a soundless blur, she returned Ty's kiss with a passion matching his. Instinct told her he needed this connection to her, physical and emotional, in order to compete. Every bit as much as he needed the lariat tied to his saddle.

The sense of contentment stealing over her told her she needed it, too. Perhaps even more than he did, for all at once her world stopped rocking wildly and righted itself.

Offering no resistance to his bold advances, she molded her body to his, relishing the sensation of his hands firmly pressed into her back, his hard muscled length as he anchored her to him, and his tongue as it swept into her mouth.

She could only imagine the number of open stares they were garnering, but she didn't care. Every harsh breath he drew, every groan issuing from deep in his chest told her neither did he.

A loud, bawdy whoop penetrated her foggy brain, returning her to reality.

"Hey, Boudeau! Hate to break up the party but you're up soon. Better get a move on."

Ty broke off their kiss, his reluctance showing in his eyes. "I want to see you tonight."

"Another date?" she asked, still holding on to him.

"Okay."

The way he said "okay" gave her reason to think he'd had something else in mind.

So did she.

"All right."

He grinned.

"On one condition."

"What's that?" He bent as if to nuzzle her neck. Her next words stopped him.

"You take first in tie-down roping."

He lifted his head. "You think I can't?"

"Not at all. But if you want to see me tonight, you'd better be bringing that belt buckle with you."

"Be ready at seven." Letting go of her, he gathered

the reins and mounted Hamm in one fluid motion. "And wear something sexy."

With that, he trotted off to the area behind the box.

Ignoring the snickering and gawking, Adele ran back to the bleachers and her seat.

She couldn't help feeling that Ty winning this event was more important than him getting back on track, and more significant than going on another date with him.

It seemed to Adele as if her whole life was suddenly poised to change.

Chapter 10

"Boudeau, you're up next!"

Ty nudged Hamm into place behind the box. The horse responded with the tiniest of cues, already in the zone and ready to go. Ty wished he could say the same for himself. Kissing Adele had affected his concentration—among other things.

That hadn't been his plan. Not intentionally. He'd only wanted to talk to her. Why, he wasn't sure now. Only that two weeks without close interaction had been too long. The need to see her, even briefly, before he went into the arena had been so powerful, he hadn't thought his actions through, simply punched in her number.

And she'd come. Just like that. Without requiring an explanation.

When he'd seen her hurrying toward him, eager anticipation brightening her expression, the part of his brain not a slave to logic had taken over, and he'd kissed her. *Really* kissed her. And it had wiped away every memory of every other woman before her.

He couldn't wait for tonight.

Except if he didn't get it together, and fast, there would be no "tonight" with her.

He had to take first place.

For her, but also for himself. Somewhere along the way, winning at roping and winning over Adele had become intermingled, and he didn't think he could separate the two.

"On deck, Boudeau."

"Sorry," Ty said, realizing his name had been called a second time. He urged Hamm closer to the box.

"You got this in the bag, son."

Ty glanced down to see Pop hobbling over. "That's what I'm hoping."

The older man gave Ty's leg an encouraging pat. "Billy Carpenter broke the barrier."

"Is that so?" Ty had missed Billy's run and the penalty. It must have happened while he and Adele were kissing.

"The only ones left who can possibly beat you are Mitch Benson and Garth Maitland."

"I'm not worried about Benson," Ty said. Lifting his head to see over the crowd, he watched the man in question throw his rope. "He chokes under pressure."

Benson's toss sailed straight and true, but when he went to tie the calf's legs, his hand accidentally slipped, costing him precious seconds. The announcer commiserated and encouraged the audience to give him a round of applause.

"That leaves Garth," Ty said, his jaw tightening.

"He goes last."

"I know."

Taking no chances, Ty checked his equipment with the thoroughness of a heart surgeon preparing for a transplant operation.

"Boudeau!"

He only had to loosen his grip on the reins slightly, and Hamm charged forward into the box, ready to go. As the big animal settled in, Ty knew he'd been right to purchase him. There wasn't a better horse around or a better horse for him. They could win today.

Hell, they could go all the way to the National Finals Rodeo in December, where participants from all over the world competed.

Pop had followed Ty as far as the fence. One of the cowboys moved aside and made room for the older man, who hoisted himself onto the bottom rail with a grunt.

Ty barely noticed. He was too preoccupied rewinding his lariat into a coil for the third time and hefting it in his hand. He didn't stop until the lariat felt exactly right.

"This probably isn't the time to tell you," Pop said, loudly enough for Ty and everyone else to hear, "but I approve of you courting my granddaughter. If that's your intention."

Caught off guard, Ty looked up. Had Pop seen them kissing? "It is my intention, sir. But I have to bring home a buckle first."

Pop laughed till he choked. "She tell you that?"

"She did. And I think she's serious."

"Then you'd better have the run of your life."

Ty couldn't agree more.

He could feel the eyes of every man standing on or straddling the fence. They knew his history, many of them having seen him lose to Garth last year. They realized today could be, make that *was*, Ty's comeback. He wasn't going to disappoint them.

Or Adele.

"Good luck, Boudeau."

"You got it in the bag, Ty."

He settled deeper into his saddle, ignoring his buddies. They weren't expecting him to reply, anyway, understanding that he was getting himself where he needed to be mentally.

A last tug on his gloves. One more inspection of his lariat and the knot that secured it to his saddle horn. A final stretch of the pigging string before he placed it between his teeth. One more hat adjustment. With each action, he narrowed his concentration until all he saw, all that mattered was his horse, the calf and the wrangler manning the gate to the chute.

"Get ready, boy," he said under his breath, giving Hamm's neck a quick pat.

Long days of honing his skills, learning about himself and his horse, were about to pay off. A burst of confidence exploded inside him, growing stronger as if he'd drunk a magical elixir.

"Go." The single clipped word accompanied a brusque nod of his head.

The gate to the chute opened with a harsh metallic swish. An instant after the calf escaped, Ty and Hamm were in motion, operating on pure adrenaline and instinct. Ty's arm came up in the air at just the right moment. The rope flew from his hand with precision and accuracy, sailing toward the running calf on a perfect gust of air. Even before the lasso reached its target, Ty was swinging his leg over the saddle, leaping off and hitting the ground at a dead run.

Hamm did his job, stepping backward and pulling the rope taut. Ty also did his job, sliding his hand along the rope as he ran forward. The instant the calf was down on its side, he wound the pigging string around its legs and threw his hands in the air to signal he was done.

He didn't need to hear the announcer or glance at the scoreboard to know he'd performed well. He could feel it in the thundering of his heart and the surge of energy racing through him.

Untying the calf, he collected his rope and pigging string, walked over to Hamm and gave the horse's neck another pat. "Thanks, partner."

Hamm bobbed his head up and down, then knocked his nose into Ty's shoulder. It seemed he was also happy with their run. The two of them made for the gate, Ty leading Hamm by the reins.

Applause broke out as Ty's official score appeared on the board. He stared, committing this moment to memory. Seven seconds flat. Good enough to put him in first place.

Ty didn't celebrate. Not yet. Garth Maitland still had to go. And while seven seconds flat was a damn fine time, Garth had beaten it before and could again today.

Stick appeared on the other side of the gate. "That was sure a nice run, Ty."

"Not bad."

"Want me to take Hamm for you?" Stick didn't add,

"So you can stay and watch the rest of the competition."

He didn't have to.

"Appreciate that."

After the teen left with the horse, Ty climbed onto the fence. He picked a spot away from the other competitors. If Garth beat him, he wanted a few minutes to himself before facing his friends.

But that wasn't going to happen. Not after the great run he'd had today.

The next contestant, a young man from Ecuador, finished at thirteen-point-three seconds. Ty hadn't been worried. The contestant after that had the potential to bump Ty out of the first place standing if he pulled off a miracle. But he didn't. The calf got loose at the last second, disqualifying him.

That left only Garth.

He was riding his regular horse and had been all weekend. The Buffalo Bill Cody Stampede might not be the biggest rodeo on the Turquoise Circuit, but he still wouldn't take a chance on a new horse.

"Folks, this cowboy needs a time of six-point-nine seconds to take over first place." The announcer's voice blared from the speakers overhead. "If anyone can do it, Garth Maitland sure can."

That was no lie.

Ty turned away from the box where Garth was going through his final equipment check, and scanned the crowd. He knew where the students from Cowboy College were sitting, and sought out Adele. At this distance it was impossible to see her face clearly. Even so, he was certain she was looking at him and not Garth.

The sound of the chute opening had Ty snapping his attention back to the box.

He willed Garth to have a good run. Not that Ty didn't want to win. But he wanted a victory because he'd earned it, not because his biggest rival performed poorly.

The calf darted toward the far end of the arena. Every movement Garth and his horse made was straight out of a textbook. Running along the rope his mount held taut, he dropped the calf to the ground and tied its legs.

The crowd roared, their applause and cheers drowning out the announcer.

Ty didn't need to hear. His gut told him the run was a good one. Better than good, it was great. Equal to his own.

But was it better?

"Ladies and gentlemen, bear with us," the announcer's voice declared. "This is close, and the officials need to be one hundred percent sure."

Ty caught sight of Garth as he reached the gate. Their gazes connected, and Garth gave the briefest of nods. Ty returned it, his silent message the same.

Good run, cowboy.

"Hold on to your hats, folks, we have it," the announcer proclaimed. "Garth Maitland's official time is seven-point-three seconds. That makes Ty Boudeau your winner today!" Cheers exploded from the stands. "With Garth Maitland in second place and Ricky Morales in third."

Ty closed his eyes and dropped his head, savoring the moment. He'd won before, plenty of times. But no victory had ever been sweeter or more hard earned.

He was, he knew now without a doubt, on his way to the top. This time he wouldn't lose at the National Finals Rodeo. He and Hamm would take home the title of World Champion and a generous sponsorship deal with it.

All at once, he was surrounded. Friends and fellow contestants pulled him off the fence, congratulating him and slapping him on the back.

"Hell of a run, Ty."

"You had me scared there for a minute, buddy, but you pulled it off."

He took it all in, his grin stretched so wide his face hurt.

"I knew you could do it." Pop appeared beside him.

"I couldn't have without your and Adele's help. I owe the both of you." Ty pulled the older man into a hug. More backslapping followed, for both him and Pop.

"Maybe I should sign up for a week at Cowboy College," a young man said jokingly.

"Maybe you should," Mitch Benson answered, his face serious.

Ty didn't think that was such a bad idea.

The speakers crackled to life again, and the announcer's voice carried across the arena. "The day's not over yet, folks. Stay in your seats, 'cause next up is the event you've been waiting for. Bull riding."

"See you in Sheridan?" Mitch asked.

Ty shook the hand he extended. "I'll be there. And having another run like today."

"I'm counting on it."

Eventually, everyone started clearing away. Some returned to their trailers to pack up, done for the weekend. Others took a place on the fence or in the bleachers to watch the bull riding.

Ty and Pop hadn't gone more than a few steps when Garth appeared in front of them.

"Congratulations," he told Ty.

"You didn't do so bad yourself today."

"First in team roping. I guess I can live with that."

"Enjoy it while it lasts. I plan on entering team roping at Sheridan."

Pop clapped Ty on the shoulder. "I'll catch up with you later, son. Garth, give your family my regards."

After Pop left, Garth asked, "Who's your partner?"

"I'm not sure yet." Louis had informed Ty earlier that he wouldn't be going to Sheridan.

"How 'bout me?"

Ty laughed. "You're not serious."

"As a heart attack. Willie's kids are getting older, and his wife doesn't want him to go on the road anymore."

Ty understood. "Team rope with you?" he repeated, surprised at how much the idea appealed to him.

"Why not?"

Why not indeed.

"I guess we could give it a try. See how we work together."

Garth grinned. "How long until you leave Seven Cedars?"

He'd been planning on leaving mid-week. Now, he wasn't so sure. "Not for a few days."

"Why don't you come by Tuesday morning? We'll give it a go."

"I'll be there."

"Seven o'clock. Main arena."

No sooner did Garth walk away, than Adele appeared. Ty had no idea how long she'd been standing there or what she'd heard. Only that he couldn't be happier to see her, or wait any longer to hold her.

"You won." She smiled shyly.

"I did." He took a step toward her. "Now, about our date—"

"There he is!"

"Whoo, hoo! Ty, you were amazing."

All at once, he was surrounded by Mike and Sandy and the other students from Cowboy College. Enduring more backslapping, handshakes and hugs, he craned his neck to catch sight of Adele. Good. She hadn't left.

"We're having a celebration potluck cookout tonight at Pop's camper." Sandy's eyes pleaded with Ty. "Say you'll be there."

"Well, I…"

"I know you're probably going out with the other contestants." Her face fell. "But please come. Just for a little while."

"Don't pressure the man," Mike admonished.

Just beyond the group, Adele smiled coyly, obviously amused.

Ty pushed back his hat. "I guess I can come for a while."

Sandy threw her arms around him.

"You'll be there, too, won't you?" one of the students asked Adele.

Her gaze, soft and warm and hinting at what the night might bring, landed on Ty.

He drew in a sharp breath.

"I wouldn't miss it for the world," she said.

Neither would he.

Adele surveyed the area beside her grandfather's truck. If not for the absence of a flickering fire and nocturnal creatures calling to each other, the setting for their gathering could have been a cookout in the woods by Little Twister Creek.

Lawn chairs and overturned crates had been set up in a circle around the portable grill, enhancing the simple but hearty meal they all shared and the conversation that flowed easily—most of it centered on Ty. Kerosene lanterns atop folding tables attracted moths, while alternately casting shadows and light on people's faces.

Ty sat at the head of the circle, relishing the moment. Well, he deserved it, thought Adele. It wasn't easy coming back from a crushing defeat like the one he'd endured. She'd been proud of him today, admiring his tenacity and drive.

Then again, there were a number of things she admired about Ty, including the natural camaraderie he had with people, drawing them to him like those lanterns did the insects. He'd known most of the students here tonight only a short time, yet he treated them like old friends, and they him. It was no surprise Iron Grip Ropes had approached him about a sponsorship deal last year. He'd have made a perfect spokesman. If he continued winning, which he would, maybe they'd approach him again.

Building custom-made saddles the quality of Charlie Kingston's was a fine occupation, but Adele couldn't help thinking Ty was better suited to doing something that got him out and about, rather than being stuck in a workroom all day.

Well, she doubted he'd be building saddles full-time for a while. Not until he retired from rodeoing, which, now that he'd discovered the previously missing connection with Hamm, wouldn't be for several years at least.

Adele went around collecting trash and depositing it in a plastic garbage bag. Some of their neighbors had already packed up their trailers and RVs and departed, leaving open spaces in the makeshift gypsy camp. Most were like her and Pop, planning to start out for home at the crack of dawn.

Pop, in his element, stole the spotlight from Ty and regaled the students with stories from back in the day when he'd competed. Everyone, including Ty, listened raptly.

Despite having had an emotional day with highs, lows and moments of downright confusion, Adele felt a sense of satisfaction. This pleasant gathering of friends, guests and people she cared about was the kind she'd envisioned when she and her grandfather first started Cowboy College.

Not that there weren't sacrifices. She had few opportunities to travel and see the country as she longed to, given all the responsibilities she shouldered.

Yet another reason she and Ty were a poor match. He would settle down eventually. In the meantime, however, he'd be going wherever his rodeo career took him, and that would be miles and miles away from Markton, Wyoming.

"Need help with that?" Sandy asked. Their potluck

dinner had consisted mostly of leftovers, topped off with ice cream and peach pies someone had purchased earlier at the market down the road.

"I'm fine," Adele said. "You go sit yourself back down."

Sandy paused, her arms crossed, and stared at the group. "I'm going to miss all this."

"We'll miss you, too."

"Tomorrow when we check out, Mike and I are going to make reservations for next summer."

"That's great. We'd love to have you back."

"We want to come at the same time Ty does."

Adele paused in the middle of securing the garbage bag with a twist tie. "I…don't think he's coming back," she said carefully.

"No?" Sandy appeared puzzled. "He said he was."

"When?"

"Just a little bit ago."

"He did?"

Adele must have given herself away, for Sandy laughed richly. "I thought that might make you happy."

"Of course it does. It's our goal for all our guests to return."

"But Ty in particular."

No, what she really wanted was for Ty to stay and not leave.

But he would. Especially after winning the gold buckle today. That was the whole reason he'd come to Cowboy College. To figure out what he'd been doing wrong, fix it, return to the circuit as soon as possible and resume his promising career.

"*You and Mike* in particular," Adele emphasized, trying to cover her slip.

"Hey, we all think it's great that you and Ty hooked up."

We all? As in the entire guest roster? Adele waited for mortification to overcome her—only it didn't. To her shock, she realized she wasn't upset that guests, and no doubt staff, too, knew she and Ty had "hooked up," as Sandy put it.

"We will see you before we leave, won't we?"

Sandy's question roused Adele from her reverie. "Of course. We'll have a goodbye party at lunch."

"What's that about a party?" Mike asked, coming up and giving his wife's waist a squeeze.

"Adele said we're having one at lunch tomorrow."

"Can I come, too?"

At the sound of Ty's voice behind her, Adele went still.

"Of course." Conscious of her audience, she set the bag of trash by the truck door for disposal later. "Everyone's invited."

"Sandy and I were thinking of going to the country and western bar up the road for something stronger than this." Mike held out his plastic bottle of iced tea. "Some of the folks were saying the band's not half-bad. You two want to go?"

"It's not a far walk," Sandy prompted.

"I don't know." Ty sent Adele a questioning look.

Technically, they had a date tonight, payment for him winning his event. If he wanted to go to the bar, she'd gladly accompany him.

The gleam in his dark eyes, coal-black in the lantern light, indicated he was thinking of something more than a few close dances and a searing kiss or two under a star-filled sky.

Was she ready for that and all the complications that went with it?

If not, she had better tell him no right now.

"Be back in a while, Pop," she called out, without looking away from Ty.

"Stay out of trouble, you two," he hollered back, an unmistakable smile in his voice.

Define trouble, Adele thought as Ty fell into step beside her.

Chapter 11

Sandy's mile-a-minute chatter hid the fact that Ty and Adele contributed very little to the conversation. Adele couldn't speak for him, but in her case, an acute case of nerves had frozen her vocal cords. Instinct told her whatever happened tonight between them would be entirely up to her. He would respect and honor any decision she made.

If only she was certain what her decision would be. *Correction.*

If only she was certain she wouldn't end up being hurt.

Sandy's prattling continued as they reached the outskirts of the makeshift gypsy camp.

"Hold on." Ty stopped in midstep and patted his jeans pocket. "I forgot my wallet in my trailer."

"We'll walk back with you," Mike offered.

"I hate to hold you up."

"You sure?" Sandy asked, her oval face lit by the parking lot lights.

"Go on ahead and find us a table."

They started out, then stopped again. "You coming?" Mike asked Adele.

Her vocal cords had yet to thaw.

"Come on." Sandy linked arms with her husband. "They'll be along in a minute." Dragging him with her, she glanced over her shoulder and chimed, "Take your time, you two."

"My trailer's this way." Ty inclined his head in the direction they'd come.

Adele nodded, swallowed and took a step.

He reached for her hand. When it was clasped firmly in his, walking wasn't nearly so difficult.

"I didn't plan this," he said, his voice low and husky. "I really did forget my wallet."

She believed him. Cowboys didn't usually carry their wallets when they competed, and Ty hadn't returned to his trailer since winning his event.

They saw many familiar faces as they navigated among the campsites. If their joined hands solicited any attention, Adele didn't care. As Sandy had pointed out, everyone at Cowboy College knew about her and Ty's attraction. So what if the rest of the world found out, too?

Suddenly, Adele wasn't indecisive anymore. Her heart, which had been whispering to her softly for weeks, now spoke loud and clear, urging her to seize the moment.

"I'm parked over there."

She followed his gaze. Ty's trailer stood alone, his neighbors having left already. Hamm, along with the other horses, was bedded down in the event stables.

Going straight to the rear wheel well, Ty located a hidden key and unlocked the side door, careful not to let it bang against the wall. At this time of night, the noise would carry half a mile.

"I won't be long," he said, and reached through the open door.

A dim light came on, illuminating the postage-stamp-size living quarters. Placing an old footstool on the ground, he grabbed the side-mounted handhold and easily hefted himself up and inside the trailer.

Adele heard the scrape of a sliding drawer. The scuffle of boots on linoleum flooring. The jingle of keys being dropped on the counter. She also heard the sound of her own boots on the footstool as she copied Ty and clasped the handhold.

He turned, his expression unreadable as he took in the sight of her standing in the trailer doorway. "The place is a little small, but I'd be happy to show you around."

Was he keeping his emotions in check? Making a joke in case he'd misinterpreted the reason she'd so boldly entered his private space? A space that could be even more private if the door was shut. Reaching behind her, she swung it closed. The clicking latch echoed loudly in the suddenly quiet interior.

So did the beating of her soaring heart.

"Adele?"

She hadn't spoken since leaving Pop's campsite, and didn't now.

Crossing the small distance separating them, she reached up and circled his neck with her arms. His eyes, which had tracked her progress, instantly went from unreadable to blazing hot.

"You know this is dangerous," he said in a rough-ened voice, pulling her close until their bodies were flush and their hips aligned.

Was it? Adele had been thinking it was exciting and daring and incredibly intoxicating. Not dangerous.

She sought his mouth, moaning softly at the first touch of his lips. Moaning again when the kiss became possessive. Heat arrowed though her, igniting every nerve in its path. This, she thought numbly, was only the beginning. There could—and would—be so much more.

Ty pushed away from her, catching her off guard, his chest heaving. "We'd better slow it down some."

Adele made a sound of protest.

"I can't take much more of this and stay sane."

They'd have to risk his sanity, she thought, a smile pulling at her lips. She liked the hard ridge of his erec-tion pressing firmly into the junction of her legs—liked it too much to stop.

Nestling closer, she rubbed her calf along his and twirled her fingers in the soft curls at the back of his neck.

As if in surrender, he leaned against the closet door behind him. "Adele, sweetheart. Please."

Please what? Leave him alone or give in to the de-sire that had been building practically since the day he arrived at Cowboy College?

She laid her palms flat on his chest. Beneath the fabric of his shirt, his heart beat fast and erratically. How much of it, she wondered, had he given to her? Enough that it would be torture for him to leave her in a few days?

Yes. She didn't require a declaration made on bended knee to know she'd come to mean something special to him. Something he wouldn't find anywhere else, regardless of where his travels took him.

She brought her hands together over the top button of his shirt and quickly unfastened it.

Before she got to the second button, he grasped her wrist, staying her motions. "Are you sure?"

Nodding, she gazed at him, hoping he saw the depths of her feelings for him reflected in her face.

"Say something, Adele. Please."

She put him out of his misery. "Make love to me, Ty."

She expected him to respond with another kiss, one designed to rob her of her ability to think coherently. He didn't. Instead, he tucked her head snugly against his chest and brushed his lips across her hair.

"I want you to know this won't be a casual fling."

Could it be anything else? He was leaving soon.

"I'll be back for you. Count on it."

His earnestness touched her.

"I'll be waiting," she said.

He kissed her then, sweetly, tenderly and with a gentleness she wouldn't have expected from a rugged, brawny cowboy like him.

Quickly, however, the kiss turned scorching. His mouth, unsatisfied with teasing and tormenting just her lips, sought out other sensitive places on her body. Her neck. The delicate skin of her earlobe. The soft hollow at the base of her throat.

Adele's limbs went weak as a needy moan escaped.

All at once Ty was tugging at her shirttail, releasing it from the waistband of her jeans. Then he reached up under the fabric and grasped her waist.

Opening his shirt, she ran her hands down his white

cotton T-shirt, enjoying the sensation of downy fabric over the taut planes of his chest. All during their sensual interplay, his lips continued exploring her sensitive regions. That stopped when her fingers brushed against his belt buckle. With a deep groan, he claimed her mouth again, stripping her shirt from her as he did.

The lighting was dim, but Ty still had a clear view of her baby-blue bra. He traced a fingertip along the lacy trim, murmuring, "Nice."

And it was. Adele might be all cowgirl on the outside, but she had an appreciation for delicate underthings.

"You told me to wear something sexy."

Emboldened by his hungry gaze, she peeled his shirt from his shoulders. He took over, shrugging it off and removing his T-shirt. She'd expected him to have a well-honed body, considering how hard he worked at roping, and she wasn't disappointed.

All at once she saw it, a lasso tattoo circling his upper right arm. It fit Ty's personality and brought a smile to her lips. "Nice," she murmured, echoing his earlier remark.

"You don't mind tattoos?"

"I have one, too."

His eyes lit up. "Where?"

She lowered the strap of her bra, revealing a tiny horse's head with flowing mane above her left breast. The same one used in the Cowboy College logo.

Ty's breath caught. Lowering his mouth, he pressed his lips to the tattoo.

Even if Adele had wanted to guard her emotions, she couldn't any longer. Not after this. Not with Ty.

She gasped when he unexpectedly tugged down the

front of her bra and cupped her freed breast. Gasped again when he circled the nipple with his tongue.

In a hurry, she grabbed at her own belt.

Ty raised his head. "No rush, sweetheart. We've got all night. Unless you still want to go to the bar with Mike and Sandy."

"Not on your life." She finished unbuckling her belt, then attacked the snap on her jeans.

"Wait." Ty covered her hands with his.

"What?"

Before her insecurities could get the better of her, he said, "I…have protection." He fumbled for the wallet on the counter, opened it and withdrew a condom.

"That's good." Stupid her. She'd been so caught up in making love with Ty, she'd forgotten about being responsible.

"I want you to know…" Again he hesitated. "This has been in my wallet awhile." He tried to grin. "In case you thought otherwise."

There were cowboys on the rodeo circuit notorious for sleeping around. And they had plenty of obliging women at their disposal. Adele believed Ty, however, and not just because he had a reputation for being one of the honorable guys. She believed him because of the genuine worry in his expression.

"I didn't think otherwise," she said. "And for the record, it's been a long while for me, too."

"Glad that's settled," he said, and kissed her again.

With all doubts erased and all barriers eradicated, they were able to revel in the feel of each other's body and the wildly erotic sensations generated by their intimate explorations. The tiny living quarters didn't allow much space for maneuvering. And without stopping to convert the dining table into a sleeping bunk, they had nowhere to lie down.

Ty showed himself to be good at improvising.

Removing the remainder of Adele's clothing, he lifted her onto the table. When she reached for him, he grabbed a pillow from the seat, placed it behind her and lowered her backward.

Starting at the horse's head tattoo, he traveled the length of her body to the V of her legs, leaving moist kisses in his wake. The skill of his mouth was matched only by the skill of his fingers. Both tantalized her unmercifully, and within minutes, she was perched on the pinnacle of release.

He didn't, however, take her over the edge, and she almost cried out in frustration when he straightened. All was forgiven when he unbuckled his jeans and stepped out of them.

She raised up on her elbows, to better see Ty in his slim fitting boxer briefs. Without the least bit of modesty, he removed them, opened the condom package and sheathed himself. Pulse soaring, she sat upright, every nerve alight with anticipation.

Except he didn't move.

"Ty? What's wrong?"

"Nothing." His dark eyes studied her from head to toe. "I just like looking at you."

He certainly knew how to prolong the agony. Or was that pleasure? Definitely pleasure. Her entire body hummed with it.

Unable to wait any longer, she arched her spine and smiled temptingly.

That did it. With an agonized groan, he grasped her legs and anchored her to him.

Adele gasped in surprise, then delight, when he entered her. Wrapping her legs around his middle, she clung to him, wanting an emotional connection with him more than she did a physical one.

Ty held back, she could tell. And as much as she wanted to tumble over the edge, she also wanted their lovemaking to last.

Murmuring sweet, sexy endearments, he bent her backward until she once again lay on the table. Covering her with his body, he kissed her deeply, his hands cupping her breasts.

Adele could wait no longer and climaxed, Ty's name on her lips. He found his own shattering release seconds later.

She clung tightly to him, savoring the aftermath of their shared storm almost as much as she had the storm itself.

Slowly, their breathing returned to normal. What could have been an awkward moment was made comfortable and easy when Ty lifted her off the table and enveloped her in a warm embrace.

"That was amazing," he said, caressing her back with strong strokes. "You're amazing."

Adele turned her face into the side of his neck. She hardly considered herself an accomplished lover. Yet it *had* been amazing with Ty. More than that, it had felt…perfect.

For a moment, she imagined them together always.

Then, too soon, reality returned.

"I suppose we should get to the bar," Adele said, easing away from Ty to look for her clothes. "Mike and Sandy are expecting us."

"Do you really want to go?"

She shook her head. "But I'm not sure I want to stand here all night. Naked, at that."

One corner of his mouth tilted up in a wicked grin. "The table converts to a bed."

She liked that idea.

Laughing together, they hurriedly removed the table-top and replaced it with a plank, then arranged the cushions into a mattress. Ty pulled a worn sleeping bag from the overhead cupboard, and they cuddled beneath it, his arm draped over her protectively and their fingers linked.

"Come with me to Ogden," he said out of the blue.

"Utah?"

"The Pioneer Days Rodeo starts the third weekend in July."

"That's only two weeks away."

"Plenty of time to pack."

"I'd love to go with you." She rolled over to face him. "More than you know. But I have to work. I can't just up and leave, not on such short notice."

"There's no one to cover for you?"

"It's our busy season."

"Then I'll skip Ogden."

"No, you won't." She pressed a light kiss to his lips. "You're winning again. You have to ride the momentum all the way to Nationals."

"I'm winning because of you."

"You always had the ability. I just helped you realize it."

"I'm coming back to Seven Cedars." He moved suddenly, throwing a leg over her and pinning her to the cushions. His hand boldly roamed her buttocks and thighs. "Don't think I'm not."

She arched into him. "I'll be waiting."

"Promise me."

A vulnerability she hadn't seen before shone in his eyes.

"I promise." The vow came easily.

"I know long-distance relationships are difficult, but we can make this work. There isn't anything I want more."

Hearing his conviction, she almost believed they could succeed where her parents had failed. Ty spent the next hour convincing her, with actions that left no doubt as to his sincerity.

Hamm entered the horse trailer without his customary balking, as if he couldn't wait to leave Cowboy College and Seven Cedars Ranch.

Adele would have preferred he put up a fight.

She'd been dreading this moment for the last five days, ever since the night she and Ty had spent together in his trailer. Standing off to the side, she watched him shut the trailer door, latch and lock it, then check the lock again just to make sure. Was he really worried that the door would swing open during the drive or simply delaying their final goodbye? He'd already missed his planned 9:00 A.M. departure time by almost an hour.

If anyone had noticed she'd spent the last four nights in Ty's cabin rather than her apartment, they said nothing. Probably because they approved of her and Ty's relationship, albeit for different reasons. Pop had more than once vocalized his desire to see Adele settled, and the employees were, she suspected, glad their boss was enjoying something other than work for a change. Reese had openly expressed her joy during Ty and Garth's first official team roping practice on Tuesday. But then, she was happily engaged to be married, and wanted all her friends to be happy, too.

"You drive careful, you hear?" Cook said. She was among the small crowd that had gathered to see Ty off.

"You're welcome back anytime." Pop's voice had a slight catch in it.

So, Adele thought, did Ty's when he answered. "I'm taking you up on that offer."

The two men started out shaking hands, but Ty pulled Pop into a bear hug. Adele felt her throat close. Five days of mental preparation obviously wasn't enough. She couldn't remember the last time she'd done anything half this hard.

"Stick, I'm counting on you to watch out for Adele and Pop while I'm gone." Ty hooked an arm around the skinny teenager's neck.

"Sure thing."

"You're a good man."

Stick's perpetual goofy grin widened.

Ty spoke to each person there, dispensing handshakes, hugs and pecks on cheeks, including one for Lani. Adele and she were on better terms, thanks in large part to Pop's recent revelations, but Adele continued to be guarded around her, unconvinced her mother had changed her ways.

Watching Lani hug Ty, Adele thought she saw genuine tears well in her mother's eyes, and she was struck with a sentimental pang. The next moment, she dismissed it. Lani knew how to put on an act with the best of them, especially around men.

Tipping his hat in one last farewell to all, Ty went to Adele and took her hand. "Walk me to my truck."

Though she generally shied away from public displays of affection, no way was he leaving without a last, lingering kiss.

Ty was of the same mind, except he carried it one step further. Amid good-natured hoots and hollers, he bent her over his arm and planted a kiss on her mouth to beat all kisses. Adele's toes were still tingling when he released her.

"I'll call you tonight."

She nodded, afraid she might cry if she tried to talk.

He reached for the door handle.

"Wait!"

Throwing her arms around him, she stood on tiptoes and pressed her face into the curve of his neck. "I'll miss you."

"Me, too, sweetheart."

Two minutes later, he was gone, his truck and trailer pulling out of the open area and heading down the long drive that would take him past the main lodge and to the highway beyond.

Adele stood there watching until the last plume of dust had dissipated. During her vigil, the others left, perhaps sensing her need to be alone.

Not yet ready to return to work, she strolled to the small barn. It had been several days since her last visit with Crackers. More than that, the quiet solitude would enable her to fortify her defenses before having to deal

with people and the inevitable well-intentioned plati-
tudes or personal questions.

Crackers nickered hello. The filly—Adele had named
her Ritz—pushed her nose up, seeking a petting. Naturally curious and playful, Ritz couldn't get enough
attention.

It was exactly the balm Adele needed to soothe her
aching heart. She'd done her best to resist Ty, and yet
she'd fallen for him. Head over heels and faster than
she'd ever imagined possible. The three weeks until he
returned were going to seem like three decades.

"There you are!"

Adele winced. *Oh, no! Why now?*

"I'm glad I found you." Lani scurried toward her, a
big, bright smile on her face.

"Hi, Mom. I was just about to get ready for class." Yes,
it was a lie, but Adele felt she'd be forgiven this once.

"There's something I need to tell you." Lani came to
a stop, looking chagrined. The expression took several
years off her face, transforming her into the attractive
woman she'd once been. Adele also noticed her mother
had filled out a little recently, the extra weight adding
a softness to her previous bone-thin frame. "I've been
stalling and stalling, and I just can't anymore."

She's leaving! Adele had been anticipating just such
an announcement for weeks.

"I'm moving." Lani's smile reappeared.

"Where to?" Adele didn't add, "this time."

"Right in town. I found an efficiency apartment to
rent. It's not much, but will do for a while. I need to
get my own place and stop mooching off you and your
grandfather."

"Oh." When did her mother start worrying about being a mooch?

"And it's close to the feed store."

Adele's stomach dropped to her knees. She should have guessed Lani wanted her own place nearby in order to carry on her affair with Henry.

"He's a married man, Mom."

"Who?"

"Henry."

"I know that."

"And it doesn't stop you?"

"From what?" Lani shook her head in confusion.

"Sleeping with him," Adele all but spit out.

"Good heavens! Is that what you think?"

"I saw you and him at the Spotted Horse."

Hurt—and disappointment?—glinted in Lani's eyes. "He offered me a job."

"A job?"

"At the feed store. His assistant manager gave notice." Lani sniffed. "I don't take up with married men. And I certainly don't take up with my boss."

"I—I…" Adele was speechless.

"I thought if I got a full-time job and my own place, that maybe you and I could, well, work things out. I've made a ton of mistakes over the years and was just trying to fix a few of them." She sniffed again. "I guess I was wrong."

"Mom." Adele struggled to find the words—any words—to say. "I'm sorry. I jumped to the wrong conclusion."

Lani's face crumpled. "I'm sorry, too. I really did want

to do the right thing for once. And when Henry offered me the job, I figured it was a good place to start."

A job and an apartment. One Lani paid for herself. Not an affair. And a chance to repair some of those burned bridges. Small steps in a very right direction.

Part of Adele resisted. Lani had never been much of a mother, disappointing her one too many times for her to be sucked in by the promise of change.

But if she didn't acknowledge her mom's efforts and support them, then perhaps she wasn't much of a daughter, either.

"It is a good place to start. I'm glad for you."

"Really?" Lani's teary eyes shone.

"And…proud."

"Oh, baby." Lani pulled her into a fierce hug. "I'm so proud of you, too. Everything you've done, the ranch, Cowboy College. Much as I tried to screw you up, you still turned out to be this incredible woman. Smart and talented and…oh, that Ty Boudeau is one lucky fellow to have you."

Slowly, very slowly, Adele returned her mother's hug. After a moment, she increased the pressure.

Maybe it was having a wonderful man like Ty in her life. Maybe it was being secure at Seven Cedars and knowing her place in the world. Whatever the reason, Adele felt some of the resentment she'd carried around for over twenty years fade, and her spirits, which had sunk so low when Ty left, gradually lift.

Chapter 12

All Ty wanted, all he'd been thinking about for the last eight hours and the last four hundred miles, was seeing Adele. Holding her, kissing her, unraveling that long braid of hers and running his fingers through her silky hair. Seven phone calls, starting this morning and ending just outside of Markton, hadn't slaked his desire to see her. If anything, they'd increased it.

The sight of the main gate leading into Seven Cedars hit Ty like a drink of cool water after a long walk in the hot desert.

He was home.

Wait a minute! When had he started thinking of Seven Cedars as home?

Since he'd left three weeks ago. Not an hour passed when he didn't imagine returning to Adele and everything he'd come to hold dear.

His gaze scanned right and left as his truck bumped along the drive and into the open area in front of the barns. He was early, but had hoped Adele would be waiting for him. They'd agreed during one of those seven phone calls that he would take Hamm to the small corral east of the arena and let him run around a bit before putting him up for the night.

A night Ty intended to spend every moment of, waking and sleeping, with Adele.

Hamm, impatient as always to be free, banged a foot on the trailer door the instant the truck came to a stop. Three minutes later, the big gelding was trotting off steam, tossing his head, and strutting his stuff for the other horses in the nearby pasture.

Ty took out his cell phone, intending to call Adele.

"He looks happy to be out."

He spun at the sound of Pop's voice behind him, and grinned broadly. "He's not the only one."

"Long drive?"

"Too long. My legs are killing me."

"How about I trade you for mine?"

Ty had noticed the older man's limp was more pronounced than before. "Hip bothering you?"

"Some. But not, I hope, for long."

"I heard you finally agreed to the replacement surgery."

Adele had given Ty the news the day after he left. It seemed Pop had postponed telling her so as not to interfere with her and Ty's time together.

"A week from Thursday," Pop said. "I wanted to wait, but that granddaughter of mine is a hard one to resist."

Ty concurred wholeheartedly.

"She's in her office if you're looking for her."

"I don't want to disturb her if she's working."

"I'm thinking she won't mind."

"Hamm needs to—"

"Go on. I'll take care of your horse."

"You sure?"

Pop scowled. "I'm not a cripple yet."

Ty needed no further persuading.

As he walked across the lobby's hardwood floor, he was reminded of his first day at the ranch and of how much had changed during the last seven weeks. He and Hamm were in perfect sync, with three shiny new buckles to show for it. Two in tie-down roping and one in team roping with Garth. That didn't count the two second-place finishes Ty had taken in steer wrestling. Altogether, the winnings were enough to bankroll him for the next six rodeos, as well as make a small but overdue payment to his parents.

And then there was Adele. He hated being apart from her, but knowing that what he was doing would eventually give them the means for a life together fueled his determination and made the long, lonely days without her bearable.

He hurried his steps, their echo resounding through the empty lobby. She must have heard him, for she appeared in the office doorway just as he was rounding the registration counter.

"You're early," she said, her face alight with excitement.

"I broke enough traffic laws to put me away for years if I'd been caught."

"I'm glad you weren't."

Not caring if anyone walked by and saw them, he clasped her in his arms. The next instant, his mouth was where it had wanted to be for hours. Days. Weeks. And he didn't hurry, despite them having only until the morning before he had to leave again for the next rodeo. This moment was worth savoring.

Except Adele had other ideas.

She didn't merely return his kiss, she took control of it, giving him a hint of what to expect later.

"That's some greeting," he said, his entire body responding to the fire in her eyes and the heat in her touch. "Mind if I leave and come back for another one?"

"Don't worry, cowboy. There's more where that came from."

He laughed, his first real one in weeks. Did she have any idea how good she made him feel? "I've missed you."

Her features abruptly crumbled, and she shielded her face with her hand.

"You're not crying, are you?"

"No." But she was.

Ty escorted her into her office, shutting the door behind them. "What's wrong, sweetheart?"

She wiped her cheek with the back of her hand. "I'm just happy to see you."

He sat down in her desk chair, then pulled her onto his lap. The chair groaned under their combined weight. "I'm happy to see you, too."

She curled into a ball, combing her fingers through his hair while he stroked her back.

"This isn't how I wanted it to be," she murmured. "I had other plans."

"From what I could tell earlier, I like your plans."

She tilted her face up to his, and he kissed her again. This time tenderly. "I don't know what's wrong with me lately. I've been so emotional."

"You have a lot going on. Pop said his surgery's next Thursday."

"Yeah. And while I can't wait for him to have it, I'm not looking forward to it." She outlined some of the details of the procedure and the daunting challenges she and her grandfather faced.

"Pop will do fine. He's not about to let a little thing like hip-replacement surgery get him down."

"You're right. I'm just not sure about me." She nestled closer with a soft sigh. "Are you hungry yet?"

"Yes." Ty lowered his head and nibbled her ear.

She wriggled away. "I meant for food. We can have an early dinner in the dining hall and then…" She ended the sentence with an inviting smile.

"Or we could 'then' first, and have a late dinner."

He'd been joking—sort of. Adele surprised and delighted him by agreeing.

After stopping briefly to check on Hamm, they sneaked off to her apartment. Or tried to. Every few minutes they ran into someone glad to see Ty and wanting to chat. A half hour later they were finally alone, secluded in Adele's bedroom and tearing off each other's clothes.

When Adele would have hurried, Ty restrained her, determined to prolong the enjoyment. Afterward, they lay with their limbs entwined in her antique brass bed, her lavender sheets strewn across their bodies, the last rays of sunlight streaming through the parted curtains of her window.

"I talked to Garth yesterday," he said, his lips brushing the soft tendrils at her temple.

"Mmm?"

"His parents and Reese are flying out to the Steamboat Springs Rodeo this weekend. They've invited you to come along."

She shook her head. "I can't."

The conversation sounded a lot like their previous one. Regardless, Ty continued. "Why not? You'd only be gone three days."

"Pop's having his surgery."

"Next Thursday. You'll be back in plenty of time."

Adele shifted. Only a little, but the two inches felt like two feet.

"There are tests he has to have. Blood work, X-rays, consultations with the doctors. The medical center's a two-hour round trip. He can't drive it alone."

"Stick could go with him."

"But he can't help Pop with all the paperwork. And believe me, between the doctor, hospital and insurance company, there's a mountain of it. On top of that, I have to meet with the barn manager and the head wrangler. Make sure Pop's work is covered while he recuperates."

Ty felt overwhelmed just listening to her, and wished there was more he could do for her.

"I'm sorry." He pulled her against him, not satisfied until those two inches separating them were reduced to a hair's width. "I'm pressuring you, and that's not my intention."

"I really wish I could come."

"Maybe I'll skip Steamboat Springs. Spend a few extra days here."

She immediately sat up and said sternly, "You'll do no such thing."

"I don't have to compete in every rodeo between now and Nationals."

"Have you qualified yet?"

"No, but—"

"Paid back your parents?"

"Not everything."

"Seriously, Ty." She groaned with exasperation. "You know better than anyone that things happen. Unexpected things. You've come too far and worked too hard to risk not qualifying."

She was right, though a part of him wished she wasn't.

"I guess we'll just have to make the most of this visit." He reached under the sheet, seeking and finding the smooth curve of her hip.

Her sigh of contentment turned into a moan of pleasure when he parted her legs.

The ring of her cell phone couldn't have come at a worse time.

"Don't answer it," he murmured, lowering his mouth to her breast.

"That's Pop's ring tone. If I don't pick up, he'll come looking for us."

Ty would have preferred weighing their options. Not Adele. She swung her legs over the side of the bed and rummaged around on the floor for her jeans.

"Yeah, Pop." She listened a moment, then held the

phone away from her mouth. "Cook's putting together a little celebration dinner for you."

"Sounds like I can't say no."

"Wise man."

He lay in bed, both pillows stuffed under his head, watching her dress.

"Come on," she urged. "We're going to be late."

"I'd rather stay here with you."

She tugged on his arm. "It's only temporary."

Was it? He and Adele hadn't spoken about the future, not specifically and not beyond Nationals this winter. He suspected that, like him, she was thinking long term.

She'd *better* be thinking long term, Ty amended as he finally rolled out of bed and reached for his clothes. Because he had zero intentions of letting her go. Now or ever.

"This way." Adele took two steps. When she heard nothing, she stopped and glanced anxiously over her shoulder. "Easy now."

"I'm all right," Pop snapped. He'd caught one front wheel of his walker on the threshold leading from the garage to the kitchen.

She resisted hurrying to his aid. He was too stubborn to accept her help even if she did. Besides, Stick stood right behind him. The teenager might be skinny, but he was strong, and more than capable of catching her grandfather if he teetered.

The wheel finally gave, hopping over the threshold, and he maneuvered the shiny red walker into the kitchen. His steps were hesitant, measured and stiff, burdened by the compression stockings he was required to wear.

Adele hurt just looking at him.

The doctor, nurses and physical therapist, however, had praised Pop's progress, stating repeatedly that he was doing well for a man his age.

A man his age!

Adele had begun to view her grandfather through different eyes and didn't like what she saw. Though in good health, he was getting older and slowing down. More of the responsibility of running the ranch and Cowboy College would fall to her, and not just during his recovery.

She prayed the next few weeks would go easier than this last one had. Talks with Pop's doctor prior to the surgery hadn't prepared her for the sight of him lying in the hospital bed surrounded by tubes and monitors, a bulky dressing on his hip and his complexion the color of paste. Her emotions, riding so close to the surface of late, had overwhelmed her, causing tears to fall at the least little provocation.

Oddly enough, it had been her mother who was there for Adele the day of the surgery, sitting with her in the family waiting area. Lani also found time to make the long drive and visit Pop twice during his hospital stay, though she remained only briefly because of her work schedule.

It was Ty, however, who had provided the most support for Adele during and after Pop's surgery. He volunteered to fly in for a day or two, but she'd have none of it, insisting he stay and continue to ride his winning streak. She'd have felt differently if Pop's surgery had been life threatening. Ty's phone calls, three a day at least, were enough for now. They gave her a break from the many nerve-racking demands placed on her, and reassured her that what they had together was special and important to him.

That didn't stop her from occasionally wondering if they'd be able to endure the continued long separations. When Ty mentioned her traveling with him on the circuit, or returning to Santa Fe to visit his parents, she allowed herself to get swept up in his excitement. Then she would look at her grandfather and accept the reality that she'd probably never travel any farther than the medical center in Cody. Not for a while, anyway.

Would Ty wait for her?

She hadn't yet found the courage to ask him.

All at once, a wave of nausea struck her. She sucked in a harsh breath and pressed a hand to her stomach. Just as quickly, the feeling subsided, and she exhaled with relief. The stress was getting to her. She'd been feeling mildly ill off and on since before Pop went in for his surgery. And tired. Some mornings, she barely had the energy to climb out of bed, requiring a second cup of coffee to get her day started. She'd be so glad when Pop got back on his feet.

"Did you remember my prescriptions from the car?" Pop stood in the middle of the kitchen, his chest rising and falling from the exertion. And all he'd done was walk from the car.

"Right here." Adele held up a small white sack.

"What about my overnight bag?"

"I'll get that later. Unless you need it this second."

"Guess not," he grumbled.

He wasn't being intentionally difficult, she knew. His doctor had warned Adele to expect periodic mood swings. In addition to the surgery taking a toll on him, there was the daunting prospect of being mostly house-bound for two to four weeks. Pop didn't do modified bed rest and restricted activity well.

"Come on, Pop," Stick said good-naturedly. "I'll help you to bed."

"All right, all right. Don't rush me."

"You want some lunch?" Adele asked.

"Not yet. Maybe later."

Her grandfather going willingly to bed and not hungry? Her worry instantly flared. He must really feel awful.

"I'll take something, if you're offering." Stick grinned sheepishly.

"Coming right up."

While he settled her grandfather in bed, she threw a quick lunch together. The aroma of grilling cheese sandwiches started her stomach roiling again. Piling the one she'd fixed for herself on Stick's plate, she heated up a bowl of canned chicken-noodle soup, hoping that would sit better.

She was just putting the lunch on the table when Ty called her cell phone.

"How's Pop? You two get home okay?"

"A little bit ago." The sexy timbre of his voice warmed her from the inside out. No matter how often he called, she never grew tired of hearing it. Especially late at night.

Stick came down the hall, spied the lunch on the table and fell on it like a typical ravenous teenager.

"How's Pop?" Adele mouthed.

"Sleeping," Stick managed to say between bites.

"Stick's here, helping out," she told Ty.

"That's good. Hey, I was thinking of coming out on Monday for a couple days."

"Aren't you in Missoula?"

"Just pulled into the fairgrounds."

Missoula was a long way from Markton. "When do you compete?"

"I'll be done Sunday afternoon by five. I checked with the airlines and can catch a late flight. A friend of mine's agreed to take care of Hamm for me. Problem is, I wouldn't land until about 10:00 P.M. your time. Is that too late?"

Yellowstone Regional Airport was over a hundred miles away. Picking up Ty added yet another task to her already extensive list. Then driving him back two days later.

But, oh, she wanted to be with him. Sleep for ten hours straight wrapped in his arms. Okay, she admitted it. Sleep wasn't the only activity she had in mind. After showing him how happy she was to see him, they'd loll around in bed all morning, not rising until the sun was high in the sky.

No, they wouldn't. She'd have to come here and check on Pop. Make sure he was doing okay.

"I—I don't know," she stammered.

"I miss you."

His longing carried across the miles, and her heart melted. "I'll be there at ten sharp waiting for you."

If necessary, she'd hire a nurse for two days. Or see if one of the wranglers' wives was interested in earning a little extra money. Pop might be more receptive to that idea.

"Wear your blue bra," Ty said in a husky drawl.

She laughed and stepped into the family room, away from Stick's prying ears. He didn't need to hear the more private details of her conversation with Ty. Some minutes later, when they disconnected, she rationalized her decision to let him come by telling herself a visit from him would boost Pop's morale.

But it was her own morale that was now soaring in anticipation. So much so that she wolfed down her reheated soup and went back for seconds.

"Call if you need me," Stick said later, on his way out the door.

"I will." Adele hoped she wouldn't have to.

While Pop continued to nap, she tidied the kitchen and emptied the car. The four-door sedan belonged to Garth's parents. They'd been kind enough to lend it to Adele and Pop while he recovered, for which she was enormously grateful. She couldn't imagine trying to wrestle her grandfather in and out of his tall truck.

When she finished unloading, she went into the old master bedroom and unpacked her few belongings. They'd agreed she would reside with Pop until he could manage on his own. She hadn't brought much with her, figuring on returning to her apartment every day for whatever she needed.

Her grandparents' bedroom had remained virtually untouched for eight years, and Adele found herself studying pictures on the wall and knickknacks on the dresser that were still where her grandmother had placed them.

It would be strange spending the night here, sleeping among the memories.

A knock on the kitchen door had her hurrying down the hall in her stocking feet.

"Coming!" she called, then remembered her grandfather was sleeping.

Whoever had shown up was comfortable enough that they'd used the back door. Probably one of the hands checking on Pop, or someone from the kitchen. Adele had arranged with Cook to have meals delivered during his convalescence.

It was none of those people.

"Hey, baby girl."

"Mom! What are you doing here? I thought you were at work."

Adele stepped back so that her mother could come inside, silently chiding the part of her that wished Lani had called first and not just shown up.

"Henry let me off early today." Lani carried a plastic grocery sack bearing the name Bush's General Store, Markton's one and only market. It probably contained a get-well present for Pop. "How are you holding up?"

"Better now that we're home."

"You look tired." Lani studied Adele with a critical and unusually maternal eye.

"Actually, I'm feeling better than I did a while ago."

"Still getting queasy?"

"Sometimes," Adele answered reluctantly. This wasn't the first time Lani had inquired about her health, and she'd begun to regret mentioning her intermittent bouts of nausea. "If you want to visit Pop, you'll have to wait or come back. He's napping."

"I really came to see you." Lani set the sack on the table.

"Something the matter?" Fresh worries immediately sprang to Adele's mind. Was her mother's job at the feed store not working out? Did she want to return to the ranch? And get her old one back?

"No. Not with me, at least." Lani's expression was kind and filled with a concern Adele hadn't seen in years. "You've not been yourself lately."

"I have a lot going on at the moment," she said, a bit testily.

"I know you do. You're tired and irritable and—"

"Stress does that to a person."

"So does pregnancy."

The comment came so far from left field, Adele couldn't immediately absorb it. "I'm…not pregnant."

"Are you sure? You have the symptoms."

"Why would you… That's ridiculous!" She wasn't about to admit to her mother that she and Ty had been intimate, or discuss the type of protection they'd used.

"If you're not pregnant, then it could be something else. Better to know for sure." Lani opened the grocery sack and withdrew a box. "I bought this for you. I figured you wouldn't want to. Not in Markton. One thing I've learned since moving here is that folks *love* to gossip."

Adele stared at the home pregnancy test, not sure what shocked her the most—her mother having the gall to butt into her personal life, or the possibility that she really was pregnant.

When was her last period?

She'd been too busy with Pop and his surgery to think about it. Now that she did, she realized she was late. By several weeks.

It couldn't be! She and Ty were careful.

But condoms weren't foolproof. And he'd said he'd been carrying that one in his wallet a long time.

Adele had to sit down before her knees buckled. With an unsteady hand, she pulled out a kitchen chair. Her mother was talking, but the words were only partially registering.

"This is one of those twin-pack early pregnancy tests. I didn't know if maybe you wanted to take one test this afternoon and then the second one tomorrow, just to be sure."

"Take the test now?"

"It's pretty simple." Through a fog, Adele watched her mother remove the kit from the package and unfold the instructions. "It's been a while since I've used one of these, but I doubt they've changed much in the last ten years."

Little by little, the enormity of the situation began to sink in. Adele could indeed be pregnant. Or not. Either way, she needed to find out.

"How does it work?" she asked in a weak voice, taking the testing kit from Lani.

While her mother read the instructions out loud, she rolled the wand between her fingers. Then she went to the hall bathroom and completed the test.

She waited the required time, sitting on the closed toilet-seat lid, an undefined ache lodged beneath her breast. Under different circumstances—if she and Ty were married, for instance—this would be a joyous occasion. Except they weren't married. They hadn't even discussed anything beyond dating.

Her mind swirled as question after question formed.

What about Pop and work and the ranch? She was only just beginning to grapple with the likelihood of having to take on additional tasks in the coming months. A child would triple her responsibilities. How would she cope?

Maybe she wouldn't have to. The results might be negative.

She gazed down at the testing wand in her hand, the plus sign clearly visible now. Even so, she squinted, doubting what her eyes saw.

Then it hit her. An emotion that could only be described as elation. It crashed over her in waves, bringing a huge smile to her face.

A baby! She was having a baby.

Adele stepped from the bathroom and into the kitchen, the testing wand extended in front of her.

Lani stood, her face expectant. An affection Adele hadn't felt for her mother in years filled her, and she impulsively opened her arms. Lani rushed to her, returning the hug *and* the affection.

"Well?" she asked when they separated.

Adele showed her the wand, and Lani, too, broke into a radiant smile.

"I'm going to be a grandmother."

Chapter 13

Adele stood in the middle of Pop's kitchen with her mother, dazed and a little in awe at the realization that she was pregnant.

Possibly pregnant, she amended. As the package instructions recommended, she should take the test again tomorrow morning just to be sure.

Except Adele *was* sure. The undefined ache she'd felt earlier had actually been her heart growing bigger with love for the tiny baby she carried. Soon her entire life would change, and in ways she could only imagine.

What about Ty's life? It would change, too. Adele had been so preoccupied with herself, she'd failed to consider him.

How, she wondered, would he react? With happiness? Anger? They'd talked about their respective families many times, but not about starting one of their own.

Certainly not this soon. Why would they? While their relationship had moved quickly, the fact was she and Ty had been dating only a couple of months, and half that time he'd been on the road.

She'd *have* to consider him, however, and soon.

But not yet. Not until she'd taken the second test and given herself a few days to reflect on her pregnancy and all the ramifications. There was also Pop and his recovery requiring her full and immediate attention.

Suddenly overwhelmed by everything she was facing, she sat back down at the table. Lani, beaming like a million-dollar lottery winner, joined her.

"How did you know?" Adele asked.

Her mom laughed. "I've been pregnant before. I recognized the symptoms."

That was a long time ago, Adele thought. Had being a mother made such an impression that Lani remembered even the smallest details twenty-eight years later?

"Did you have a lot of morning sickness?"

"With you? Heavens, no. I never felt better. With the…" Lani paused, guilt reflected in her eyes. The moment didn't last. Forcing a smile, she picked up right where she'd left off. "Some women are sick day and night."

The remark her mother had made earlier about home pregnancy tests not changing much in ten years came back to Adele.

"Were you pregnant more than once?"

Lani's eyes closed and her posture sagged. "Me and my big mouth."

"Mom?"

"I never wanted you to find out."

"What happened?"

"After you were born, I got pregnant again. But I lost the baby. A little boy."

"I'm so sorry. How terrible for you."

"It was hard. On your dad, too. Neither of us talked much about it, but soon after that he started drinking heavily."

"Why didn't you tell me?"

Lani patted Adele's hand, the first spontaneously caring gesture she'd made in years. If any barriers had remained between them, they vanished in that moment.

"It wasn't a burden I wanted you to bear."

"What happened ten years ago?"

Lani wiped her misty eyes and shook her head as if chiding herself for once again saying too much. "I got pregnant yet again, if you can believe it. But I guess it wasn't meant to be, because before I could even tell the baby's father, I miscarried." She let out a wistful sigh. "I had nothing but trouble after that. Female trouble. I finally got a hysterectomy this past March."

A hysterectomy? Was that the reason her mother had looked so thin and frail when she'd first arrived at Seven Cedars?

"But enough of that talk. You don't need to be hearing any of it. Not now." She patted Adele's cheek. "You're going to have a beautiful, healthy baby, and I'm going to be a grandmother. You should make an appointment with an obstetrician right away."

"I will." Maybe she could arrange that for next week, when she drove Pop to the medical center for his checkup and physical therapy.

"Not that it's any of my business, but when are you going to tell Ty?"

Adele didn't know how to answer her mother.

If she told him she was pregnant, he might quit rodeoing. No, he *would* quit. He'd probably propose, too, and move to Seven Cedars, believing marrying her to be the right and honorable thing to do.

She couldn't let him. Not that the idea of marrying Ty wasn't appealing…and there was the baby to consider. But what about the championship? He'd lost once before, when it was just within his grasp. Then there were his parents. They could really use the money he owed them. If he won, he could repay them every dime. For a man with Ty's pride, settling his debts was not just important, it was imperative.

Mentally counting backward, Adele determined that she was around six weeks pregnant, give or take. Plenty of time before she had to decide what to do. Before she began showing.

She suddenly remembered he was flying in Sunday evening. How could she see him, look at him, *be* with him, and not think of the baby? Maybe she should call him and postpone his trip, citing Pop as an excuse. Give herself a little more time to come to grips with… everything.

"I don't know when I'll tell him," Adele murmured contemplatively. "I want to see the doctor first. Make sure the baby's okay."

"Oh, honey bun." Lani's features fell. "I've scared you with my stories, and I shouldn't have. Shame on me."

"I'm glad you told me." Adele welcomed the change

in subject. "It explains a lot. I've been blaming you, and to a lesser degree, Dad, for things that weren't your fault. I think I have a lot of making up to do with both of you."

"That's sweet of you to say, but the truth is, I was a lousy mother. I hope you won't hold that against me, because I intend to be the best grandmother in the world."

"Good." Adele inhaled deeply. "I'm going to need a lot of help."

They reached across the table and shared another hug, only to be interrupted by a loud banging noise from down the hall.

"Pop!" Adele sprang from her chair.

Lani followed her to his bedroom. They were both aghast to find him sitting up in bed, his lap table on the floor and his walker leaning at a crooked angle.

"What are you doing?" Adele cried.

"Trying to get up. What the hell does it look like?" he barked, his face flushed a deep crimson.

"Are you in pain?" She glanced at the nightstand, where she'd left his medications, then at the clock. His next dose wasn't due for another two hours.

"Hell, yes, I'm in pain. I just had my hip replaced with some damn metal contraption."

"Oh, Pop," she soothed, wishing she could wave her hand and magically erase his suffering.

To her surprise, he let out a choked sob. "Why didn't you tell me you were having a baby?"

He must have heard her and Lani talking in the kitchen!

Before Adele could tell him she'd just found out herself, she was slammed with a wave of intense nausea, and barely reached the hall bathroom in time.

"Hey, Boudeau." A man Ty had handily beaten in steer wrestling that morning jogged toward him, tugging the brim of his ball cap down against the pouring rain. "What's the rush?" he hollered.

"Besides this weather?" Ty tossed his overnight bag into the backseat of Garth's pickup truck. It landed atop a plastic crate, rain gear, a laptop case and a well-worn duffel bag.

"A bunch of us are heading to the Chuck Box Bar and Grill," the man said upon reaching Ty. "You and Maitland want to come along?"

"Thanks, but we can't." He slammed the truck door shut, sidestepping a rapidly growing puddle. "I've got a plane to catch in two hours, and thirty miles to drive."

Garth had volunteered to drive him to the airport. Barring any traffic delays due to the rain, or longs lines at airport security, he had just enough time to make his flight.

"Guess I'll see you in Fort Benton."

"That you will."

Lifting the collar of his jacket, the man departed, his hunched form leaping over streams of running water.

Luckily for the participants, the weather had held for most of the rodeo. Saddle bronc riding, the last event of the day, had turned into a mud-flying free-for-all, and the closing ceremony was canceled. Ty hadn't minded. He'd grabbed his winnings and buckle—only one this weekend—and hightailed it to where he'd parked, meeting the friend who had agreed to drive his truck and trailer to her place in the next town over. Ty had known Nancy and her brother for years, and was confident Hamm couldn't have a better caretaker. When Ty returned from seeing Adele, Nancy would meet him at the airport and give him a lift to her place. From there, he would continue on to Fort Benton.

A lot of trouble and a lot of favors called in, but Ty felt it would be worth everything and more to see Adele.

He'd originally arranged for Nancy to drive him to the airport, but when Garth got wind of Ty's plans, he'd insisted on taking her place. A consolation prize, perhaps, for beating the pants off Ty earlier today.

And speaking of Garth...

Ty checked the time on his cell phone, cupping his hand to protect it from the rain. Where the heck was he? If they didn't head out soon, Ty might miss his plane.

He turned to see Garth running toward him, water exploding in great sheets from his boots as they hit the ground. Ty hated to think how soaked his friend's feet must be getting. Hopefully, he had an extra pair of shoes buried in that pile of stuff in his backseat.

"Sorry I'm late. I needed a pick-me-up for the road." Garth lifted his rain poncho and removed two large travel cups of coffee he'd been carrying. By some miracle, they'd survived the journey intact.

Ty took the one Garth held out to him. "Thanks." He hoped the hot liquid would act like high-octane fuel, combating the sluggishness brought on by two days of intense competition and not enough sleep.

They climbed into the truck and began slowly traversing the muddy lake that had once been the parking area. Deep ruts hampered their progress. Ty had to force himself to keep from checking the time every few minutes. There was nothing he could do about the weather, so he might as well relax.

Yeah, right.

He tried distracting himself by guzzling coffee and listening, at least a little, to Garth ramble on about Reese and their upcoming wedding.

"We finally set a date. Valentine's Day. Reese insisted we wait until after Nationals. You're coming to the wedding, aren't you?"

"You still going to want me there when I take away your title?"

"After this weekend, I wouldn't bet on that."

Both men laughed. Ty wasn't worried. He might not have won every event today, but his scores were good enough to put him one step closer to qualifying for the National Finals Rodeo.

They were about a mile down the road when Ty's cell phone rang. His pulse jumped at seeing Adele's name flashing on the display. In a few hours, they'd be together. He dreaded thinking about the months stretching ahead of them until December. Instead of becoming easier, the separations were harder and harder. When he returned to Markton for Garth's wedding—and he would, win or lose—he planned on staying a full month with Adele. Maybe by then he could convince her to go with him to visit his parents.

"Hey, girl. How you doing?"

"Hanging in there."

Slouching in the seat, he readied himself for a long talk. While he couldn't pinpoint anything specific, she'd sounded odd the last few days. When he questioned her, she'd blamed her grandfather. Ty understood. Taking care of Pop couldn't be easy, though Adele swore he was doing remarkably well.

Ty promised himself she'd get as much rest as possible during his visit, even if it meant he had to play nursemaid to Pop. As long as he and Adele had their nights together…

"You have no idea how good it is to hear your voice," he said.

Beside him, Garth made a sound of disgust, as if to imply Ty was nothing but a sucker for a pretty woman. The grin he wore, however, said Ty was in good company.

The two them were a pair, and Ty had to chuckle. Like Garth, he'd found the woman of his dreams. Ty also thought he might have found the place where he wanted to settle down for the rest of his life. Much as he loved Santa Fe, Wyoming had a lot more to offer. When he wasn't on the circuit, he could teach roping. Construct saddles in his spare time. Train with Garth. Woo Adele.

Life couldn't get any better. Except maybe with winning the title of World Champion.

"How'd you do today?" Adele asked.

"First in team roping. Second in steer wrestling." He shot Garth a dirty look. "Fourth in tie-down roping."

"Not bad."

"Fort Benton's going to be a whole 'nother story."

"You think," Garth muttered.

Ty ignored him, preferring to concentrate on Adele. "What's the latest on Pop?"

"Improving."

"Your mom?"

"Fine."

Her monosyllabic answers bothered him. "Is everything okay?"

"Great."

"What about Ritz?"

"Getting big."

Just when he was beginning to really worry, she asked, "Have you left for the airport yet?"

"On our way. Should be there in about forty-five minutes." She didn't immediately reply, and he thought they might have lost their connection. "You there?"

"Yeah." Another long pause followed. "Ty, I hate to ask this of you…."

"What's wrong?" Alerted by her tone, he sat bolt upright.

"Is there any chance you can postpone your trip?"

"Postpone? Why?"

Garth glanced over at him questioningly. Ty shrugged, not sure yet what was happening.

"I'm sorry." Adele sounded as if she was on the verge of crying.

"Sweetheart, what happened?"

"Nothing. It's just not a good time. Pop requires so much care—"

"I thought you said he was improving."

"Did I? Well, he is. I mean, the surgery site's healing. The, um, physical therapy isn't progressing at the speed the doctor wants."

"You told me yesterday he was almost ready for a cane."

"He is. He will be. Eventually. The therapists want me to take him in for an extra session this week."

"I'll go with you. Heck, I'll take him. You can stay home and nap. I know you're working your tail off." He wished she'd relinquish even a small amount of her grandfather's care to someone else rather than doing it all herself.

"It's not only Pop. We have…we have new calves arriving tomorrow, which I need to oversee. And the grain shipment's being delivered on Thursday."

"Can't the barn manager handle that?"

"He's, um, sick. The flu."

With sudden certainty, Ty knew Adele was lying. The question was why?

He immediately assumed the worst, and his stomach tightened into a knot. "You don't want to see me?"

"Of course I do!"

Ty sensed Garth's curious gaze on him, but he couldn't be bothered with his friend right now.

"I'm just so overwhelmed." A tiny sob had crept into her voice. "I really do want to see you."

For the first time since she'd called, he felt she truly meant what she said. "I want that, too. Like crazy."

"Next week will be better," she added, suddenly more composed. "Or the week after. By then Pop should be getting around better, and won't be so demanding."

"Is he giving you that much of a hard time?"

"More than you know," she answered tiredly.

Perhaps Ty was reading too much into her request. It could be exactly as she claimed, and she wanted him to come out when her grandfather was more self-sufficient and her own energy not so depleted.

It occurred to him to fly out anyway, regardless of what she said. Every bone in his body longed to do just that.

"Please, Ty," she implored. "I need a little more time."

Desperate as he was to see her, he wouldn't make her life more difficult. "I'll reschedule my flight for next week."

"Or two weeks."

He'd be in Albuquerque then. And his family had talked about coming out to watch him compete. No problem. He'd find a way to make it work. "All right. Two weeks."

"Thank you."

"Hey, Stick called me the other day."

"He did?" She sounded alarmed.

"Said he was trying to get you to hire his cousin."

"Oh, yeah."

"Asked me if I—"

"Ty, I've got to go."

"Is it Pop?"

"Y-yes. He's calling me. Sorry. Bye."

Ty flipped his phone shut and stared out the window at the downpour.

"Everything okay?" Garth asked, taking his eyes momentarily off the road.

"I'm not sure." Ty removed his cowboy hat and flung it on the truck floor with more force than necessary. "Any way you can turn this vehicle around? We need to head back."

"Forget something?"

"Seems I'm not flying out today."

After a quick explanation, Ty called the airlines.

Then he phoned Nancy. She expressed sympathy over his canceled trip, and readily agreed to meet him and Garth at the rodeo grounds.

"I appreciate all your help," he told Garth, then picked up his hat, brushed it off and returned it to his head.

"No problem."

After another mile, he said, "You know Adele pretty well, right?"

"Since we were kids."

"Tell me, how is she at handling stress?"

"You kidding? She's a rock. I remember when she and Pop started Cowboy College. Everything they had to go through to get it off the ground. And when her grandmother died, Adele was the one who held Pop together. He'd have drowned in his own grief without her."

Ty frowned.

"Why?"

"She's having a difficult time coping with Pop's hip-replacement surgery. I guess he's being irritable and demanding."

"When isn't he? She's used to that."

Yeah, she was.

"And she's got all kinds of help there," Garth continued. "Built-in food service, housekeeping and drivers if she needs them. There's not an employee on the ranch who wouldn't pitch in if she asked them."

That was what Ty thought, too. "So why is she acting the way she is?"

Garth mulled the question over. "You really want my opinion?"

"I wouldn't ask if I didn't."

"There's something else going on," he said, confirming Ty's suspicions. "Something she's not telling you."

Pop hobbled into Adele's office without knocking, awkwardly closing the door behind him. During the three and a half weeks since his surgery, he'd graduated from the walker to a cane, and was getting around quite well.

Enough that he'd decided two days ago he was ready to resume his previous responsibilities. Adele would have none of it, convinced he'd trip on something and injure his brand-new hip. Stick had been assigned to drive Pop wherever he wanted to go in the golf cart, and to keep an eye on him. Fortunately for Adele's nerves, Pop tired easily and had yet to do more than chat with the barn manager, watch a few classes and check out the new grain shipment.

He also made trips to her office to inquire about the running of the ranch.

She bore those visits as patiently as possible.

Except when he asked about the baby. Other than to respond that she was feeling well despite continued morning sickness, she clammed up. Pop gave new meaning to the word *relentless* and was constantly pushing her to do what he thought was right, namely tell Ty about the baby and, as Pop put it, make an honest woman out of her.

She refused to argue, as determined as her grandfather to handle the situation her own way. Which, at the moment, was to do and say nothing.

"Hey, Pop. What brings you here?" She smiled brightly, already knowing the answer and bracing herself for a string of questions about reservations, food orders and class schedules.

"What time is Ty arriving?" He bent and grabbed her visitor's chair, pulling it away from the wall.

Adele automatically leaped up to help him.

"Sit your fanny down," he grumped. "I can manage. Don't need you hovering every second of the day." And he did manage. Just fine.

Was it true? Did she hover?

Probably.

She sat poised on the edge of her seat until Pop leaned his cane against her file cabinet, exhaling lustily as he did.

"We had two new reservations," she said, facing her computer and moving her mouse. "At this rate—"

"When is Ty getting in?" he repeated.

"After lunch sometime," Adele answered, hoping her tone gave no indication how nervous she was about his visit.

"Where's he staying?"

"Room nine's vacant."

"It's a little small for him."

"Better than his horse trailer."

At the mention of Ty's trailer, Adele was inundated with memories of when they'd made love in his tiny living quarters. Consulting the calendar after her trip to the obstetrician's office, she felt certain that was the night she'd gotten pregnant.

"If you need to rent the room out, he can bunk in my house."

"I don't need to rent it out."

She didn't mention that Ty would probably stay with her.

"You going to tell him about the baby?" Pop had asked the question no less than two dozen times.

Her answer was always the same. "Eventually."

"Eventually over the next two days or eventually sometime before the kid's born?"

"I'll tell him when the moment's right."

He grumbled an expletive under his breath. "You can't hide this forever."

"No. But I can for a while."

"Dellie," Pop warned.

She opened her mouth to object, then promptly closed it at the sight of his watery eyes. Struck by a rush of tender emotions, she got up and went to him, stooping over to give him a loving hug.

"I can't believe I'm going to be a great-grandfather," he mumbled. "Your grandmother would be overjoyed. God, I wish she was here."

"Me, too." Adele swallowed a sob.

"I know you think I'm being a crotchety old busy-body."

"Did I say that?"

"I only want what's best for you and the baby. And that's a father. A father *and* a husband."

Adele returned to her desk chair. "You need to let me and Ty work this out between us."

"Don't know why you're taking so long," Pop complained, back to his former grumpy self.

She didn't mind. He put on a gruff front, but deep down he was a sentimental slob.

"I need time, Pop. This is a big deal. Life altering. For both of us."

"Are you afraid he's going to leave you high and dry?"

"No. Just the opposite, in fact."

"As it should be. He has a responsibility." Her grandfather's voice rose.

Adele glanced worriedly at the office door, then shushed him. "But not one he asked for or planned on so soon in our relationship," she said in a subdued voice.

"He's a good man, Dellie. He'll take care of you and the baby."

"I know. But an unplanned pregnancy isn't an automatic reason to rush into marriage. There are other things to consider. Other people."

"Just because your folks were lousy parents, don't assume you and Ty will be, too."

Her grandfather's words sliced into her, opening wounds she thought were finally closed.

"That's not it."

"Are you sure?"

"Yes," she replied. Only she wasn't. Not entirely.

Already she loved the baby with every breath she drew, and wanted more than anything for him or her to have a better childhood than she'd had. Two parents, Adele knew, was no guarantee for happiness.

Her cell phone abruptly rang. "It's Ty," she told her grandfather, after checking the screen, and answered with a forced but chipper, "Hello."

"I'm pulling in the drive."

"Already!"

"I couldn't wait to see you."

His enthusiasm was catching. "I can't wait to see you, either."

"Where are you?"

"My office."

"Meet me out front in two minutes."

Adele was instantly on her feet. "You coming?" she asked Pop, after disconnecting.

"Naw. You go on. I'll meet up with him later."

"Promise me you won't say anything about the baby until I've talked to him."

Pop grumbled his assent.

She was out the door and halfway across the lobby when she remembered she hadn't made sure he could rise from the chair without assistance. Starting back, she halted when he appeared in her office doorway.

"Get going." He shooed her away. "I'm fine."

Standing on the front porch, she watched Ty's truck approach, toy-size at first, then growing larger as it neared.

He had come home to Seven Cedars. And *her*.

All at once, happiness bubbled up inside her, vanquishing her earlier doubts and insecurities. Whatever obstacles they faced, and there were a lot of them, they'd find a solution. Together. The sight of his grinning face, full of gladness and affection, further convinced her that nothing was impossible.

She ran down the steps and into his arms the instant he climbed out of his truck.

"I have some great news!"

"So do I," he said, giving her a smacking kiss on the lips.

She laughed, giddy with delight. "You go first."

"Big Sky Trailers has offered me a sponsorship contract with a bonus if I win at Nationals."

"They did?"

"It's only a one-year contract to start, but they're talking magazine ads and even cable TV spots if all goes well."

"That's...wonderful."

"I'll have to go to Texas for the month of January. That's where their headquarters is located."

Adele's heart went from beating wildly to skipping painfully. So much for springing her announcement on him.

"Can you believe it?" He lifted her off her feet, swung her in a circle and gave her another kiss. "Hey, I missed breakfast this morning and I'm starving. Any chance the dining hall's still open? We can talk about why you've been avoiding me over lunch."

Chapter 14

Pop had joined Adele and Ty for lunch. With his mouth set in a grim line, he sat listening to Ty expound on the details of the Big Sky Trailers sponsorship contract, which were exciting to say the least.

Exciting for Ty.

"If I win at Nationals, they want to feature me and Hamm in their advertising campaign." He seemed to have forgotten all about her news. Perhaps that was for the best. "Even more incentive for me to win," he said with single-minded determination.

Ty was well on the way to getting everything he wanted. Not at all like when he'd first come to Cowboy College…what? Nearly three months ago.

Adele was partially responsible for the transformation. Little had she known at the time that helping him fix his problems with Hamm and launch a career comeback would return to hurt her.

Little had she known she'd fall in love with him.

She pressed a hand to her breast, trying to soothe the ragged pain beneath it. Given the chance to do it all over again, she'd change nothing. Not loving him and certainly not having his baby.

"Of course, I'll be here for Garth and Reese's wedding," he continued, finishing the last of his steak sandwich.

Pop hadn't ordered any food, and Adele only picked at her shrimp salad. Ty didn't appear to notice their lack of appetites.

"That's good," she said, mentally calculating which stage she'd be in her pregnancy come Valentine's Day. No hiding it then. Even if she tried, someone was bound to say something.

"Why don't you come with me to Texas?" He reached under the table and rested a hand on her knee, his eyes alight with boyish charm. "You can visit your dad. Big Sky's headquarters is only a couple hours from where he lives."

When Adele didn't immediately respond, Pop made a disgruntled sound, which Ty misinterpreted.

"Sorry, Pop. I should've talked to you first about stealing her away."

"Not my decision," he muttered crustily.

It was on the tip of Adele's tongue to explain her grandfather's dour mood, only she couldn't think of anything to say without mentioning the baby. Instead, she asked Ty, "Is this what you want? The sponsorship contract?"

He gave her a surprised look. "It's a great opportunity. And not just because of the money."

She nodded. No argument there. "I thought you wanted to build saddles."

"Charlie's shop will be there when I'm ready."

Adele couldn't help but wonder if he planned to include her in his long-term goals. He'd made no mention of the future other than her accompanying him to Texas in January.

Wasn't she just as guilty of making plans without him? Not the same, she told herself. She *was* thinking of him.

Ty would quit competing and give up a lucrative sponsorship the moment he learned about the baby. It wasn't fair, not when he'd worked so hard and so long to achieve his dream. Neither was it fair to make his parents wait additional months, perhaps years, for the money he owed them. Especially when they could really use it and had already been exceedingly patient.

She could see why the Big Sky's marketing people had approached Ty. Not only was his meteoric return to roping catching the attention of fans, he was a great spokesperson, possessing good looks, talent and a natural charm. Not to mention a gorgeous and athletic horse. Some ropers competed their whole lives and had little to show for it. Ty could, if all went well, build an impressive career from this one sponsorship offer.

She wouldn't be the one to take it from him.

"We don't have to decide anything right this second," she said cheerfully, attempting to smooth out the awkward pause.

Her smile must have appeared as fake as it felt, for Ty stopped eating, set his fork down and turned to her.

"I haven't signed the contract yet. I can always change my mind."

"It's a great offer. You'd be a fool not to take it."

Pop's closed hand came down a little too hard on the table.

Ty's gaze darted to him, then back to Adele. "Yes, but I don't want to be away from you."

"We'll talk more tonight," she told him, her fake smile still firmly in place.

Pop grumbled angrily and, leaning heavily on his cane, rose from the table. Without a word, he limped away.

"I guess I upset him."

"It's not you." Adele also stood, and patted Ty's shoulder. "I'll be right back."

He stopped her by snaring her wrist. "Are we okay? Are *you* okay?"

She didn't answer him. "Give me a few minutes alone with Pop, will you?"

His eyes followed her as she hurried out of the dining hall. She could only guess what he was thinking.

Spying Pop outside, she called to him. "Wait."

He halted, but one glance at his fierce expression had her wishing she'd let him go on ahead without her.

"You need to tell him about the baby," he barked when she was within earshot.

"Not so loud." She tugged on his arm imploringly. "You know what will happen if I do. He'll stay here and give up the Big Sky sponsorship contract. Quit team roping with Garth. Probably propose to me."

"As he should!"

"What makes you think I want to marry him?"

Pop gaped at her. "Why the hell not?"

Adele grimaced and moved in front of him, as if that would stop his voice from carrying to the guests nearby. "He already lost one championship and one career opportunity. I don't want to be the reason he loses a second one. I certainly don't want to be the reason his mother loses her real estate business."

"We could lend him the—"

"Do you think for one second Ty would take money from us?"

"He might. If you two were married."

"No, he won't. He has too much pride. Just like he'll quit competing if I tell him about the baby. He'd want any child of his to have two parents at home. Like he did. Like I didn't."

Pop grumbled.

"I can't risk Ty coming to resent me for taking everything away from him. And he will, even if he doesn't mean to. Worse, he might come to resent our child."

"Dellie."

She hugged her grandfather, hating the frailty in his frame, which hadn't been there before. "The best day of my life was when I came here to live permanently." The best day until she'd learned she was pregnant. "I want my child to grow up with everything you and Grandma gave me. A good home, security, wide-open spaces and the best horses in the state to ride." She wiped her damp cheeks.

"I can't take the place of a father."

"You did for me."

"I still think you should tell Ty." Though Pop continued insisting, much of the fight had gone out of him.

"I will someday, but not right now."

He ruffled her hair as he had when she was young. "I love you, Dellie."

"I love you, too, Grandpa."

He chuckled, though it was filled with sadness. "You haven't called me Grandpa since you were fourteen."

"Maybe I should start again."

"Whatever excuse you're going to give Ty, you'd better think fast." Pop tilted his head toward the lobby door. "Because here he comes."

Adele's pulse spiked at the sight of Ty striding in her direction, looking every bit like a man who wouldn't settle until he knew what the heck was going on.

Adele didn't have a destination in mind when she and Ty started walking. After a few minutes, she noticed their feet were taking them to the corral where Stick had placed Hamm while they had lunch with Pop. Probably because the corral was away from the ranch hands and guests, and gave them a modicum of privacy.

"What's wrong?" Ty demanded when they neared the fence. Given how poorly he was concealing his frustration, she was impressed he'd waited. "And this time, Adele, I want an answer. No more sidestepping."

Having little experience in breaking up with men, she decided quick and clean was the best approach.

Easier on you, too, a small voice inside her whispered.

True. But why prolong the agony?

Sticking to her hastily concocted plan, she blurted, "I've recently realized I'm not cut out for a long-distance relationship."

Ty visibly jerked and his eyes widened, but when he spoke, his words were measured, as if he was weighing each one. "It's only been a couple of months."

Good point. And if not for the baby, she'd be willing to give their arrangement a considerably longer trial period.

"I don't need any more time. This isn't working out for me."

"I'd have come two weeks ago. You're the one who told me not to."

"Pop just had surgery."

"And I respected your wishes. Now, all of a sudden, you tell me it's not working out, and act as if it's my fault, when you're the one pushing me away."

He was absolutely right.

Nonetheless, Adele continued, afraid her courage would desert her. "You have every right to be angry at me."

"I'm not angry, I'm confused."

She could see it clouding his eyes, along with the hurt she was inflicting.

Damn. She'd been in such a hurry, she hadn't considered he might put up a fight. She was, however, committed to finish what she'd begun. They would both come away from this bruised and possibly a little embittered, but everyone would be better off in the long run.

"The reason my parents' marriage fell apart was because Dad only stayed home a few months of the year."

"Is that what you want?" Ty asked. "For us to get married?"

It was her turn to jerk. "No!"

"Why not?"

She drew a shallow breath. Anything deeper was impossible, not with the huge knot of pain pressing against her ribs. "Seven Cedars is my home, and Cowboy College is my business. I'm not leaving either of them. Asking you to give up your home and your dream isn't right, either."

"I don't get it." He rubbed the back of his neck, his jaw working furiously. "Why can't we continue the way we are?"

"Because my heart shatters every time you leave and every time you hang up the phone after calling me." That much, at least, was completely true.

"And you think the answer is to break up with me?"

Adele involuntarily crossed her arms over her middle. "Yes."

"Have you met somebody else?"

"Of course not!"

He shook his head, his brows forming a deep V. "This makes no sense."

Hamm must have sensed the seriousness of their mood. Rather than trot in circles as usual, he stood solemnly in the center of the corral, head lowered, tail swishing, his breath stirring up small dust clouds.

"I'm sorry," Adele murmured.

"Just like that? You break up with me out of the blue, tell me you're sorry, and I'm supposed to be okay with it?" Ty might not have been angry before, but he definitely was now.

"Please try and see this from my side."

"How much does this have to do with the sponsorship offer from Big Sky?"

He'd finally put two and two together.

"Some," she admitted.

"Because I'll be gone the month of January?"

"Nationals isn't until late December. Add January,

when you'll be in Texas, and you're asking me to wait half a year."

"We'd see each other every few weeks."

"For a day or two."

"I have a break over the holidays."

"What about next year?"

"Who says I'll compete next year?"

"You know you will. You told me you wanted to compete until you physically couldn't anymore."

"I…" He hesitated and shifted awkwardly.

Was this the moment she'd been hoping for? When he'd tell her he loved her? She chewed her bottom lip, waiting…and waiting.

"I…care about you. A lot. I'm not ready for this to end."

If he only knew how much she wasn't ready for this to end, either.

She could always tell him she'd had a change of heart. They would kiss, make up and pretend this morning had never happened.

Except what would that accomplish other than delaying the inevitable? Unless she was prepared to tell him about the baby, be the reason he quit competing, forfeited the championship, postponed paying back his parents, she had to let him go. Now.

"I'm being selfish, I know that," she said. "The idea of ending up like my mother… I won't let that happen to me."

"I'm not your father."

"No, but you'll be gone as much as he was."

"I just don't understand why you can't come with me sometimes. I'm not asking you to leave the ranch for weeks on end."

"You saw Pop. He can't get through a day without taking a nap. How's he going to run this place by himself, even for a weekend? We're also smack-dab in the middle of our busy season."

"Those are excuses." He narrowed his eyes, as if trying to read more into what she said. "If you really wanted to take a few vacation days, you could."

"They're valid excuses." Adele refused to wilt under his penetrating stare. "I can't turn my back on my family and my business. A lot of people depend on me."

"So do I."

He depended on her? For what? Help with his horse? A place to crash between competitions? Disappointment sliced through her.

"I wish things were different."

"You're not giving me a choice." His anger had returned, lending his voice a steely edge.

"And what choice would that be? Have me wait for you for what could be years? Give up my life here, my home and my business? Leave my ailing grandfather? That's asking a lot."

Her words were harsh, as she'd intended. In response, his expression closed, like a door slamming shut.

She clenched her hands into fists and held them at her sides. It was the only way to prevent herself from going to him.

"Can we sleep on it? Talk again in the morning?"

His request was utterly reasonable. Except Adele knew if their breakup wasn't a swift one, she ran the risk of reconsidering and relenting. Or allowing Pop to sway her, as he would surely try to do if Ty stayed on the ranch. Even overnight.

"It won't make any difference."

She swore he flinched.

In that moment, Adele hated herself.

"If you ever—"

"I have to go."

Turning on her heel, she walked the entire distance to her apartment, without once stopping or looking back. Thankfully, Ty didn't follow her, saving her from having to test her willpower.

Oh, God, what must he think of her?

How could she have been so cruel?

In the solitude of her bedroom, she cried until a bout of nausea sent her running to the bathroom. A while later, Pop called to check on her and to let her know Ty had loaded Hamm and pulled out about thirty minutes earlier, telling no one where he was going.

Adele suspected he needed a friend about now and might head over to see Garth.

"Are you sure you didn't make a mistake, Dellie?" Pop asked.

She might have been able to lie to Ty, but her grandfather was a different story. "No, I'm not sure at all."

"When he finds out, and he will eventually, he's going to be mad."

She could deal with that. What she couldn't deal with was Ty hating her. And he very well could after what she'd done to him.

Chapter 15

"What's with you, bro? You suck today."

Ty's little sister, Dana, couldn't be more right. In the three weeks since Adele had given him his walking papers, he could hardly put his boots on the correct feet, much less rope. He wasn't just back to where he'd been after Nationals last year, he was worse. Worse than worse. He couldn't rope a calf if it climbed up in the saddle with him. Even Hamm snorted in disgust whenever Ty approached.

Dana circled the big gelding, studying him intently. "I don't see a thing wrong with him," she said, shaking her head contemplatively. "He's in great shape."

"I was afraid of that."

Dana had met up with Ty the evening before. He was in St. George for the Lions Dixie Roundup Rodeo. She'd traveled to a town twenty miles over the hill for a job interview with a prestigious equine hospital. Though he knew her side trip to St. George was a thinly disguised attempt to check up on him at the request of their parents, he was still glad to see her. Last night, over a couple of beers, she'd offered to examine Hamm, on the slim chance Ty's recent string of losses was due to an injury or illness.

As he'd expected, he had no one to blame but himself.

"What are you going to do?" Dana asked.

"About what?"

She ticked off the items on her fingers. "Competing tomorrow. Big Sky's offer. Adele."

"Nothing."

"Not a good answer."

"Keep trudging along."

She made a face. "Excuse my language, but you need to get your shit together."

He did. His standings were slipping. Fast. At this rate, he wouldn't qualify for Nationals. Big Sky's people had started getting a little antsy. If Ty didn't win or place in the top three soon, they might pull out of their contract, citing the clause that gave them the right to do so if he didn't perform at a certain level.

So much for paying his parents back in one lump sum.

His folks would cut him some slack. Continue being patient.

Ty, however, was fast losing all patience with himself. This wasn't how it was supposed to be.

"Have you talked to Adele since she kicked you to the curb?"

Ty winced. "Do you have to be so blunt?"

"Yes. Everyone's been walking on eggshells around

you, afraid of saying the wrong thing because you might have a meltdown or cry or something. I say you need a good shaking up."

They were in the barn at the rodeo fairgrounds, standing in Hamm's stall. Leaving it, they latched the door behind them and headed down the aisle. Ty had competed yesterday in both team and tie-down roping, doing badly in the former, his lasso missing the calf by a good foot. Garth didn't say much afterward, taking the disqualification in stride. Ty half wished his partner would blow up at him. Maybe then he wouldn't feel so guilty.

Amazingly, he hadn't done quite so terribly in tie-down roping, currently holding sixth place. A position that landed him in the final round later today.

Big Sky Trailers, however, wasn't interested in a spokesman who came in sixth.

"The answer is no, I haven't spoken to Adele, and I'm not going to."

"Why not?" Dana pressed. "You're nuts about her."

"I won't beg."

He would, actually, if he thought it would do any good. Hell, he'd get down on his knees. But Adele's cold tone during their last meeting still haunted him, and he doubted she'd softened her stance since then.

"Who said anything about begging?" Dana sent him a conspiratorial smile. "I had sweet-talking in mind. And flowers."

Wildflowers. That's what he had given Adele before, and she'd liked them very much.

Ty pushed the memory away to a dark corner in his mind.

While Dana continued to yap about the pros and

cons of various tokens of affection, they cut behind
the main arena, bypassing the food and vendor booths
and hordes of people milling about. By nine o'clock tonight, the rodeo would be over and the grounds resembling a ghost town.

Much the way Ty's insides felt.

He'd replayed his last conversation with Adele repeatedly in his head, unable to shake the feeling she
hadn't been entirely honest with him. Try as he might,
he could detect nothing specific in her words or actions,
except one. When he'd said he depended on her, she
had instantly withdrawn, emotionally and physically.

What a fool he'd been. Given a second chance, he
would have hauled her into his arms, told her he loved
her and kidnapped her to his trailer so they could relive
their first night together.

Because he did love her. Ty realized that now. Much
too late, unfortunately.

"Markton's a four-hour drive from here," Dana was
saying. "You could head over tonight after the rodeo."

"I can't."

"I'll come with you," she added, as if she hadn't
heard him.

His temper flared. "Butt out, sis."

They stopped and faced each other, Dana with her
hands on her hips, Ty with his teeth grinding together.

"Well, you need to do something. Cowboy College
fixed you before. Maybe it can again."

Cowboy College? Or Adele?

He'd gone to Seven Cedars looking for that missing
magical element that would turn Hamm and his good
partnership to an unstoppable one. And he'd found it.

Not in the minor discoveries he'd made, such as how Hamm moved or which eye he took aim with. Ty had found it with Adele. Her belief in him and his desire to make her proud of him were what had inspired him to push himself harder than he ever had before.

"You're right," he told his sister, his anger dissolving. Not that he ever stayed angry at Dana long. "Cowboy College did fix me."

She grinned. "So, what are we waiting for? Let's go."

"If I do, I'd have to be willing to give up rodeoing, Nationals and the Big Sky sponsorship contract. For good. Adele doesn't want a man who's on the road all the time. That's why she kicked me to the curb in the first place."

Dana's expression turned serious. "Are you willing to do that?"

It was, he realized, the million-dollar question.

Adele drove straight from Pop's house to the main lodge and parked in front, leaving her truck sitting at a crooked angle. She'd been looking for her grandfather all over the ranch for the better part of an hour, with no luck. He hadn't shown up for class after breakfast, and according to everyone she asked, no one had seen hide nor hair of him all morning. Her mild concern over his abrupt disappearance was quickly blossoming into outright worry.

Where could he be?

Climbing the steps to the main lodge, she called his cell phone for the tenth time, angrily pressing the disconnect button when it went straight to his voice mail.

Did his battery die, or had he shut off his phone?

Not for the first time she wondered how much his disappearance had to do with their argument last night. Ever since Ty left Pop had been nagging her to tell him about the baby. Try as she might, she couldn't blame her grandfather. He was old-fashioned and set in his ways, and believed a man should be responsible for his children.

As Ty did.

Her throat ached at the thought of him. Not an hour passed that she didn't miss him and second-guess her decision to send him packing. It was crazy how completely he'd become a part of her life in just a few months.

Then again, with the baby she was carrying, he'd be a part of her life always. Even if he didn't know it.

Pushing thoughts of Ty to the back of her mind as she crossed the lobby, she concentrated on Pop. Wherever he was, he must have his truck. It wasn't in his garage or in his usual parking space at the barn.

After peeking in her office—a long shot, but she tried anyway—she went down the hall to the kitchen. If she didn't find him there, she was going into town and would scour it end to end. That failing, she was calling the sheriff. They probably wouldn't do anything, not until Pop had been missing twenty-four hours. Hopefully, they would put the word out to look for him and his vehicle. Especially when she explained about his bad arthritis and recent hip-replacement surgery.

All at once, she had a brainstorm. The Maitlands would help her search for Pop. She pulled out her cell phone to call Garth, only to pause. They were at the rodeo in St. George. Garth had mentioned the other day he and his family were all going.

Ty was there, too.

Returning her cell phone to her pocket, she pushed open the door to the kitchen and entered. The staff was busy preparing for lunch, and she didn't want to get in the way.

"Sorry to bother you," she called out. Heads turned in response. "Has anyone seen Pop?"

"Not since breakfast." Confirming nods accompanied the dishwasher's reply.

"Okay." Adele's spirits plummeted even as her worry escalated to new heights. "If anyone does see or hear from him, tell him to call me right away."

As she was leaving, she ran into Cook coming out of the walk-in freezer.

"What are you doing here, girl?" With her generous girth and perpetually red complexion, Cook resembled an overgrown cherub.

"Trying to find Pop."

"Well, he's not here." The woman chuckled.

"I know."

"He went to St. George. Left about a half hour ago."

"What?" Adele's jaw quite literally dropped. "You're kidding."

Cook looked perplexed, then alarmed. "Didn't he tell you?"

"No." Adele was torn between relief and irritation. Relief won out.

"He asked me to pack him a lunch. Said he'd be home by dinnertime."

"What was he thinking? He can't drive that far. Not at his age and with his hip."

"I'm sorry, Adele. I had no idea he didn't tell you."

This wasn't Cook's fault. Adele tried to remain calm, knowing she'd have more luck stopping a moving freight train than Pop when he set his mind on something.

And Adele was fairly certain she knew what that something was.

He had gone to track down Ty and tell him about the baby.

Dammit. He had no right.

"I'm going after him," she told Cook, calculating how much of a head start her grandfather had on her. Luckily, he always drove five to ten miles under the speed limit. "I'll let you know when I find him."

Once in her truck, Adele made a series of phone calls. First to the barn manager, instructing him to have Stick cover the day's classes. Next, she called Garth and, getting his voice mail, left a message for him to keep an eye out for Pop at the rodeo. Lastly, she contacted the sheriff's office, just in case Pop had an accident or his truck broke down on the highway.

She considered calling Ty, then chickened out. He'd want to know why Pop was coming to see him, and Adele wasn't ready to explain.

In town, she stopped at the gas station to fill up. Just as she was returning the nozzle to the pump, her mother pulled up in her pint-size economy car and rolled down the window.

"Hey, Dellie. I was just on my way to see you. I know

it's probably a little early for this, but I brought some nursery—"

"I can't talk now. Pop took off without telling me. He's on his way to St. George to find Ty. I'm going after him."

Lani didn't hesitate. "I'll come with you."

Until very recently, Adele would have refused to let her mother accompany her anywhere.

Not today.

"Park your car over there, and let's go."

Ty and Dana would have made better time getting Hamm to the warm-up arena if not for being waylaid by Mike and Sandy.

"What are you guys doing here?" Ty greeted his friends and former fellow students warmly.

"Mike surprised me with tickets," Sandy gushed.

Ty introduced Dana, and the four of them chatted amiably. Well, Dana did most of the chatting. Ty's mind was occupied elsewhere.

Funny how knowing what to do gave a man a sense of peace. As soon as he finished his event this afternoon, he'd load up and hit the road again.

Garth meandered over while they were talking, leading his own horse.

"You on your way to warm up?" he asked Ty, after saying hello to Mike, Sandy and Dana.

Ty started to answer, then was distracted by the sight of Pop emerging from the crowd and coming toward him. Ty's first thought was that Pop's limp had significantly lessened. The hip-replacement surgery was obviously a success.

"Hey, Pop." He smiled, ridiculously pleased to see the older man. "What are you doing here?"

At his greeting, everyone in their group turned, matching smiles on their faces.

Ignoring them, Pop came straight at Ty, his wizened features fixed in a purposeful scowl, his stride deliberate. "I need to have a word with you, young man."

A word? Young man?

"Sure." Ty handed Hamm's reins to Dana and stepped forward. "Is something the matter?"

"This is for taking advantage of my little girl."

Before Ty could respond, Pop's fist connected with his jaw in a lightning fast right hook worthy of a man one-third his age.

Ty's head snapped to the side. Pain radiated through his entire face, neck and shoulders, and he stumbled backward from the force of the blow.

Sandy let out a little scream.

Ty shook his head, dazed and more than a little confused. It didn't occur to him to retaliate.

"And this is for leaving her in a fix."

Pop's left fist plowed into Ty's stomach, knocking the wind clean out of him and sending him sprawling to the ground, flat on his rear.

"Stop him," Dana cried.

"Hey, that's enough."

Ty heard Garth and his sister over the dense ringing in his ears, and had a vague impression of Garth scuffling with Pop and pulling him away. Thank God. Pop might be seventy-seven and suffering from debilitating arthritis, but he still packed a mean punch.

"What do you mean, I left her in a fix?" he sputtered, his knees bent and his throbbing head cradled in his hands. Fortunately, the ringing in his ears had started to subside.

"Dellie's pregnant."

"She is?" Squinting, he looked up at Pop, an action that sent fresh waves of pain pulsing through him.

"You're going to be a father."

"I am?" The blows he'd taken must have dulled his thinking, for nothing made sense.

"You all right?"

Mike's face appeared, and Ty had the impression of hands tenderly and expertly probing him all over for injuries. He was also aware of a growing audience.

"I don't know," he slurred, trying not to move his sore mouth.

"Sandy." Mike pulled a handkerchief from his back pocket. "Put some ice from your drink in this." She did and Mike pressed the ice pack to Ty's jaw, while Dana hovered nearby.

Garth knelt down beside Ty, his face splitting in a wide grin. "Congratulations, pal."

"She never said anything." Ty looked around for Pop. "I swear, if she had, I wouldn't have left her."

Suddenly, Garth, Dana, Mike and Sandy all stood and stepped away. Ty's vision had cleared enough for him to see Adele emerging from the crowd and running toward him, her mother and a security guard not far behind.

"What happened? Ty, are you okay?"

Adele took Garth's place, kneeling beside Ty. Mike went to talk to the security guard.

"Did you fall?" she asked, her touch more tender and more welcome than Mike's.

"Your grandfather slugged me. Twice."

"Pop!" Adele turned and sent her grandfather an infuriated glare. "I apologize for him," she said, returning her attention to Ty.

"How come you didn't tell me you're pregnant?"

"I—I...because I was afraid you'd quit rodeoing."

"Hell, yes, I will."

"You can't."

"I'm not leaving my—"

"You will not lose the championship again. You hear me? Too much is riding on it."

The side of his mouth that didn't ache pulled up in a smile. "Kind of bossy, aren't you?"

"I was wrong, Ty." She lowered her gaze. "I should have told you about the baby."

"Yes, you should have."

"It's just that you've worked so hard to get to this point, and you deserve to win."

"You deserve to have the father of your baby there with you when you need him." The fog around him had lifted. In fact, his head was clearer than it had been in weeks.

"What are you—"

"Shut up." Cupping her face in his hands, he drew her to him for a kiss that would have lasted longer if his mouth didn't hurt so much. "Help me up," he demanded when they broke apart.

"Are you sure you should? You could have broken something."

He beckoned to Garth to give him a boost. "I'm not going to propose to you sitting on my ass in the dirt."

"Propose!" Adele gasped. "We need to talk first."

"Plenty of time for that later." Pop sidled over to them.

"This is what you wanted." Adele stared at him accusingly.

"Damn straight," he said with undisguised satisfaction.

Sandy didn't hide her tears as she squeezed Mike's arm. "Isn't this romantic?"

Ty wasn't sure how getting the tar beaten out of him was romantic.

"Wait until Mom and Dad hear!" Dana exclaimed with glee, and whipped out her cell phone, taking pictures to commemorate the moment.

Adele rose along with Ty as Garth pulled him to his feet. He wobbled only for as long as it took him to put an arm around her and nestle her against him.

"I know there's a lot we need to figure out." Everything that had happened during his last visit to Seven Cedars suddenly made sense. And now that he understood her concerns, he would do everything in his power to lay them to rest. "We'll do it one day, one problem at a time."

"I don't want you marrying me because you feel obligated."

"I'm not. I love you, Adele. And I should have told you that weeks ago." He could see a trace of uncertainty in her expression. "Would it help you to know I was planning on driving to Seven Cedars tonight after the rodeo?"

"You were?"

"And when I got there, I was going to demand you give us a second chance."

"Oh, Ty. I love you, too."

"I'm glad you said that." He tugged her closer, threading his fingers in her hair. "So, how 'bout a September wedding?"

"Not so fast, cowboy." She leaned back, appraising him critically. "There's a little matter of the World tie-down roping and team roping championships."

"I thought we agreed—"

"We did no such thing. You're going to finish out the season. The baby will wait until then."

"What if I can't?" He felt his grin expand.

"You can come home every couple of weeks. And I'll fly out to see you. Once. Maybe twice." She was grinning, too. "If you win the championship, and only if you win, then I'll consider marrying you."

Her challenge was like the one she'd issued him at the Cowboy College jackpot. Then, it had been a dinner date at stake. Today, it was the rest of their lives.

"You think I can't?"

"I know you can't unless you qualify," she answered smugly.

Ty accepted his fallen hat from Garth, slapped it against his leg to knock off the dust and put in back on his head. "Seems I have an event to win."

"You sure you're up to it?" Mike asked with doctorly concern.

"I am." Ty only had eyes for Adele. "And when I do win, then we'll talk about *my* list of requirements."

She raised her brows in surprise. "Such as?"

"If I'm going to retire after Nationals, we make some changes at Cowboy College. I want to expand the program to include professional ropers. With three experts in residence, we can attract an entirely new clientele."

"And one on the way," Lani added. "With genes like theirs, how could the kid not be a roper?"

"I like it." Pop smiled approvingly and draped an arm around Lani.

"Me, too." Adele stood on tiptoes to give Ty's cheek a tender kiss.

"Hate to break up the party, buddy," Garth said, "but we'd better get a move on." He swung up into the saddle.

"No taking it easy on me just because I'm injured and newly engaged," Ty warned his friend.

"I wouldn't dream of it."

Much as Ty hated to, he left Adele to join Garth in the warm-up arena.

An hour later, the announcer's voice blared from the speakers, proclaiming Ty the tie-down roping winner. Amid the applause and cheers that followed, he shouted the news that Ty had set an arena record with his last run.

Ty hardly heard the man. He was too busy kissing his wife-to-be and the mother of his child, and planning their future, one that included the realization of all their dreams, a display cabinet full of gold belt buckles and a three-generation legacy to pass on to their children.

* * * * *

Rebecca Winters lives in Salt Lake City, Utah. With canyons and high alpine meadows full of wildflowers, she never runs out of places to explore. They, plus her favorite vacation spots in Europe, often end up as backgrounds for her romance novels—because writing is her passion, along with her family and church. Rebecca loves to hear from readers. If you wish to email her, please visit her website at rebeccawinters.net.

Books by Rebecca Winters

Harlequin Romance

Escape to Provence

Falling for Her French Tycoon

The Princess Brides

The Princess's New Year Wedding
The Prince's Forbidden Bride
How to Propose to a Princess

Holiday with a Billionaire

Captivated by the Brooding Billionaire
Falling for the Venetian Billionaire
Wedding the Greek Billionaire
The Magnate's Holiday Proposal

Visit the Author Profile page at Harlequin.com for more titles.

THE WYOMING COWBOY

Rebecca Winters

I want to dedicate this series to the courageous men and women serving in our armed forces, who've willingly put their lives in harm's way to keep the rest of us safe. God bless all of you.

Chapter 1

Carson Lundgren was sitting in the hospital ward's common room watching the final moments of the NAS-CAR race when he heard a disturbance. Annoyed, he turned his head to see Dr. Rimer passing out a document to the eight vets assembled. What in blazes was going on?

"Ray? You're closest to the TV. Would you mind shutting it off?"

Ray nodded and put an end to one of the few distractions the men looked forward to.

"Thank you. You'll all be going home tomorrow, so

I urge you gentlemen to read this and take what you can from it to heart. It's a good letter written by a former serviceman. I like a lot of things it says. While you're doing that, I'll go find our special guest and bring him in."

Special guest?

The guys eyed each other with resignation. Who knew how long this would take? They were all anxious to watch the end of the race. Carson looked down to scan the page.

> *Consider how different and difficult it is to go from a life of service, where every day has a mission, and someone depends on you to make life-and-death decisions, to a life with civilians who are making decisions about what client to call back first or what is the best outfit to wear to work.*

Life would be different, all right. In Carson's case he didn't need to worry about choosing the proper clothes. He was going back to his Wyoming ranch, where a shirt and jeans had been his uniform before he'd signed up for the Marines. It would be his uniform again, now that he was out of the service.

> *In the beginning it feels as if you are so much more experienced than the people around you, and in a lot of ways you are. But that kind of thinking will only further alienate you from others. Practicing humility is the best possible advice I can give to help with reintegration into civilian life.*

Carson did feel more "experienced." He'd seen things in the war that he could never explain to people who hadn't gone through the same thing.

Veterans need to recognize that even a short tour in a combat zone can have an effect on them. While it takes everyone some time to recover after coming home, those who have seen, or been directly affected by a traumatic or horrific event (using your own definition or a generally accepted definition of such an event), need to be able to reconcile that it may have an impact on their lives and relationships with others after the deployment is over.

Since Carson had no family and his grandfather was dead, he didn't need to worry about that.

Seeking help is not a sign of weakness, no more than asking your buddy to cover your backside. The body may heal from scars and wounds readily, but the scars and wounds of trauma can last much longer and are more difficult to heal.

Difficult? A caustic laugh escaped from him. The cough he'd developed in Afghanistan would never go away, and no one could convince him otherwise.

I promise that, in time, you will see that your civilian counterparts are skilled and have a perspective that you may not have ever considered. And through a respect for what they do and what they have done, you will learn that you, too, are valued and respected.

Carson had always respected the ranch staff and knew he could count on their support.

Just as you are on edge in the beginning, they too may be a little unsure of how to treat you and how to act around you.

They'd treat him just the same as always.

So, take the first step. Be patient, be kind and be humble, and you will see that the transition is much easier.

"Gentlemen?" Dr. Rimer came back in the room where most of them were coughing because of the same affliction. He was followed by a five-star general decked out in full-dress uniform. Carson glanced at his buddies, Ross and Buck, wondering what was going on.

"I'm pleased and honored to introduce General Aldous Cook. He's anxious to talk to you men recovering in the unit. He's been asked to do some investigating for the Senate committee examining the troubling findings of the *Millennium Cohort Study of 2009*."

The eight of them got to their feet and saluted him before shaking his hand.

The General smiled. "Be seated, gentlemen. I'm honored to be in your presence and want to thank you for your invaluable service to our country." He cleared his throat. "I understand you're all going home tomorrow and have a great deal on your minds so I'll make this quick.

"As you're well aware, a significant number of returning American veterans like yourselves have reported respiratory problems that started during deployment to Iraq and Afghanistan. The study of 2009 revealed that fourteen percent of the deployed troops reported new breathing problems, compared with ten percent among those who hadn't deployed.

"Though the percentage difference seems small when extrapolated for the two million troops who've been deployed since 2001, the survey suggested that at least 80,000 additional soldiers have developed post-deployment breathing problems.

"There's a fierce debate under way over just how long-lasting and severe these problems really are. We're tracking the numbers accrued among the troops based in Southern Afghanistan since 2009, particularly the Marines.

"After ruling out other factors, it's apparent that the powerful dust storms, plus the fine dust from metals, toxins and burn pits used to incinerate garbage at military bases, are the potential culprits. Steps need to be taken to reduce the hazards, and I'm concerned that this exposure isn't getting the serious review it needs.

"Dr. Rimer has indicated you've all improved since you've been here, but we'll continue to track your progress. He assures me that with time, most of you will overcome your coughing and shortness of breath."

Tell us another fairy tale, General.

"My concern is that every one of you receives the

post-deployment care you need for as long as you need it. I'm fighting for you in the congressional hearings."

Along with the others, Carson stood up and applauded. At least the General had bothered to come to the hospital in person and make an attempt to get at the root of the problem. Carson admired him for that. The General chatted with each of them for a few minutes, then left. With the end of the NASCAR race now missed, everyone left the lounge except Carson and his two roommates, Ross and Buck.

They hadn't known each other until six weeks ago, when the three of them had been flown here from their various divisions and diagnosed with acute dyspnea. But even if they were hacking, coughing and wheezing, at least they'd arrived at the hospital on their own two feet. It tore them up that some of their buddies—especially those who'd been married with families—hadn't made it through the war.

The behavioral psychologist who'd been working with them suggested that, once they were discharged, they should find a positive way to work through their survivor's guilt.

In addition to the guilt Carson already struggled with for personal reasons, he was barely functioning. During the long hours of the night when they couldn't sleep, they'd talked about the wives and children who'd lost husbands and fathers from their own squads. If the three of them could think of a way to help those families, maybe they could forgive themselves for coming home alive.

At one point in their nocturnal discussions, Carson threw out an idea that began to percolate and gain ground. "What if we invited the fatherless kids to my ranch for a summer vacation? The ranch has lots of outdoor activities for kids who may not have spent much time out-of-doors. We could take them fishing and camping, not to mention horseback riding and hiking."

Ross sat up in his bed. "All of those are good confidence builders. Heaven knows those children will have lost some confidence. How many kids are you talking about?"

"I don't know."

"Do you have enough room for guests?"

"No. We'd have to live in the ranch house, so that wouldn't work. We'd have to put up some cabins."

"I could build them with your help," Buck offered. "Construction is what I was raised to do."

"I'm afraid I don't have much money."

Buck said, "I have a little I've put away."

"I have some, too," Ross chimed in. "Looking down the road, we'd have to hire and pay a cook and provide maid service."

Encouraged, Carson said, "No matter what, we'll have to start out small."

"Their moms will have to bring them."

"You're right, Buck. How long should they come for?"

"This is a bit of an experiment, so how about we try a week with one family and see how it goes?"

"For working mothers, I think a week sounds about right," Ross theorized. "One thing we can do is help the kids if they need to talk about death, since we've been through a lot of grief counseling ourselves."

"Good point. That's one thing we know how to do. What ages are we talking about?"

"I'm thinking about my nieces and nephews," Buck murmured. "How about little guys who are really missing their dads? Like six on up to maybe ten."

Carson nodded. "That sounds about right. They'd be school age. Younger than six might be too young."

"Agreed," they all concurred.

Before long, enthusiasm for the project they envisioned wouldn't let them alone. They soon found themselves plotting to turn Carson's ranch into a dude ranch where tourists could come along with the families of fatherless children. They would establish a fund to take care of the costs. If their pilot program went well through the summer, they'd talk about keeping it open year-round.

Their plan was a good one and sounded feasible, except for one thing. None of them had gone home yet. Anything could happen when Buck and Ross were reunited with their families. Their parents had dreams for them when their beloved sons returned to their former lives. For that reason, Carson wasn't holding his breath—what little he had at the moment. He had to admit the inhalers were helping. When he'd first been brought in, he'd been gasping for every breath and thought each was his last.

Of the three men, Carson was the only one who didn't have living family. The grandfather who'd raised him had passed away five months ago of a surprise heart attack, leaving the ranch and its problems to him. Not even his grandfather's doctor had seen it coming.

Carson had flown home on emergency family leave to bury him.

In that regard, he wouldn't have to run their brainchild past the older man he'd abandoned when he'd entered the military. At the time he hadn't seen it as abandonment. They'd corresponded and phoned whenever possible, but in the end Carson wasn't there for his grandfather when the chips were down. Now it was too late to make it up to the man he'd loved.

"Tomorrow's the big day, guys." Once they were all discharged from the hospital in the morning, he knew anything could happen to change his friends' focus.

Buck nodded. "I'll join you before the week is out."

Maybe. But knowing Buck was the oldest son in a large, close-knit family who wanted and needed him back in the construction business, maybe not. "Give me a call and I'll pick you up at the airport. What about you, Ross?"

"Three days at the most."

"You think?"

He eyed him narrowly. "I *know.*"

Put like that, Carson could believe him, but his family who'd made their mark in oil for generations would have its way of pressuring the favorite son who'd made it home from the war. His politician father had long laid hopes for him set in stone. Time would tell if their master plan would get off the ground.

"I can hear the carts arriving with our dinner. Let's get back to the room and eat before our final session with the shrink."

It couldn't come soon enough for any of them. The war had been their world for a long time. Tomorrow they'd leave it forever. But fear clutched him in the gut that it would never leave them.

MAY 2
Sandusky, Ohio

At three o'clock, Tracy Baretta left her office to pick up Johnny from elementary school. When she joined the line of cars waiting for the kids to come out, she hoped she'd see Clara Brewster. Her son, Nate, was a cute boy who'd invited Johnny to his birthday party last month. Johnny hadn't wanted to go, but Tracy had made him.

Maybe Nate would like to come home with her and Johnny to play, but she didn't see him or his mom. Her disappointment changed to a dull pain when she had to wait until all the kids had been picked up before her skinny, dark-haired first grader exited the school doors alone.

He purposely hung back from the others. His behavior had her worried sick. She'd been setting up some playdates with a few of the other boys in his first-grade class, but they hadn't worked out well.

Johnny preferred to be alone and stay home with her after school. He'd become a very quiet child since Tony's death and was way too attached to her. The psychologist told her to keep finding ways to get him to interact with other kids and not take no for an answer, but she wasn't gaining ground.

He got in the rear seat with his backpack and strapped himself in. She looked over her shoulder at him. "How was school today, honey?"

"We had a substitute."

"Was she fun?"

"It was a man. I didn't like him."

She eyed him in the rearview mirror. "Why do you say that?"

"He made me sit with Danny."

"Isn't he a nice boy?"

"He calls me squirt."

His tear-filled voice brought out every savage maternal instinct to protect him. Praying for inspiration she said, "Do you want to know something?"

"What?"

"Your father was one of the shortest kids in his class when he was your age. By high school he was five feet ten." The perfect size for Tracy. "That'll happen to you, too. Do you think your father was a squirt?"

"No," he muttered.

"Then forget what Danny said. When we go to Grandma's house, she'll show you lots of pictures to make you feel better."

Of course Johnny couldn't forget. Silence filled the car for the rest of the drive home to their small rental house. She parked in front of the garage. While he scrambled out of the back, she retrieved the mail and they entered through the front door.

Once inside, he raced for the kitchen. "Wash your hands before you eat anything!" He was always hungry for sweets after school.

While her six-year-old grumbled and ran into the bathroom, Tracy went to the kitchen and poured him a glass of milk before she sorted through the mail, mostly ads and bills. Among the assortment she saw a handwritten envelope addressed to Mrs. Anthony Baretta. It had a Jackson, Wyoming, postmark.

She didn't know anyone in Wyoming. Her glance took in the return address. Lundgren's Teton Valley Dude Ranch was printed inside the logo of a mountain peak.

A dude ranch? She'd heard of them all her life, but she'd never been to one. Truth be told, she'd never traveled west of the Mississippi. Every trip had been to Florida, the East Coast, New York City, the Jersey Shore or Toronto. Tony had promised Johnny that when he got out of the service next year, they'd take a big driving trip west, all the way to Disneyland. Another pain shot through her.

She took a deep breath, curious to know who would be writing to her from Wyoming. After slitting the envelope open, she pulled out the handwritten letter.

> *Dear Mrs. Baretta,*
> *My name is Carson Lundgren. You don't know me from Adam. I served as a marine in Afghanistan before I got out of the service.*

The word Afghanistan swam before her eyes. *Tony.* She closed them tightly to stop the tears and sank down on one of the kitchen chairs. Her husband had been gone eleven months, yet she knew she would always experience this crushing pain when she thought of him.

"Mom? Can I have a peanut-butter cookie?" He'd drunk his milk.

"How about string cheese or an apple instead?"

"No-o," he moaned.

"Johnny—" she said in a firm voice.

"Can I have some for dinner?"

"If you eat everything else first."

"Okay." She heard him rummage in the fridge for the cheese before he left the kitchen to watch his favorite afternoon cartoons.

When he'd disappeared into the living room, she wiped her eyes and continued reading.

> *Buck Summerhays and Ross Livingston, former marines, are in business with me on the Teton Valley Dude Ranch. We put our heads together and decided to contact the families of the fallen soldiers from our various units.*
>
> *Your courageous husband, Anthony Baretta, served our country with honor and distinction. Now, we'd like to honor him by offering you and your son John an all-expenses-paid, one-week vacation at the dude ranch anytime in June, July or August. We'll pay for your airfare and any other travel expenses.*

Tracy's eyes widened in total wonder.

> *You're welcome to contact your husband's division commander. His office helped us obtain your address. If you're interested and have questions, please phone our office at the number below. We've also listed our website. Visit it to see the brochure we've prepared. We'll be happy to email you any additional information.*

Please know how anxious we are to give some-
thing back to you after Anthony's great sacrifice.
With warmest regards,
Carson Lundgren

His words made her throat swell with emotion. With
the letter still open, she phoned the commander's office
and learned that the offer was completely legitimate.
His assistant had nothing but praise for such a worthy
cause and hoped she and her son would be able to take
advantage of it.

Tracy's thoughts flew to her plans for the summer.
When school was out, it was decided she and Johnny
would spend six weeks in Cleveland with Tony's parents. They saw Tony in their grandson and were living
for a long visit. So was Tracy, who'd been orphaned at
eighteen and had no other family.

Luckily, she had June and the first half of July off
from her job as technology facilitator for the Sandusky
school district. Both she and Johnny needed a huge dose
of family love, and they would get it. Grandma planned
for them to stay in Tony's old room with all his stuff.
Johnny would adore that.

The Barettas were a big Italian-American family
with aunts, uncles and lots of cousins. Two of Johnny's uncles were policemen and the other three were
firefighters, like their father. *Like Tony, before he'd
joined the Marines to help pay for a college education.*

Their loving kindness had saved her life, and Johnny's, when news of the tragedy had come. He needed
that love and support more than ever. She wondered

what his reaction would be when he heard what this new invitation was about.

But before she did anything else, she called her sister-in-law Natalie to feel her out. When Tracy read her the letter, Natalie cried, "You've got to be kidding me! A dude ranch? Oh, my gosh, Tracy. You'll have the time of your life. Ask Ruth. She went to one in Montana with my folks a few years ago. Remember?"

"Vaguely."

"Yeah. It was a working ranch and they helped feed animals and went on trail rides and stuff. She got to help herd some cows."

"I don't think this is that kind of a ranch, but I don't know for sure. The thing is, Johnny's been difficult for so long, I don't think he'd even like the idea of it."

"If you want, I'll tell Cory about it. I could have him call Johnny and tell him he's thinks it would be super cool."

"That might work. Johnny loves Cory and usually goes along with anything his favorite cousin says."

"Cory will want to go with him. But seriously, Tracy, I can't believe what a wonderful thing these ex-marines have decided to do. You hear a lot of talk about remembering our fallen heroes, but this is the first time I've heard of a group of soldiers doing something like this."

"I know. Believe me, I'm blown away by this letter. If Tony knew, he'd be so touched." The tears came. She couldn't stop them. "There's just one problem. The folks are expecting Johnny and me to visit there as soon as school is out. Since my vacation is over in mid-July, I would have to make arrangements to do this trip before then."

"True." Natalie's voice trailed. "It will cut into the time you planned with Mom and Dad Baretta."

"Yes. You know how they're looking forward to spending time with Johnny."

"Well, don't say anything to them until you find out if he wants to go."

"You're right. First things first. I'll let you know what happens. Thanks for being there and being my best friend."

"Ditto to you. *Ciao.*"

Deciding there was no time like the present to find out, Tracy picked up the letter and walked into the living room. Johnny was spread out on the floor with his turtle pillow-pet watching *Tom and Jerry.*

"Honey, do you mind if I shut off the TV? There's something I want to talk to you about."

He turned to look at her out of eyes as dark a brown as Tony's. She picked up the remote and turned the set off before sitting down on the couch. "We just got an invitation in the mail to do something we've never done before. It was sent by some men who used to be marines, like your father."

That seemed to pique his interest enough to sit up cross-legged. "Are they going to have a party?" In his child's world, an invitation meant a party. Since Tony's death he'd shied away from them. He seemed to have lost his confidence. It killed her.

"No. Let me read this to you."

He sat quietly until she'd finished. "What's a dude ranch?"

"It's a place to go horseback riding and probably lots of other things."

Her son had never been on a horse. Neither had she.
"You mean like a cowboy?" She nodded. "Where is it?"

"In Wyoming."

"Where's that?"

"If you're interested, I'll show you on the computer."

"Okay."

He followed her into her bedroom where she had
her laptop. In a second she'd brought up a map of the
United States. "We live here, in Ohio." She pointed to
Cleveland. "Now, watch my finger. You have to cross
Indiana, Illinois, Iowa and South Dakota to get to Wy-
oming, right here."

She could hear his mind working. "How long would
we be gone?"

"A week."

"That's a long time." His voice wobbled. "I don't
want to go."

Tracy had been afraid of that answer, but she understood. It meant leaving the only security he'd ever
known. Going to stay with his aunt Natalie and play
with his cousin Cory, or having an overnighter on the
weekend with his grandparents, who only lived an hour
away, was different.

"We don't have to. These men know your daddy died
and they'd like to do something nice for you, but it's
your decision, Johnny. Before I turn off the computer,
would you like to see some pictures Mr. Lundgren sent
so you could see what it looks like?"

He sighed. "I guess."

Tracy typed in the web address and clicked. Up
popped a colored photograph of the Teton Mountain
Range with a few pockets of snow. The scene was so

spectacular she let out a slight gasp. In the bottom of the picture was the layout of the Teton Valley Dude Ranch surrounded by sage.

A "whoa" from Johnny told her his attention had been captured. She read the description below the picture out loud.

"The dude ranch is located along the legendary Snake River in the shadow of the magnificent Teton Mountain Range. It's just five miles from the town of Jackson, a sophisticated mountain resort. Fifteen minutes away are world-class skiing areas.

"This 1,700-acre ranch operates as a cattle ranch with its own elk and deer herds, eagles and bears. There's fishing along the three miles of the Snake. At elevations from 6,200 to 7,300 feet, summers bring average temperatures of eighty degrees and low humidity.

"Mountaineering, fly-fishing, white-water rafting, wildlife expeditions, horseback riding, photo safaris, hiking and camping trips, stargazing, bird watching, ballooning, a visit to the rodeo, are all included when you stay on the ranch. Among the amenities you'll enjoy are a game room, a swimming pool, a babysitting service, laundry services and the use of a car for local transportation."

Johnny nudged her. "What's white water?"

She'd been deep in thought. "There's a picture here of some people in a raft running the rapids. Take a look."

His eyes widened. "You mean we'd do that if we went there?"

"If we wanted to."

He looked up at her. "When would we go?"

So he *was* interested. She felt a sudden lift of her

spirits. "How about as soon as school is out? After our trip is over, we'll fly back to Cleveland and stay with Grandma and Grandpa for a month. Why don't you think about it, and let me know tonight before you go to bed?"

"Can I see the rest of the pictures?"

"Sure. You know how to work the computer. While you do that, I'm going to start dinner." With her fingers crossed, she got up from her swivel chair so he could sit and look at everything. He needed something to bring him out of his shell. Maybe a trip like this would help.

A half hour later he came running into the kitchen where she'd made spaghetti. "Mom—you should see the elks. They have giant horns!"

"You mean antlers."

"Oh, yeah. I forgot."

She hunkered down and gave him a hug. "It's pretty exciting stuff, huh."

He stared at her with a solemn expression. "Do you want to go?"

Oh, my precious son. "If *you* do."

JUNE 7
Jackson, Wyoming

It was late Friday afternoon when the small plane from Salt Lake City, Utah, started to make its descent. The pilot came on over the intercom. "Ladies and gentlemen, you're about to land at the only commercial airport located inside a U.S. national park."

Johnny reached for Tracy's hand.

"We're flying over the Greater Yellowstone region

with forests, mountains, wilderness areas and lakes as far as the eye can see. Ahead is the majestic Teton Range. You'll see the Snake River and the plains around it in a patchwork of colors."

Tracy found it all glorious beyond description, but when the Grand Teton came into view, knifing into the atmosphere, every passenger was struck dumb with awe.

"If you'll look below, we're coming up on Jackson Hole."

Seeing it for the first time, Tracy could understand the reason for its name. It was a narrow valley surrounded by mountains and probably presented a challenge for the pilot to land safely. She clung to Johnny's hand. Before long, their plane touched down on the tarmac and taxied to the gate.

After it came to a stop, she unclasped their seat belts. "Are you all right, honey?"

He nodded. "That was scary."

"I agree, but we're here safe and sound now." She reached for her purse above the seat. "Let's go."

They followed the other eight passengers out the exit to the tiny terminal. The second they entered the one-story building, she heard a deep male voice call her name.

Tracy looked to her left and saw a tall, lean cowboy in jeans and a Western shirt. With his hard-muscled physique, he stood out from everyone else around him. This was no actor from a Western movie set. From his well-worn black Stetson to his cowboy boots, everything about him shouted authentic.

Johnny hugged her side. "Who's that?" he whispered.

The thirtyish-looking stranger must have heard him because he walked over and reached out to shake Johnny's hand. "My name's Carson Lundgren. I'm the man who sent your mom the letter inviting you to the ranch. You have to be John." His eyes traveled over Tracy's son with a compassion she could feel.

He nodded.

"Have you found your stomach yet, or is it still up in the air?" His question made Johnny laugh. He couldn't have said anything to break the ice faster. "I'll tell you a secret. When I was your age and my grandpa took me on my first plane ride around the Teton Valley, I didn't find my stomach for a week, but you get used to it."

While her son was studying him in amazement, his hot blue gaze switched to Tracy. Her medium height meant she had to look up at him. He removed his hat, revealing a head of dark blond hair, attractively disheveled.

"Mrs. Baretta, it's a pleasure to meet you and your son."

"We're excited to be here, Mr. Lundgren, and honored by the invitation. Please call us Johnny and Tracy."

"Terrific. You can call me Carson." He coughed for a few seconds. "Forgive me. I do that quite often. Something I picked up overseas. It's not contagious."

Johnny's head tipped back to look at him. "You used to be a marine like my dad, huh?"

"Yup. I have a picture of him and his buddies." He pulled a wallet from his pocket. Inside was a small packet of photos. He handed one to Johnny. "I didn't know him, because I'd just been transferred in from another detail when the picture was taken. But I learned

Tony Baretta came from a long line of firefighters and had the reputation of being the toughest marine in the unit. You can keep it."

"Thanks." His young voice trembled. "I loved him."

"Of course you did, just like I loved my grandpa."

"What about your dad?"

"My parents were killed in a freak flood when I was a baby. My grandparents raised me. After my grandma died, it was just Grandpa and me."

"Didn't you have cousins?"

"Nope. How about you?"

He looked at Tracy. "How many do I have, Mom?"

"Let me think. Twenty-two-and-a-half at the present counting."

Carson's brows lifted. "You're lucky. I would have given anything for just one."

That sounded like a lonely statement. Tracy looked over Johnny's shoulder while he studied the photograph. She counted a dozen soldiers in uniform. When she found Tony, her eyes glazed over.

Johnny's next remark surprised her because it wasn't about his father. "You look different in a helmet."

"We were just a bunch of metal heads." Johnny laughed again. "None of us liked them much, but the gear kept us protected."

"I like your cowboy hat better," Johnny said before putting the picture in his pocket.

Carson grinned. The rugged rancher was one striking male. "Shall we get you a hat like it on our way to the ranch?"

"Could we?" Tracy hadn't seen him exhibit this kind of excitement in over a year.

"Of course. You can't live on a dude ranch without your duds."

"What are duds?"

"Everything I'm wearing plus a lot of other things."

"What other things?"

"Chaps and gloves for bull riding."

"Do you ride *bulls?*" Johnny's eyes grew huge.

"I used to when I was training for the rodeo."

"Can I see one?"

"Sure. I'm planning on taking you to the Jackson rodeo on the last night you're here. You'll see barrel racing and steer wrestling too."

"Mom!" Johnny cried out with uncontained excitement.

"Come on, partner. Let's get your luggage and we'll go shopping."

"As long as you let me pay for everything," Tracy interjected.

He shook his head. "While you're here, we take care of everything for the kids."

"I can't allow that," she insisted. "A free vacation is one thing, but I'll be buying whatever Johnny wants or needs while we're here."

His blue eyes flickered before he shoved his hat back on. "Yes, ma'am."

Johnny had to hurry to keep up with the larger-than-life cowboy whose long powerful legs reached the baggage claim in a few strides.

"I bet you're hungry. Do you like buffalo burgers?"

"Buffalo?"

Tracy tried to hide her smile. Her son turned to her. "Mom? Are there really buffalo burgers?"

"Yes, but I've never eaten one."

He looked at Carson. "Are they good?"

"Do you like hamburgers?"

"Yes."

"Then you don't have anything to worry about." His lips twitched when he glanced at Tracy. "Which bags are yours?"

"The two blue ones and the matching shoulder bag."

"Here you go." He handed Johnny the shoulder bag and he reached for the other two. "The van's right outside." Her son had to be surprised, but she noticed he carried the bag like a man and kept up with Carson.

They walked outside into a beautiful, still evening. She loved the dry air, but could tell they were at a much higher elevation than they were used to. The mountain range loomed over the valley, so close she felt dwarfed by it.

Their host shot her a concerned glance. "Are you all right, Tracy?"

"I'm fine."

"The air's thinner than you're used to in Ohio."

"It isn't that as much as the mountains. They're so close to us, I feel like they're pressing in."

"I had the same feeling in reverse when we reached Afghanistan and I got off the plane with no mountains in sight where we landed. I felt like I was in a constant state of free-fall. Without landmarks, it took me a while to get my bearings."

"Coming from a paradise like this, I can't even imagine it. Tony and I grew up on Lake Erie. He told me that after he got there, with no water in sight, he went into shock."

"We all did," Carson murmured. "On every level."

She hadn't talked to anyone about Tony's war experiences in a long time and hadn't wanted to. But this was different, because Carson had made a connection by being there, too. With that photo in his pocket, her son wouldn't forget, either.

He guided them to the dark green van. It was easy to spot, with the same logo on the side she'd seen on the envelope. He stowed their luggage in the rear, then helped her and Johnny into the backseat.

"First we'll head to the Silver Dollar Grill for some grub."

"What's grub?"

"That's what the ranch hands call food. After that, we'll drive over to the Boot Corral and get you outfitted. I think they even sell some mustangs."

"What are those?"

"Cap guns. When I was little I had a mustang and played like I was Hopalong Cassidy."

"Who was he?"

"Hoppy was a straight shooter and my favorite cowboy."

His dark head jerked around to Tracy. "Did you ever see Hoppy?"

Her quick-study son was soaking up all this fascinating information like a sponge. "When I was a little girl my father had some old Western movies and we'd watch them. Hoppy was the good guy who always played fair. He had white hair and wore a black cowboy hat."

"Hey—" He looked at Carson. "So do you!" Johnny cried in delight.

"Yup. I wanted to be just like him."

Tracy smiled. "He had two partners. One old duffer was called Gabby, and the young one was called Lucky. I was crazy about Lucky. He was tall and good-looking."

Johnny giggled.

"All the girls loved Lucky," Carson commented. "That was mushy stuff."

"Yeah," her son agreed with him.

"Now we know where Lucky got his name, don't we." Carson winked at her. "I have a couple of old Western movies on CD, and you can see him in action."

"Can we watch it tonight?"

"No, young man," Tracy intervened. "When we get to the ranch, we're both going straight to bed. It's been a long day."

"Your mom's right, Johnny. Tonight we'll load you up with one of those mustangs Hoppy used to use and all the ammo you want. In a few days, when I take you out riding, we'll scout for bad guys."

"I've never been on a horse."

"Never?"

"No."

Those blue eyes flicked to Tracy. "How about you?"

She shook her head. "I'm afraid we're a pair of the greenest greenhorns you ever met. When I saw your dude ranch logo on the envelope, I never dreamed Johnny and I would end up spending time on one."

His chuckle slid in under the radar to resonate through her. "With a couple of lessons that problem will be rectified and you can explore to your heart's content. There's no place like it on Earth. My grandfather used to tell me that, but it wasn't until I came home for his funeral last November that I realized what he meant." She heard the tremor in his voice.

He'd had a recent loss, too. Tracy sensed he was still suffering.

Carson broke their gaze and looked back at Johnny. "We have four ponies. I think I know the one that will be yours while you're here."

"Yippee!" Until this moment Tracy hadn't thought her son's face would ever light up like that again.

"You can name her," he added.

Johnny looked perplexed. "I don't know any girl names for a horse."

"You think about it tonight, and tell me tomorrow."

"Okay."

Carson smiled at both of them before closing the door. She heard him cough again before he walked around the car and got in behind the wheel. Something he'd picked up after being deployed, he'd said.

"What makes you cough so much?"

He looked over at Johnny. "There were a lot of contaminants in the air in Afghanistan. Stuff like smoke and toxins. Some of the soldiers breathed too many bad fumes and our lungs were injured. When I got sick, I was sent to a hospital in Maryland for special treatment. That's where I met Ross and Buck. We became such good friends, we decided to go into business together after we got home."

"Oh. Does it hurt?" Johnny almost whispered the last word.

"It did in the beginning, but not so much now. We're a lot better than we used to be."

"I'm glad."

Her sweet boy.

"Me too, son."

War was a ghastly reality of life. Carson and his friends were some of the fortunate ones who came home alive. She admired them for getting on with living despite their problem, for unselfishly wanting to make a difference in her life and Johnny's. What generous, remarkable men....

As he drove them toward the town, she stared out the window. With night coming on, the Tetons formed a giant silhouette against the growing darkness. She shivered in reaction.

Instead of Johnny, who carried on an animated conversation with their host about horses and breeds, *she* was the one who felt oddly troubled for being so far away from home and everything familiar to her. This new world had taken her by surprise in ways she couldn't understand or explain.

Chapter 2

Carson pulled the van in front of the newly erected cabin designated for the Baretta family. He'd asked one of the girls from town who did housekeeping to keep the lights on after she left. Earlier he'd made certain there were snacks for the Barettas, and in the minifridge he'd stored plenty of juices and sodas.

It had grown quiet during the drive from Jackson to the ranch. When he looked in the rearview mirror, he saw Johnny was fast asleep. The cute little guy had finally conked out.

Carson got out and opened the rear door of the van. His gaze met Tracy's. He handed her the key. "If you'll open the door, I'll carry him inside."

She gathered the sacks with their purchases and hurried ahead of him. The front room consisted of a living room with a couch and chairs and a fireplace. On one wall was an entertainment center with a TV, DVD player and a supply of family movies for the guests. Against the other wall was a rectangular table and chairs. A coffeemaker and a microwave sat on one end near the minifridge.

The back hallway divided into two bedrooms and a bathroom. He swept past her to one of the bedrooms and deposited Johnny on one of the twin beds. He didn't weigh a lot. The boy was built like his father and had the brunette hair and brown eyes of his Italian ancestry.

He was Tony Baretta's son, all right. You wouldn't think he belonged to his blonde mother until you saw his facial features. Pure northern European, like hers. An appealing combination.

As for Tracy Baretta with her gray-green eyes, she was just plain appealing. Unexpectedly lovely. Womanly.

In the guys' desire to make this week memorable for their family, he simply hadn't counted on...*her*.

While she started taking off Johnny's shoes, Carson went back outside to bring in the luggage. "If you need anything, just pick up the phone and one of the staff will answer, day or night. Tomorrow morning, walk over to the main ranch house. We serve breakfast there from six to nine in the big dining room. Lunch is from twelve to two and dinner from five to eight.

"I'll watch for you and introduce you to the guys. They're anxious to meet you. After that, we'll plan your day. For your information, different sets of tourists are staying in the other cabins, but you're the only family here at our invitation for this coming week. In another month we're expecting our next family."

She followed him to the front door of the cabin. "Thank you for everything, Carson." Her voice cracked. "To be honest, I'm overwhelmed. You and your friends are so good to do what you're doing. I could never repay you for this." Tears glistened in her eyes. "From the time you met us at the airport, my son has been a different child. That picture meant everything to him."

To her, too, he wagered.

"Losing your husband has been a traumatic experience for you. My friends and I know that. Even though anyone in the military, and their family, is aware that death can come, no one's ready for it. When our division heard about Tony, we all suffered because he left a wife and child. We're like brothers out there. When one gets hurt, we all hurt."

She nodded. "Tony talked a lot about his buddies. He was so proud to serve with you."

"That goes both ways. There's no way we can bring him back to you, but we'd like to put a smile back on your son's face, if only for a little while. I promise that while you're here, we'll treat him with sensitivity and try to keep him as happy and safe as is humanly possible."

She smiled warmly. "I know you will." He could feel her sincerity.

"We have other guests coming to the ranch all the time, but you and Johnny are our special visitors. No one knows that we've nicknamed this place the Daddy Dude Ranch. What we hope to do is try to lend ourselves out as dads to take some of the burden off you."

Her hazel eyes glistened with tears. "You've already done that. Did you see Johnny in that shop earlier, walking around in those Western clothes with that huge smile on his face? He put that cowboy hat on just the way you wear yours and tried walking like you do in his new cowboy boots. I never saw anything so cute in my life."

"You're right about that." Carson thought he'd never seen anything so beautiful as the woman standing in front of him.

"That mustang we bought was like giving him a bag of Oreos with just the centers."

Carson chuckled. "He likes those?"

"He has a terrible sweet tooth."

"Didn't we all?"

"Probably. Let me say once again how honored I feel that you picked our family. It was a great thrill to receive your letter. Already I can tell Johnny is thriving on this kind of attention. What you're doing is inspirational."

From the light behind them, he could pick out gold and silver filaments in the hair she wore fastened at her nape. Opposites had attracted to produce Johnny. Carson was having trouble concentrating on their conversation.

"Thank you, Tracy. He's a terrific boy."

"For a man who's never had children, you're so good with him. Where did you learn those skills?"

"That's because my grandfather was the best and put up with me and my friends. If it rubbed off on me, then I'm glad."

"So am I. Johnny's having a marvelous time."

"I had a wonderful evening, too, believe me. If I didn't say it before, welcome to the Teton Valley Ranch. Now I'll wish you good-night."

He left quickly and headed for the van. It was a short drive to the main house where he'd been raised. He pulled in back and entered through the rear door. Ross was still in the den working on the accounts when Carson walked down the hall.

"Hey—" Ross called to him. "How did everything go with the Baretta family?"

"Hang on while I grab a cup of coffee and I'll tell you."

"I could use one, too. I'll come with you." They walked down another hall to the kitchen, both coughing up a storm en route.

"Where's Buck?"

"In town, getting some more materials to do repairs on the bunkhouse. He should have been back by now."

"Unless he made a stop at Bubba's Barbecue to see you-know-who."

"Since his last date with Nicole after she got off work, I don't think he's interested after all. She called here twice today. He didn't return the calls."

"Why am I not surprised?" Buck was a confirmed bachelor, as were they all.

Carson grabbed a donut. The cook, who lived in town, had gone home for the night. They had the kitchen to themselves. No sooner had he brewed a fresh pot of coffee than they heard Buck coughing before he appeared in the doorway.

In a minute the three of them filled their mugs and sat down at the old oak table where Carson had eaten most of the meals in his life with his grandparents. Until he'd gone into the Marines. But he didn't want to think about that right now. The guys wanted to know how things had gone at the airport.

"Johnny Baretta is the cutest little six-year-old you ever saw in your life." He filled them in on the details. "He swallowed a couple of bites of that buffalo burger like a man."

They smiled. "How about his mom?" Buck asked.

Carson took a long swig of his coffee. How to answer them... "Nice."

Ross burst into laughter. "That's it? Nice?"

No. That *wasn't* it. "When you meet her in the morning at breakfast, you can make your own assessment." He knew exactly how they'd react. "She's very grateful."

Both men eyed him with speculation. Buck drained his mug. "What's the plan for tomorrow?"

"After breakfast I'll take them over to the barn and give them a riding lesson. Later in the day I thought they'd appreciate a drive around the ranch to get their bearings, and we'll go from there. What about you?"

"I'm going to get the repairs done on the bunkhouse in the morning. Then I'll be taking the Holden party on an overnight campout. We'll be back the next day."

Ross got up from the table to wash their mugs. "The Harris party is planning to do some fly fishing. If Johnny wants to join us, come and find me."

"That boy is game for anything." Tony Baretta had been a lucky man in many ways. He shouldn't have been the one to get killed by a roadside bomb. Carson could still hear Johnny say, *I loved my dad.* The sound of the boy's broken heart would always haunt him.

He pushed himself away from the table, causing Buck to give him a second glance. "What's up?"

Carson grimaced. "When we thought up this idea, we hadn't met these people. It was pure hell to look into that little guy's eyes last night and see the sadness. I hadn't counted on caring so m—" Another coughing spell attacked him, preventing him from finishing his thought.

He needed his inhaler and headed for the hall. "I'll see you two in the morning." Ross would do a security check and lock up.

Carson had taken over his grandfather's room on the ground floor. The other two had bedrooms on the second floor. It was a temporary arrangement. At the end of the summer they'd assess their dude ranch experiment. If they decided it wasn't working, either or both of them could still work on the ranch and make Wyoming their permanent home. He'd already told them they could build their own houses on the property.

Once he reached the bedroom, he inhaled his medication and then took a shower followed by a sleeping pill. Tonight he needed to be knocked out. His old friend "guilt" was back with a double punch. He couldn't make up to his grandfather for the years away, and no power on earth could bring Johnny's father back.

Carson must have been out of his mind to think a week on the ranch was going to make a dent in that boy's pain. He knew for sure Tracy was barely functioning, but she was a mother who'd do anything to help her child get on with living. She had that hidden strength women were famous for. He could only admire her and lament his lack of it.

After getting into bed, he lay back against the pillow with a troubled sigh. He realized it was too late to decide not to go through with the dude ranch idea for the fallen soldiers' families. He and the guys had put three months of hard labor into their project to get everything ready. The Barettas had already arrived and were now asleep in one of the new cabins.

They had their work cut out for them, but Carson was afraid they'd fall short of their desire to make a difference. In fact he was *terrified*.

The next morning Tracy pulled on a pair of jeans and a sage-colored cotton sweater. It had a crew neck and long sleeves. She'd done some shopping before this trip. If it got hot later in the day, she'd switch to a blouse. The cowboy boots she'd bought last evening felt strange and would take some getting used to.

After giving her hair a good brush, she fastened it at the nape with a tortoise-shell clip. Once she'd put on lotion and applied lipstick, a shade between coral and pink, she was ready for the day.

"Who's hungry for breakfast?" she asked, coming out of the bathroom into the sunny room with its yellow and white motif. But it was a silly question because Johnny didn't hear her. He'd been dressed for half an hour in his new duds, complete with a black cowboy hat and boots, and was busy loading his mustang again. Already he'd gone through a couple of rolls of caps, waking her up with a start.

She'd bought him three dozen rolls to keep him supplied, but at this rate he'd go through them by the end of the day. It was a good thing the cabins weren't too close together.

Tracy slipped the key in her pocket. "Come on, honey." She opened the door and immediately let out a gasp as she came face-to-face with the Grand Teton. In the morning sun it looked so different from last night when she'd had the sensation of it closing in on her. Against an impossibly blue sky, she'd never seen anything as glorious in her life.

Between the vista of mountains and the strong scent of sage filling the dry air, Tracy felt as if they'd been transported to another world. Even Johnny stopped fiddling with his cap gun to look. "Those sure are tall mountains!"

"They're magnificent!"

She locked the door and they started walking along the dirt road to the sprawling two-story ranch house in the distance. It was the kind you saw in pictures of the Old West, owned by some legendary cattle king.

"I hope they have cereal."

Tracy hoped they didn't. He needed to get off candy and sugar-coated cereal, his favorites when he could get away with it. His grandmother made all kinds of fabulous pasta, but he only liked boring mac and cheese out of the box. "Carson mentioned eggs, bacon and buckwheat pancakes."

"What's buckwheat?"

She smiled. "You'll have to ask him." The poor man had already answered a hundred questions last evening. She'd been surprised at his patience with her son.

Her eyes took in the tourist log cabins where she saw cars parked. Many of the outbuildings were farther away. Last night, Carson had pointed out the ranch manager's complex with homes and bunkhouses. He'd mentioned a shed for machinery and hay, a calving barn, horse barn and corrals, but it had been too dark to pick everything out. To Tracy the hundred-year-old ranch resembled a small city.

At least a dozen vehicles, from trucks, vans, and four-wheel-drives to a Jeep without a top and several cars, were parked at the rear of the ranch house. She kept walking with Johnny to the front, admiring the workmanship and the weathered timbers. The house had several decks, with a grove of trees to the side to provide shade. The first Lundgren knew what he was doing, to stake out his claim in this paradise.

They rounded the corner and walked up the steps to the entrance. An office was located to the left of the rustic foyer. At a glance to the right, the huge great room with a stone fireplace led into a big dining room with wagon-wheel chandeliers.

"Hi! Can I help you?"

Johnny walked over to the college-aged girl behind the counter. "Hi! We're waiting for Carson."

The friendly brunette leaned over to smile at him. "You must be Johnny Baretta from Ohio."

"Yup. What's your name?"

"Susan. Anything you need, you ask me. Mr. Lundgren told me to tell you to go right on through to the dining room and he'd meet you there."

"Thank you," Tracy spoke for both of them.

"Welcome to the ranch, Mrs. Baretta."

"We're thrilled to be here. Come on, honey."

They were almost to the dining room when a handsome, fit-looking man, probably Carson's age and height, came forward. Though he wore a plaid shirt and jeans, with his shorter cropped black hair she could imagine him in Marine gear. His brown eyes played over her with male interest before they lit on Johnny.

"I'm Ross Livingston, Carson's friend. You must be the brave guy who ate a buffalo burger last night."

"Well…" He looked at Tracy. "Not all of it," Johnny answered honestly. "It was too big."

"I know, and I'm impressed you got through most of it."

Tracy laughed and he joined her, provoking the same kind of cough she'd heard come out of Carson. "Excuse me," he said after it had subsided. "It's not contagious in case you were worried."

"We're not. Carson already explained."

"Good. He got detained on the phone, but he should be here in a minute. Come into the dining room with me, Johnny, and we'll get you served."

They followed him. "Do you know if they have cereal?"

"Sure. What kind do you like?"

"Froot Loops."

"You're in luck."

"Goody!"

Tracy refrained from bursting his bubble. Tomorrow they'd choose something else.

Ross guided them across dark, vintage hardwood floors in keeping with the Western flavor to an empty table with a red-and-white-checked cloth. A vase of fresh white daisies had been placed on each table. She found this setting charming.

When he helped them to be seated, he took a chair and handed them Saturday's menu from the holder. "In a minute the waitress will come to take your order."

She scanned the menu.

"Mom? Do they have hot chocolate?"

Tracy couldn't lie. "Yes."

"Then that's what I want with my cereal."

"I'll let you have it if you'll eat some meat. There's sausage, bacon or ham."

"And brook trout," Ross interjected, smiling into her eyes as he said it.

She chuckled. "I think after the buffalo burger, we'll hold off on the fish for another day."

As he broke into laughter, the waitress came to the table, but she hadn't come alone. Their host had arrived without his hat, wearing another Western shirt in a tan color. The chiseled angles of his hard-boned features drew her gaze for the second time in twelve hours. He was all male.

"Carson!"

"Hey, partner—" He sat down next to Ross and made the introductions.

"Where's your hat?"

"I'll put it on after breakfast."

"I want to keep mine on."

"Except that it might be hard to eat with it," Tracy declared. "Let me put it on the empty chair until after."

"Okay."

The waitress took their orders and left.

Ross got up from the table. "Hey, Johnny, while you're waiting for your food, I'll take you out to the foyer and show you something amazing before I leave. Since I've already eaten, I have a group of guests waiting for me to take them fishing."

"What is it?" Ross had aroused his curiosity.

"Come with me and see."

"I'll be right back, Mom."

"Okay."

As they walked away, she heard Ross say, "I'm glad you came, Johnny. We're going to have a lot of fun while you and your mom are here."

"Your friend is nice," Tracy told Carson.

He studied her features for a moment, seeming to reflect on what she'd said. "He's the best. Right now he's showing Johnny the big moose head that was mounted years before I was born. It's the granddaddy of them all, but you don't see it until you're leaving to go outside."

"He's fascinated by the big animals."

"Did your husband hunt, or any of your family?"

"No."

"I've never been much of a hunter, either, but my grandfather allowed licensed hunters to use the land during the hunting season, so I do, too. I much prefer to see the elk and deer alive. There's great opportunity here to photograph the animals. I'll show Johnny lots of spots. He can hide in the trees and take pictures of squirrels and rabbits, all the cute little forest creatures."

"He'll go crazy."

"That's the idea."

To her consternation, Tracy found herself studying his rugged features and looked away. "There's so much to do here, it's hard to know where to start. When I read your brochure on the internet, I couldn't believe it."

He had an amazing white smile. "Most people can't do it all. They find something they love and stick to it. That'll be the trick with Johnny. We'll try him out on several things and see what he likes most."

"Mom—" He came running back into the dining room, bringing her back to the present. "You've got to see this moose! It's humongous!" That was Cory's favorite word.

"I promise I'll get a look at it when we go outside."

"Its head is as big as the Pierce's minicar!"

Carson threw back his head and laughed so hard, everyone in the room looked over. As for Tracy, she felt his rich male belly laugh clear through her stomach to her toes. The laugh set off another of his coughing spells. His blue eyes zeroed in on her. "Who are the Pierces?"

"Our neighbors down the street in Sandusky."

Johnny sat back down. "Ross thinks he looks like a supersize Bullwinkle."

"He's that, all right."

Tracy smiled at him. "I have a feeling you and Ross are both big teases. Can I presume your other friend is just as bad?"

"He has his moments," he drawled. "You'll meet Buck tomorrow when he's back from taking some guests on an overnight campout."

"Can we go on one of those?"

Carson's brilliant blue gaze switched to Johnny. "I'm planning on it."

Johnny's face lit up. "I want to see that elk with the giant antlers."

"You liked that picture?"

"Yeah. It was awesome."

"I couldn't agree more, but I don't know if he's still around. My grandpa took that picture a few years ago. Tell you what. When we're out driving and hiking, we'll look for him."

The waitress came with their food. Tracy's omelet was superb. She ate all of it and was gratified to see Johnny finish his ham. Carson put away steak and eggs, then got up from the table.

"Give me five minutes and I'll meet you out in front in the Jeep. We'll drive over to the barn." He coughed for a moment. "Normally we'd walk, but I'm planning to give you a tour of the property after your riding lesson. It'll save time. The restrooms are down the hall from the front desk."

"Thank you. The breakfast was delicious by the way."

"I'm glad you enjoyed it." He turned to leave.

"See you in a minute, Carson! Don't forget your hat!"

That kid made him chuckle. He'd done a lot of it since last evening. More than he'd done in a long time.

He walked through the doors to the kitchen and nodded to the staff. After putting some bottled water and half a dozen oranges and plums in a bag, he headed down another hall to the bedroom for his Stetson.

Making certain he had his cell on him, he headed out the rear door of the ranch with more energy than usual. Susan would phone him if there were any problems. After stashing the bag in the backseat, he started the engine and took off.

Try as he might, when he drove around the gravel drive to the front, he couldn't take his eyes off Tracy Baretta. From the length of her sinuous body to her blond hair gleaming in the morning sun, she was a knockout. But she didn't seem to know it. That was part of her attraction.

"There's nothing wrong with looking," his grandfather used to say to him. "But if a woman's off-limits, then that's the way you keep it." Carson had adopted that motto and it had kept him out of a hell of a lot of trouble.

This woman was Tony Baretta's widow and still grieving for him.

Shut it off, Lundgren.

Johnny started toward him. "Can I ride in front with you?"

"You bet." He jumped out and went around to open both doors for them, trying to take his own advice as he helped Tracy into the backseat.

Once they got going, Johnny let out a whoop of excitement. "I've never ridden in a Jeep before. This is more fun than riding on a fire engine."

"I don't believe it."

"It's true!"

Carson glanced at him. "I've never been on one."

"If you come back to Ohio, my uncles will let you go on their ladder truck."

"Sounds pretty exciting. But wait till you ride a horse. You'll love it so much, you won't want to do anything else."

"What's your horse's name?"

"I've had a lot of them. My latest one is a gelding named Blueberry. He's a blue roan."

Johnny giggled. "You have a blue horse?"

"Seeing's believing. Wait till you meet your palomino. She's a creamy gold color with a white mane and tail." *Almost as beautiful as your mother.* "Have you thought of a name yet?"

"No."

"That's okay. It'll come to you."

They headed for the barn. He'd talked to Bert ahead of time. The pony had been put in the corral so Johnny would see it first off. He drove the Jeep around till they came to the entrance to the corral. There stood the pony in the sun. Carson stopped the Jeep.

"Oh, Johnny—look at that adorable pony!"

The boy stared for the longest time before scrambling out of the front seat. He'd left his mustang behind.

"Wait!" His mother hurried after him, but he'd already reached the fencing before she caught up to him.

Carson joined them. "Isn't she a little beauty?"

Johnny's head jerked toward him. The excitement on his face was worth a thousand words. "I'm going to call her Goldie."

"That's the perfect name for her." The pony walked right over to them. "Good morning, Goldie. This is Johnny. He's flown a long way to meet you."

Carson lifted the boy so he could reach over the railing. "You notice that pretty white marking? That's her forelock. Watch what happens when I rub it. She's gentle and likes being touched."

The pony nickered and nudged closer. "See?"

Johnny giggled and carefully put out his hand to imitate Carson's gesture. He got the same reaction from Goldie who moved her head up and down, nickering more intensely this time.

"She loves it and wants you to do it some more."

As he patted the horse with increasing confidence, Tracy flashed Carson a smile. It came from her eyes as well as her mouth. That was a first.

He dragged his glance away with reluctance. "Come

into the barn with me, Johnny. We'll go in the tack room to pick out her saddle."

"Tack room?"

Carson shared another smile with Tracy. "It's a room where we keep the saddles and bridles for the horses."

"Oh." Johnny jumped down. "We'll be right back, Mom."

Carson had a hunch the boy was hooked. You never knew. Some kids showed little interest or were too scared and didn't want to ride. This little guy was tough. *Like his father.*

"I'll be waiting."

Johnny asked a dozen questions while they gathered everything, impressing Carson with his bright mind that wanted to learn. This was a new world for Carson who, as an adult, had never spent time taking care of anyone's child. He found Johnny totally entertaining and quite wonderful.

As a kid, Carson had grown up around the children whose parents worked on the ranch, and of course, the neighbor's kids. A couple of the boys, including his best friend Jean-Paul, wanted to be rodeo champions. So did Carson, whose grandfather had been a champion and taught him everything he knew.

In between chores and school, they'd spent their free time on the back of a horse, learning how to be bull-doggers and bull riders. As they grew older there were girls, and later on women, prize money and championships. But it still wasn't enough. He'd wanted to get out and see the world. He'd joined the Marines on a whim, wanting a new arena.

Through it all, Carson had taken and taken, never

giving anything back. The pain over his own selfishness would never go away, but Johnny's enthusiasm wouldn't allow him time to wallow in it.

He carried the equipment to the corral and put the bridle on Goldie. Johnny stood by him, watching in fascination. "Here you go. Hold the reins while I get her saddled."

The pony moved forward and nudged Johnny. He laughed and was probably scared to death, but he held on. "She likes you or she wouldn't do that. You'll get used to it."

Carson threw on the blanket, then the saddle. "Okay. Now I'd like you to walk around the corral leading Goldie. Just walk normally, holding on to the reins. She'll follow. It will help her to learn to trust you, because she's nervous. Do you want me to walk with you, or do you want to do it yourself?"

He thought for a minute. "I can do it."

"Fine."

The whole time this went on, Carson was aware of his mother watching in silence from the fence as her brave son did a slow walk around the enclosure without a misstep. At one point she took some pictures with her cell phone.

"Great job, Johnny. Now walk her to that feeding bag. Dig in and pull out a handful of oats. If you hold them out to her with your hand flat, she'll eat them without hurting you, but it'll tickle."

Johnny laughed nervously, but he did what Carson told him to do. In a minute he was giggling while the pony enjoyed her treat. "It feels funny." He heard Tracy laugh from the sidelines.

"You've made a friend for life, Johnny. Think you're ready to get up on her?" The boy nodded. "Okay." Now the next lesson was about to begin. "I'm going to seat you in the saddle, then I'll adjust the stirrups." Carson lifted him. "You hold on to the reins and the pommel. Are you all right? I know it seems a long way up. Did you ever fall off the tricky bars at school?"

"Yes."

"Well, this is a lot safer because you've got this pony under you and she loves you. She doesn't want you to fall. Okay if I let go of you?"

"Okay," he said in a shaky voice.

Carson took a few steps back, ready to catch him if he suddenly wanted to get off. But he didn't. "Good man."

"You look like a real cowboy!" his mother called out. "I'm so proud of you!"

"Thanks."

Moving to the front of the pony Carson said, "I'm going to take hold of the bridle and walk Goldie. You keep holding on to the pommel so you can feel what it's like to ride her. Does that sound okay to you?"

Johnny nodded, but was biting his lip.

"We'll only go a few feet, then we'll stop."

"Okay," the boy murmured.

Carson started to walk. Goldie cooperated. When he stopped, she stopped. "How did that feel? Do you want to keep going?"

"Yes."

"Good for you. I've seen ten-year-olds out here who started bawling their heads off for their moms about now." He moved again and just kept going until they'd circled the corral. "You just passed your first lesson with flying colors, Johnny." He heard clapping and cheers from Tracy.

A big smile broke out on his face. "Thanks. Can I go around by myself now?"

That's what he'd been hoping to hear, but you never knew. "Why not? Let me show you how to hold the reins. If she goes too fast, just pull back on them a little. Ready?" He nodded.

"I'm going to give Goldie a little tap on her hind quarters to get her going. Okay?"

"Yup."

Suddenly they were off at the same speed as before, but without his help. Carson walked over to the fence where Tracy was hanging over it.

"Hey—I'm doing it. I'm riding!" he cried out.

"You sure are," she called back. "I can't believe it!"

"It's easy, Mom." He circled one more time. "Now it's your turn."

Carson saw the expression on her face and chuckled. "Yeah, Mom. It's easy. Now it's time for you. Better not let your son show you up."

"He already has. I'm quaking in my new leather boots."

"I shivered my first time, too, but I promise it will be okay. Annie's a gentle, sure-footed mare."

She got down off the fence and walked around to enter the corral. Carson waited until Goldie had come up to him before he removed the boy's feet from the stirrups and pulled him off. "Give her a rub on the forelock, then she'll know you had a good time."

Johnny did his bidding without any hesitation. "Can I give her some more oats?"

"Of course." He handed him the reins. "Go ahead. You know what to do."

While he walked her over to the feed bag, Carson called to Bert to bring out Annie, and then he made the introductions. "Bert Rawlins, this is Tracy Baretta. Bert has been running the stable for years."

Tracy shook his hand. "It's a pleasure to meet you."

"The feeling's mutual, ma'am. Annie's saddled and ready to go."

Carson reached for the reins and handed them to Tracy. "Let's see how good a teacher I am."

There was more green than gray in her eyes today. They were suspiciously bright. "You already know. My son's over there feeding that pony like he's been living on this ranch for a month."

Nothing could have pleased Carson more. He watched her move in front of the bay and rub her forelock. She nickered on cue.

"This is my first time, Annie. Don't let me down." Pulling on the reins, she started walking around the corral just as her son had done.

Carson decided the brown horse with the black mane and tail provided the perfect foil for her gleaming blond hair. When she came around, he helped her into the saddle and adjusted her stirrups. "Would you like me to walk you around?"

"I think I'll be all right." What did they say about a mother walking into a burning building for her child?

He handed her the reins and gave the horse's rump a tap. Annie knew what to do and started walking. Halfway around the arena, Carson knew Tracy would be all right.

"Hey, Mom—it's fun, huh?"

"It will be when I've had a few more lessons."

Annie kept walking toward Carson. He looked up at Tracy. "Want to go around one more time, pulling on the reins to the right or left?"

"Sure."

He was sure she didn't, but she was game.

"This time, give her a nudge with your heels and she'll go."

The second she made contact, Annie started out. It surprised Tracy, knocking her off balance, but she righted herself in a hurry.

"If she's going too fast, pull on the reins and she'll slow down."

Little by little she made it around the enclosure, urging the horse in one direction, then another.

"You're doing great, Mom!"

"You both are. I think that will be all for today."

Carson signaled Bert to take care of the horses. "Come on, Johnny." He walked over to help Tracy, but she was too quick for him. She flung her leg over and got down on her own. Whether she did it without thinking or didn't want help, he didn't know.

"Are we going for a Jeep ride now?"

"Would you like that, partner?"

"Yes. Then can we come back to see Goldie? I think she'll miss me."

Johnny was showing the first signs of a horse lover. Either it was in you, or it wasn't. "I'm sure she will."

The three of them got back in the Jeep. For the next

hour, he gave them a tour of the property so they could get their bearings. Johnny talked up a storm while a quieter Tracy sat back and took in the sights. As they neared the ranch house, his cell phone rang. The caller ID indicated it was the district ranger for the Bridger-Teton National Forest.

"Excuse me for a minute. I have to take this," he said to them before answering. "Dave? What's up?"

"There's a man-made fire started up on the western edge of the forest bordering your property."

Carson grimaced. Tourist season always brought on a slew of forest fires.

"I've assembled two crews and am asking for any volunteers who can help stamp it out to meet up at the shadow rock trailhead," Dave continued. "There's not much wind. I think we can contain it before it spreads."

Before hanging up, Carson said, "I'll rustle up as many of the hands as I can and we'll be there shortly."

This would happen today, of all days. The hell of it was, with his disease, he didn't dare help fight the fire. Smoke was his enemy. All he could do was bring help and wear his oxygen apparatus.

Johnny looked at him. "Do you think I can take another ride on Goldie after dinner? I want to turn her in different directions and do stuff with her."

"I suppose that's up to your mother." Carson's gaze flicked to Tracy. "Did you hear that, Mom? What do you say?"

Chapter 3

Tracy heard it. In fact, she heard and saw so many things already, she was starting to experience turmoil. Johnny was eating up all the attention Carson showered on him. It would continue nonstop until next Saturday when they flew home.

With all their own family and work responsibilities, none of Johnny's uncles could give him this kind of time. Not even Tony had spent every waking hour with their son in the due course of a day. No father did, unless they were on vacation. Even then there were other distractions.

Few fathers had the skills or showed the infinite patience of this ex-marine rancher who seemed to be going above and beyond any expectations. He had to be a dream come true for her son, who'd been emotionally starving for a male role model since Tony's death.

When she'd accepted the invitation to come to the ranch, she hadn't realized these former soldiers would spend their own personal time this way. She had assumed the ranch staff would offer activities to entertain them. Period.

This was different.

Carson was different.

By giving Johnny that photo of his father, Carson had formed a bond with her son that wasn't going to go away. Carson might not see what was happening, but every moment invested for Johnny's sake increased her son's interest.

Tracy couldn't allow that to happen. Before long they'd be leaving this place, never to return. Johnny was still dealing with his father's death. They didn't need another crisis after they got home. She had to do something quickly to fix things before he got too attached to this incredible man. Tracy had to acknowledge that, so far, he *was* incredible, which was exactly what made her so uneasy.

While he'd driven them around the breathtaking property, giving them fruit and water, she'd sat in the back of the Jeep planning what she would say to Carson when she could get him alone. Another lesson at the corral after dinner was not an option.

Tonight after they'd eaten, she and Johnny would watch a movie in their cabin until he fell asleep. Then she'd phone Carson and have an important talk with him. Once he understood her concerns, he would make certain his partners spent equal time with Johnny. By the time he pulled up in front of their cabin to let them out, she felt more relaxed about her decision.

"I kept you longer than planned, but we're still in time for lunch."

Johnny looked up at him. "What are you going to have, Carson?"

"I think a grilled cheese sandwich and a salad."

"Me, too."

Since when? Tracy mused.

Carson tipped his Stetson. "See you two inside."

She slid out, not wanting to analyze why what he just did gave her a strange feeling in her tummy, as Johnny was wont to say. "Come on, honey. Don't forget your mustang."

To her relief, Carson drove off. "Let's use the restroom first, then maybe we'll find some other kids and you can play with them."

A few minutes later they entered the dining room. Ross was seated at a larger table with some tourists, including a couple of children. He waved her over. "Come and sit with us, Tracy. We're all going to do some more fishing after we eat and hope you'll join us."

Bless you, Ross.

"Johnny? Meet Sam Harris, who's seven, and Rachel Harris, who's nine. They're from Florida. This is Johnny Baretta from Ohio. He's six."

"I'm almost seven!"

Tracy smiled. "That's true. Your birthday is in a month." He'd be one of the older ones in his class in the fall.

After they sat down, Ross finished introducing her to Monica and Ralph Harris, who were marine biologists. The Tetons had to be a complete change of scenery for them, too.

Soon the waitress came over and took everyone's order. Carson still hadn't come. Tracy knew Johnny was looking for him.

Sam, the towheaded boy, glanced at Johnny. "How long are you here for?"

"A week."

"Same here. Then our parents have to get back to work."

"Oh."

"Where's your dad?" Rachel asked.

Johnny had faced this question many times, but Tracy knew it was always painful for him. "He died in the war."

"That's too bad," she said, sounding genuinely sad. "Do you like to fish?"

"My dad took me a couple of times."

"We'll catch our limit this afternoon," Ross chimed in, no doubt anxious to change the topic of conversation.

By the time lunch arrived, Carson had come into the dining room and walked over to their table, but he didn't sit down. Ross introduced him to everyone while they ate. "Mr. Lundgren's great-great-grandfather purchased this land in 1908 and made it into the Teton Valley Ranch."

"The ranch house was a lot smaller than this in the beginning," Carson informed them.

"You're sure lucky to live here," Sam uttered.

"We're lucky you came to visit."

Carson always knew the right thing to say to make everyone feel good.

"To my regret, something's come up and I won't be able to join you this afternoon, but Ross is an expert and will show all of you where to catch the biggest fish. When you bring them in, we'll ask the cook to fix them for your dinner. There's no better-tasting trout than a German brown."

"He ought to know," Ross interjected. "He was fishing the Snake with his grandpa when he was just a toddler."

Everyone laughed except Johnny, who'd become exceptionally quiet.

"Enjoy your day. See you later," Carson said. His glance included Tracy and Johnny before he hurried out of the dining room.

"Where's he going?" her son whispered.

"I don't know, honey." Something had come up. Though he'd shown nothing tangible, she'd felt his tension. "He runs this ranch with his friends and has a lot of other things to do." *Thank heaven.*

"Do we have to go fishing?" He'd only eaten half of his grilled cheese and didn't touch the green salad, which was no surprise.

"Yes." Her automatic instinct had been to say no, because she was afraid to push him too hard. But right now she decided to take the psychologist's advice and practice a little tough love. "It'll be fun for both of us. I've never been fly fishing and want to try it."

"Okay," he finally muttered. At least he hadn't fought her on it. "But I bet I don't catch one."

"I bet you do. Think how fun it will be to phone your grandparents tonight and tell them everything."

This was the way their vacation was supposed to be. Doing all sorts of activities with different people. Unfortunately, Carson had gotten there first and had spoiled her son. Nothing and no one was more exciting than he was, even Tracy recognized that.

Ross got up from the table. "I'll bring the van in front and we'll go." He came around to her side. "Is everything all right?" He'd assumed there'd been a hard moment at the table for Johnny. He'd assumed correctly, but for the wrong reason. She couldn't tell Ross what was really going on inside Johnny, not when these wonderful marines were doing everything in their power to bring her son some happiness.

She smiled at him. For once this wasn't about Tony, or Johnny's sensitivity to a child's question. This was about Carson. "Everything's fine. Honestly. See you in a minute."

Sam got out of his chair and came over to Johnny, who was putting another roll of caps into his mustang. "Where did you get that cap gun?"

"In Jackson. Carson took us."

He turned to his parents. "Can we go into town and buy one?"

"I want one, too," Rachel chimed in.

Their mother gave Tracy that "what are you going to do?" look. Tracy liked her. "Maybe after we're through fishing."

Tracy took her son aside. "Why don't you go out front and let them shoot your gun for a minute?"

"Do I have to?"

"No, but it's a good way to make friends, don't you think?"

A big sigh escaped. "I guess." He turned to Sam. "Do you guys want to try shooting some caps outside?"

"Heck, yes!"

They both ran out and Rachel followed. Tracy walked over to the parents who thanked her.

"I'm glad Johnny has someone to play with. After dinner we could all drive into town and take you to the Boot Corral. You can get a cap gun and cowboy hats there, in fact, everything Western."

"That's a wonderful idea!"

"I'm afraid my son would sleep in all his gear and new cowboy boots if I let him."

Both Harrises grinned as they headed out of the dining room for the foyer. "This is a fabulous place," Ralph commented. "I wish we could stay a month."

Tracy understood how he felt. She was grateful his children would be here for Johnny. If she could drum up enough activities that included them until they flew home, maybe a talk with Carson wasn't necessary. She needed to let things play out naturally before she got paranoid. No doubt other families with children would be staying here, too, and her worries would go away.

The next time Johnny brought up Carson's name, she'd impress upon him that the owner of the ranch had too many responsibilities to be on hand all hours of the day.

Unfortunately, his name surfaced after their wonderful trout dinner when they'd all decided to go into town and do some shopping.

"I don't want to go, Mom. Carson's going to give me another lesson on Goldie."

"But he's not here, honey. We'll have to wait until tomorrow. Tell you what. After we get back from town, you and the kids can go swimming. How does that sound?"

He thought about it for a minute before he said, "Okay." Convincing him was like pulling teeth, but he liked the Harris children well enough to give in.

As it turned out, once they were back from town loaded with hats, guns and more ammo than they could use in a week, they realized it was too cool outside to swim. Monica suggested they play Ping-Pong in the game room off the dining room.

Tracy agreed and told Johnny to go along with them. She'd come back to the ranch house as soon as she'd freshened up. When she walked in the bedroom for their jackets, her cell phone rang. She checked the caller ID. It had to be her mother-in-law calling.

"Hello, Sylvia?"

"No, it's Natalie. We came over for dinner before we leave on our trip in the morning. I'm using her phone to call because I can't find mine. How are you doing by now? Or, more to the point, how's Giovanni? Is he begging to go back home? I've wondered how he would handle things. I guess you realize our father-in-law is worried about him."

That was no news. Since Tony's death, his father had tried to step in as father and grandfather.

"If you want to know the truth, things are going so well it's got me scared."

"What do you mean?"

"Mr. Lundgren might be a former marine, but he's the owner of this ranch and is this amazing cowboy who's showing Johnny the time of his life. My son has a new hero."

"Already?"

"I'm afraid so. You wouldn't recognize him."

"Why afraid?"

"That was a wrong choice of words."

"I don't think so. How old is this guy?"

Natalie always got to the crux. "Maybe twenty-nine, thirty. I don't know."

"Is he a hunk?"

"Nat—"

"He *is!*"

"Listen. I'd love to talk more, but I don't have time. This nice couple with two children is watching out for Johnny in the game room and he's waiting for me."

"You mean he's playing on his own without *you?*"

"I know that sounds unbelievable. In a nutshell, he's had his first horseback ride on the most beautiful golden pony you've ever seen, and he's in love with her."

"Her?"

"He named her Goldie. You should see him riding around in the saddle like a pro, all decked out in Western gear and a cowboy hat. We'll bring the same outfit home for Cory."

"You actually got him over his fear long enough to ride a horse?" She sounded incredulous. Tracy understood. Since Tony's death, Johnny showed reluctance to try anything new.

"Mr. Lundgren gave him his first lesson."

"How did he accomplish that?"

Tracy told her about the photo of his father Carson had given him at the airport. "That was the magic connection that built his trust."

"You're right. He sounds like some wonderful guy. What's his wife like?"

Tracy gripped the phone tighter. "He's not married.

Now, I really have to go. Have a great time on your trip to New York. We'll talk when I get back. Give our love to the family. *Ciao,* Nat."

There were no words to describe the ex-marine that would do him justice, so it was better not to try. No sooner had she disconnected than the phone on the bedside table started ringing. She assumed it was the front desk calling. Maybe it was Monica. She picked up. "Hello?"

"Hi, Tracy. It's Carson. Am I disturbing you?"

His deep voice rumbled through her. She sank down on her twin bed. After discussing him with Natalie, she needed the support. "Not at all. I was just on my way over to the ranch house to play Ping-Pong with the others."

"That sounds fun," he said before he started coughing. "I'm sorry about today. I'd fully intended to take you fishing and give Johnny another horseback riding lesson."

She gripped the phone a little tighter. "Please don't worry about that. Ross did the honors. Even *I* caught a twelve-incher. It was my first time fly fishing. I must admit it was a real thrill to feel that tug and reel it in."

"How did it taste?"

"Absolutely delicious."

"That's good," he murmured before coughing again.

She moistened her lips nervously for no good reason. "I take it you had to deal with an emergency."

"You could say that. A couple of college kids out backpacking in the forest didn't do a good enough job of putting out their campfire. It took several crews of rangers and forest service workers to keep it from spreading too far onto ranch property."

Her breath caught. That was why she'd felt his tension at the table. "How much did it burn?"

"Only a few acres this time."

"*This* time?"

"It happens every year." Suddenly he was hacking again. "Some fires are more devastating than others."

"Does that mean you were breathing smoke all day?"

"No. I rounded up the hands and drove them to the fire in shifts, but I took oxygen with me."

"Even so, you shouldn't have been near there with your problem," she said before she realized her voice was shaking.

"There was no one else to do the job. Undeserving as I am, I have to try to save what my grandfather willed to me."

She got to her feet. "What do you mean by undeserving?"

"Forget my ramblings. It slipped out by accident."

"And I heard it, which means you inhaled too much smoke today and don't feel well. You ought to be in bed."

"A good night's sleep is all I need. I'll let you go so you can join your son. It would be better not to tell him about the fire."

"Agreed." She couldn't let him hang up yet. "Carson, how long were you in the hospital?"

"About five weeks. From the end of January to the beginning of March."

"Were you all suffering from the same illness?"

"On our ward, yes."

His cough worried her. "Are you getting better?"

"We're certainly better than we were when we were flown in."

"I mean, are you going to get well?"

"We don't know."

She frowned. "You mean the doctor can't tell you?"

"Not really. They're doing studies on us. The day before we left the hospital, a general came to talk to us about asking Congress for the funding to help our cause."

"The Congress doesn't do enough," she muttered.

"Well, at least he came to our floor and said he's rooting for us, so that's better than nothing."

"Then you could have a lifelong ailment."

"That's right, but we can live with it, even if no one else can. The ranch house gets pretty noisy when the three of us have a coughing fit together."

He tried to make light of it, but she wasn't laughing. "You're very brave."

"If you want to talk brave, let's talk about your husband. Why did he join the Marines?"

"His best friend went into the military and got killed by friendly gunfire. It tore Tony apart. He decided to join up to finish what his friend had started. We were already married, but I could tell he wanted it more than anything. We were lucky to go to Japan together before he was deployed to Afghanistan. It doesn't happen often that a marine can go there with his wife."

"You're right."

"During 9/11 I saw those firefighters run into those torched buildings and I wondered how they did it. Then I met Tony and understood. It's in his genes, I guess."

"Those genes saved lives, Tracy. That's why you can't talk about him in the same breath you talk about me and the guys. We're no heroes."

But they were.

"You shouldn't have gone near that fire today."

"That's the second time you've said it."

"I'm sorry. Johnny's been worried about you, too."

"Tracy," he said in a deep voice, "I appreciate your concern more than you know. I haven't had anyone worry about me in a long time. Thanks for caring. We'll see each other at breakfast. Good night."

He hung up too fast for her to wish him the same. Afraid he'd be up all night coughing, she knew that if she didn't hurry to the game room she'd brood over his condition. And his state of mind, which was none of her business and shouldn't be her concern. But to her chagrin, she couldn't think about anything else on her way to the ranch house.

Carson had medicated himself before going to bed, but he woke up late Sunday morning feeling only slightly better. It wasn't just his physical condition due to the smoke he'd inhaled the day before, despite the oxygen. When he'd phoned Tracy last night, he hadn't realized how vulnerable he'd been at the time. His sickness had worn him down and caused him to reveal a little of his inner turmoil, something he regretted.

She was a guest on the ranch. He was supposed to be helping to lift her burden for the week instead of talking about himself.

He grabbed his cell phone to call his ranch foreman and get an update on the progress with the fencing in the upper pasture. After they chatted for a few minutes, he dragged his body out of bed to shower and shave.

Once dressed, he walked through the ranch house to the kitchen and poured himself some coffee. He talked to the cook and kitchen help while he drank it, then entered the dining room and discovered a few guests still eating, but no sign of Tracy or Johnny. Ross would know what was going on.

Carson went to the office, but the place was empty. Since Buck wouldn't be back until lunchtime, he headed for the foyer to talk to Susan. "How's everything going?"

"Great!"

"Have you seen Ross?"

"Yes. Another couple of groups went fishing with him. Did you know that by this evening we'll be all booked up?"

"That's the kind of news I like to hear."

Like most ranches, the cattle operation on the Teton Valley Ranch had little, if any, margin. But the value of the land kept rising faster than the liability from raising cattle. It was either sell the hay, grass and cows to someone else, or borrow on the land when the market was down. In time he hoped the dude ranch idea would bring in its own source of revenue.

"Johnny Baretta was asking about you this morning. He can't wait for another horseback riding lesson."

That news pleased him even more. "Do you have any idea where he and his mother might be?"

"I heard him and the Harris children talking about going swimming. You should have seen how cute they all looked in their cowboy outfits when they came in for breakfast."

"I can imagine. Talk to you later."

He walked outside and headed around the other side of the house to the pool area. The swimming pool had been Buck's idea and was a real winner for children and people who simply wanted to laze about. The kids' shouts of laughter reached his ears before he came upon the two families enjoying the water.

"Carson!"

Johnny's shriek of excitement took him by surprise and touched him. "Hey, partner."

The boy scrambled out of the pool and came running over to him. Above his dark, wet hair he saw Tracy's silvery-gold head as she trod water. Their eyes met for a brief moment, causing a totally foreign adrenaline rush. "Can we go horseback riding now?"

"That's the plan," he said before breaking the eye contact.

Like clockwork, the other two children hurried over to him dripping water. "Will you take us riding, too?"

He chuckled. It brought on another coughing spell. "Of course. Anyone who wants a lesson, meet me at the corral in fifteen minutes!" he called out so the parents would hear him. They waved back in acknowledgment. As he turned to leave, he heard Rachel ask Johnny why Carson coughed so much.

"Because he breathed all this bad stuff in the war."

"What kind of stuff?" Sam wanted to know.

"Smoke and other junk."

"Ew. I hope I never have to go."

"I wish my dad had never joined the Marines." Johnny's mournful comment tore Carson apart.

He hurried back inside the ranch house to grab a bite of breakfast in the kitchen. While he downed bacon and eggs, he phoned Bert and asked him to start saddling Goldie and two of the other ponies.

After they hung up, he packed some food and drinks in a basket. In a minute, he left through the back door and placed the basket in the back of the truck, then climbed in. The interior still smelled of acrid smoke.

If the kids wanted some fun after their lesson, he'd let them get in the back and he'd drive them to the pasture to see the cattle. When he'd been a boy, he'd enjoyed walking around the new calves and figured they would, too.

When he reached the barn, he saddled Annie, but held off getting more horses ready for the Harrises. They might not want to ride, only watch their children.

Another lesson for Tracy and her son ought to be enough for them to take a short ride down by the Snake River tomorrow. With enough practice, they'd be able to enjoy half-day rides around the property.

If Johnny could handle it, they'd camp out in the Bridger-Teton forest where there were breathtaking vistas of the surrounding country. Even if the journey would be bittersweet, he longed to show them his favorite places. Since joining the Marines, he hadn't done any of this.

Once Annie's bridle was on, he grasped the reins and walked her outside to the corral where Bert had assembled the ponies. In the distance, he saw the children running along the dirt road toward them. All three were dressed in their cowboy outfits.

Johnny reached him first. "Do you think Goldie missed me?"

"Why don't you give her forelock a rub and find out?"

Without hesitation he approached the golden palomino. "Hi, Goldie. It's me." He reached out to touch her. The pony nickered and nudged him affectionately. "Hey—" He turned to Carson. "Did you see that? She really likes me!"

While Burt grinned, Carson burst into laughter. It ended in a coughing spasm, but he didn't care. "She sure does."

"I'm going to feed her some oats." Seizing the reins without fear, he walked her over to the feed bag.

Knowing Bert would keep an eye on him, Carson approached the fence. Beneath the brim of his Stetson, his gaze fell on Tracy whose damp hair was caught back with a hair band. This morning she wore a tangerine-colored knit top and jeans her beautiful figure did amazing things for. "Are you ready for your next lesson?"

"I think so." Her smoky green eyes smiled at him before she entered the corral.

"Would you like some help mounting?"

"Thank you, but I'd like to see if I can do this on my own first."

This was the second time she hadn't wanted him to get too close. The first time he might have imagined it, but the second time led him to believe she was avoiding contact. He forced himself to look at the Harrises, who'd just come walking up.

"Should I ask Bert to saddle some horses for you?"

They shook their heads. Ralph leaned over the fence. "We've been riding before. Right now, we just want to see how the kids do."

"Understood." He turned to Johnny. "Hey, partner—why don't you help me show Rachel and Sam what you do before you get on."

"Sure! Which pony do you guys want?"

"That was a good question to ask them, Johnny."

Sam cried, "Can I have the brown one with the black tail?"

"Bruno is a great choice."

"I like the one with the little ears and big eyes. It's so cute."

Carson nodded. "That dappled gray filly is all yours, Rachel. Her name is Mitzi."

The children loved the names.

"Okay, Johnny. What do they do now?"

"They have to rub their noses so the ponies will know they like them."

The next few minutes were pure revelation as Tracy's son took the kids through the drill, step by step, until they were ready to mount.

Ridiculous as it was, Carson felt a tug on his emotions because Johnny had learned his lesson so quickly and was being such a perfect riding instructor. He glanced at Tracy several times. Without her saying anything, he knew she was bursting with motherly pride.

Soon all four of them were astride their horses. They circled the corral several times and played Follow the Leader in figure eights, Johnny's idea. Carson lounged against the fence next to the Harrises, entertained by the children who appeared to be having a terrific time. Since Tracy rode with them, Carson had a legitimate reason to study her without seeming obvious.

He threw out a few suggestions here and there, to help them use their reins properly, but for the most part, the lesson was a big success. Eventually he called a halt.

"It's time for a rest," he announced and was met with sounds of protest. "Bert will help you down. I know it's fun, but you need a break and so do the ponies. I'll give you another lesson before dinner. Right now, I thought you might like to ride to the upper pasture with me and see some Texas Longhorns."

Johnny looked perplexed. "What are those?"

"Beef cattle."

"We're not in Texas!" Sam pointed out.

"Nope, but they were brought from there to this part of the country years ago. Want to get a look at the herd?"

"Yeah!" they said with a collective voice.

He turned to the Harrises. "I'll bring them back for lunch. You can come along, or you're welcome do something else."

Ralph smiled. "If you don't mind, I think we'd like to take a walk."

"Good. Then we'll meet you back at the ranch around one o'clock."

While they talked to their children about being on their best behavior, Carson walked over to Tracy who'd once again gotten off her horse without assistance. "Are you going to ride with us?"

"Please, Mom?" Johnny's brown eyes beseeched her.

Apparently she had reservations. Maybe she hadn't

been around other men since her husband's funeral and didn't feel comfortable with him or any man yet. Operating on that assumption he said, "I was going to let the kids ride in the truck bed. If you're with them, you can keep a close eye on what goes on. Those bales of hay will make a good seat for you."

She averted her eyes. "That ought to be a lot of fun."

Johnny jumped up and down with glee. "Hey, guys—we're going to ride in the back of the truck!" The other two sounded equally excited.

Pleased she'd capitulated, Carson walked over to the truck and lowered the tailgate. One by one he lifted the children inside. Before she could refuse him, he picked her up by the waist and set her down carefully. Their arms brushed against each other in the process, sending warmth through his body. After she scrambled to her feet, he closed the tailgate and hurried around to the cab.

With his pulse still racing, he started the engine and took off down the road, passing the Harrises. The children sat on the bales and clung to the sides of the truck while they called out and waved. Through the truck's rear window, Carson caught glimpses of her profile as she took in the scenery. Haunted by her utter femininity, he tried to concentrate on something else. Anything else.

There'd been a slew of women in his life from his teens on. One or two had held his interest through part of a summer, but much to his grandfather's displeasure, he'd never had the urge to settle down. It had been the same in the military.

Carson couldn't relate to the Anthony Barettas of this world, who were already happily married when deployed. Though foreign women held a certain fascination for Carson, those feelings were overshadowed by his interest in exotic places and the need to experience a different thrill.

Then came the day when his restlessness for new adventures took a literal hit from the deathly stench of war. Suffocation sucked the life out of him, extinguishing former pleasures, even his desire to be with a woman. Of no use to the military any longer, he'd been discharged early but had returned to the ranch too late to make up to his grandfather for the lost time.

Since he'd flown home from Maryland, the idea of inviting the Baretta family and others like them to the ranch had been the only thing helping him hold on to his sanity. Giving them a little pleasure might help vindicate his worthless existence, if only for a time.

Never in his wildest imagination did he expect Tony Baretta's widow to be the woman who would arouse feelings that, to his shock, must have been lying dormant since he'd become an adult.

Somehow, in his gut, he'd sensed her importance in his life from the moment they'd met at the airport. Nothing remotely like this had ever happened to him before. He couldn't explain what was going on inside him, let alone his interest in one little boy. But whatever he was experiencing was so real he could taste it and feel it.

Next Saturday they'd be flying back to Ohio. He already felt empty at the thought of it, which made no sense at all.

Chapter 4

After passing through heavily scented sage and roll-ing meadows, the truck wound its way up the slopes of the forest. The smell of the hay bales mingled with the fresh fragrance of the pines, filling the dry air with their distinctive perfume.

To the delight of both Tracy and the children, they spotted elk and moose along the way. Carson slowed down the truck so they could get a good look. Rabbits hopped through the undergrowth. The birdsong was so noisy among the trees, it was like a virtual aviary. Squirrels scrambled through the boughs of the pines. Chipmunks chattered. Bees zoomed back and forth.

Tracy looked all around her. The earth was alive.

Life was burgeoning on every front. She could feel it creeping into her, bringing on new sensations that were almost painful in their intensity, sensations she'd thought never to experience again.

For so long she'd felt like the flower in the little vase Johnny had brought home from school for Mother's Day. The pink rose had done its best, but after a week it had dried up. She kept it in the kitchen window as a reminder of her son's sweet gift. Every time she looked at it, she saw herself in the wasted stem and pitiful-looking petals—a woman who was all dried up and incapable of being revived.

Or so she'd thought....

After following a long curve through the trees, they came out on another slope of grassy meadow where she lost count of the cattle after reaching the two hundred mark. They came in every color. In the distance she saw a few hands and a border collie keeping an eye on the herd. Carson brought the truck to a stop and got out.

"Oh," Rachel half crooned. "Some of the mothers have babies."

Tracy had seen them. With puffy white clouds dotting the sky above the alpine pasture, it was a serene, heavenly sight of animals in harmony with nature. "They're adorable."

Carson walked around to undo the tailgate. Beneath his cowboy hat, his eyes glowed like blue topaz as he glanced at her. "Every animal, whether it be a pony or a calf, represents a miracle of nature. Don't you think?"

"Yes," she murmured, unexpectedly moved by his words and the beauty of her surroundings.

Johnny's giggle brought her head around. "Look at the funny calf. She's running away."

"Buster won't let her get far." Carson lowered the children to the ground. Tracy stayed put on her bale of hay. "Wouldn't you like to walk around with us?"

"They won't hurt you, Mom."

She chuckled. "I know. But from up here I can get some pictures of you guys first." Tracy pulled out her cell phone to make her point. "I'll join you in a minute." She didn't want Carson's help getting down. To her chagrin she still felt his touch from earlier when he'd lifted her in.

After she'd snapped half a dozen shots, she sat down on the tailgate and jumped to the ground. The children had followed Carson, who walked them through the herd, answering their myriad questions. Why were some of the calves speckled and their mothers weren't? How come they drank so much water? He was a born teacher, exhibiting more patience than she possessed.

Soon the dog ran up to them, delighting the kids. Tracy trailed behind, trying not to be too startled when some of the cows decided to move to a different spot or made long lowing sounds.

Carson cornered one of the beige-colored calves and held it so the children could pet it. Their expressions were so priceless, she pulled out her camera and took a couple of more pictures for herself and the Harrises, who would love to see these.

The hour passed quickly. When he finally announced it was time to get back to the ranch house, the children didn't want to go. He promised them they could come again in a few days.

"Do you think that calf will remember us?" Johnny wanted to know. All the children had to run to keep up with his long strides. Luckily their cowboy hats were held on with ties and didn't fall off.

As Tracy looked at Carson waiting for his answer, their

gazes collided. "I wouldn't be surprised. The real question is, will you remember which calf you played with?"

"Sure," Sam piped up. "It had brown eyes."

A half smile appeared on Carson's mouth, drawing Tracy's attention when it shouldn't have. "I'm afraid they all have brown eyes. Every once in a while a blue-eyed calf is born here, but their irises turn brown after a couple of months."

Rachel stared up at him. "Do you think there might be one with blue eyes in this herd?"

"Maybe. Tell you what. The next time I bring you up here, you guys can check all the calves' eyes. I'll give you a prize if you can find a blue pair."

"Hooray!" the children cried.

On that exciting note, he lifted them into the truck and shut the tailgate without reaching for Tracy.

Perhaps he wasn't thinking when he did it, but it meant she'd be riding in the cab with him. He must have been reading her mind because he said, "Riding on top of a hay bale might work one way, but you've got more horseback riding to do and deserve a break." Flashing her a quick smile, he turned to the kids.

"That basket in the corner has water and fruit for you guys. How about handing your mom a bottle, Johnny?"

"Okay. Do you want one, too?"

"I sure do. Thanks. Your mom's going to ride in front with me. That means everyone sits down the whole time and holds on tight to the side."

"We will," they said in unison.

"That's good. We don't want any accidents."

"Please be careful," Tracy urged the kids.

"Mom—we're not babies!"

Carson's chuckle turned into a coughing spell as he helped her into the passenger side of the truck. Their fingers brushed when he handed her the bottle of water. This awareness of him was ridiculous, but all she could do was pretend otherwise.

He shut the door and went around to the driver's side. She could still smell residual smoke from yesterday's forest fire. Carson should have been spared that.

Before he got in, he drank from his bottle. She watched the muscles working in his bronzed throat. He must have been thirsty, because he drained it. After tossing it in the basket in back, he slid behind the wheel.

She drank half of hers, not so much from thirst but because she needed to occupy herself with some activity. "What do you call the color of that calf the children were petting?"

"Slate dun."

"I knew it couldn't be beige."

In her peripheral vision, she noticed him grin. "In a herd of Longhorns you'll see about every color of the rainbow represented, including stripes and spots."

"Thank you for giving us this experience." She took a deep breath of mountain air. "There's so much to learn. Johnny's going to go home loaded with information and impress his relatives. That's saying a lot since they always sound like they know everything about everything and don't hold back expressing it."

His chuckle filled the cab. "Is he homesick yet?"

"I thought he would be. When we were flying into Jackson, I was afraid he would want to turn right around and go back. But nothing could be further from the truth. The second he caught sight of the tall dude who told him he'd take him shopping for some duds like his, he's been a changed child. For your information, tall doesn't run in the Baretta family. Neither does a Western twang."

He darted her a quick glance. "Johnny wasn't outgoing before?"

"He was…until Tony died. Since then he's been in a reclusive state. The psychologist has been working with me to try to bring him out of his shell. When I get back to Ohio, I'm going to give him your business card and tell him to send all his trauma patients to the Teton Valley Dude Ranch. It's already doing wonders for his psyche."

"That's gratifying to hear, but let's not talk about your going home yet. You just barely got here. I'm glad we're alone so you can tell me what kinds of things he wants to do the most. I don't want him to be frightened of anything."

"Well, I can tell you right now he's crazy about Goldie and would probably spend all his days riding, pretending he's a cowboy."

"He seems to be a natural around her."

"That's because of the way you introduced him to horseback riding. You've given him back some of the confidence he's lost this last year. That was a masterful stroke when you handed him the reins and suggested he walk the pony around first so she would get used to him. In your subtle way, you sent the hint that Goldie was nervous, thereby taking the fear from Johnny.

"I held my breath waiting for him to drop the reins and run over to me. To my shock, he carried on like a trouper. When he was riding her around, he wore the biggest smile I've seen in over a year. That's your doing, Carson. You have no idea the wonders you've accomplished with him already. I'm afraid you're going to get tired of my thanking you all the time."

"That's not going to happen. If my grandpa could hear our conversation, he'd be gratified by your compliment since he was the one who taught me everything I know about horses and kids."

She bit her lip. "You miss him terribly, don't you?"

"Yes. He and my grandmother were kind, wonderful people. They didn't deserve to be burdened with a headstrong, selfish grandson so early in life."

Tracy took another drink of water. "There's that word *deserve* again. Don't you know every child is selfish? The whole world revolves around them until they grow up and hopefully learn what life's really about."

His hands tightened on the steering wheel. "Except I grew up too late. I should never have left him alone."

"Did he try to keep you from going into the Marines?"

"No. Just the opposite in fact," he said before another coughing spell ensued.

"He sounds like a wise man who knew you had to find your own path. Tony's two brothers who wanted to be police officers instead of firemen got a lot of flack from the rest of the family, especially from their father. He thought there was no other way to live, but two of his sons had other ideas. It has left resentments that seem to deepen."

"That's too bad. How did he handle Tony going into the Marines?"

"He didn't like it. But by then Tony was a firefighter and planned to come back to it when he got out of the service. As long as his sons fell in line, he was happy. To this day, he's still angry with the other two. He needed to take lessons from your grandfather."

"Unfortunately nothing removes my guilt. I was his only family left."

"It sounds like he wanted *you* to be happy. That was more important to him. He took on a sacred trust when he took over your upbringing. I feel the same way now that Tony's gone. It's up to me to guide my son. I'm terrified I'll make mistakes. What worries me is the struggle Johnny's going to have later on."

"In what way?"

"His grandfather will expect him to grow up and take his place among the Baretta firefighters. Imagine his shock when we go home and Johnny announces he's going to be a cowboy like his friend Carson when he grows up."

Her comment seemed to remove some of the stress lines around his mouth that could grow hard or soft depending on his emotions. "These are early days, Tracy. Your son's going to go through a dozen different stages before he becomes a man."

She moaned. "Let's hope he doesn't end up suffering from your problem."

His brows furrowed. "What do you mean?"

Tracy looked through the back window to make sure the children were all right.

"I've been keeping an eye on them," he murmured, reading her mind again. Of course he had. He had a handle on everything, inspiring confidence in everyone, old or young.

"I don't want Johnny to be afraid to reach out for his dreams for fear of leaving me on my own. He's especially aware of it since learning I lost my parents at eighteen. Sometimes he shows signs of being overly protective. A few months ago he told me he would never leave me and planned to take care of me all my life."

"There's a sweetness in that boy."

"Don't I know it, but I refuse to exploit it. That's one of the main reasons why I decided to accept your invitation to come to the ranch. If I don't help him to live life the way he should, then I'm failing as a mother. You and your friends have done a greater service for our family than you can possibly imagine. I know I said this before. You were inspired, and I—I'm indebted to you." Her voice caught.

He sat back in the seat. "After so much heartache, do you have any idea how much I admire you for carrying on? Tell me something. How did you continue to function after your parents were killed? I can't imagine losing them both at the same time."

"We had fantastic neighbors and friends at our church. Between them and my close friends, they became my support group and helped me while I was in college. Then I met Tony and was swept into his family."

He cast her a glance. "Swept off your feet, too?"

She nodded. "Natalie, my sister-in-law who's married to Joe, one of the out-of-favor police officers in the family, has become my closest friend. They have an eight-year-old son, Cory, who gets along famously with Johnny. I've been very blessed, so I can't complain."

After a silence Carson said, "What's the other reason you decided to accept our offer?"

"To be honest, I was becoming as much of a recluse as Johnny." She told him about the Mother's Day flower.

"Your letter jerked me out of the limbo I'd been wallowing in. Once I caught sight of the Tetons in the brochure, I lost my breath. Like your stomach that flew around in the air for a week after your first flight with your grandpa, I haven't been able to get my breath back since."

"After a visit to the Tetons, some people remain in that state."

"Especially you, who came home from war struggling for yours. You and your friends have paid a heavy price. I admire you more than you know."

She'd been struggling, too, but it was from trying to keep her distance from him, which was turning out to be impossible. Tracy didn't understand everything going on inside him, but she realized that keeping her distance from him would be the wrong thing to do at the moment. Johnny was beginning to thrive. In a strange way she recognized they were all emotionally crippled because of the war and needed each other to get stronger.

"Do you mind if I ask you a personal question?"

"Go ahead."

"Why isn't there a Mrs. Lundgren?"

"You wouldn't like to hear the truth."

"Try me."

"The psychiatrist at the hospital did an evaluation on all of us. That was his first question to me. When I told him I preferred new adventures to being tied down, he told me I was an angry man."

"Angry—*you?*"

Carson laughed. "That was my response, too. He told me that was a crock. He said I'd been angry all my life because my parents died. That anger took the form of flight, whether it was sports, travel, the military. He said I was too angry to settle down. But with this illness that cramped my style, it was time I came to grips with it and let it go, or I'd self-destruct."

"And have you let it go?"

"I'm trying, but when I think of what I did to my grandfather, I can't forgive myself. There's so much I've wanted to say to him."

"Don't you think he knew why you were struggling? Did he ever try to talk to you about it?"

"Thousands of times, but I always told him we'd talk later. Of course that never happened. Then the opportunity was gone."

"As my in-laws used to tell me when I wallowed in grief over my parents' death, 'You'll be together in heaven and can talk everything over then, Tracy.' I've come to believe that. One day you'll have that talk with your grandfather."

"I'd like to believe it, but you've got more faith than I have."

Tracy sat there, pained for him and unable to do anything about it. Quiet reigned inside the cab as they drove through the sage. The children, on the other hand, were whooping it up, firing their cap guns. Johnny was becoming her exuberant child again. She had to pray it wasn't solely because of Carson.

The Harris family couldn't have come to the ranch at a better time. Tracy would involve them in as many activities as possible, because every new distraction helped.

As they drove around to the front of the ranch house, a cowboy with an impressive physique whom she hadn't seen before stood talking to some guests. He had to be the third ex-marine.

The moment he saw Carson, he left them and walked over to the truck. He removed his hat and peered in his friend's open window, allowing his green eyes to take her in. He wore his curly light-brown hair longer than the other two men and was every bit as attractive.

"Welcome to the ranch, Mrs. Baretta. We've been looking forward to your visit." His remark ended with the usual cough. The sound of it wounded Tracy because she knew at what cost they'd served their country.

"Tracy? This is Buck Summerhays. Now you've met all three amigos."

"It's a privilege, Mr. Summerhays. Johnny and I can't thank you enough for making us so welcome."

"The honor of meeting Tony Baretta's family is ours. Call me Buck."

Carson opened the door. "Come on. I want you to meet Johnny and the other two children."

While he got out, Tracy hurriedly opened her door and jumped down, not wanting any assistance. Everyone congregated at the rear of the truck. The men helped the children down, and Carson made the introductions.

Buck shut the tailgate before turning to everyone. "Where have you dudes been?"

"To see the cows," Sam spoke up.

Rachel nodded. "Next time we're going to look for calves with blue eyes. Carson's going to give us a prize if we find one."

His lips twitched. "Is that so." His gaze fell on Johnny. "Now that you've been to the pasture, what do you want to do this afternoon after lunch?"

"I'd like to ride Goldie some more."

"Who's that?"

"My pony."

"Ah." His twinkling eyes sent Carson a silent message. "I was thinking I'd take you guys on a float trip down the river."

"That sounds exciting," Tracy intervened. "How about we all do that with Buck? After dinner you can have another horseback ride before bed."

"Yeah!"

Johnny wasn't quite as enthusiastic as the other two, but he didn't put up an argument for which she was thankful. "Then come on. Let's go in and wash our hands really well. After that we'll find your parents and eat." She herded the children inside the ranch house so the men could talk in private.

Carson noticed Buck's eyes linger on Tracy as she disappeared inside the doors. He knew what his buddy was going to say before he said it.

"You're a cool one." He switched his gaze to Carson with a secretive smile. "*Nice* has to be the understatement of all time."

"Her son's nice, too."

"I can see that." Suddenly his expression sobered. "Tony Baretta shouldn't have had to die."

His throat swelled with emotion for their suffering. "Amen." After more coughing he said, "I'll park the truck around back."

"I'll come with you."

In a minute they'd washed up and entered the kitchen to eat lunch.

"How was the pack trip?"

"It went without a hitch, but I noticed there are a lot of tourists already."

"There'll be a ton more as we get into summer."

They devoured their club sandwiches. "I'm thinking that on this first float trip we'll stay away from any rapids. If they enjoy it, then we'll do a more adventurous one in a few days."

"Sounds good."

"Ross is busy fishing with another group for the afternoon. Are you going to come?" Buck eyed Carson over the rim of his coffee cup.

"No. I need to lie down for a couple of hours."

Buck frowned. "Come to think of it, you don't seem yourself. What's going on?"

Carson brought him up to speed on the forest fire. "I kept the mask on as much as possible, but I still took in too much smoke."

"You shouldn't have gone near there."

"That's what Tracy said." He could still hear the concern in her voice.

His buddy's brows lifted in surprise. "Did you tell her about the fire?"

"I had to so she wouldn't think I was abandoning Johnny. When I called her to explain, I was hacking almost as badly as when we were first brought into the hospital. If I ever needed proof of how bad it is for us, yesterday did it. None of us should ever get anywhere close to a fire if we can possibly help it."

"Tell me about it. Last night I had a few coughing spasms myself and realized I needed to stay away from the campfire."

"We need to take oxygen and inhalers with us everywhere, in case we're caught in a bad situation."

"Agreed."

"Tell Johnny and the kids I have ranch business and will meet them at the corral after dinner for another lesson. Let Willy know I'm here if an emergency arises." The part-time apprentice mechanic from Jackson alternated shifts with Susan and Patty at the front desk for the extra money.

"Will do. Take it easy." He looked worried.

Carson got up from the table. "I've learned my lesson. See you tonight."

He left the kitchen and headed for his bedroom. Though he was a little more tired than usual after yesterday's incident, he was using it as an excuse to stay away from Tracy. Carson felt like he was on a seesaw with her.

Sometimes she seemed to invite more intimate conversation, particularly when she talked about not wanting to manipulate her son's feelings. Despite the blow that had changed her life, she had a healthy desire to be the best mom possible. He felt her love for Johnny, and it humbled him.

But other times, she'd keep her distance. He didn't know how to penetrate that invisible wall she threw up, no doubt to protect herself.

She'd married into a family that kept her and Johnny close. If she'd done any dating since her husband's death, it couldn't have made much of an impact. Otherwise, she wouldn't have left Ohio to come here for a week.

He stretched out on the bed. The more he thought

about it, the more he was convinced this was her first experience being around a man again in such an isolated environment. A few more days together and he'd find out if she saw him in any other light than her host while she was on vacation.

This was new territory for him, too. He needed to take it slow and easy. Like the stallion he'd broken in at nineteen, you had to become friends first. The trick was to watch and key in to all the signals before you made any kind of move. One wrong step and the opportunity could be lost for a long time. Maybe forever.

And there was Johnny.

It was one thing to be the man who taught him how to horseback ride. But it was something else again if he sensed someone was trying to get close to his mother. She'd said Johnny showed signs of being overly protective.

No man would ever be able to replace his father. It would take her son's approval and tremendous courage on Carson's part before he could begin to establish a personal relationship with her, even if she were willing.

Last but not least would be the great obstacle of the Baretta family, who would resent another man infiltrating their ranks. Worse would be their fear of Carson influencing Tony's son. He was their beloved flesh and blood.

Frustrated, he turned on his side. His thoughts went back to a certain conversation his grandfather had initiated.

"What are you looking for in a woman?"

"That's the whole point. I'm not."

"You don't want children some day?"

"I don't know."

"One of the things I love most about you is your honesty, Carson. Wherever the military takes you, don't ever lose that quality no matter what."

"Grandpa, are you really okay about my becoming a marine?"

"The only thing I can imagine being worse than your staying home for me when you want to be elsewhere, would be for me to have to leave the ranch when it's the only place I want to be. Does that answer your question?"

Oh yes, it answered it, all right. Carson had gone to do his tour of duty until it was cut short because he could no longer perform. Then he'd come home to the birthright his grandfather had bequeathed him without asking anything in return.

What tragic irony to be back for good, wanting to tell his grandfather that, at last, he could answer those questions. He wanted that talk so badly, tears stung his eyes. But it was too late to tell him what this woman and her son already meant to him.

When he couldn't stand it any longer, he got up to shower and change clothes. There was always ranch business that required his attention. Work had proved to be the panacea to keep most of his demons at bay. But when he left his room, instead of heading for the den, he turned in the other direction and kept on walking right out the back door to his truck.

After reaching the barn, he saddled Blueberry. On his way out he saw Bert and told him he'd be back at seven to give the children another riding lesson. The other man said he'd have the ponies ready.

Carson thanked him and rode off. His horse needed the exercise, and needing the release, Carson rode hard to a rise overlooking the Snake River. In his opinion, this spot on the property captured the view of the grand-daddy Teton at its most magnificent angle. He'd often wondered why his ancestor, Silas Lundgren, hadn't cho-sen to build the original ranch house here.

While he sat astride Blueberry, his mind's eye could imagine a house of glass, bringing the elements inside every room. Not a large house. Just the right size for a family to grow. Maybe a loft a little boy and his dog would love. From their perch they could watch a storm settle in over the Tetons, or follow the dive of an eagle intent on its prey.

The master bedroom would have the same view, with the added splendor of a grassy meadow filled with wild-flowers coming right up to the windows. While she marveled over the sight, he would marvel over *her,* morning, noon and night.

A cough eventually forced him to let go of his vi-sion. When he checked his watch, he saw it was almost seven o'clock. He had to give his horse another workout in order not to be too late.

As he came galloping up to the corral, he saw Tracy's hair gleaming in the evening rays of the sun. She was surrounded by both families, mounted and ready for another lesson. He brought Blueberry to a sliding stop.

"Wow—" Johnny exclaimed from the top of Goldie. "Will you teach me how to do that? It was awesome!"

Chapter 5

The man and horse truly were one.

Talk about rugged elegance personified in its purest form!

Except for Johnny, everyone else sitting on their mounts was speechless. Tracy realized she was staring and looked away, but she'd never get that picture of him out of her mind. The quintessential cowboy had been indelibly inscribed there.

"If you'll follow me," came his deep voice, "we'll take a short ride past the cabins. On the way back, I have a surprise for you."

"Won't you tell us?" Sam called to him.

"No," his sister chided him. "Then it won't be a surprise."

Tracy exchanged an amused glance with the Harrises. The three of them rode behind the children.

Johnny caught up to Carson. Two cowboys—one short, one tall—both wearing black Stetsons. She would love to hear their conversation, but the only sound drifting back was the occasional cough.

To see her son riding so proudly on his pony next to his mentor brought tears to her eyes. They'd been here such a short time, yet already he was loving this and showed no fear. Coming to the Tetons had been the right thing to do!

In the last twelve hours she hadn't heard him talk once about his father. In truth, Tony hadn't been actively in her thoughts, either. Neither she nor Johnny had memories here. The new setting and experiences had pushed the past to the background for a little while. As Natalie had reminded her, this was what the right kind of vacation was supposed to do for you.

Tracy hadn't believed it was possible, but this evening she was confronted with living proof that Johnny was enjoying life again. So was she. The old adage about a mother being as happy as her saddest child could have been coined with her and her son in mind. But not tonight. *Not tonight.*

At one point, Carson turned his horse around. Flashing everyone a glance he said, "We're going to head back now. The first person to figure out my surprise gets to choose the video for us to watch in the game room afterward."

The children cried out with excitement and urged their horses around, which took a little doing. Carson gave them some pointers. Tracy listened to his instructions so she wouldn't be the only one who had trouble handling her horse.

Pretty soon they were all facing west. Sam's hand went up like he was in school. Johnny's hand followed too late.

"Tell us what you think, Sam."

"The mountains have turned into giants!"

"That's what *I* was going to say," Johnny muttered. Tracy hoped he wouldn't pout.

Carson's horse danced in place. "They do look pretty imposing, but I'm still waiting for the special answer."

"*I* know."

"Go ahead, Rachel."

"The sun has gone down behind them, lighting up the whole sky with colors."

"Congratulations! It's the greatest sight this side of the Continental Divide." Carson lifted his hat in a sweeping gesture, delighting her. "The lovely young cowgirl on Mitzi wins the prize."

After the grownups clapped, Monica let out a sigh. "It's probably the most beautiful sunset I've ever seen, and we've watched thousands of them over the ocean in Florida, haven't we, Ralph."

"You can say that again."

Tracy agreed with them, especially the way the orangey-pink tones painted Carson's face before his hat went back on.

A sly smile broke the corner of his mouth. "First person to reach the corral wins a new currycomb."

Sam's brows wrinkled. "A curry what?"

"A kind of comb to clean your ponies after a ride. They love it."

"Come on!" Johnny shouted and made some clicking sounds with his tongue the way Carson had shown him. Goldie obeyed and started walking. In her heart of hearts, Tracy wanted her son to win.

In the end, the ponies hurried after Goldie. They kept up with each other and rode in together. Carson smiled at them. "You *all* win."

"Yay!"

While Bert helped the children down and unsaddled their ponies, Carson went into the barn and brought them each their prizes. Once he'd dismounted, he removed the tack from his horse and showed them how to move the round metal combs in circles. They got to work with a diligence any parents could be proud of. Then they watered the horses and gave them oats.

He was a master teacher. Tonight they'd learned lessons they'd never forget—how to appreciate a beautiful sunset, how to care for an animal, how to handle competition. The list went on and on, increasing her admiration for him.

"Who wants a ride back to the house?"

"We do!"

"Then come on." He punctuated it with a cough. "There's room for everyone in the back."

The men lifted the children. While Ralph helped Monica, Carson picked up Tracy. This time the contact of their thighs brushing against each other flowed through her like a current of electricity. She tried to suppress her gasp but feared he'd heard it.

On the short trip through the sage, the kids sang. They sounded happy, and Tracy started singing with them. It took her back to her youth. She'd had a pretty idyllic childhood. When Carson pulled the truck up in front of the house, she didn't want the moment to end.

Ralph moved first and helped everyone down, including Tracy. That was good. She didn't dare get that close to Carson again tonight. He'd kept the engine idling and said he'd see them in a minute before he took off around the back of the house. Everyone hurried inside to wash up.

Soon Carson joined them, bringing sodas from the kitchen. He sat on one of the leather chairs while the rest of them gathered round the big screen on two large leather couches. Fortunately, they had the game room to themselves.

To the boys' disappointment, Rachel chose *The Princess Bride,* but Tracy enjoyed it and got the feeling all the grownups did, too. Before it was over, both Sam and Johnny's eyes had closed. Ralph took his son home, leaving Rachel to finish the film with her mom.

Carson eyed Tracy. "Johnny's had a big day, too. I'll walk you to your cabin."

Her heart jumped at the idea of being alone with him, but to turn him down would cause attention. Instead, she said good-night to the others and followed him out of the ranch house while he held Johnny's hand. Her son was pretty groggy all the way to the cabin.

Tracy had to laugh when he staggered into the bedroom. Carson looked on with a smile as she got him changed into pajamas and tucked him into bed without a visit to the bathroom. "My son is zonked."

He nodded. "Johnny's gone nonstop all day. This altitude wears a man out."

She turned off the light and they went into the front room where another bout of coughing ensued. Tracy darted him an anxious glance. "You should be in bed, too."

Carson cocked his head. "Is that your polite way of trying to get me to leave?"

She hadn't expected that question. "No—" she answered rather too emotionally, revealing her guilt. "Not at all."

"Good, because I rested earlier and now I'm not tired." He removed his hat and tossed it on the table.

"Please help yourself to any of the snacks." She folded her legs under her and sank down on the end of the couch.

"Don't mind if I do." He reached for the pine nuts. The next thing she knew, he'd lounged back in one of the overstuffed chairs, extending his long legs. "We need to have a little talk."

Alarmed, she sat forward. "Is there something wrong?"

"I don't know. You tell me." Between narrowed lids his eyes burned a hot blue, searing her insides.

"I don't understand."

He stopped munching. "I think you do. You need to be honest with me. Are you uncomfortable around me?"

She swallowed with difficulty, looking everywhere except at him. "If I've made you feel that way, then it's purely unintentional. I'm so sorry."

"So you do admit there's a problem."

Tracy got to her feet. "Not with you," she murmured.

"Johnny, then?"

Her eyes widened. "How can you even ask me that?"

The question seemed to please him because the muscles in his face relaxed. "Does your family wish you hadn't come?"

"I know my in-laws were astounded you and your friends had made such an opportunity available in honor of their son. They were really touched, but I believe they thought Johnny would want to turn right around and come home."

One brow dipped. "Is that what you thought, too?"

"When I first told Johnny about the letter, he said he didn't want to go. I knew why. Wyoming sounded too far away."

"What did you do to change his mind?"

"I asked him if he at least wanted to see the brochure you sent. He agreed to take a look. The second he saw that photo of the Tetons, he was blown away."

Their gazes fused. "Those mountains have a profound effect on everyone."

"Then he wanted to know about white water. But something extraordinary happened when he saw that gigantic elk with the huge *horns*..." Carson chuckled. "He looked at me and I felt his soul peer into mine before he asked me if I wanted to go. He always asks me first how I feel when he wants something but is afraid to tell me.

"I still wasn't sure how he'd feel after he got here. In retrospect, even if he'd wanted to turn right around, that airplane trip from Salt Lake would have put him off flying for a while."

Carson's smile widened, giving her heart another workout.

"My sister-in-law Natalie thought it was a fantastic opportunity and urged me to accept the invitation, but I don't know how my in-laws really felt about my taking their grandson to another part of the continent."

The tension grew. "Now that you've ruled out all of that, we're back to my original question, the one you still haven't answered."

Naturally he hadn't forgotten where this conversation had been headed and wouldn't leave the cabin while he waited for the truth. "As you've probably divined, *I'm* the problem."

"Why?"

He had a side to him that could be blunt and direct when the occasion demanded. It caught her off guard. "I guess there was one thing I hadn't thought about before we left. After we arrived here, it took me by surprise."

"Explain what you mean." He wasn't going to let this go.

She took a fortifying breath. "I assumed we'd be coming to a vacation spot with all the activities mentioned, but it has turned out to be…more."

"In what regard?"

"I—I didn't expect the one-on-one treatment," her voice faltered.

"From me and my buddies?"

"Yes."

He got to his feet. "But that was the whole point."

Tracy nodded. "I realize that now. But for some reason, I didn't think your business enterprise meant it would be a hands-on experience involving you so personally."

His brows met in a frown. "A dude ranch is meant to cater to the individual. If the three of us weren't here, there'd be others giving you the same attention. After losing your husband, does it bother you to be around other males again? Is that what this is about? I've half suspected as much."

She felt her face growing red as an apple.

"Have you even been out with a man since he died?"

"I've been to faculty functions with men, but they've always been in groups."

"In other words, no, you haven't."

"No," she whispered.

"And now you're suddenly thrown together with three bachelors practically 24/7." He put his hands on his hips in a totally male stance. "I get it. And I'll tell you something."

At this juncture, she felt like too much of a fool to know what to say, so she let him talk.

"I haven't been out with a woman since I was transported from the Middle East to Walter Reed Medical Center. When we were discharged, I felt like I was going home to die. The only thing that kept me going was this plan I dreamed up with Ross and Buck to bring a little happiness to the families who were suffering the loss of a husband and father.

"Lady—when I saw you walk through the airport terminal, I was as unprepared as you were. It was one thing to visualize Anthony Baretta's widow and his son in my mind, but quite another to be confronted with the sight of you in the flesh."

Tracy lowered her head. "After thinking of you in the abstract, the sight of you was pretty overwhelming, too," she confessed. "I guess we'd been picturing three marines in uniform whom we'd get to meet at some point during our stay so we could thank you. Instead, we were greeted by the king of the cowboys, as Johnny refers to you in private. He wasn't prepared, either, and clung to me for a long moment."

"I remember," he said in a husky-sounding voice before another cough came on. "From a distance, he was your husband's replica. That is, until I saw both your faces close up."

She eyed him covertly. Close up or at a distance, Carson Lundgren was no man's replica. He was an original with a stature to match the mountains outside the cabin door. "I'm glad we had this conversation. I feel much better about everything."

"So do I. From now on we each understand where the other is coming from. It'll make everything easier."

Not necessarily. Not while her pulse was racing too hard.

"Pardon the expression, but you and Johnny are our guinea pigs in this venture. The next family we've invited will be arriving next month. Because of you, we'll be much better prepared for the emotional upheaval created by war, whatever it is. Thank you for being honest with me. It means more than you know."

"Thank you for a wonderful day."

His eyes deepened in color. "There's more to come tomorrow, if you're up for it. But after Johnny's experience flying into Jackson, maybe not."

She took an extra breath. "You're talking about a hot-air-balloon ride? The kind mentioned in your brochure?"

"It's an unprecedented way to experience the Teton Valley. Buck will be taking some groups up."

"I'd love to go, but I'll have to feel out Johnny in the

morning before breakfast. If it's mentioned at the table and the other children want to g—"

"I hear you," he broke in. "Johnny might be afraid, but will be too scared to admit it. I don't want to put him under any pressure. When you know how he feels, call the front desk. They'll put you through to me. If necessary, I'll give Buck a heads-up."

"Thank you. You have unusual understanding of children."

"I was a child once and had my share of fears to deal with. Peer pressure was a killer. I'm thinking that if he doesn't like the balloon idea, then we'll take a longer horseback ride tomorrow and enjoy an overnight campout on the property." He put his hat back on, ready to leave. For once she wasn't ready to let him go, but she had to.

"I can tell you right now he'll be in ecstasy over that option."

"Good. If it turns out to be successful, then he'll probably be ready to do another one in Teton Park. We'll take the horses up to String Lake. It's a great place to swim and hike around."

"Sounds heavenly."

She had to remember that he was working out the rest of their vacation agenda rather than making a date with her. Yet that's what it felt like. Her reaction was ridiculous considering she was a mother of twenty-seven instead of some vulnerable nineteen-year-old.

The only time she'd ever felt like this before was when she'd driven to Cleveland with some of her girlfriends from college. They were having a picnic at

Lakefront State Park when a crew of firefighters had pulled up to eat their lunch and toss a football around. The cutest guy in the group started flirting with her. Mr. Personality. He could talk his way in or out of anything. Tony was a mover who told her after one date that he was going to marry her.

When she thought of Carson, there was no point of comparison because he wasn't pursuing her. That was why she was a fool trying to make one.

"All we've talked about is Johnny's pleasure. Since this vacation is for you, too, why don't you tell me something you'd like to do while you're here?"

She laughed gently. "If he's happy, then that's what makes me happy, but I have to admit I enjoy riding. I had no idea I'd like it this much. You're a great teacher."

"That's nice to hear."

"It's true." After a brief pause because she suddenly felt tongue-tied, she wished him goodnight. He tipped his hat and left.

Tracy closed the door behind him and locked it. Though he'd walked away as if he was glad the air had been cleared, she was afraid she'd offended him. It was humiliating to realize he'd figured out her lame hang-up about being around a man again before she'd articulated it.

To make certain she didn't get the wrong idea about him, Carson had revealed his own surprise at meeting *her.* Then, in the nicest way possible, he'd let her have it by spelling it out she wasn't the only one suffering emotional fallout from the war.

When she finally got into bed, she felt worse than a fool.

* * *

When Tracy stepped out of the shower, she could hear Johnny talking to someone. Throwing on a robe, she walked into the bedroom just as he put her cell phone on the bedside table.

"Who was that, honey?"

"Grandma and Grandpa."

"Why didn't you tell me?"

"Because you were in the bathroom. They said they'd call back tomorrow morning 'cos they were in a hurry."

"How are they?"

"Fine. They want to see me ride Goldie. I told them Carson's been teaching me and took us to get my cowboy outfit and cap gun." He ran over and gave her an exuberant hug. "I'm having the best time of my whole life!"

"I'm so glad."

"When are we going home?"

Uh-oh. "Next Saturday morning. Why? Are you missing them too much?"

"No. What's today?"

"Monday." Time was flying.

She could hear him counting in his head. "So we have five more days?"

"Yes."

"Goody! I don't want to go home. I can't leave Goldie."

Tracy knew he'd said it in the heat of the moment, and she was happy about it, but the implication for what it might portend for the future stole some of her happiness.

Though home would be wonderfully familiar to her son after they got back, he would suffer his first attack of culture shock, because nothing in Sandusky or Cleveland compared remotely to Wyoming's Teton Valley.

"Mom? Do you like it here?"

That was one of his trick questions. He needed to find out what *she* really thought before he expressed exactly what *he* thought. No doubt her in-laws had asked him the same question.

She ruffled his hair. "What do you think? I got on a horse, didn't I?"

"Yes," he answered in a quiet tone.

Something else was definitely on his mind, but she didn't know if he was ready to broach it yet, so she asked him a question. "How would you like to go up in a hot-air balloon today and see the whole area?"

Tracy had to wait a long time for the answer she knew was coming. "Do you?" That lackluster question told her everything.

"I don't know. There are so many things to do here, it's hard to pick. We could fish or swim, or go on a hike."

No response.

"Maybe we ought to have a break and drive into town to do some sightseeing. I'll buy you some more caps."

"I don't want to do that," he muttered.

"Or…we could go horseback riding. I like it."

He shot up in her bed. His dark brown eyes had ignited. "I *love* it."

His reaction was no surprise, but the intensity of it had come from some part deep inside of him. "Then it's settled. Hurry and have your bath. After we're dressed we'll have breakfast and walk over to the corral."

Johnny pressed a big kiss right on her mouth. That

told her everything she needed to know before he scrambled out of her bed to the bathroom. When he was out of earshot, she called the front desk and was quickly put through to Carson.

"Good morning, Tracy." His voice sounded an octave lower, sending vibrations through her. Maybe it was due to his coughing, or maybe he sounded like that when he first awakened. "What's the verdict for today?"

She smiled. "Surely you don't need to ask."

"Well that answer suits me just fine, since there's nothing I'd rather do than be on the back of a horse. I'll tell Buck to go on without you. After you've eaten breakfast, I'll come by the cabin. You'll need saddle-bags to pack your things to stay overnight and go swimming."

"Swimming?"

"Yes. We'll be camping next to a small lake on the property. If Johnny has a camera, tell him to bring it. He'll have a field day taking pictures of the wildlife I was talking to you about."

An unbidden thrill of excitement ran through her. "We'll hurry."

Forty-five minutes later Carson swung by the cabin in the Jeep, having sent some of the hands to the lake to make preparations for everyone. Johnny was outside shooting off caps.

"Carson!" Like a heat-seeking missile, Tracy's boy came running in his cowboy hat. "Mom said we're going on a campout!" He clasped him around the waist, hugging him with such surprising strength, his hat fell off. Johnny had never been this demonstrative before.

Without hesitation, Carson hugged him back. "We sure are, partner," he answered in an unsteady voice, loving the feel of those young arms clinging to him. Nothing had ever felt so good.

As he started coughing, he looked up and saw Tracy on the porch step, but was unable to read her expression. She'd told him Johnny was protective of her. Without saying more than that, Carson got the point. Her son had a tendency to guard her.

But she couldn't have missed witnessing his exuberance with Carson just now. It had probably shocked her as much as it had him. Needing to return the situation to normal as fast as possible, he reached in the back of the Jeep and handed Johnny some gear.

"These saddlebags are for your stuff. The bigger one is for your mom. Will you take them into the cabin so she can pack what you need?"

"Sure."

"Remember to bring a jacket."

He flashed him a huge smile. "I will. I'll be right back."

Carson kept his distance and lounged against the side of the Jeep to wait. Pretty soon they came out. Johnny carried both bags and handed them to Carson to put in the back. It warmed his heart to see the boy was a quick learner.

"Can I ride in front, Mom?"

"If it's all right with Carson."

"Anything goes around here. Come on." He opened both passenger doors for them, avoiding eye contact with her. So much for the talk they'd had last night. Considering he was more aware of her than ever, it had accomplished absolutely nothing. "We'll drive to the barn and mount up."

"How come Rachel and Sam didn't come to breakfast?"

In the rearview mirror he noticed a pair of hazel eyes fastened on him.

"They ate early and went on an activity with Buck. He'll bring them to the camp later, but they won't be riding up with us."

"Hooray!"

"Johnny—" his mother scolded. "That wasn't nice to say."

"I'm sorry, but their ponies always come right up to mine."

Carson glanced at him in surprise. "So you noticed." He had natural horse sense. Everything the boy said and did pleased him.

"Yeah. They get in the way."

"I know what you mean. When it happens again, I'll teach you a simple trick so they'll leave Goldie alone."

"Thanks! How come they do that?"

"Have you ever heard of the three blind mice who hung around together?"

Johnny giggled. "Yes."

"That's what the ponies do, because they're friends. When you're on Goldie, you have to show them who's the boss."

"But how?"

"Have you ever heard the expression giddyup?"

"Yup."

"Well, you're going to practice saying that to Goldie today. And when you say it, you're going to nudge her sides with your heels. That'll make her go faster. Pretty soon she'll start to go faster every time you say the word and you won't need to use your heels. When she understands, then you wait until you're riding with the other kids. If their ponies start to crowd in on you, just call out 'giddyup' and see what happens."

"But what if that makes the other ponies go faster, too?"

Carson threw his head back and laughed, producing another cough. When it subsided, he could still hear Tracy's laughter. "That's a very astute question, partner. In all probability it will, so you'll have to ride even harder and make a lot of noise. But you'll also need to be prepared to pull on the reins so you don't lose control."

"That's going to be fun!"

Johnny bounced up and down on the seat all the way to the barn where their horses and pony were saddled. Carson parked the Jeep outside before grabbing the bags, including his own. He fastened a set behind each saddle while Bert helped Tracy and Johnny to mount.

Bert waved them off. "Have a good ride!"

"Thanks. We will!" Johnny called back. "See ya tomorrow, Bert."

"Okay, young fella."

Add another fan to Johnny Baretta's list. To charm old Bert wasn't an easy feat. So far the waitresses and desk staff, not to mention Carson's buddies, found him delightful.

Carson hadn't personally known Anthony Baretta, but he had a reputation in their division for being well liked and easy to get along with. Like father, like son.

Carson led them along a track through the sage in

a northeastly direction. Johnny followed, and Tracy brought up the rear. When they'd been going for a while, he fell back alongside Johnny and told him to start working on Goldie.

The first few times the boy said giddyup, he didn't use his heels fast enough and nothing happened. Johnny's frustration started to build.

"You have to be patient and listen to Carson, honey."

"But I *am* listening, Mom."

"Sure you are," Carson encouraged him. "The trick is to use your heels at exactly the same time you call out. Try a louder voice the next time."

"What if it doesn't work?"

"Then you keep trying until it does. Did I ever tell you about the first time I learned to ride a bull?"

"No. What happened?"

"I was training for the junior bull-riding competition. It was awful. I got unseated so fast every time, I was ready to cry."

"Did you?" came the solemn question.

"Almost. But then I looked at my grandpa. He was just standing there by the gate with a smile, telling me to try it again."

"What did you do?"

"I got so mad, I walked back behind the barrier and climbed on another bull. When the gate opened, I concentrated on what I'd learned, and guess what? I stayed on long enough for the other cowboys watching to clap."

"I bet your grandpa was happy."

"Yup, but not as happy as I was."

"I think I'll wait a little while before I try again," he announced.

Carson understood Johnny's sentiments well enough. He'd been there and done that many times before. "That's fine. We're in no hurry."

Tracy drew up along the other side of her son. "I hope you don't wait too long. We're coming to the forest."

Carson could sense her desire for Johnny to conquer this moment. It managed to fire her son who got a determined look on his cute face. All of a sudden they heard a loud giddyup rend the air and Goldie took off trotting. Johnny let out a yelp.

"Pull on the reins and she'll stop."

To Carson's delight, Johnny had the presence of mind to follow through and ended up doing everything right. He turned his pony toward them. "She *minded* me."

"Yup." Carson couldn't be more proud if Johnny were his own son. "Now she knows who's boss."

"You were amazing, honey!"

"Thanks."

When Tracy beamed like that, her beauty took Carson's breath. She stared at him through glistening eyes. "You've worked magic with him."

"He's *your* son, don't forget."

"I can't take any credit for this. His confidence level is through the roof. How do I thank you?"

"With that smile, you already have."

"Hey, you guys—aren't you coming?"

Johnny's question broke the odd stillness that had suddenly enveloped them. Both their shoulders shook with laughter at the same time. "What's the hurry?" Carson called out when he could find his voice.

"I want to keep riding."

"You mean you're not tired yet?"

"Tired? No way! Come on! Goldie wants to keep going."

"We're coming. Since you're in the lead, we'll continue to follow you."

"What if I get lost?"

"Hey, partner—we can't get lost. This is my back yard."

"Back yard!" Johnny laughed hysterically. "You're so funny, Carson."

He blinked. "No one in the world has ever said that to me before."

"Sometimes you really are," Tracy concurred. "As my son has found out, it's a very appealing side of you."

Carson felt an adrenalin rush. *Is that what you think too, Tracy?*

"Mom? How come you guys keep talking?"

He heard her clear her throat. "Because we're waiting for you to get going." She darted Carson an amused glance.

"Oh."

With less trouble than he'd demonstrated earlier, Johnny turned the palomino around and headed into the forest. The three of them were on the move once more, this time with Tracy at Carson's side. But after they got into the thick of the pines, the trail became less discernible in spots. Carson pulled alongside Johnny. His mother stayed right behind them.

"Seen any bad guys yet?"

"No, but I'm keeping a lookout."

"Got your mustang handy?"

"It's in my pocket. How far is the lake?"

"We wind up the slope for two more miles."

"What's it called?"

"I call it Secret Lake."

"Who else knows about it?"

"Only my best friends."

"You mean Ross and Buck?"

"That's right. And a few others. It's my favorite place. I can't let just anybody come up here. Otherwise it wouldn't be a secret."

Johnny looked over at him with those serious dark eyes. "Thanks for bringing me. I'm having the funnest time of my whole life."

Chapter 6

It was the second time Tracy's son had expressed the very sentiment she felt. She had to admit she was enjoying this trip a lot more than she'd anticipated. But along with this newfound excitement, her guilt was increasing.

Strictly speaking, it wasn't the guilt some war widows experienced, making them cling to the memory of their husbands. The love she and Tony shared would always be in her heart. They'd talked about the possibility of his dying, and she'd promised him she would move on if—heaven forbid—something happened to him. Since that horrible day, she'd been doing her best to make a full life for herself and Johnny.

This was a different kind of guilt, because she *didn't* feel guilty about enjoying Carson's company. To be honest, she was attracted to him. Very attracted.

Her biggest fear was that he'd already sensed it. Last

night he'd sounded relieved after they'd had their talk. As he'd explained, when he and his friends had put their plan into action, they'd done it purely to brighten up the lives of a few families affected by the war.

Neither Carson nor his friends wanted or expected some love-starved woman with a child to come on to them because she'd lost her husband. The thought had to have crossed his mind when they'd first met at the airport.

According to Carson, the three men had been bachelors when they'd joined the Marines. And they were still living that lifestyle outside of this special project that was bringing so much joy to Johnny's life. Since Tracy couldn't help what they were thinking, there was no point in being embarrassed. What she needed to do was be friends with all of them, the way she was with Tony's brothers. That was going to be especially hard when she was around Carson, but she could do it. And she would!

"Mom—there's the lake!"

Johnny's exultant cry jolted her back to the moment. They'd moved on ahead of her. "Good for you for finding it! Does it look like Lake Erie with lots of barges and a lighthouse?" she teased.

"Heck, no. It's little, with pine trees all around it."

She smiled. "Can you see any fish?"

"Can you?" she heard him ask Carson. *Oh, Johnny.* Her son was so predictable.

"See all those dark things moving around?"

"Yeah."

"The lake is full of rainbow trout."

"I don't see their rainbows."

"You will when you catch one." Carson was ever the patient teacher. "We'll cook it for your dinner tonight."

"Won't there be anything else to eat?" was her son's forlorn reply.

Carson's laughter warmed new places inside her. "We've got lots of stuff."

"That's good."

Tracy drew closer to them.

"Hey—I can see some tents and a table! Someone else is camping here." He didn't sound happy about that.

Carson laughed again. "Yup. That someone is *you,* partner. Those tents have already been set up for us."

"Whoa!"

"Maybe you'd like to sleep in that three-man tent with Sam and Rachel."

"Oh, yeah. I forgot they were coming. Where will you sleep?"

"Right next to you guys in my tent."

"What about my mom?"

"There's a tent for her and one for the Harrises. The one on the end is for Buck."

"But there are six tents."

"Yup. The extra one is where we keep the food and all the supplies we'll need. After we take care of the horses, we'll fix ourselves some lunch."

"Goody."

Their entertaining conversation was music to Tracy's ears. She finally broke through the heavy cover of pines to discover a small body of deep green water bathed by the sun. "This place looks enchanted."

While Carson put out some hay and water for the horses, he slanted her a hooded look. "It is."

She felt a shiver run through her. They'd already dismounted and he'd removed the saddles and bags.

"Come over here, Mom. I'll tie your reins to this tree the way Carson showed me."

"Such wonderful service deserves a kiss." She got down off her horse and planted one on her son's cheek.

"The latrine is around the other side in the trees, away from the camping area," he informed her.

Latrine. Since their arrival in Jackson, Johnny's vocabulary must have increased by a couple of hundred words at least. He was becoming a veritable fount of knowledge.

"Thanks. I'll keep that in mind." Without being asked, Tracy picked up their bags. "I'll take these."

"Put mine in the big tent."

"Didn't you forget to say something?"

"Oh, yeah. Please. I forgot."

"I know, but it's so much nicer when you remember."

Carson's eyes smiled at her before she started walking along the tree-lined shore toward the tents pitched some distance away. She undid the tie on the screen and entered the big one where three sleeping bags and extra blankets were rolled out. It was getting hot out, but the temperature inside was still pleasant.

She emptied his saddlebag and put his things in little stacks against the side of his sleeping bag. Then she left and picked out one of the other tents for herself. It didn't take her long to unpack.

When she emerged, she discovered Carson putting out picnic food on the camp table beneath some pine boughs to give them shade. Johnny had the duty of setting up the camp chairs.

Tracy approached them and looked all around. "With the smell of the pines so strong, this is what I call heaven on earth." She eyed her son. "Do you know how lucky we are, Johnny? Can you believe Carson and his friends have gone to all this trouble for us? We're going to have to think of something really special to do for them."

"I know."

They settled down to eat.

"Guess what?" Carson said after swallowing his second roast beef sandwich. "You've already done something special."

Johnny stopped chewing on his sandwich. "No, we haven't."

"Want to bet? You accepted our invitation to come. We hoped you and your mom would like the idea." He darted her a penetrating glance. "That's all the payment we needed."

Carson.

"At first I didn't want to." Her son was nothing if not honest.

"I don't blame you. I'd have been scared to go someplace where I'd never been before. I think you were very brave to come."

"I'm not brave, but my mom is."

"She sure is." In an unexpected gesture, Carson pulled out his phone and clicked on the photo gallery. "Now take a look at this." He handed it to Johnny.

"That's me riding Goldie!"

"Yup. How many kids do you know your age who can go on a trail ride in the mountains on their own pony?" Tracy hadn't seen him take a picture. She was amazed. Had he taken one of her, too?

Johnny's brown gaze switched from the photo to study Carson. "I don't know any."

"Neither do I. So don't ever tell me Tony Baretta's son isn't brave." Carson's expression grew serious. "You're just like your dad and I'm proud to know you."

The conviction in his tone shook Tracy to the core and affected Johnny to the point of tears. They didn't fall, but they shimmered on the tips of his lashes with every heartbeat. "I'm proud of you, too. You're sick all the time and still do *everything.*"

If Tracy wasn't mistaken, Carson's eyes had a suspicious sheen. As for herself, a huge lump had lodged in her throat.

"If everyone's finished eating, what do you say we put the rest of the food in the bear locker and go for a swim? Remember we have to fasten it tight. Occasionally a black bear or a grizzly forages through this area, but unlikely you'll ever see one."

Johnny looked at Tracy. "Don't worry, Mom. Carson brought bear spray. He'll keep us safe."

She lifted her gaze to a pair of blue eyes that blinded her with their intensity. "I have no doubt of it."

The three of them made short work of cleaning up and went to their respective tents to change into their bathing suits. When Johnny was dressed, he came running with his beach sandals and towel to her tent. She'd put a beach cover-up over her one-piece blue floral suit.

Before leaving Sandusky, she'd searched half a dozen shops to find something modest. Other women didn't mind being scantily clad, but she wasn't comfortable walking around like that.

Once she'd covered them in sunscreen, she grabbed

her towel and they both left the tent in search of Carson. He'd beaten them to the shore and was blowing up a huge inner tube with a pump. Johnny squealed in delight.

The only thing more eye-catching than the sight of this pristine mountain lake was Carson Lundgren dressed in nothing more than his swimming trunks. Tracy had trouble not staring at such an amazing, hard-packed specimen of male beauty.

She felt his keen gaze play over her before he said, "Johnny? I want you to wear the life jacket I left on the table. Even if you're a good swimmer, I'll feel much better if you wear it while we're out here. Don't be fooled by this lake. You can only wade in a few feet, then it drops off fast to thirty feet."

Johnny's dark head swung around. "Okay." He ran over and put it on. Tracy made sure he'd fastened it correctly.

"I think we're ready!" Carson announced. He tossed the tube in the water, then dove in and came up in the center with a lopsided smile that knocked her off balance. "Come on in, and we'll go for a ride."

Johnny needed no urging and started running. Tracy threw off her cover-up and followed him in. "Oh—this water's colder than I thought!"

"It's good for you," Carson said, and then promptly coughed. The moment was so funny she was still laughing when he helped her and Johnny to grab on to the tube. Once they were all comfortable, he propelled them around.

They must have been out there close to an hour, soaking up the sun and identifying wildlife. Sometimes they swam away from the tube. Carson flew through the water like a fish and played games with them. When everyone was exhausted, they went back to shore to dry off and get a cold drink.

"I think it's time for a little rest."

"But Mom, I have to go talk to Goldie. She's missed me."

"You can see her in a little while. Come on. It's time to get out of the sun."

"What are you going to do, Carson?"

He'd been coughing. "I've got a few phone calls to make, partner. It won't be long before Buck arrives with the Harrises."

Tracy didn't know how he was able to spend so much time with them when he had the whole operation of his cattle ranch to worry about. "Thank you for another wonderful day, Carson."

He flicked her a shuttered glance. "It's only half over."

She knew that, yet the fact that he'd mentioned it filled her with fresh excitement. With an arm around Johnny, Tracy walked him to her tent, but stopped by his to get him a change of clothes. Once he was dressed, he lay down on top of her roomy sleeping bag. After she got dressed, she joined him. In two seconds, he was asleep.

Tracy lay there wondering if Carson's calls were all business. Since he'd come home from war, surely he'd been with women he'd met in Jackson or through his business contacts, even if it hadn't been an official date. That would go for his friends, too. Any woman lucky enough to capture his interest would be wondering why he hadn't been as available lately.

When she realized where her thoughts had wandered, she sat up, impatient with herself for caring what he did in his off time. She was supposed to be thinking of him as a friend, but her feelings weren't remotely like anything she felt for her brothers-in-law.

He would have been a charmer during the years he was competing in the rodeo. He had to be driving a lot of women crazy, these days, too. Carson was driving one woman crazy right here on the ranch and she didn't know what to do about it. Tracy had to admit those blue eyes and the half smile he sometimes flashed were playing havoc with her emotions.

After she'd met Tony, nothing had kept her from responding to him in an open, free way. Now, she had a son who came first in her life and the situation with Carson was so different it was almost painful. If he had feelings for her—sometimes, when he looked at her, she felt that he did—he hadn't acted on them. But then again, he was naturally kind and generous. She didn't dare read more into a smile or an intense look than was meant. He'd told her that she and Johnny were their guinea pigs.

The daunting thought occurred to her that Carson's emotions weren't invested, which explained why he never did anything overtly personal. Next month, another family devastated by the war would be arriving. He and his friends would welcome them and be as kind and attentive as they'd been to Johnny and her.

Maybe he'd meet a widow this summer who would be so desirable to him, he'd reach out to her because he couldn't help himself. Tracy groaned. What kind of woman might she be?

Tomorrow was Tuesday, and they only had four more days here. With her attraction to Carson growing, she'd found herself dreading the march of time, just like Johnny. But it suddenly dawned on her that without some signal from him, those days would seem like a lifetime.

Another worse thought intruded when she heard voices in the distance. Johnny heard them, too, and sat up, rubbing his eyes. She reached for her watch, which she'd taken off to go swimming. It was four-thirty. Buck appeared to have arrived with the others.

What if Carson had picked up on certain vibes from Tracy and had been including the Harris family in all their activities to keep everything on an even keel?

Was it true?

Maybe she was wrong, since she didn't know Carson's mind, but she cringed to think it could be a possibility.

"Hey, Johnny!" Sam was right outside her tent. "What are you doing? We're going swimming!"

"I'm coming, but I've got to get my suit back on!"

"Okay. Hurry!"

Off came his clothes. Soon he was ready. "Aren't you coming, Mom?"

"In a minute. You go on."

In case Carson was up for more play time in the lake, she decided against going swimming again. Grabbing her hairbrush and Johnny's beach towel, she left the tent and walked toward the others. Monica and Ralph waved to her. They were already in the water with the inner tube. "Come on in!"

"I just barely got out! How was the balloon ride?"

"Fantastic! You should try it before you leave the Tetons."

"Maybe I will!"

The children were clustered around Carson and Buck, who were handing out life jackets. She sat down in a camp chair, ostensibly to keep an eye on the children. But it was hard to focus when there were two tall, well-built ex-marines ready to enter the water. She finally closed her eyes and gave her damp hair a good brushing while she soaked in the heat.

The color of Tracy's hair shimmering in the sun was indescribable. The fine strands could be real silver and gold intertwined. While the kids played with the Harrises, Carson kept his eyes above the waterline to take in the curves of her exquisitely proportioned body.

Buck emerged from the depths next to him, coughing up a storm. "I agree she's quite a sight," he whispered when he'd caught a breath. "When are you going to do something about it?"

"Is it that obvious?"

"Not to anyone but me and Ross."

"We didn't invite her family to the ranch for me to make a pass."

Buck scowled. "Hey, it's me you're talking to. I damn well know that. Tell me the truth. You haven't gotten any signals from her that she'd like you to?"

"I don't know. It's hard to read her. She's warm and friendly enough when she's with Johnny, which is most of the time."

"Maybe we need to arrange something this evening so she isn't with him. Time is fleeting. Saturday will be here before you know it."

Carson threw back his head. "Thanks for making my day, Buck."

"Just trying to help things along for a buddy."

"Sorry for snapping."

"Forget it. There's only one cure for your problem. I'll tell ghost stories in the kids' tent after everyone goes to bed. No adults allowed. While the Harrises retire to their tent, you and Tracy can sit around and talk. That ought to give you plenty of time to get creative."

"She'll probably go to her tent."

After a pause Buck said, "Like I said, get creative and follow her."

"That's been my idea since the moment we set up camp."

"Then I don't see a problem."

"I wish I didn't."

"Don't let me down, buddy. You take first watch tonight and see where it leads. Wake me up when it's my turn." Buck did a backflip away from him and swam underwater to surprise the kids.

That was easy enough for his friend to say, but Carson intended to follow through, all the same. The hourglass was emptying every second. He needed to mind his grandfather's advice when he'd been teaching Carson how to wrestle steers. "Put your fear away and seize the moment without hesitation, otherwise the opportunity is lost."

Tonight might be one of the few opportunities left

to find out what was going on inside her. Armed with a plan, it helped him get through the rest of the evening.

While Carson and Buck explained why they were wearing canisters of oxygen and masks, Ralph Harris volunteered to build a small fire along the shoreline away from everyone. It would help them to avoid breathing too much smoke.

Instead of rainbow trout, they served roasted Teton hot dogs and Snake River marshmallows. The menu was a huge hit and met with Johnny's wholehearted approval.

With their meal finally over, Carson put the food away. Ralph volunteered to douse the fire and make sure there'd be no sparks. Now that it was time for bed, Buck made his exciting announcement and the children scurried to the big tent for stories.

The Harrises eventually said good-night. Before Tracy could say the same thing, Carson told her he'd walk her to the latrine. "In case Bigfoot is lurking."

"Carson!"

He stood chuckling at a distance until she came out. "Maybe you'd better sit with me and have a soda until you're not so jumpy."

"Are you intentionally trying to frighten me?"

His pulse rate sped up. "Is it working?"

"Yes."

"That's good. I don't feel like being alone on a perfect night like this."

"It's incredible."

He liked the sound of that. They walked back to the camp in companionable silence. Carson waited for her to tell him she really was tired and needed to go to bed. Instead she sat down near him, staring out at the water.

Before dinner she'd put on a navy pullover with long sleeves over her jeans. Everything she wore suited her. Earlier, while she'd been roasting her hot dog and the flames from the fire were turning to embers, they'd cast a glow that brought out the creamy beauty of her complexion. She'd left her hair free, flowing to her shoulders. It had a lot of natural curl. He'd never met a more feminine woman.

"Tracy?"

Her gaze swerved to his. "What is it? I can tell something's on your mind."

He'd been about as subtle as a sledgehammer. "How would you like to go into Jackson with me tomorrow night?"

"You mean me and Johnny?"

"No. Just you. I want to take you dancing."

After a slight hesitation, she smiled. "I don't recall that being listed on your brochure."

He took a deep breath. Damn if it didn't always cause him to cough. "It isn't. I'm asking you out on a date, strictly off the record. If the answer's no, tell me now and we'll pretend I never brought it up."

She looked pensive. "I'm afraid I'm not a very good dancer."

Carson still hadn't been given the right answer. As far as he was concerned, this evening was definitely over. He got to his feet, too filled with disappointment to sit still. "Do I take it that's a no?"

"No!"

His heart gave a big kick at her emphatic response. "So it's a yes?"

"Yes, but let me warn you now, I'm out of practice."

"It's been a while for me, too." He studied her classic features in the near darkness. "If you remember, we listed babysitting on the brochure. Do you think Johnny could handle that?"

"I think he could, but I'd rather feel out Monica. Maybe we can trade nights. If she's willing to let Johnny stay at their cabin tomorrow night, I'll tend her children at mine the following night."

It thrilled him that Tracy was so ready with a solution. He was beginning to get the impression she wanted this date as much as he did. Otherwise, she wouldn't have agreed to go out alone with him. "Sounds like a plan that will make our little cowboys and girls happy."

A gentle laugh escaped. "Johnny really likes them."

"They're great kids." He reached for the flashlight on the table. "Plan on wearing something dressy."

"I only brought one outfit that would qualify, but I didn't think I'd wear it."

"I'll wear something a little dressier, too. Come on. It's late. I'll take you to your tent."

"I'd appreciate that." She got up and started walking. "Will you shine the light inside to make sure Bigfoot's brother isn't waiting for me?"

He smiled to himself. "I'll do that and one better. Buck and I are taking turns tonight keeping watch so everyone's safe." Once they reached her tent, he made a thorough inspection. "It's all right to go in."

As she stepped past him, their arms brushed. It was all he could do not to pull her to him.

She turned to him in the darkness. "Thank you for everything, Carson." Her voice sounded husky. "With two ex-marines guarding each other and all of us, I won't have a care in the world tonight."

He needed to get away from her *now*. "Keep the flashlight with you. If Johnny wakes up and wants you, one of us will bring him to you. See you in the morning, Tracy."

With the adrenalin pumping through him, Carson headed for the food tent and grabbed another flashlight from the box. Needing some exercise, he took a walk to check on the horses and make sure all was well.

Their little group had been making enough noise all day to scare off any bears. But on the off chance that one was hungry enough to come around and investigate, he was taking every precaution to safeguard their guests. The thought of anything happening to Tracy or Johnny in his care was anathema to him. He'd never had such intense feelings before.

With time on his hands, he got on the phone and chatted with Ross. They talked about plans for the rest of the week. There were bookings for regular guests extending into August already. It appeared their brainchild was showing the promise of success.

This kind of news should make Carson happy. It *was* making him happy, but he had two people on his mind who were sleeping in tents very close to him. He was going out of his mind thinking about them leaving so soon and told Ross as much. That's when he heard a child's voice cry out, *"Mom—"*

It could have been any one of the three children. "Ross? One of the kids is awake. Got to go."

He took off for the bigger tent and almost ran into Buck who was holding Johnny's hand. The second the little guy saw him, he cried Carson's name and ran into his arms.

Carson got down on his haunches to hug him tight. "It's okay, Johnny. You were just having a bad dream."

"Mommy and I were at this big airport looking for you, but we couldn't find you. I kept calling for you, but you never came. Then I couldn't find my mom."

Carson looked up at Buck who'd heard everything. They'd both assumed the ghost stories had given him nightmares. Maybe they had. But Carson had featured in this one and Johnny had been looking for him.

It seemed Carson wasn't the only one hating the thought of Johnny and Tracy leaving the Tetons this coming weekend. The implication sent a shockwave through his body and wasn't lost on Buck, either.

Mercifully, the other kids stayed asleep.

"I'll take over now," Buck murmured.

Carson nodded. "Come on, Johnny. Let's go find your mom."

The boy put a trusting hand in Carson's and they walked to her tent. "Tracy?" he called to her from the opening. She stirred and sat up. "Johnny had a bad dream and wants to sleep with you."

"Oh, honey, come here." Johnny ran to her. Carson turned to leave, but Johnny's cry stopped him. "Don't go, Carson!" He sounded frantic.

"Johnny, Carson needs to go to his tent and get some sleep."

"He can sleep right here by me. Please, Mommy. I don't want him to leave."

In order to avoid a bigger disturbance he said, "Tell you what, partner. I'll stay here until you fall asleep. How's that?"

"You promise you won't go away?"

"Not until after I hear you snoring."

"I don't snore. Do I, Mom?"

She laughed softly. "Sometimes."

Tracy turned on the flashlight to find the blanket. "I'm not using this, Carson. Why don't you put this down next to Johnny." She was wearing pajamas with little footballs on them and looked adorable.

As Johnny might say, this was the funnest sleepover in the whole world.

Carson arranged the blanket into a pillow and stretched out. Their close quarters made everything cozy.

Tracy kissed her boy who'd climbed into the sleeping bag with her. "Do you want me to leave the light on?"

"Heck, no. Carson's here."

Tears stung Carson's eyes.

Tracy turned it off. "What kind of a bad dream was it?"

Johnny told her exactly what he'd told Carson.

He heard her deep sigh. "I've had dreams where I couldn't find somebody."

"You have?"

"Me, too," Carson interjected.

"Well, we're all here now and it's time to go back to sleep."

"Mom?"

"Yes?"

"I don't want to go home."

Carson's heart skipped a beat.

"Shh. We'll talk about it in the morning."

"Promise?"

"Promise."

"I love you, Mom."

"I love *you*, honey."

"Good night, Carson. I love you, too."

Carson closed his eyes tightly. "The feeling's mutual, partner. Good night." What else could he have said that wouldn't have upset Tracy?

When he'd had thoughts earlier in the day of being in the tent with her, he never dreamed he'd end up here in the middle of the night under these circumstances. In order to prove to her he wouldn't take advantage of the situation, he waited until he could tell they were asleep, then he crept out of the tent. He found Buck sitting on one of the chairs with his legs propped on another one.

"Go to bed, Buck. I'll never sleep tonight."

"Why not, besides the obvious?"

Carson brought him up to speed. "I'm afraid this plan of ours may be backfiring big-time. We were supposed to give them a fun vacation, but now he says he doesn't want to go home. I know you're going to say he'll get over it, but until he does, Tracy's probably going to wish she'd never come."

"Speaking of Tracy, what happened out there tonight when you two were alone?"

"I asked her to go dancing with me tomorrow night. She said yes." The "yes" came out a little louder because he had to cough.

Buck moved his legs to the ground. "You weren't really surprised, were you?"

"I don't know. Ever since she got here, I've been turned inside out."

He got to his feet and stretched. "Do you wish she hadn't come?"

"If this becomes a nightmare for her because of Johnny, then yes. I have no doubt it was his father he was looking for."

"I'm sure you're right. It's only natural. But she chose to accept our invitation. There's a risk in everything and nothing's perfect in this imperfect world. You have to know they've been having a wonderful time."

"But at what cost?"

"That's your old guilt talking, Carson. You've got to stop taking on what can't be helped."

Buck was right. "I don't know how to do that."

"It's the only flaw I find in you. See you in the morning."

Chapter 7

"Come on, honey." Johnny was slow putting on his cowboy boots this morning. "Now that we've had breakfast, they're calling us to pack up." So far he hadn't talked about his bad dream last night. That was good, because now wasn't the time for the serious discussion with him about Carson.

Johnny reached for his cowboy hat and put it on. "Do we have to go back to the ranch today?"

"Yes." She finished putting his things in the saddlebag.

"But I like it here."

"There are a lot more fun things we're going to do. Remember what Buck said while he was cooking our pancakes? Ross is taking us on a hike over in Teton Park. We haven't been there yet."

"Why isn't Carson coming with us?"

"You know why. He has business matters to take care of today."

"I'd rather stay home and ride Goldie."

Home?

"You can ride her after dinner. Here. You carry your saddlebag and I'll bring mine."

After fastening her hair back with a clip, she opened the tent flap and they joined everyone congregated by the horses. She could hear the men coughing. Carson's black Stetson stood out as he finished saddling Goldie. He darted her a private glance before his blue gaze fell on Johnny. He took the bag from him and attached it.

"Up you go, partner." He helped him mount and handed him the reins.

"Who's going to take down our tents and stuff?"

"Some of my ranch hands. They came yesterday to set everything up for us."

"Oh."

"Remember what to do when the other ponies crowd in," he whispered. Tracy heard that and smiled.

Johnny's face brightened. "Yup."

Carson moved to Tracy's horse, Annie, who was ready to go. In a deft move he fastened Tracy's saddlebag. While she mounted, he undid the reins and put them in her hands, giving them a little squeeze.

Tracy had been so excited about the date he'd made with her last night, she'd had trouble getting to sleep. When he'd brought Johnny to the tent in the middle of the night, his presence had made it impossible for her to settle back down. With that squeeze just now, she felt breathless.

He mounted his horse with effortless masculine precision. "Is everyone ready?"

"I am!" Sam called out.

"How about you, Rachel?"

"I've been ready for a long time." Her comment produced chuckles from everyone, including her parents.

"Then let's move out." Carson sounded like the hero in a Western film. Johnny fell in line right behind him, followed by the other kids, then the parents. Tracy stayed in front of Buck, who brought up the rear. A wagon train without a wagon. She loved it. In fact, she loved it too much. She was as bad as Johnny.

At first when they moved through the forest, she thought it was the trees making it seem darker than usual. But she soon realized clouds had moved in over the Tetons, blotting out the sun's rays. She felt the temperature drop. The sight of clouds after so many days of sunshine came as a surprise.

She dropped back to ride alongside Buck. "We had blue sky at breakfast. I can't believe how fast the weather has changed. Do you think there's going to be a storm?"

He nodded. "This cold front has moved in with more force than I'd anticipated. If it keeps up, we may not be able to go on that hike today."

Johnny wouldn't mind that at all. But he wouldn't like it if he couldn't go riding. "In that case, it'll be a good day for the children to play in the game room. A marathon Monopoly session will keep them occupied."

He laughed. "When we were young, my brothers and I used to play it all night. It drove my parents crazy."

"Where did you grow up, Buck?"

"Colorado Springs."

"I've heard it's beautiful there."

"It is, but I've decided nothing beats this place." A cough followed.

"How long do you plan to stay here?"

He flicked her an enigmatic glance. "If our business venture bears fruit, I'll build a home here and put down roots."

"What did you do before you went into the Marines?"

Buck's eyes got a faraway look. "My dad's in the construction business. Our family didn't know anything else."

"I see."

There was so much he didn't say, she heard pain and decided not to question him further. "While I have the chance, I want to thank you for all you've done to make this trip possible for Johnny and me. This is a once-in-a-lifetime adventure that so few people will ever enjoy. We won't forget your kindness and generosity for as long as we live."

"We're glad you're having such a good time. It makes everything we've done worthwhile, believe me."

While they'd been talking, they'd come out of the trees into the sagebrush. The track widened. "I'm going to ride up to Johnny and see how he's doing."

"Go right ahead. It's been a pleasure talking to you."

"For me, too, Buck."

She spurred her horse on past the others, delighted at the sight of her son moving along so comfortably on Goldie. Before he saw her, she whipped out her phone and took some more pictures of everyone. Carson was right in front of Johnny so he got into the pictures, too, without his knowledge.

As she put her phone away, she noticed the ponies edging up on Goldie. It really was funny how they wanted to be by her. In a minute they'd reached Johnny. She couldn't wait to see what would happen.

"Hey, Carson—here they come!"

His mentor moved to the side of the track to make room for him. She watched Johnny brace himself before he cried, "Giddyup!" and kicked his heels at the same time. Goldie was a smart little girl and trotted off, leaving the others behind. Sam and Rachel looked totally surprised.

Unable to help herself, Tracy urged her horse forward so she could catch up to her son. Once abreast of him she said, "Well done, cowboy."

"Did you see that, Mom?" Excitement filled his countenance.

"I sure did."

By now, Carson had caught up on his other side. "Thanks for teaching me that trick, Carson."

"Any time, partner."

Over Johnny's hat her gaze fused with Carson's. She could tell he was proud of her son. So was she. It was one of those incredible moments. "At this point I feel like we're actors in a movie on location out West."

He grinned. "We *are* out West, but instead of the Ponderosa, our star actor, Johnny Baretta, is headed with his posse for the Teton Valley Ranch on his wonder pony, Goldie!"

Johnny giggled. "You're so funny, Carson."

Oh, Carson—you're so wonderful, it hurts.

During this halcyon moment, they all heard thunder, the kind that could put a crack in those glorious mountains in the far distance. It kept echoing up and down the valley.

"Whoa!" Johnny cried out along with the other kids.

Carson whistled. "Now that's the kind of thunder that grows hair on a man's chest." Johnny burst into uproarious laughter. It set the tone for the ride in, calming any fears the children might have had. Their host turned in the saddle. "First person to reach the corral gets a banana split for lunch!"

"Goody!"

By the time the barn came into view, sheet lightning was illuminating the dark clouds that had settled in over the area. Tracy shot Carson a glance. "I've never seen anything so spectacular."

"During a storm it gets pretty exciting around here."

Almost as exciting as he was.

The first drops of rain pelted them as they rode into the barn to dismount. Bert came out of his office and helped the children down. Buck smiled at everyone. "Looks like we got home in the nick of time."

Ralph eyed the children. "I wonder who won?"

"Carson," all three kids said in unison.

He shook his head. "You were all there right behind me. I say everyone gets a banana split."

"Hooray!"

While the men removed the saddles and bridles, Johnny walked over to Carson. "Do you think the horses got scared?" Sometimes Tracy marveled over her son's sensitivity.

"After that first clap of thunder, I think they were a little fidgety, but since we didn't show any fear, they did fine out there. Tell you what. I'm going to take everyone back to the ranch house in the Jeep. But we'll have to make two trips. Why don't you kids come with me first, because I know you're hungry."

"Whoopie!"

Tracy watched them follow Carson into the drenching rain. She walked over to Ralph and Monica. This was the perfect time to talk to them in private. "Now we're alone for a minute, I have something to ask you, but please don't worry if you don't feel it's something you want to do."

When she told them, Monica's face lit up. "We were just going to approach you about the same thing. The kids like each other and trust you."

"Johnny thinks you guys are great, too. This is perfect. I'll babysit for you tomorrow night."

"Thank you. We're dying to go into Jackson and have a little time alone."

Tracy could relate to that. She gathered the two saddle-bags while they waited for Carson's return. Tonight was going to be a special time with a very special man and she planned to enjoy it to the fullest. After she and Johnny were back in Ohio, it would be a memory she would pull out and relive when the going got tough again. But she didn't want to think about the tough part right now.

Carson had only seen Tracy in jeans or a bathing suit. When she opened the cabin door at seven-thirty, he was treated to a vision of a different kind. With her blond hair loose, the champagne-colored skirt and gauzy blouse looked sensational on her. Soft and dreamy. Her high-heeled sandals showed off her shapely legs.

"Carson—" Her hazel eyes played over him longer than usual. "I almost didn't recognize you in a regu-

lar suit minus the boots and hat. I don't think Johnny would, either."

"A man has to be civilized around here once in a while. Are you ready?"

"Yes," she said quietly. "I'll grab my purse and jacket."

They left the cabin and he helped her into his Altima. The storm had passed, leaving everything cooler. He loved the smell of the sage after the rain. "Is Johnny all right with this?"

"I wondered about it when I broached the subject this afternoon. When he found out he'd be staying at the Harris's cabin until I got back, he didn't exactly mind we were going somewhere without him. Of course, I had to promise I'd come and get him."

"Of course." Carson started the engine and drove off. "Since you've told me how protective he can be, I guess I wondered if he put up a fuss that I'm taking you out."

"Are you kidding? The king of the cowboys?"

Her comment removed the bands constricting his lungs. The result was another bout of coughing. "After his nightmare, I worried his father was on his mind."

"I'm sure he was, subconsciously, but he didn't mention Tony at all. In fact, he hasn't talked about him once since our arrival here. That tells me you and your friends have achieved your goal to bring our family some happiness. Today made it evident that my son has come out of his shell. Your goodness and generosity are the sole reason for that. I told Buck the same thing earlier today."

Carson had noticed the two of them talking as they'd headed back to the ranch. "And what about you, Tracy? Are you enjoying yourself?"

"You know very well that question doesn't need an answer. I could never imagine myself being with another man again. Yet I found myself saying yes when you invited me out. I thought, why not? If Johnny could get on a small plane and dive-bomb into Jackson Hole, then it was time I took a risk. That should tell you a lot."

It did, but it wasn't enough. Patience had never been Carson's strong suit. "I'm taking you to the Hermitage, a French restaurant I haven't been to since my return from Maryland. It's in the Spring Creek Ranch area, a thousand feet above the valley floor.

"The view is superb. I thought you might like a change from authentic Western and enjoy some great French food along with a live band that plays a lot of romantic French songs. On Friday night after the rodeo, I'll take you and Johnny to a fun place for Western music and line dancing. Everyone gets in on the act in their duds. He'll be in his element."

He felt her eyes on him. "Be careful, Carson. You're spoiling us too much. If you treat all the families who come here at your invitation the way you're treating me and Johnny, no one will ever want to leave."

"Can I quote you on that when the time comes?" He pulled up to the crowded restaurant and turned off the engine. Luckily he'd made reservations. Even in the semidarkness, he saw color fill her cheeks.

She looked away. "You know what I meant."

"My friends and I appreciate the compliment." Levering himself from the car, he went around to help her out. The place had been built to resemble one of those religious retreats in the French Alps. He ushered her through the heavy wooden doors. The high ceilings and huge picture windows were unexpected and provided a contemporary twist.

"Carson! I couldn't believe it when I heard you'd made a reservation." A wiry older man came rushing over to the entry and kissed him on both cheeks. "Are you on leave? I haven't seen you since your *grand-père*'s funeral."

"I've left the military, Maurice, and am back for good."

"That's the best news I've heard in a long time."

His throat swelled with emotion. "It's good to see you."

"And who is this ravishing creature?"

"Please meet Tracy Baretta, one of the guests staying at the ranch with her son. Tracy, this is Maurice Chappuis, the owner."

The restaurateur's warm brown eyes studied her for a long moment. "How do you do, Tracy."

"It's very nice to meet you."

Carson would have said more, but a coughing spell stopped him. Maurice frowned. "That doesn't sound good."

"I got it when I was overseas, but I'm not contagious, so don't worry." He glanced at Tracy. "His son Jean-Paul and I were friends back in high school. Jean-Paul was a local bull riding legend. Maurice came to all our competitions. What's he up to these days?"

"Same thing as usual. Helping me here and on the ranch. Except…he got married four months ago and they're expecting!"

"You're kidding!" Carson was truly happy for him.

Maurice crossed himself. "He's off tonight. When I tell him who walked in here, he'll be overjoyed."

"Tell him to come by the ranch and bring his wife."

"I will. Now come. Sit, sit, sit. Only the best champagne in the house for you. I don't need to tell you we serve the best coq au vin in the world, and we have a new *chanteur* performing with the band. He does wonderful Charles Aznavour renditions."

"That's why we're here." He gave Maurice another hug. Seeing him like this brought the past hurtling back. Once again his guilt took over. Jean-Paul hadn't gone away. He wasn't restless, as Carson had been. Once his rodeo days were over, he'd stayed in Jackson. He'd built a life here, helping his father. Now he had a wife.

After Maurice seated Tracy, Carson took the seat opposite her at the window with its amazing view of the valley. The wine steward came over to pour them champagne. When he was gone, she eyed her dinner companion with concern.

"Maurice is wonderful, but I can tell something's wrong." Her naturally arched brows lifted. "Memories?"

He nodded soberly. "Too many. They all came rushing in at once."

"I know the feeling. When you handed that photograph to Johnny at the airport, and I saw Tony, it was like instant immersion into a former life."

"Immersion's a good word." He drank some champagne. "Mmm. You should try this. It's like velvet."

But she remained still. "You loved your grandfather, didn't you?"

"Yes."

"Then why do I sense so much sadness?"

"You know the old saying, act in haste and repent at leisure? That's me. But I don't want to talk about me tonight." He lifted his wineglass. "I'm dining with a beautiful woman and don't want anything to spoil it. Here's to an unforgettable evening."

She lifted her glass to touch his, and then sipped. "Oh—" She smiled. "That's really good."

"Isn't it?"

The waiter brought their meal and a basket of freshly baked croissants. Maurice didn't usually serve these with dinner, but he knew how much Carson loved them.

"You have to try one of these. They literally melt in your mouth. I've eaten a dozen of them in one sitting before."

She took a bite. "I believe you."

While they ate their meal, he saw the dance band assemble across the room. A man in a turtleneck and jacket took over the mic. "Ladies and gentlemen," he said in heavily accented French. "I've been told we have a very special guest in the restaurant tonight. Monsieur Lundgren, it is up to you to choose our first number before the dancing starts."

Carson chuckled. Trust Maurice to pull this. He glanced at Tracy, whose smile haunted him. "Go on. I'm curious to know what you pick."

"How about, 'Yesterday When I Was Young'?"

Many people in the restaurant clapped because they knew the song, too. Once the man started to sing, Carson's eyes slid to Tracy's. Their eyes didn't leave each other until the singing was over.

"I first heard that song before I was sent to the hospital," he told her. "Remember the opening lines about being young and the taste of life sweet on the tongue, of treating life as if it were a foolish game?" She nodded. "All of it burned through me like a red-hot poker. That's what I'd done, and now that time was gone.

"I looked back at my own life, knowing I could never return to those times. I felt older than my grandfather who'd passed away. Opportunities had been missed. Too late I learned that the *now* of life is the essence."

Her eyes filled and she reached across the table to squeeze his hand gently.

"Let's dance." Carson stood, and reached for her to join him.

They gravitated to each other on the dance floor. When he pulled her into his arms she whispered, "You're still young, Carson."

He drew her tighter against him without saying anything. They danced every dance. He forgot the time, the place. Carson needed the warmth of her lissome body. With each movement he inhaled her sweet fragrance and felt every breath she took.

"I need to be alone with you, Tracy. Let's get out of here." He felt a tremor shake her body as he led her back to the table. Once he'd left some bills, he ushered her out of the restaurant to the car.

A few residue clouds obscured the moon. Except for his coughing, they drove back to the ranch in silence. It was after eleven, but there was no way this evening was over. Maybe she wouldn't like it, but he pulled around to the rear of the ranch house and shut off the engine.

"This is my home. I'd like you to see how I live. I want you to come in and be with me for a while. If that doesn't—"

"It's what I'd like, too," she broke in. He sensed she

wanted to be with him. What surprised him was how forthright she was. That's the way the whole night had gone.

He got out and went around to help her from the car. "The guys live upstairs. I have the back of the house to myself."

They walked down the hall to his bedroom, where Buck had done some remodeling for him. His grandfather's former room had been turned into a suite with its own sitting room and bathroom, but Carson wasn't thinking about that right now. He started to help her off with her jacket, but the moment he touched her, he couldn't help kissing the side of her neck.

"So help me, I promised myself I wouldn't do this, but I don't seem to have any control when I get close to you."

She twisted around until she faced him. That beautiful face. "Neither do I."

"Tracy—"

Carson lowered his head and covered her mouth with his own, exultant that at last he was tasting her. The singing line of her mouth had been tempting him for days. By some miracle she was kissing him back and she went on giving kiss after kiss. Like their dancing, they couldn't stop. It felt too wonderful to love this way.

He'd been empty for too many years. He wanted to go slow, but he didn't know how. She wasn't helping him. This merging of lips and bodies was so powerful, their desire for each other took on a life of its own. Carson didn't remember picking her up and carrying her to the bed. But there she was, lying on the mattress, looking up at him with a longing he could hardly credit was for him.

After crushing her mouth once more, he lifted his head, but he was out of breath. "I brought you here to... to do this...and to talk."

"I know," she half moaned. "That's why I came. We *have* to talk."

"How are we supposed to do that now? Do you have any idea how much I want to make love to you?"

"That makes two of us." Her voice trembled. "Don't hate me too much if I confess that I wanted you to kiss me to see if what I was feeling was real."

"You mean I was an experiment."

"Yes. But so was I to you—be honest about that." Her eyes beseeched him to understand. "After Tony, I—"

"You don't need to explain anything to me," he cut in. "I've been wondering about that, too, but no longer. It's real, all right." He buried his face in her fragrant hair.

"What's happened to us proves there's life after death. Until I met you, I didn't believe it. Oh, Carson." She covered his face with kisses.

He found her mouth again, starving for her. "Now we *have* to believe it, because it's evident we're both hungry for each other. There's been an awareness between us from the first instant. Whether it's an infatuation that will burn out, only time will tell, but at least we can admit to what we're feeling right now and go on from here."

A tortured look entered her eyes. "We can't go on. This has to end tonight and you know it."

"Tonight?"

He rolled her on top of him, searching the depths

of her eyes. "We've only just begun and we have three more precious days and nights together. How can you say it has to end now? How do we do that, Tracy?"

"Because we can't afford to start something we can't finish."

"Who says we can't?" he cried fiercely. "It already started Friday evening. Don't you know I don't ever want you to go home? You can't! Not when we feel this way about each other. For two people to connect the way we have is so rare, we have to hold on to it and nurture it. If I've learned nothing else, that's what war has taught me. Can you deny it?"

"Carson!" she said in genuine shock. "I couldn't possibly stay."

"That's because you're afraid."

"All right, yes. I am, for too many reasons to mention!"

"So am I. Petrified. This is new for me, too."

"We've only known each other a few days."

"That's the whole point, isn't it? How can we really get to know each other unless you stay? In order to give us a chance, I'd like you and Johnny to live in the cabin for as long as you want, until Christmas, even. That way you'll have seen all the seasons come and go except spring—which is enchanting. With weather like ours, it's important you experience it. By then, we'll know if you're ready to pack your bags or not."

She knew the "or not" meant he was talking about marriage, but he didn't say it in order not to scare her over something she wasn't ready for yet. With her, it would have to be all or nothing. He'd marry her in the morning, but he was going to give her plenty of time to get used to the idea.

Carson groaned when she started to ease herself away from him. He reached for her, but she slid to the edge of the bed and stood up. "If it were just me, I might consider staying on in Jackson at a motel for another week to see more of you. But we're talking about Johnny, too."

He got to his feet. "Exactly. He needs time to get to know the real me and see if he likes the man who's not just a cowboy. He's told me several times he doesn't want to go home. Whether he really meant it or not, he said it, and that's a start in the right direction."

She shook her head. "It just wouldn't work."

"Of course it would. We need to see where this leads."

"It might lead nowhere!" she exclaimed. "You could end up not liking me. We might find out we're not good for each other."

"Johnny may end up despising me, and you may discover you're bored and hate this lifestyle," Carson agreed. "But that's the risk we'll have to take because a fire's been lit, Tracy, and you can't ignore it."

"I'm not. I'm only trying to think with my head and not with emotions or hormones."

"That would be impossible. They all work together. I know we have to head for the Harrises' cabin, but before we walk out of here, I want you to think hard about something." He grasped her upper arms. "Will you listen?"

"Of course."

"I let my grandfather down when he was alive, but now that I'm back, I intend to keep this ranch going for my own sake as well as to honor him. The only way you and I can be together is for you to come to me. If you let fear take over, you'll be throwing away something precious. Are you willing to take that chance?"

"You make it all sound so easy, but it isn't. For one thing, I have my career."

He folded his arms so he wouldn't crush her in his arms again. "The Teton School District would welcome credentials like yours. Johnny could attend any one of six elementary schools. He'll make friends there and with the neighbors. We're only fifteen minutes away from town."

"Carson, I couldn't just stay on your property for six months."

"Then pay me rent like you do your landlord in Sandusky."

"But you built these cabins for tourists. Johnny and I would be taking up one of them. It wouldn't be fair to you and your friends after all the work you've done to make this into a dude ranch."

"I've already contacted the architect to build another one." The house of glass near the river.

"Your friends will hardly welcome the news that the family you invited here has decided to stay on. You three have started a new business together and don't need that complication."

He grimaced. "I'd hardly call you a complication, Tracy. But I know why you're throwing up all these excuses. For you to stay here will cause a major earthquake in the Baretta family. Don't bother to deny it, because I know it's true."

"They'd have a difficult time if Johnny weren't there."

"Your family could come out here for visits. They'd always be welcome."

"They're very set in their ways and don't travel often."

"What's really wrong that you're not telling me?"

She lowered her head. "They wouldn't approve."

"I get it," he fired back. "But their son has been laid to rest and their daughter-in-law has the right to get on with her life the way she sees best."

"You don't know what they're like." She raised anxious eyes to him. "My in-laws are good Catholics."

An angry laugh escaped his lips. "What would they prefer? That I fly home with you and assure them that while you're staying on my ranch, you won't be living in sin with me?"

The second she blanched, he realized his mistake and gathered her into his arms where she fit against his as if she'd been made for him. Rocking her back and forth he whispered, "Forgive me for saying that. Already you're seeing a side of me that probably makes you glad you're leaving on Saturday. I know I sound desperate. It's because I am."

Carson found her mouth and drank deeply. He would have gone on kissing her indefinitely, but he had to cough. After it subsided he said, "Have I told you what a wonderful son you have? Last night he wanted me to stay in your tent. You have no idea what that meant to me." He lowered his mouth to kiss her again and tasted salt from her tears.

In the next instant she put her hands on his chest to stop him. "We can't do this, Carson. It's midnight. We have to go for Johnny."

He drew in his breath. "I know, but I have to have

one more of these." Cupping her face in his hands, he savored another heart-stopping kiss from her lips. Her response told him things she wasn't ready to admit yet. Carson needed to be able to do this for the rest of their lives. In his gut, he knew that if she didn't end up being his wife there would be other women to provide a distraction, but he'd never marry one of them.

Ross had put it into words while they were working on the cabins in April. "You're probably one of those 'one woman' men you hear about. My great-grandfather was exactly like that. A crusty bachelor who came out to Texas from the East to find oil and make his fortune. Big business and politics were the only things on his mind.

"According to the story, he saw my great-grandmother picking bluebonnets in a field. She looked like a vision and he presented himself to her. It was history from there."

Carson had experienced a similar vision when Tracy had walked into the airline terminal. He was ready to make his own history, but he needed this woman and her son for it to happen. They made him want to be a better person because they were life to him.

Chapter 8

"Mom? My stomach hurts."

Tracy turned in the bed to look at Johnny, who was still under his covers. Normally he was up by this time, shooting off his cap gun. "You look pale. What kind of treats did you eat last night?"

"Sam's mom made popcorn."

"Is that all you ate?"

"No. When she put me in the bedroom with Sam, he had a bag of mini chocolate bars and we ate some."

"I bet his mother didn't know about those."

"She didn't. He told me we had to keep it a secret."

"So how many did you really eat?"

"All of them."

"No wonder you're sick. Do you think you're going to throw up?"

"Yes."

She pushed the covers aside and jumped out of bed. He started running and beat her to the bathroom in time to empty his stomach. Tracy waited till he was through, then she helped him wash out his mouth.

"I still don't feel good."

"I'm not surprised. I want you to get back in bed."

"But Carson was going to take us all riding this morning. Goldie will wonder where I am." He burst into tears, the first he'd shed since coming here.

Just the mention of Carson's name set her trembling. Last night the Harrises had left the cabin door unlocked. Carson had stolen in and brought Johnny out to the car. Her son had been sound asleep. When they reached her cabin, he'd put Johnny to bed and had left without touching her. For the rest of the night she'd ached for him until it turned into literal pain.

"I'll tell him you're not feeling well. Maybe by this afternoon you'll feel better and then we can go over to the corral."

"Will you tell him to come and see me?"

"Honey, he has other guests to take care of. In the meantime, we'll wait to see if you throw up again. If you don't, I'll get you some toast and there's Sprite in the fridge." The cabin had been stocked with enough snacks and fruit for her to skip breakfast in the dining room. "Would you like to lie down on the couch in the other room so you can watch a movie?"

"Okay."

Tracy took a blanket and pillow from his bed and tried to make him comfortable. She looked through the DVDs. "Do you want *The Hobbit* or Harry Potter?"

"I don't care."

That was his nausea talking. When it passed, then he'd ask her questions about her night out with Carson. She popped in the Harry Potter DVD.

"When are you going to call him?"

She glanced at her watch. It was quarter after eight. "In a little while. Let's give him time to eat his breakfast first." In truth she had no idea what time he ate. She'd phone him at nine.

"Don't tell Sam's mom what we did or she might get mad."

"She's so nice I'm sure she'll understand. I have to call her to let her know you won't be riding with her children this morning."

His eyes were closed. "Okay."

"I'll only be in the bedroom for a minute." She hurried in the other room and phoned the front desk. They put her call through.

"Monica? I'm glad I caught you. How are the children this morning?"

"That's funny you'd ask. Rachel's fine, but Sam says he's not feeling well."

"Neither is Johnny." In the next breath Tracy told her about the overload of chocolate.

"That little monkey of mine. I'm so sorry."

"You don't need to apologize, Monica. My son was equally guilty. I think they've learned their lesson. I just wanted you to know we won't be going riding this morning. Maybe not at all today."

"I agree we'll have to give riding a miss. I'll call Carson and let him know the situation."

Good idea.

Tracy wasn't ready to face him yet, not even over

the phone. "Thank you, but don't think this changes our plan for me to tend your children. How about tomorrow night instead of tonight? Hopefully everyone will be well by then."

"That would be wonderful, if you're sure."

"Absolutely. I had a lovely time last night and want you and your husband to enjoy your evening, too. Why don't I treat tomorrow night like a special campout for the children? Our last one before we all have to leave the ranch. There's a bed for everyone here and we've got the couch. That way, you and Ralph don't have to come home until you want."

"Do you mean it?"

"Of course."

"You're one in a million, Tracy."

"So are you. We'll talk later."

After hanging up, Tracy padded into the other room. Johnny had fallen asleep again. That was good. Hopefully when he awakened, he'd feel a little better. She left the DVD on, hoping it might distract her.

Last night, while she'd been dancing with Carson, she'd wanted him to kiss her so badly, she couldn't wait to leave and go home with him. But what happened after that had shaken her world and she needed to talk to her sister-in-law, the only one who wouldn't judge her or the situation. Much as she wanted to phone Natalie, she couldn't. It wouldn't be fair to intrude on their vacation. Tracy needed to work this out on her own.

While she sat there brooding, she didn't feel like getting dressed yet. Instead she walked over to the table to make herself some coffee. It was something to do while her son slept on. Among the snacks she found a granola bar. While she ate, she sat down at the table to watch the movie and sip the hot brew.

Though she stared at the TV screen, her thoughts were full of last night's conversation with Carson and the way he made her feel while they'd kissed each other in mindless passion.

Much as she might want a repeat of that rapture for the rest of her life, Tracy couldn't just stay on here. What he'd suggested was impossible. Once she'd met Tony, the Barettas had become her whole family. They weren't simply her in-laws. With the loss of their son, they'd clung to Tracy and she to them. She didn't know what she and Johnny would have done without them.

They'd be so hurt if she told them she'd be staying on in the Tetons for a while. Her plans to visit them in Cleveland would have to be put off until later in the summer. She couldn't do that to them, no matter how much she dreaded the thought of leaving Carson.

What he'd said was true. If there was any chance that a lasting, meaningful relationship could develop, they needed to explore those feelings. Would they be as strong as their physical attraction for each other?

The way she felt right now, she couldn't imagine that attraction ever burning out, but she knew it could happen. One of the couples she and Tony had been friends with after they'd moved to Sandusky had recently divorced. They'd seemed to be so in love.

She needed to put last night's events away. For Tracy to want to be with a man she'd only just met and who lived thousands of miles away was ludicrous. The more she thought about it, the more she realized it would be the height of selfishness to stay here. Johnny might be having the time of his life on this vacation, but he needed loving family surrounding him. She couldn't keep him away from that.

Tracy had been blessed with a loving marriage to Tony. Now it was up to her to give Johnny the life they'd envisioned for their boy. One that included his favorite cousin, Cory, plus his other cousins, loving aunts and uncles, adoring grandparents. Good friends from the neighborhood and school would come with time.

From the deep fathoms of her troubling thoughts, she heard a knock on the door. Maybe it was Rachel with a message from Sam. Afraid it might wake up Johnny, she padded over to the door in her Cleveland Browns pajamas and opened it.

Bright blue eyes greeted her. "Dr. Lundgren at your service, Mrs. Baretta. My receptionist informed me I needed to make a house call on a new patient. She tells me he overdosed on Kisses. I can relate to that. In fact I'm still suffering the effects because I've become addicted to them."

Carson...

Heat swept through her body into her face.

"Hey—Carson?" Johnny called from the couch with excitement while she was trying to recover her breath.

"Yup. I've brought some stuff to make you feel better."

Johnny hurried to the door. He didn't look as pale as before. "What is it?"

Carson reached into the sack he carried. "Some Popsicles when you're ready for one."

"Thanks! I threw up this morning, but I'm feeling a little better now."

"That's good. Maybe you'd like to watch the DVDs I brought of Hoppy."

"Goody!"

Tracy was completely flustered, having been caught in her pajamas with her hair disheveled. "Well, aren't you a lucky boy. Thank you, Carson. Please come in. I'll get dressed and be out shortly." She flew through the cabin to her bedroom and shut the door.

When she emerged a few minutes later in jeans and a blouse, the two of them were on the couch. Johnny was sucking happily on a banana Popsicle while he told Carson how he got sick. Tracy thought he might throw it up later, but at least he was taking in some liquid.

"A long time ago I remember eating too many Tootsie Rolls and got a stomachache for a whole day. I still can't eat one."

"I did the same thing on some fudge cookies," Tracy admitted.

Carson's gaze drifted over her. "Sounds like you're both chocolate addicts. By the way, I like the mother–son outfits."

Johnny spoke before she could. "My aunt Natalie gave these to us for Christmas. She and Cory have a pair, too. We love the Cleveland Browns."

"How about their quarterback, Colt McCoy?"

"Yeah." They high-fived each other.

"You're not going to leave are you?" Johnny cried when Carson unexpectedly got to his feet.

"Nope. I was going to put in one of the DVDs for you to watch."

"Good. I don't want you to go. Mom said you had a lot of other stuff to do today."

He walked over to the player. Glancing at them over his shoulder he said, "I was planning on taking you guys riding, but since that's out, I thought I'd hang out with you till you're feeling better."

"I probably won't be better all day." Her son was milking this for all it was worth.

Tracy didn't dare look at Carson or she'd burst out laughing. Instead she reached for an apple and sat down in the chair, putting her legs beneath her. In seconds he'd exchanged the DVDs in the player, and one of the old cowboy movies with the kind of music written for the early Westerns came on the screen.

"William Boyd," she said aloud. Seeing the actor's name brought back memories of the past with her parents.

Johnny frowned. "I thought his name was Hoppy."

"That's the character he plays in the film, honey."

"Oh."

"I wonder if Lucky is as cute as I remember," she teased. A little imp of mischief prompted her to see if she could get a rise out of Carson.

She wasn't disappointed when his gaze narrowed on her. "Why don't we take a vote at the end of the show?"

The by-play passed over Johnny. He moved his pillow so he could lie against Carson's leg. It was exactly the kind of thing he would do when he watched TV with Tony and got sleepy. Tracy couldn't believe how comfortable her son was with Carson, who seemed to take all this in as the natural course of events.

Before long, Hoppy and his friends came riding into town at full speed.

"There he is, riding his horse, Topper—" Carson

blurted, sounding as excited as a kid. "To me, he was the greatest superhero in the world."

Johnny sat up. "But that guy in the black cowboy hat looks like a grandfather!"

Laughter burst out of Carson so hard it brought on a coughing spasm.

Tracy's shoulders shook. "He really does look old now that you think about it, but Lucky's still as cute as ever."

"That white hat's too big on him, Mom. He looks like a nerd. What's his horse's name?"

"Zipper."

Johnny giggled. As for Carson, he had a struggle to stop laughing. "Well, Mom, I'm afraid I have to throw in my vote with Johnny. That makes two of us who disagree with you."

"You guys are just jealous."

"How come you like Hoppy so much?" Johnny's tone was serious.

She watched Carson's features sober. "I don't remember my dad. When I saw Hoppy's films, I imagined my dad being like him. A great cowboy who was really good, really courageous and always fair. My grandpa was like that, too. I was lucky to be raised by him."

"Yeah," Johnny murmured.

"You know something? You were lucky to have your father for as long as you did."

"I know."

"And now you have your grandfather."

"Yup. He's awesome. Carson? Do you miss your grandpa?"

"Yes. Very much. I bet you've missed yours this trip, too."

"Nope, 'cos he's not dead." *Shock*. "I can call him and Grandma whenever I want."

"I envy you."

Tracy felt Carson's pain. They needed to get off the subject. "You two are missing the show." She doubted anyone was really concentrating on it, but the room fell quiet until the end of the movie. When it was over, she got up to turn it off. "Are you getting hungry, Johnny?"

"No. Can I have another Popsicle?"

That was a good sign the nausea was subsiding. She picked up the paper with the sticks and threw them in the wastepaper basket, then drew another treat out of the small freezer. "Is cherry okay?"

"Yes."

He still wasn't well if this was all he could tolerate, but at least he hadn't been sick again. When she turned, she noticed Carson was already on his feet. She had a hunch he was leaving and her spirits plummeted. He looked down at Johnny.

"I hate to go, but I have to take some guests riding this afternoon. When I'm through, I'll phone to find out if you're hungry. If so, I'll bring you and your mom some dinner."

"I wish you didn't have to leave." He looked crestfallen to the point of tears.

"Can you thank him for the Popsicles and the movies?"

Johnny nodded. "Thanks, Carson."

"You're welcome." He flicked a glance to Tracy. "I'll have one of the kitchen staff bring you lunch."

"You don't have to do that. There's plenty to eat here."

"I want to do it," he insisted. "Does a club sandwich sound good?"

"Wonderful."

"Great. I'll have her bring some soda crackers, too."

There wasn't anything Carson couldn't, wouldn't or didn't do. *He* was the superhero.

After he left, gloom settled over the cabin. Johnny lay there watching cartoons while she tried to interest herself in the book she'd brought. Except for the arrival of her lunch, it turned out to be the longest day either of them had lived through in a long time.

On a happier note, by midafternoon Johnny was hungry enough to eat the crackers and drink some Sprite. Things were improving. Though neither of them said it, they were both living for the evening when Carson had promised to come back.

When he finally arrived, he brought them country-fried steak and the trimmings, plus chicken-noodle soup and toast for Johnny. The sight of him walking through the cabin door dressed in a black crew neck shirt and jeans changed the rhythm of her heart.

He'd also brought a colorful puzzle of all the planets. Johnny adored it and they worked on it until his head drooped. Tracy had been counting the minutes until she could put him into bed. The thought of being alone at last with Carson was the only thing driving her.

With a heart thudding out of control, Carson sat on the couch, waiting for her. When she appeared he whispered, "Come over here."

Tracy moved toward him. He caught hold of her hand and pulled her down so she lay in his arms. The fragrance of her strawberry shampoo seduced him almost as much as the feel of her warm body cuddled up to his.

A deep sigh escaped his lips as they swept over each feature of her face. "I've been dreaming about being with you like this since you first arrived. After last night, it's a miracle I functioned at all today. You're a beautiful creature, Tracy."

She smiled. "Men always say that about a woman, but the well-kept secret is that every woman knows there's nothing more beautiful than a man who possesses all the right attributes. *You,* Carson Lundgren, were given an unfair number of them."

"As long as you think that, I'll never complain." Unable to stand it any longer, he started to devour her mouth with slow, deliberate kisses that shook them both. He wrapped his legs around her gorgeous limbs, needing to feel every inch of her.

She explored his arms and back with growing urgency. When her hands cupped the back of his neck to bring him even closer, he realized what a sensuous woman he held in his arms. It filled him with an ecstasy he'd never known before. This was an experience he couldn't compare to anything else.

"I want to take you to bed so badly I can hardly bear it, but this isn't the place, not with Johnny sleeping in the next room."

Tracy covered his face with kisses. "It's a good thing he's nearby, because you've done something to me. I don't think I'll ever be the same, even when I'm back in Ohio."

"If your craving is as strong as mine, then you won't be going anywhere."

"You sounded fierce just now." She gave him a teasing smile before kissing him long and hard.

He finally lifted his mouth from hers. "You know why that is. We're not playing a game." A cough came out of him. "This is for real."

"Carson—" She framed his face with her hands. "I'm trying to be as honest with you as I know how to be. As you can see, I'm completely enamored with you. I spent all night asking myself questions—why this should be, and why it would happen now.

"Tony's only been gone a year. So many things have been going through my mind. Am I feeling this because this is my first experience with another man since he died and I'm missing physical fulfillment? Is this rugged Western cowboy so different from any man I've ever known, that I'm blinded by the comparison? When the newness wears off, will he be disenchanted by my Ohio roots?"

He smoothed some silvery-gold strands off her cheek. "To be brutally honest, I've been asking the same questions, and others. Why am I taken with a woman who will keep another man in her heart forever? Why have I met a woman who has a son she'll always put first? Am I crazy to want to deal with all that, knowing she's bonded to her husband's family?"

A tortured expression broke out on her face. "The way you put it, it does sound crazy. As I told you last night, you're young with your whole life ahead of you. Some single, Western woman who's never met the right man is going to come along and knock your socks off.

You'll be the only man in her heart. The two of you will start a new family together."

Carson grimaced. "As long as you're playing what-if, can you imagine the irony of another widow with a child, like yourself, coming to the ranch this summer and sweeping me off my feet? A woman with the wisdom to grab at a second chance for happiness?"

Shadows darkened her eyes. "Actually, I can. I've been haunted by that very possibility since last night."

He raised himself up. "Are you willing to risk it and fly back to Ohio on Saturday, away from me? Before you find out what joy you might be depriving the three of us of?"

She shook her head. "You don't know Johnny. This trip represents a huge change for him.

"In the heat of the moment he'd agree to do whatever I wanted, but in time his true feelings will surface. When they do, it could be traumatic for him if he wants to go home because he misses the family too much, but feels guilty because he doesn't want to hurt your feelings.

"I don't question his affection for you, Carson. But he'll feel the pull of family the longer he's out here. I'd rather spare him that kind of pain."

Her words gutted him. He got up from the couch, unconsciously raking a hand through his hair. "You know your son the way I never will. I have no say when it comes to your mother's intuition. It's clear to me you've made up your mind. Have no fear I'll try to persuade you further."

Tracy looked wounded as she slid off the couch. "You know I'm right," her voice trembled.

He wheeled around. "No. I don't know that. What I do know is that when you leave, you'll be preventing us from learning the truth. For the rest of our lives we'll have that question mark hanging over us. But as we've discovered by surviving the war, life goes on."

"Carson," she pleaded.

"Carson what? You've said it all, Tracy. Now I've got to go. If Johnny feels well in the morning, bring him to the barn after breakfast. I'm driving the kids to the upper pasture. My foreman has been in touch with some other ranchers and has found a cow with a blue-eyed calf for me. I'd like one of the kids to find it."

Tears glistened in her eyes. "They'll be overjoyed."

"I still need to come up with a prize. Do you think a pair of chaps?"

She wiped the tears away with the heel of her hand. "You already know the answer to that question."

He tried to ignore her emotion. "After lunch, I'll take them horseback riding. As for Friday, I'll be doing some ranching business during the day, but Ross or Buck will take them riding for the last time. I'm still good to drive them to the rodeo on Friday evening."

"Johnny's living for it," she whispered.

"I think he'll enjoy it. On Saturday morning, I'll be running you and the Harrises to the airport in the van. With the children leaving at the same time, it should make things easier all the way around. I expect I'll see you in the morning."

Carson started for the door, but saw movement in his peripheral vision. "Don't come any closer." *Not ever again.*

He left the cabin, suppressing a cough until he got

outside. When it subsided, he climbed in the Jeep with-out looking back. En route to Jackson, he phoned Ross and told him he was going into town in case anyone needed him.

"You sound like hell."

"That's where I am."

"If you want company, I'll tell Buck I'm joining you."

"Thanks, Ross, but I'm not fit to be around anyone."

"Tracy's still leaving on Saturday?"

"Yup."

"Sorry, bud."

"I'll live, unfortunately."

Carson hung up and continued driving to Jackson where he headed for the Aspen Cemetery. The small resting place was closed at sunset, but that didn't stop him. He pulled off the road and hopped a fence. His parents and grandparents were buried in the same plot up on the hillside near some evergreens. This was the first time he'd been here since the funeral.

The moon had come up and illuminated the dou-ble headstones. In a few strides he reached them and hunkered down to read the names and dates. *Beloved Son and Daughter* was inscribed on his parents' gran-ite stone. It had been here for twenty-eight years. How many times had Carson come to this sacred place as a youth to talk to them?

For his grandparents, he'd had the words inscribed, *Our Last Ride Will Be to Heaven.* Carson had heard his grandfather say it often enough while he was alive. He could hear him saying it now and wept.

Finally, blinking back the tears, his gaze fell on the grassy spot next to it. One day it would be Carson's own grave. When someone buried him here, there'd only be a single headstone. That would be the end of the Lundgren line.

"Sorry, Grandpa. I finally met that woman you were asking me about. But like everything else important that happened in my life, I got there too late. Marriage isn't in my destiny. But I swear I'll take care of the ranch so you're not disappointed in me."

If the guys were still in business with him when the end came, he had no doubt they'd be married with families. He'd deed them the title and their families could carry on the Lundgren legacy. They been brought together at a low ebb in their lives and had formed an unbreakable bond.

But if it turned out they wanted and needed to go back to their former lives after this experiment was over, he'd will the property to the Chappuis family. Maurice had been like a surrogate uncle to him. Jean-Paul had been his best friend in his early days. Carson couldn't think of anyone he'd want more to inherit. No family had ever worked harder to carve out a life here. Either way, the ranch would be in the best of hands.

Having made his peace, he returned to the ranch. Two more days and she'd be gone. He would have to play the congenial host to Johnny without the boy knowing Carson's pain. The whole point of inviting their family here in the first place was to bring a little happiness into their lives. To that end he was still fully committed.

Chapter 9

"I found one!"

From her perch on a hay bale, Tracy heard Sam's shout of delight. The calf with the blue eyes had been discovered.

Carson praised everyone for looking, but Sam was proclaimed the winner. In a few minutes Johnny came running through the herd to the truck. He'd recovered from his stomach upset but was now afflicted with another problem. When she pulled him into the truck bed, he was fighting tears.

"What's wrong, honey?" As if she didn't know.

"I wanted to find it."

"I know, but so did Rachel."

"Carson's going to give him a pair of chaps."

"Think how happy it will make him."

"But I wanted to be the one so he'd be proud of me."
He broke down and flung himself at her.

With that last remark, her heart ached for him. "He's always proud of you. You know what I think? You're a little tired after being sick yesterday."

"No, I'm not."

"Then hurry and dry your eyes because everyone's coming. You don't want anyone to see how you feel. Why don't you go over to the basket and get us both some water?"

"Okay," he muttered.

The kids came running over to the truck. Carson lifted them inside. She saw him glance at Johnny with concern, then his gaze swerved to her. It was the first time all morning he'd actually looked at her. When they'd arrived at the pasture, she'd already decided to stay put in the truck so she wouldn't have to interact with Carson any more than she had to.

When he'd left her cabin last night, she'd known he'd be keeping his distance until they left Wyoming, but this new estrangement was killing her.

Afraid he knew it, she gave Sam a hug. "Congratulations! You must have sharp eyes!"

"Yeah." He smiled. "I couldn't believe it."

"I wish I found it first," Rachel lamented.

Tracy nodded. "We all know how you feel. Better luck next time." She turned to Johnny. "Why don't you hand everyone a drink while you're at it, honey? You've all worked hard in this hot sun."

He passed the drinks around, but his face was devoid of animation.

Carson closed the tailgate. "If everyone's in, we'll head back to the ranch for lunch."

He walked around to the front, draining his water

bottle. Once he'd emptied it he called out, "Catch, Johnny!" and tossed it into the back of the truck before climbing into the cab.

By some miracle her son nabbed it, causing a smile to spread on his face.

On the way back, Tracy chatted with the children about the coming sleepover. Soda was allowed, but no candy. What movie did they want to watch? What board games did they want her to choose from the game room? To her relief, Johnny started to settle down and be his friendlier self. Knowing Rachel had lost out, too, helped a little.

When Carson let them out of the back of the truck after they'd arrived in front of the ranch house, Tracy moved right with the kids and jumped down from the end before Carson could reach for her. It was a bittersweet relief to hurry inside with them, knowing he'd disappear for a while.

The kids had the routine down pat. Bathroom first, to wash their hands. As they emerged into the foyer a few minutes later, Tracy heard a familiar female voice call out, "Giovanni! Look at you in those cowboy clothes!"

Her mind reeled.

No-o.

It couldn't be.

But it was. No one else called him by their pet name for him.

"Grandma?"

"Yes! Grandma and Papa. Come and give us a hug. We've missed you so much!"

Tracy was so unprepared for this, she almost fainted. Johnny sounded equally shocked, but he ran to them.

His grandmother kissed him several times, and then his grandfather picked him up and hugged him hard. Both of them were attractive and had dark hair with some silver showing. Sylvia was even wearing a pantsuit, something she rarely did.

It was painful for Tracy to watch the interaction, because conflicting emotions were swamping her. To see them here so removed from their world...

She didn't know what all had gone on to bring them to Wyoming when her vacation wasn't over yet, but she had a strong inkling.

Between Johnny's conversation with them on the phone the other day, and her conversation with Natalie, her in-laws were curious enough to get on a plane and come. It was totally unlike them.

She felt the other kids' eyes on her, needing an explanation. "Children? I'd like you to meet Johnny's grandparents from Ohio, Sylvia and Vincent Baretta. Dad and Mom? Please meet Rachel and Sam Harris from Florida. We've all become friends while we've been staying here."

"Oh, it's so nice to meet Johnny's friends," her mother-in-law said, patting their cheeks.

Her father-in-law still held Johnny while he reached for Tracy and kissed her. "After our talk with Giovanni the other morning, we decided to surprise you."

"You certainly did that." She still couldn't believe they'd come.

"Hi!" Monica had just appeared in the foyer with Ralph. "What's all the excitement?"

"These are my grandparents!" Johnny announced. "They came to see me ride Goldie!"

Okay. The pieces of the puzzle were starting to come together.

"Do you like my cowboy hat and boots? Carson took us to the store to get them."

Sylvia clapped her hands. "You look wonderful! Who's Carson?"

"He owns this whole ranch, Grandma. He rides bulls in the rodeo and is king of the cowboys!" Johnny's eyes shone like stars.

Tracy needed to do something quick. "Mom and Dad Baretta? Please meet Monica and Ralph Harris." They walked over and shook hands.

Monica smiled. "What a thrill for you, Johnny!"

"Yeah. Wait till I tell Carson! Let's hurry and eat. I'll take you over to the corral after lunch. He takes us riding every day! This morning he drove us to the pasture!"

"And guess what?" Rachel looked at her parents. "Sam found the blue-eyed calf."

"Yes, and Carson's going to give me a brand new pair of chaps to take home for winning."

"Good for you." Ralph patted his son on the back.

"We don't want to go home," Sam told his parents. "Carson told us about all these neat hikes we can go on in the Tetons. We just barely got here."

"I don't want to go home, either." Johnny took up the mantra. "Carson said the ponies will miss us. We can't leave them, Mom!"

Tracy heard her mother-in-law give the nervous little laugh she sometimes made when she didn't quite know what was going on. Johnny's grandfather lowered him to the floor. Still reeling, she said, "Why don't we go in the dining room for lunch, and then we can talk."

The room was fairly crowded. Tracy found two tables close together. While the Harrises took one of them, she guided her in-laws to the other. Johnny sat down between his grandparents, talking a mile a minute. Carson this and Carson that.

After their waitress took the orders, Tracy was finally able to ask a few questions. "When did you get here?"

Vincent had been quiet most of the time. "We flew into Salt Lake from Cleveland, then caught a flight to Jackson last evening and stayed at a motel. Today we rented a car and drove over here to surprise you."

"Well, it's wonderful to see you." Her voice trembled. It really was, but she was still incredulous.

"These mountains are overpowering!" Sylvia exclaimed. "It's beautiful here, but I can tell we're in a much higher altitude."

"I love it here!" Johnny blurted. "It's my favorite place in the whole world."

Tracy saw a look of surprise in her in-laws' eyes. She had an idea they, too, were in shock over the change in their formerly withdrawn grandson. Suddenly Johnny jumped up from the table.

"Hey, Carson—" He ran over to the tall cowboy in the black Stetson and plaid shirt walking toward them and hugged him around the waist. "My grandma and grandpa came to see me. Will you take us all riding?"

"Sure I will," Tracy heard him say as if it were the most normal thing in the world that her in-laws had shown up unannounced and uninvited.

Johnny made the introductions. Vincent stood up to shake Carson's hand. "It was a great thing you and your fellow marines did, inviting Tracy and Giovanni here, Mr. Lundgren. Thank you for honoring our son this way. We're very grateful to you for showing our grandson such a good time."

"We certainly are," Sylvia chimed in.

"The honor has been all ours, Mr. and Mrs. Baretta. I'd be happy to introduce you to my business partners, but they're both out with other guests at the moment. It pleases me to tell you that Johnny has turned into quite a horseman already." He coughed. "I'll be over at the corral when you want to see him ride."

"We'll be right over after we eat."

"Please feel free to use all the facilities while you're here."

"That's very generous of you. Sylvia and I are staying in Jackson. We decided we'd join our family and take them to Yellowstone Park before we fly back home together. It will be a new adventure for all of us."

A gasp escaped Tracy's throat, causing Carson to glance at her briefly, but she couldn't read anything in those blue slits. Johnny hurried over to Tracy. He put his lips against her ear. "I don't want to go to Yellowstone."

"We'll talk about this later," she murmured. "Sit down and eat your lunch."

Carson tipped his hat, and then stopped at the Harrises' table to talk to them for a minute before he left the dining room in a few long, swift strides. Tracy's heart dropped to her feet. A subdued Johnny sat down, but he only played with his hamburger.

Sylvia patted his hand. "We got a suite with another room so you can stay with us tonight."

"We can't, Grandma. We're having a sleepover at our cabin with Rachel and Sam." This time Tracy saw definite hurt in Sylvia's eyes. Vincent's face had closed up.

"I'm afraid I promised Monica and Ralph," Tracy explained.

"They babysat me while Mom and Carson went out to dinner." Johnny was a veritable encyclopedia of information, but every word that came out of his mouth caused his grandparents grief.

"Well then, we'll have to do it on Friday night."

"But Carson's taking us to the rodeo!"

Tracy needed to put a stop to this, but didn't know how. "When are you flying back?"

"Tuesday," Vincent informed her. "If you call the airline, you can change your flight so we can all fly home together."

Johnny slumped down in his seat. "I don't want to go home."

Though she couldn't condone his behavior, she understood it. "Mom and Dad?" They looked hurt and confused. "If you'll excuse us, we'll meet you at the corral. Drive your car over to the barn. You can't miss it and we'll be waiting for you. Come on, Johnny."

He bolted out of his chair without giving his grandparents a kiss and ran over to the other kids. It wounded her for their sake, but the damage was done now. Soon the three children preceded Tracy out of the dining room. She needed a talk with her son, but this wasn't the time.

Tracy saw Carson's Jeep outside the barn before they

reached the corral. Bert had already saddled the ponies. Carson came out leading Annie and Blueberry.

Tracy stood at the fence. While the children waited for Bert to help them mount, she watched Carson help Johnny. The play of male muscles in his arms and across his back held her mesmerized.

She heard the sound of a car and turned in time to see her in-laws get out and walk over to her. "You're in for a treat," she promised them. "We've done a lot of riding."

"Watch me!" Johnny called out to his grandparents.

All three children rode well, but Johnny stole the show as he walked Goldie around the corral like an old hand. She saw the pride in her in-laws' eyes. "You look wonderful!" they both called out to him. Vincent had tears in his eyes.

Johnny's face was beaming. "She's *my* pony."

"She's beautiful," Sylvia cried.

"Come on and ride, Grandpa. Carson's going to take us down to the Snake River and back."

"Why don't you go?" Tracy urged him. "You can ride the horse I've been riding. Sylvia and I will stay here until you get back." This would be a good time to feel out her mother-in-law over their unexpected arrival.

Johnny's invitation must have put Vincent in a better mood because he said, "I think I will."

"What about you, Sylvia? Maybe you'd like to ride, too?"

"Not me. You go ahead, Vincent. Tracy and I will have a good visit while you're gone."

It sounded like Sylvia wanted to talk to Tracy in private. They'd had a definite agenda in coming out here. Vincent was curious about the man who'd caused this change in his grandson. This would give him a chance to get a feel for him. They'd probably talk about the war and the circumstances leading up to Tony's death.

As for Carson, a picture was worth more than a thousands words of explanation from her. During the ride with Vincent, he'd come to know and understand better the dynamics that made up the Baretta family. He'd already learned a lot from their surprise visit.

The two men spoke for a minute before Vincent climbed in the saddle. He'd ridden horses in parades with the other firefighters and looked good up there. He always did, especially when he had to dress in his formal uniform. She realized Tony would have looked a lot like him if he'd had the opportunity to live a full life.

Oddly enough, that sharp pain at the remembrance of her husband was missing. The only pain she was feeling right now was a deep, soul-wrenching kind of pain as she watched the king of the cowboys mount his horse with effortless grace. From beneath the brim of his hat, he shot Tracy a piercing glance. "We'll be gone a couple of hours. I'll bring everyone back in the Jeep."

She took a deep breath. "We'll be waiting."

On that note he nodded and led everyone out of the corral, away from her.

This is what you wanted, Tracy, so why the anguish? Except that it wasn't what she wanted. She'd been looking forward to the ride this afternoon with each breath she took. Every second with Carson was precious until they had to leave.

When she couldn't see them anymore for the tears she was fighting, she walked toward the car. "Come on,

Sylvia. I'll drive us back to our cabin and fix you a cup of coffee." Her mother-in-law was a big coffee drinker.

"I like the sound of that." Sylvia handed her the keys. "This is very beautiful country," she said as they drove through the sage. "When we saw the brochure on the internet, I couldn't appreciate it the way I do now."

"You have to be here and see those Tetons to realize the grandeur."

"You love it here as much as Johnny does, don't you?"

With that serious inflection in Sylvia's voice, it was the kind of question that deserved a totally honest answer. "Yes."

Tracy pulled the car up to the cabin and they went inside. "The bathroom is through there, Sylvia. While you freshen up, I'll fix us some coffee." Her mother-in-law liked it with cream and sugar. Tracy added a few snacks to a tray and put it on the coffee table.

A few minutes later they were both ensconced on the couch. "This is a very charming cabin, sunny. So was the dining room at the ranch house. You say this whole ranch belongs to Mr. Lundgren?"

Instead of the usual chitchat about family, Sylvia had zeroed in on Carson. Tracy couldn't say she was surprised. "Yes. The Teton Valley Ranch has been in their family since the early 1900s. His grandparents raised him here after his parents were killed. Carson's grandfather died recently and left him everything."

"Johnny told us he isn't married. He's certainly young to have so much responsibility."

Oh, Sylvia... "There's no one more capable."

"Obviously. Why does he cough so much?"

Tracy explained about him and his friends who'd met at Walter Reed. "Because of their illness, they were discharged from the military and decided to make this place into a dude ranch.

"Next month, another family they're honoring will be arriving. The plan is to take care of several more war widows with children by the time summer is over. They're quite remarkable men."

"I agree."

Tracy moistened her lips nervously. "Sylvia, why didn't you let me know you were coming?"

"I wanted to, but Vincent felt it would be more fun to surprise you. You know how much he loves Johnny. Every time he looks at him, he sees Tony. It was hard for him to see you two leave on this trip."

"And hard for you, too, I bet," Tracy added.

Sylvia teared up. "Yes, but I was glad for you to have this opportunity and told him. He was morose after you left. It came as a shock to hear Johnny talk about this man over the phone. He didn't mention his father once."

I know.

"That upset Vincent so much, especially after we'd heard Natalie telling Sally about this exciting cowboy you met. After we got off the phone with Johnny, Vincent called to make reservations to fly out here."

It was exactly as Tracy had thought. Her father-in-law had felt threatened.

"Don't be upset with Vincent, Tracy. He's different since Tony died, because he doesn't want anything to change. He wants to be there for you and Johnny."

"I know that, Sylvia, and I love him for it."

"But you didn't like our coming here out of the blue.

If you could have seen your face." She reached over to squeeze Tracy's hand. "I don't need to ask what this man means to Johnny. What I want to know is, how much does he mean to you?"

Tracy's heart was thudding so hard, she had to get up from the couch. "I— It's hard to put into words," her voice faltered.

"That means it's serious."

She wheeled around. "It could be," she answered with all the truth in her, "but I don't mean to hurt you or Dad. You know Tony was my life."

"Hey—you forget I'm a woman, too." She got to her feet. "Our son has been dead for a year. I have eyes in my head. When this tall, blue-eyed god walked toward our table in the dining room, he made *my* heart leap."

"Oh, Sylvia—" Tracy reached out and hugged her mother-in-law. She'd never loved her more than at this moment. For a few minutes they both cried. Finally Tracy pulled away and wiped her eyes. "He's asked me to stay on so we can really get to know each other."

"Does Johnny know this?"

"No, and I don't want him to know." Having broken down this far, Tracy decided to tell Sylvia everything and ended up admitting all her reservations. "After losing Tony, if it didn't work out, Johnny could be severely damaged. I told Carson it wouldn't work and that's the way we've left it."

"If, if—" Sylvia exclaimed dramatically. "You can't worry about the ifs! Do you remember Frankie, who was killed two years ago battling that warehouse fire?"

"Yes. It was horrible."

"No one thought his wife and daughters would get

over it. One of the other firefighters looked out for her, and six months later they were married and expecting a baby of their own. These things happen and they should! What if she'd said she couldn't risk it? Now she has a father for her girls and a new baby with this man she loves."

Tracy was struggling. "How do you think Frankie's parents felt about it?"

"At first they had a hard time. Now they're fine with it."

She looked at Sylvia. "Can you honestly see Vincent being fine with this? Carson's not a firefighter. His life is here, running this ranch. If I were to get to know him better, Johnny and I would have to stay out here, otherwise a relationship wouldn't be possible."

Sylvia's brows lifted. "You worry too much. Yes, Vincent is having difficulty letting go, but this situation isn't about your father-in-law or me. You let *me* worry about him. This is about *your* life and Johnny's, what's best for the two of you. In time you'll get your answer."

"You're the wisest woman I know. I love you, Sylvia."

"I love you, too. I always will. Since neither Vincent nor I have ever been to Yellowstone, he has his heart set on taking Johnny to see the Old Faithful geyser. Why don't we all leave for the park after the rodeo? He has us booked at Grant Village. That will give us Saturday, Sunday and Monday together. Then we'll drive you back here to the ranch and leave Tuesday. Perhaps by then you'll know your mind better."

It was a good plan. Three days with his grandparents, and Johnny might realize he was ready to go home to

Ohio, especially when he remembered Sam and Rachel would be gone. Three days away from Carson would give Tracy some perspective, too. At the moment she had none.

"Will you come to our sleepover?"

Carson smiled at Johnny as he helped him off his pony. "I'll do better than that. I'll bring pizza for your going-away party."

Johnny frowned. "What do you mean?"

"You're leaving for Yellowstone after the rodeo, so I thought we'd celebrate tonight."

"But we'll be back."

"I don't know what your mother's plans are, Johnny." Out of the corner of his eye, he watched his grandfather dismount. Carson hated to admit it, but he was a good man who obviously adored his grandson and couldn't wait to get him home to Ohio.

Carson's gut twisted when he thought back to his conversation with Tracy, who loved her in-laws. Their hold on her and Johnny was fairly absolute. "I'll bring enough for your grandparents, too." He turned to the others. "Let's get you guys home so you can get ready for the pizza party."

"Yay!" the others cried, but not Johnny.

Everyone got in the Jeep and they took off. He dropped Sam and Rachel at their cabin, and then headed for Tracy's. The rental car was out in front. She'd been there all afternoon with her mother-in-law. It was no accident her in-laws had decided to show up. She'd been right about Tony's family. They were very protective. *You don't have a chance in hell, Lundgren.*

Mr. Baretta sat next to Carson. When he stopped the truck, the older man turned to him. "It's been a privilege to go riding with you. I can see Johnny has been in the best of hands." He shook Carson's hand and got out to help his grandson.

Since he couldn't handle seeing Tracy right now, Carson went straight to the ranch house without looking back. He made a beeline for the kitchen and put in an order for pizza for six. While he was at it, he'd bring the chaps for Sam.

He saw Ross and Buck in the office. "I'm glad you're both here." He walked inside and shut the door.

Ross eyed him curiously. "The Harrises told us Johnny's grandparents showed up."

"You heard right."

"That's interesting," Buck muttered on a cough. "What's going on?"

"They've missed Johnny and came to get him. Under the circumstances, I need a favor."

"Anything."

"You know I'm taking the kids to the rodeo tomorrow night, but during the day I need to work with the foreman. Ross, will you take the kids riding? I'll get one of the staff to take the other guests fishing."

His dark brows furrowed. "Johnny's not going to like it. You know that."

"It's the only way to handle it. Tracy expects me to help make the parting easier for him. Her father-in-law let me know they're leaving for Yellowstone right after the rodeo and will be flying back to Salt Lake from there. I've decided that it'll be the best to say goodbye with a crowd around."

"I get it. Of course I'll do it. Did Tracy know they were coming?"

"I don't think so. It was supposed to be a surprise, but I can't be sure. It doesn't matter, does it? They're here, and Tracy will be leaving tomorrow for good."

The guys stared hard at him. "It *does* matter if she didn't want them to show up," Buck said.

"Want to make a bet? I spent part of the afternoon with Tony Baretta's father. He's a crusty fire chief from a long line of firefighters and he's tougher than nails. It kind of explains Tony," Carson bit out. A coughing spell followed. It was always worse for all of them this time of day. "I've got to get my inhaler. I'll see you guys later."

Carson went to his bedroom to medicate himself. After his shower, he left for Jackson to buy those chaps for Sam. He'd buy two more pair, for Rachel and Johnny, but he'd tell Monica and Tracy to hide them in their suitcases so they'd find them after they got home. The last thing he wanted was to take away the fun from Sam who'd been the winner.

He would miss those kids like crazy. It was then he realized what a huge transformation he'd undergone since Tracy had arrived. But he couldn't allow himself to think about that right now.

Later, as he was coming out of the Boot Corral with his purchases, he bumped into Carly Bishoff. "Hey, Carly." He tipped his hat to her. "How's the best barrel racer in Teton County? I hear you're going to win tomorrow night."

"You're planning to be there?"

"I am."

The good-looking redhead flashed him a winning

smile. "I'd be a lot better if you ever gave me a call. I've been waiting since high school. Do you want to hook up after the rodeo?" She'd thrown that invitation out before, but he'd never taken her up on it.

"Why not?" he asked, shocking himself. It was his pain speaking, but he couldn't take it back. Tomorrow night he needed help, or he wouldn't get through it after Tracy and Johnny drove off.

"Did I hear you right, cowboy?"

"You sure did."

"Then you know where to find me after."

"It's a date."

He headed for his Jeep, already regretting what he'd done. She was a great girl. Hell and hell.

With the pizza order ready, he was able to pick it up and head straight for the Harrises' cabin. When he knocked on their door, Monica greeted him. He learned the kids had already gone and Ralph was in the shower. Carson was in luck.

"Will you hide these from Rachel until you get back to Florida? I'm giving Sam his prize tonight."

"She'll be thrilled!" Monica exclaimed. "Honestly, Carson, you've made this a dream vacation. We'll never forget."

"Neither will I, believe me. See you tomorrow when we all leave for the rodeo."

"We can't wait."

"Have fun tonight."

"Thanks to Tracy, we definitely will. She's a wonderful person."

She's more than that. "I couldn't agree more. Good night."

The children were running around outside shooting their cap guns when Carson pulled up to Tracy's cabin. The Barettas' rental car was parked along the side. They all came running up to the Jeep.

"Pizza delivery!" he called out.

The kids whooped it up and scrambled around to take the cartons inside.

"Just a minute, Sam," he called him back. "This present is for you." He handed him a sack with the chaps.

Sam looked inside and broke into a big smile. "Thanks, Carson! Wait till I show my parents!"

He ran into the cabin with Rachel and Johnny. Carson followed them. He needed to tell Tracy to come out to the Jeep so he could secretly give her Johnny's present, but she saved him the trouble by coming outside. For the moment, they were alone. She was so beautiful, he couldn't stop staring.

"H-Hi." She sounded out of breath. "I can't believe you brought pizza."

"It's a going-away party. What else could I do?"

Her hazel eyes went suspiciously bright. "Johnny's been worried about that."

He grimaced. "I haven't been too happy about it myself. What did you tell him?"

"Nothing I said has comforted him."

"He'll be all right once you're on the road with your in-laws. I bought him chaps, but I suggest you put them in the rental car so the other kids don't see them. He wanted to win."

"Johnny hasn't gotten over it. Do you know why? Because he wanted you to be proud of him."

His throat swelled. "He's the best, Tracy."

When she took the sack from him, he could feel her tremble. "Won't you stay and eat with us? Vincent said the ride was a special treat for him. That's all because of you."

"I'm glad, but didn't you know seven is a crowd when you're already a party of six?" he asked pointedly, half hoping she'd beg him to stay. But of course she didn't, and he would have been forced to turn her down anyway. "Ross will take the kids riding tomorrow. If you and your in-laws want to meet me in front of the ranch house at quarter after four, you can follow me to the rodeo grounds. It starts at five. Have a fun sleepover. If there's anything you need, call the desk. Good night."

Chapter 10

If a horse had kicked her in the stomach, knocking her flat, Tracy couldn't have been more incapacitated as Carson got back in his Jeep and drove off without hesitation. She would never see him alone again. Being at the rodeo with him, surrounded by family and hundreds of other people, wasn't the same thing.

This was it! With children and in-laws to entertain, she couldn't run after him right now. And even if she could, what would she say? The talk with Sylvia had taken away a lot of her guilt to do with the family, but she was no closer to making a decision. Johnny was the key. She had to put him above every other consideration.

If she decided to stay on, how long would it be before Johnny wanted to go home? But if she went home, and he ended up grieving for Carson as well as his father, it could end up a nightmare.

In agony, she went back in the cabin to supervise the evening's activities.

Her in-laws stayed until it was time to get the children to bed. They planned to come by at ten tomorrow to take everyone fishing, including the Harris children who enjoyed Johnny's grandparents a lot. Sylvia and Vincent really were the greatest. With so many grandchildren, they'd had enough practice.

On the surface Johnny went along and entered into the fun as much as he could because he loved his grandparents, but his heart wasn't in it. Tracy knew her son. The light Carson had put there had gone out again, because Johnny knew they would be leaving the ranch for good tomorrow.

How much could she trust it to be a crush on Carson that he'd get over in a few weeks? Or could it be the real thing? She'd been asking herself the same question where her feelings for Carson were concerned, but the answer was easy. When he'd driven away in the Jeep, she'd felt her heart go with him. Somehow during this last week he'd stolen it from her. Now that it was his, she couldn't take it back. She didn't want to.

What if Johnny were suffering the same way? Children were so open and honest. That night at the lake after Johnny's nightmare, he'd told Carson he loved him before saying good-night. At the time, she'd assumed he'd said it because his emotions were in turmoil after such a bad dream.

But now Tracy wasn't so sure. She thought back to the many times Johnny had spent with his uncles. He loved being with them and had wonderful experiences, but she couldn't recall him ever saying he *loved* them to their faces in a one-on-one situation with no one else around. Only a certain cowboy held that honor, but he was gone.

Her thoughts came full circle to that night at the lake. When Johnny's declaration of love for Carson came blurting out, she realized it had to have been born in the deepest recesses of his soul.

With that memory weighing her down, she finally got everyone to bed. They'd planned for Rachel to sleep on the couch so Johnny and Sam could share the other bedroom. But in the end, Johnny said he wanted to sleep with her.

Rachel and Sam were happy enough to share the other bedroom. Long after the lights went out and all was quiet, she heard subdued noises coming from Johnny's bed. She listened hard. He was crying.

She raised herself up on one elbow. "That's not a happy sound I can hear. Want to talk about it?"

"No."

"No? How come?"

He turned away from her. "I just don't."

"Do you wish your grandparents hadn't come?"

"No. I'm glad they came so they could see me ride Goldie."

"They're very proud of you."

"I know."

She bit her lip, loving this wonderful son of hers who was suffering a major heartache. Trying to get to the bottom of it she said, "I bet you wish your dad could see you ride."

"Grandma says he can see me from heaven."

He'd said it so matter-of-factly, Tracy didn't know

what to think. "I *know* he can, and I know he's very proud of you."

"Carson says I'm a natural. What does that mean?"

They were back to Carson. "It means you look like you were born on a horse and are getting to be an expert."

"But I won't be an expert, 'cos we're leaving tomorrow and I'll never see Goldie again. I don't want to go riding with Ross tomorrow."

"Then we don't have to."

"I don't want to go to the rodeo, either."

By now she was sitting up in her bed. "Why not?"

"I just don't."

Her spirits plunged. "But Carson's taking us."

"He can take Rachel and Sam. He likes *them*."

Tracy got out of bed and climbed into his. His pillow was wet. "Okay. Tell me what's really bothering you, honey, otherwise neither of us is going to get any sleep."

Suddenly he turned toward her and hugged her while he sobbed. Great heaving sobs that shook the bed.

"Honey—" Tracy rocked him for a long time. "What's wrong? Please tell me."

"C-Carson doesn't like me, Mom."

If the moment weren't so critical, she would have laughed. "You mean because Sam won the chaps?"

"No-o." He couldn't stop crying.

"He brought you some chaps, too, but he asked me to hide them until we got back to Ohio. It's his present to you."

"I don't want them."

"Why?"

"He only did that 'cos he thinks I'm a big baby."

"Johnny—" In her shock, she realized something deeper was going on here. "How do you know he doesn't like you?"

"He's not even going to take me riding tomorrow."

"But that's because he has ranch business."

"No, he doesn't."

"Johnny Baretta—I can't believe you just said that."

"It's true, Mom. He wouldn't stay for the party. He's glad Grandma and Grandpa came. Now he doesn't have to be with me."

Where on earth had he gotten this idea that Carson had rejected him? Carson had done everything but stand on his head to give her son the time of his life. But since her talk with Carson the other night, plus the arrival of her in-laws, he'd backed off. *All because of you, Tracy.*

Tormented with fresh guilt, she said, "What if we weren't leaving?"

"I *want* to leave."

Since when? There was something else going on here. She would get to the bottom of it if it killed her. "Tell me the truth, honey. Did Carson do something that hurt you?"

Instead of words, more sobs answered her question. She couldn't imagine what this was all about. "I have to know, Johnny." She ached for him. "Please tell me."

Tracy had to wait to get her answer. Long after the tears dried up, she heard, "W-When I told him I loved him, he didn't tell me back."

"You mean the night when we were in the tent out camping?"

"Yes."

"But he *did* tell you."

He shot up in bed. "No, he didn't!"

"Yes he did. I remember distinctly. He said, 'The feeling's mutual, partner.'"

"What does that mean?"

Good heavens! "Honey—it meant he felt the same way."

"Then why didn't he say it?"

By now she was praying for inspiration. "Maybe he thought you weren't ready to hear the exact words back. Maybe he was afraid you only wanted to hear those words from your father."

"Why? I *love* him! Now that Dad's gone, he's my favorite person in the whole world!"

"I know that," she said in a quiet tone, too overcome to say more.

"I wish you loved him, too." Her son's voice cracked.

Her eyes widened. "You do?"

"Yes, but I know you loved Dad and always will."

She wrapped her arm around him. "I will always love your father, but that doesn't mean I can't love someone else again one day."

He jerked back to life, sending her an unmistakable message. "It doesn't?"

"No."

"Do you think you could love Carson? I know you like him because you went to dinner with him."

Oh, Johnny... "I like him a lot."

"He likes you, too. I can tell."

Her pulse was racing. "How?"

"You know. Stuff."

"What stuff?"

"He told me you were prettier than Goldie."

"He did?" A smile found its way to her lips.

"Yup. And he said you were a better mom than any woman he had ever known. He said my dad was lucky 'cos you were the kind of a woman a man wanted to marry. But he's afraid a woman wouldn't want to marry him."

Tracy had no idea all this had gone on out of her hearing. "Why would he think that?"

"'Cos he's got a disease. He says no woman wants to marry an old war vet who goes around coughing all the time. That's not true, is it, Mom?"

"No. Of course not. Tell you what, honey. Your grandparents flew all the way out here to be with you, so let's enjoy being with them until they have to fly home to Ohio. After we see them off at the airport, we'll bring their rental car back here and surprise Carson."

"Then we don't have to go home with them?"

"No." *Absolutely not.* "But don't let Carson know what we plan to do, otherwise it won't be a surprise."

"I *know*," he said in that unique way of his. "Oh, Mom. I love you!" He threw his arms around her once more.

After a long hug she said, "Now it's time to sleep. We'll talk some more in the morning after the kids go home."

"Okay."

They kissed good-night and she got back in her own bed, praying for morning to get here as fast as possible. She wouldn't be able to breathe until they'd come back from Yellowstone.

After the rodeo, everyone congregated in the parking lot; the Harrises, the Barettas and Carson. The dreaded time had come for everyone to say goodbye.

"Did you like the rodeo, guys?"

"Yeah!" Sam was still jumping up and down with excitement in his jeans and chaps. "Especially the bulls!"

"They're so big!" Johnny exclaimed.

Rachel smiled up at Carson. "I liked the barrel racing. That looked so fun."

"Maybe if you keep riding after you get home to Florida, you'll be able to do it one day." He looked at the Harrises. "If you'll climb in the Jeep, I'll run you back to the ranch."

The kids all said goodbye to each other. Tracy hugged the Harrises. Carson heard them exchange email addresses. Then it was time to help her and Johnny get in the back of the Barettas' rental car. They were all packed and ready for their trip to Yellowstone.

He couldn't hug Johnny the way he wanted to, not in front of everyone. Instead, he shook his hand. "It's been a pleasure getting to know the son of Tony Baretta. We had a great time together, didn't we, partner?"

"Yup." Johnny's eyes teared up, but he didn't cry. He knew his grandparents were watching and took the parting like a man. "Thanks for everything, Carson. Be sure and give Goldie some oats for me tomorrow. Tell her I'll miss her."

"I sure will. She'll miss you, too." That boy was taking a piece of him away. Carson didn't know he could love a child this much. He shut the door and walked around to say goodbye to Tracy. She'd already gotten in but hadn't closed the door yet.

Her eyes lifted to his. "We'll never forget what you've done for us, Carson. We thanked Ross and Buck earlier, but please thank them again. You and your buddies accomplished your objective to help a grieving family heal in ways you can't possibly comprehend. Our gratitude knows no bounds."

"That's good to hear and means more than you know. We had a lot of fun, too," he said on a cough. That was the understatement of all time. Carson didn't know how much more of this he could take.

He shut her door and walked to Mr. Baretta's open window. "There's still some daylight left, Vincent. Drive safely and enjoy."

"I'm sure we will. Thank you again, Carson. This was a great thing you did for Tracy and Johnny, one they'll remember forever." The two men shook hands.

He nodded to Sylvia. "It was a real pleasure meeting Johnny's grandmother."

"We enjoyed getting to know you, too, Carson. Goodbye and thank you."

Unable to bear it, Carson headed for his Jeep. Out of the rear window of the rental car he saw Tracy's gorgeous face. Her eyes glistened with tears. As he walked around the back end he spied Johnny's soulful brown eyes staring at him through the window. Tony Baretta's eyes. He belonged to the Baretta clan. So did Tracy.

The week from heaven had turned into the lifetime from hell.

On Monday, the family went back to watch Old Faithful go off. They'd seen it the day before, but Johnny wanted to see it again.

"Whoa!" he cried out when the geyser shot up into the air. It really was fantastic. But Tracy had something else on her mind that couldn't be put off any longer.

Once they returned to Grant Village, she would have to open up the discussion that wouldn't surprise Sylvia. But it was going to shock and hurt Vincent. Luckily she knew she had her mother-in-law's blessing.

They all grabbed a bite to eat and went back to their adjoining rooms. While she was alone with Johnny, she said, "I'm going to tell your grandparents we're not going back to Ohio with them. They need to know, because we need to leave for Jackson. Your grandparents will need a good night's sleep at the motel there before they fly home tomorrow."

He jumped up and down. "I can't wait to see Carson!" He hugged her so hard, he almost knocked her over.

She needed no other answer. Though his grandparents would be leaving, the only person on his mind was Carson. She couldn't wait to see him, either. After three days' deprivation, she was dying for him.

"Okay. Let's go to their room." She tapped on the door and they told her to come in.

Sylvia was resting on the bed. Vincent sat at the table, looking at a map of Yellowstone. He glanced up. "What would you two like to do now?"

"We'd like to talk to you if it's all right." That caused her mother-in-law to sit up.

Vincent smiled. "Come on in and sit down."

"Thanks. This is hard for me to say, because I love you so much and would never want to hurt you, but I can't go back to Ohio yet. Carson has asked me and Johnny to stay on so we can get to know each other better."

"He *did?*" Johnny looked shocked.

"Yes. It was the night he took me out to dinner. I didn't tell you then, because I needed time to think about it."

But happy tears were already gushing down his cheeks. "Then he really does love us!"

"Yes. I believe he does." She had a hard time swallowing. "The problem is, we've only been here a week. That's why we need more time."

Her father-in-law stared at her. "How come it's taken until today for you to tell us? Sylvia confided in me the other day. We've been waiting."

There was a light in his eyes, making her heart beat faster.

"Why do you think we flew out here in the first place? Natalie told us you'd met a man. When Johnny got on the phone with us, we knew it was for real. We couldn't let this go on without sizing him up."

He got to his feet and came over to hug her. "Our grandson was right. Carson Lundgren is awesome. You'd be a fool not to stay. Tony's gone, and we'll love him forever, but Sylvia and I knew this day would have to come. We just didn't know you'd fall for the king of the cowboys."

"Oh, Dad!"

It was a love fest all around with Johnny hugging his grandmother.

Three hours later, Vincent drove them to the ranch house and dropped them off in front. It was almost nine in the evening. After more hugs, kisses and promises to phone, they carried their bags into the foyer. Tracy's legs were trembling so hard, she could scarcely walk. Johnny was all decked out in his cowboy stuff.

Susan was at the front desk. When she looked up, she blinked. "Hi! We all thought you'd left! Did you leave something behind?"

Yes. Our hearts.

"As a matter of fact, we did. Is Carson around?"

"He's over at the barn with the vet. One of the horses went lame this afternoon."

Johnny stared up at Tracy. "I hope it's not Goldie."

"No," Susan said. "It's not any of the ponies."

"That's good."

Tracy smiled at Susan. "Do you mind if we leave our bags out here? We won't be long."

"Of course you can. I'll put them behind the desk for now."

"Thank you." Reaching for Johnny's hand she said, "Come on, honey. Let's go find him."

They left the ranch house at a run and kept running all the way to the barn. There was an unfamiliar truck outside. The vet's most likely. The sound of coughing let her know the location of the stall before they saw the light from it.

She ventured closer, but kept out of sight. The two men were conversing. "Let's wait till they're through," she whispered to Johnny.

Their voices drifted outside the stall. "Magpie will be all right, Carson. Let her rest for a few days, and then see if her limp is improving. This capped hock isn't serious. If she gets worse, call me."

"Will do. Thanks, Jesse."

"You bet."

Tracy and Johnny stood in the shadows. They watched the other man leave the barn. Her son looked up at her with eyes that glowed in the semidarkness. "Can I tell him we're here?" he whispered.

The blood was pounding in her ears. "Tell him whatever you want, honey."

While Tracy peeked, he moved carefully until he was behind Carson who was talking to the horse and rubbing her forelock to comfort her. What a man. What a fabulous man.

"Carson?"

He spun around so fast, Johnny backed away. The look on Carson's face was one of absolute shock. *"Johnny—"* Like lightning, he hunkered down in front of her son. "What are you doing here?" His voice sounded unsteady. Closer to the source of the light, Carson showed a definite pallor.

"Mom and I decided we want to stay. Grandma and Grandpa dropped us off before they went back to Jackson."

"You mean, until tomorrow?"

"No. They're going back to Ohio. We're going to stay here. Don't you want us to?"

In the next breath Carson crushed her son in his powerful arms. "Don't I *want* you to—" he cried. "Do you have any idea how much I love you and your mom?"

"We love you, too!" came Johnny's fervent cry as he wrapped his arms tightly around Carson's neck.

"Every second since the rodeo I've been praying you'd come back."

"We would have come sooner, but we had to wait till they brought us back from Yellowstone. My grandparents think you're awesome!"

Carson's eyes played over Johnny as if he couldn't

believe what he was seeing or hearing. "Where's your mom?"

Her heart almost failed her. "Right here." Tracy stepped into the light. "We came as soon as we could. It's probably too early in our relationship to be saying this, but I love you, Carson. I've known it all along, but it took Johnny to say it first. You know the old saying… a child shall lead them."

His eyes burned like the blue flames in a fire. He got to his feet. "I know the saying and believe it." She heard his sharp intake of breath. "Let's go home." His voice sounded husky as he turned off the light. Sliding an arm around her shoulders, he grasped Johnny's hand and they left the barn. "If I'm dreaming this up, then we're all in it together because I'm never letting you go."

"Is anyone using our cabin?" Johnny wanted to know.

"Yes."

"Then where will we stay?"

"With me."

Tracy's joy spiked.

"You mean in the ranch house?"

"Yup."

"Goody. I love it in there, but I've never seen where you sleep."

"You're going to find out right now, but it'll be temporary because I'm building us a house in my favorite spot by the river, smack-dab in the middle of a flowering meadow."

"You are?"

"It will have a loft where you can sleep and see the Grand Teton right out your window. I was thinking of getting a dog."

Johnny squealed. "Can I have a Boston terrier? Nate has one." Tracy didn't know that. She hadn't heard the other boy's name for a long time.

"What a great choice. He can sleep with you in the loft. You'll be able to see the mountains from every window." He squeezed Tracy's hip, sending a jolt through her like a current of electricity.

The sweet smell of sage rose up from the valley floor, increasing her euphoria. The moon had come up, distilling its serene beauty over a landscape Tracy had learned to love with a fierceness that surprised her.

When they walked in the foyer, Susan jumped to her feet. "Hi, Carson. Looks like they found you."

He sent Tracy a private message. "That they did. Just so you know, they're staying with me."

"Our luggage is behind the counter," Johnny announced. "I'll get it."

Her son was acting like a man. That was Carson's influence. He carried the cases around, but held on to the shoulder bag. Carson picked them up. "Let's go, partner. You want to open that door at the end of the hall past the restrooms?"

"Sure."

Once again Carson was allowing her into his inner sanctum, but this time there was all the difference in the world, because she wouldn't be leaving it.

He led them down a hall till he came to a bedroom on his left. "In here, Johnny. This is where you and your mom will stay for now." The room was rustic and cozy with twin beds and an en suite bathroom. Carson set the bags down on the wood floor and turned to her.

"When we planned the dude ranch, we decided

we'd use this guest bedroom if there was ever an over-flow. Little did I know when I sent you that letter…" He couldn't finish the sentence, but he said everything with his eyes. Her emotions were so overpowering she couldn't talk, either.

"Hey, Carson—can I see your room?"

"You bet. Follow me." They went across the hall to his suite where she'd been before. Her eyes slid to the bed where the fire between them had ignited, only to be stifled. Thank heaven this was now. The thought of another separation from Carson just meant pain to her.

"This is a big room!"

"My grandparents lived in here."

"Look at all these pictures!" Johnny ran around staring at them. "Hey, Mom—here are pictures of Carson when he was little, riding a pony like me! But there's no saddle. I want to learn to ride without a saddle. That's so cool."

"We'll try it out in a few days."

"What was your pony's name?"

"Confetti, because she was spotty."

"How cute," Tracy murmured as Carson came to stand behind her. He looped his strong arms around her neck, pressing kisses into her hair. He felt so wonderful, she couldn't wait to be alone with him.

"My grandparents took pictures of me constantly. You'll see me at every gawky stage."

"These are when you were in the Marines."

"Yup. My parents' and grandparents' pictures are on the other walls."

Johnny hurried over to look at them. "Is this your dad?"

The picture he was pointing to was in an oval frame. "Yes. He was twelve there."

"You kind of look like him."

"I've been told I resemble my mother more. See their wedding picture over on the left?"

Johnny moved to get a glance. "You do look a lot like her!"

This was an exciting night, but Johnny needed to get to bed. She needed him to go to sleep because she was going to die of longing for Carson if he didn't. "Honey? I'm sure Carson will let you look at everything tomorrow. But right now it's time for bed."

"Okay." He looked at Carson. "Will you come with me and Mom?"

"I was hoping you'd ask because I'd like to do it every night from now on. Let's go, partner."

Tracy moved ahead and pulled his pajamas out of his suitcase. Once his teeth were brushed, he climbed under the covers of the twin bed nearest the bathroom. While she stood by him, Carson set Johnny's cowboy hat on the dresser and sat down at his side.

"Do you know I never thought I'd get married or have a family?"

"I know. 'Cos you're afraid you'll cough too much and a woman won't like it, but Mom says it doesn't matter to her."

Carson shot her a penetrating glance. "Then I'm the luckiest man alive." He looked back at him. "I know I'm not your father, Johnny. I could never take his place, but I want you to know I love you as much as if you were my own son."

"I love you, too." Johnny sat up and gave him another squeeze before he settled back down against the pillow.

"Okay. It's time to go to sleep now. I'll stay with you while Carson closes up the ranch house and turns out the lights." In truth, Tracy had no idea of his routine, but until her son passed out, she couldn't go into Carson's room.

He got to his feet and tousled Johnny's hair. "I know a little filly who's going to be very happy when you show up to ride her tomorrow."

"I bet she's really missed me."

"You have no idea. Goodnight, partner. See you in the morning."

Carson's gaze slid to Tracy's. His eyes blazed with the promise of what was to come.

Chapter 11

Carson's elation was too great. He dashed down the hall and up the stairs. After coughing his head off, he called out to the guys. They emerged from their rooms in various states of undress.

Buck stared at him as if he were seeing an apparition. "What's happened to you? I hardly recognize the walking corpse."

"You might well ask."

"Something's up." Ross walked around him. "If I didn't know better…"

He nodded to both of them. "Tracy came back tonight with Johnny. They love me. They're here to stay and her in-laws gave us their blessing."

Slow smiles broke out on their faces. They slapped him on the back. "Congratulations. When's the wedding?"

"I haven't even been alone with her yet. She's putting Johnny to bed. I've installed them in the guest bedroom across from me. After tonight I'll know our plans better."

"What in the hell are you doing up here?"

"Trying to give her time to get him to sleep. Until we can be alone, I don't dare get anywhere near her. Besides, the three of us have a business arrangement. I don't want you to think my personal plans change anything."

Buck nodded. "We know that."

"If you want our blessing, you've got it." Ross gave him another pat on the shoulder. "Now, you've got thirty seconds to get out of here!"

Carson's eyes smarted. "Thanks, guys. I couldn't have made it out of the hospital without you."

Ross's brow quirked. "If you didn't know it yet, you saved my life with your offer to come here."

"Amen," Buck muttered. "We were dead meat when we arrived at the hospital. It took meeting you guys to make me believe there was still some hope. If Tracy's willing to take you on, inhaler and all, then you're one lucky dude."

"She's a keeper."

"She is," Carson murmured. "Unless there's a fire, I'm unavailable till morning."

He heard hoots and wolf whistles as he started down the stairs.

Tracy heard him coming and hurried out of the bedroom. Johnny had finally dropped off. When they saw each other, they both started running. He picked her up and swung her around before carrying her into his bedroom.

"I need your mouth more than I need life," he cried softly. They mouths met and clung with a refined savagery while they tried to satisfy their hunger. But it was unquenchable as they found out when they ended up on the bed.

"Oh, Tracy…" His voice was ragged. "When you drove away the other night, I literally thought I wasn't going to make it through the night, let alone the rest of my life. Earlier, when you told me you'd be leaving after the rodeo, I happened to meet the redheaded barrel racer in town and she asked me to meet her after it was over. I told her I would because my pain was so bad.

"But I couldn't. Instead I got a message to her that something else had come up and I went on a drive in the truck. I ended up at the pasture, if you can believe it, not even realizing where I was until I got there."

"Oh, my darling." She covered his face with kisses. "Sylvia and I had an illuminating talk before we ever left for Yellowstone. She knew what was in my heart and urged me to do what I wanted. She was wonderful. But it was Johnny who turned everything around. He said he wanted to go home because you didn't love him."

"What?"

"I know. Can you believe it? But children are so literal, and when he told you he loved you in the tent, you didn't say the same words back. He decided you didn't want him around."

"I was afraid to say it back before."

"I know. You didn't want to raise any hopes with him, and I love you for that. So when I translated what you said about the feeling being mutual, he was a changed child. I told him I loved you, too, but we needed to go to the park with his grandparents and I'd have a talk with Vincent.

"As it turned out, Sylvia had already told him the truth, and he told me I'd be a fool if I didn't stay on with you. That was music to my ears. You really did win them over, and they can see how happy you make me and Johnny. But I have to tell you, you make me so happy, I'm jumping out of my skin."

"Then jump into mine, sweetheart." They kissed over and over again, long and hard, slow and gentle, still not quite believing this was happening.

"I'm the luckiest woman alive to have met you. I don't know how I could have been so blessed.

"Besides being a hero in every sense of the word, you're absolutely the most gorgeous man, you know. I haven't been able to take my eyes off you since we got here."

"Let's talk gorgeous, shall we?" He rolled over on top of her. "That day at the lake, I could have eaten you alive."

"Then we were both having the same problem. The only trouble with falling in love when you have a son who's my shadow, is finding any time alone. Even now, he's just across the hall and could wake up at any moment."

"I know that." He ran his fingers through her silky hair. "It's probably a good thing. We need a chaperone if we're going to do this thing by the book. I've decided that's exactly what we're going to do."

"Don't I have any say in it?"

"Yes. Please don't make us wait months to get married. After what we both went through during the war, life's too precious to waste time when something this fantastic comes along. *You're* fantastic, my love."

"How about a month?"

His groan came out on a cough.

"I wish we could get married tonight, but a month will give any of the family long enough to make plans if they want to fly out for the wedding. Do you think you can wait that long?"

"I can do anything as long you'll be my wife. I guess I'd better make this official. Will you marry me, Tracy? This is going to be forever."

"Yes, yes, yes! You've made me the happiest woman on earth. Last night while I was lying in bed, tossing and turning for want of you, I started imagining married life with you. I—I always wanted another baby. A little brother or sister for Johnny, but maybe I'm getting way ahead of myself. It's just that you're already the most remarkable father to Johnny. But—"

"But what?" He stifled the word with his lips. "I think you and I were having the same dream last night, but I didn't stop with one child."

"Oh, darling—" She crushed him in her arms. "Johnny's so crazy about you. To have more babies with you— Life with you is going to be glorious!" She stared into those brilliant blue eyes. "Love me, darling. I need you so badly."

"You don't know the half of it."

Hours later, they surfaced. "Did I ever tell you the advice my grandfather gave me years ago?"

"No," she whispered into his neck.

"He told me I could look at a woman, but if she wasn't available, then that was all I could do. I'm afraid that advice got thrown out the window when you walked into the terminal."

She kissed his hard jaw. "You were inspired to invite

all those special families here. It's a great thing you're doing, but I honestly believe I was guided here to you."

"I know you were. When the idea first came to me in the hospital, it came fully fledged, like some power had planted it there."

"I believe that. I wouldn't be surprised if your grandfather had a hand in it, because he could see what was coming and wanted you to find true happiness."

"Tracy…" He murmured her name over and over. "I want to believe it because I know I've found it with you."

"I feel the same way, and I know that wherever Tony is, he's happy for us, too."

He hugged her possessively. "Don't leave me yet. We have at least an hour before sunup."

"I'll only stay a little longer, because you never know about Johnny."

"Then let's go use the other twin bed in your room, so we can enjoy this precious time without worry."

But it didn't work out so well. Carson finally fell asleep, face down, but coughed enough that by six o'clock Johnny woke up and looked over at the two of them. Tracy smiled at him. "Good morning."

"Hey—did you guys stay in here with me all night?"

Carson opened one eye and turned over. "We did for part of the night. How did you sleep, partner?"

"Good." He scrambled out of bed to get his cap gun.

"Guess what? There's a ten-year-old girl staying at your old cabin named Julie."

"Did her dad die, too?"

"No. She and her parents are tourists staying for a few days. I'm going to need you to show her how to ride."

"Has she ever been on a horse?"

"I don't know. We'll have to ask Ross."

"I think she'd better ride Mitzi."

Tracy lost the battle of tears and wiped them away furiously. "Johnny? Carson and I talked everything over last night. We're going to get married in a month."

He frowned. "How come we have to wait a month?"

Carson chuckled. "Yeah, Mom," he whispered in her ear.

"To give the family time to come if they want."

"Can I call Cory and tell him?"

"Of course. You can call everyone and invite them."

Johnny walked over to their bed. "Carson?"

By the inflection in his voice, it sounded serious. Carson sat up. "What is it?"

"When you get married, can I call you Dad?"

Carson had to clear his throat several times. "I'd be honored if you did, but only if you want to."

"I do!"

"How about if after the wedding I call you son? That's how I think of you already."

"I want to be your son," he said soberly. "Can I tell Grandma and Grandpa about…well, you know."

"Of course. I want everyone to know how happy I am."

"I'm happy, too."

"Come here, Johnny, and give me a hug."

Tracy's son flew into his arms. She sat up and threw her arms around both of them. Life simply didn't get any better than this.

* * * * *

*Before he testifies in an important case, businessman
Michael "Mikey" Fiore hides out in Jacobsville, Texas,
and crosses paths with softly beautiful Bernadette, who
seems burdened with her own secrets. Their bond grows
into passion...until shocking truths surface.*

Read on for a sneak peek at
Texas Proud,
the latest book in
#1 New York Times *bestselling author Diana Palmer's
Long, Tall Texans series!*

Mikey's fingers contracted. "Suppose I told you that the
hotel I own is actually a casino," he said slowly, "and it's
in Las Vegas?"

Bernie's eyes widened. "You own a casino in Las
Vegas?" she exclaimed. "Wow!"

He laughed, surprised at her easy acceptance. "I run it
legit, too," he added. "No fixes, no hidden switches, no
cheating. Drives the feds nuts, because they can't find
anything to pin on me there."

"The feds?" she asked.

He drew in a breath. "I told you, I'm a bad man." He
felt guilty about it, dirty. His fingers caressed hers as they

neared Graylings, the huge mansion where his cousin lived with the heir to the Grayling racehorse stables.

Her fingers curled trustingly around his. "And I told you that the past doesn't matter," she said stubbornly. Her heart was running wild. "Not at all. I don't care how bad you've been."

His own heart stopped and then ran away. His teeth clenched. "I don't even think you're real, Bernie," he whispered. "I think I dreamed you."

She flushed and smiled. "Thanks."

He glanced in the rearview mirror. "What I'd give for just five minutes alone with you right now," he said tautly. "Fat chance," he added as he noticed the sedan tailing casually behind them.

She felt all aglow inside. She wanted that, too. Maybe they could find a quiet place to be alone, even for just a few minutes. She wanted to kiss him until her mouth hurt.

Don't miss
Texas Proud *by Diana Palmer,*
available October 2020 wherever
Harlequin Special Edition books and ebooks are sold.

Harlequin.com

HARLEQUIN

Heartfelt or suspenseful, inspiring or passionate, Harlequin has your happily-ever-after.

With new books published every month, you are sure to find the satisfying escape you know you deserve.

HNEWS2020

Love Harlequin romance?

DISCOVER.

Be the first to find out about promotions, news and exclusive content!

Facebook.com/HarlequinBooks

Twitter.com/HarlequinBooks

Instagram.com/HarlequinBooks

Pinterest.com/HarlequinBooks

ReaderService.com

EXPLORE.

Sign up for the Harlequin e-newsletter and download a free book from any series at **TryHarlequin.com**

CONNECT.

Join our Harlequin community to share your thoughts and connect with other romance readers! **Facebook.com/groups/HarlequinConnection**